Kiss it Better

P.F. SCOTT

My name is Paula and I write books because I love it!

The process of creating a storyline and characters is my favourite part of all. I write all the time, I hardly miss a day, for me it's an outlet, almost like a therapy of sorts... *a bit of me time!*

I live in Melbourne, Australia. I'm married with two grown up children and my fur baby co-writer, Alby.

Secrets Series
P.F. SCOTT

For lovers of love.

The biggest secret of all.

Chapter One

Eve let herself go to his sensual touch, his loving hand stroked her hair away from her face lovingly, his soft lips kissing and licking at hers lustfully. Gasping from his intoxicating love and touch, she ran her palms up his masculine arms, clenching his shoulders, her longing emotion spilled into a sexually fueled state of no return. Nails digging into his beautiful skin as she accepting him inside her needy body. Inhaling his precious scent deep into her lungs, it was happiness as she knew it. Then suddenly it was too perfect, and Eve knew it had to be a dream.

Opening her eyes, reality flooded her. Hot and sweaty, her hair stuck to the side of her face where tears had fallen. Eve's chest sunk to her stomach as she gazed up at the brilliant chandelier hanging above her. Dreams were all she had… dreams of him loving her. For the most part, her dreams were blissful, right up until the point she realised it was only a dream. Her precious and sensual dreams had become part of her coping mechanism with Evan's death, so her psychologist kept telling her so.

It was a new day, and the world wasn't about to wait for Eve to get her shit together. Jumping out of bed and taking a shower; the smell of coffee and fresh pastries filled the house, making her smile on her way downstairs to have breakfast with her grandmother.

Crisp white tablecloths adorned with burgundy and pink flowers, antique gold cutlery, gold rimmed champagne, wine and water glasses, and white linen laced edged napkins. Everything was perfect as always when Eve set the tables for a wedding. Chateau Balingarde had never had as many weddings on the books as in the past few years. Louis and Vivienne put it down to a modern marketing campaign and updated business plan that they had worked tirelessly on with Eve. They had revived the soul of the chateau and vineyard, making it a sought-after wedding location. Together they had literally spent years overhauling the entire estate, restructuring the business, restoring the chateau, and surrounding buildings, and nurturing the vineyard. Brining family history into the modern age. It had paid off; the chateau was flourishing in every way. Eve's passion and love for the chateau had derived from a young age, as a child it was full of fun and adventure, as she got older it became a place to find herself and heal her broken soul, on more than one occasion.

Today's wedding was for international guest, the guest house was already full and had been for the past two days, in one hour the festivities would begin. A romantic ceremony under the big old trees in front of the chateau where Eve lived with her grandmother and Louis. A string quartet would play in the background as the guests enjoyed drinks and canapes and breathtaking views before heading into the old cellar for the evening reception.

Eve wore a fitted nude cocktail dress that conservatively hugged her womanly curves, nude pumps and her long dark curls pulled tightly back into a sleek long plat that went all the way down her back. At twenty-four years old she was confidently feminine and still as sweet as ever. Her supple cinnamon skin, her curvaceous body, the long hair, and alluring almond eyes made her an exotic vision. Everyone gravitated towards her mysterious sultriness and calm demeanor, this overpowered the deep heartache. She hid the pain very well. Unless you knew Eve's tragic past, you would never know.

On the days like today, when she'd woke after dreaming of Evan, she had a heavier heart, but there was no time to feel sorry for herself, she had to get on with her day and would do so with grace. Her life in France was very simple, she worked a few hours every day and read most nights, thankfully her grandmother had shelves full of old French erotic fiction novels, which entertained her to no end, it was an education in itself, reading Vivienne's books. She'd moved to France only weeks after Evan's death, the first few years hadn't been great, she'd gone through waves of self-destruction, not eating, drinking too much, and shutting herself off from the world. As always her grandmother had unconditionally seen her through the hard times. The woman was an angel!

In her own words, Eve was now fine. Which for anyone who knew her, was code for 'not that good.' She'd never get over losing Evan or Rafael, she'd just got used to it.

Tomorrow, after the wedding; all the guests would leave by noon and the chateau would be back in go slow mode until the next wedding. Tomorrow afternoon Eve was leaving to spend the week in London with Quinn - her friend, what their relationship was, didn't really have a label. She really had no idea what she and Dr. Quinn Portman were to each other. Things with Quinn were easy, they didn't expect anything from each other, their friendship was based on good company and no commitment, they'd never had sex.

Eve met Quinn at his parents' home on her second visit to London after moving to France. She was visiting Clive and Henrietta who had been very good to her following the untimely death of their friend Evan. They had been great friends with him when they had lived in Sydney, even selling their beloved Villa Rosado to him as a gift to Eve. That's how Eve had met the eccentric older couple who had now become her great friends.

The very first time she'd met Quinn, who was old enough to be her father, he asked her out for a drink, much to his parents horror. She called him the very next day and met him for dinner, great conversation, and many drinks near his home in Notting Hill, they'd talked and talked.

Her flight to London from Bordeaux got her there at five pm, an hour and forty-five minutes later and Eve was in London with Quinn. The peculiar dynamics of their friendship, for want of a better word, had everyone baffled. The issue was the age gape and that they were great friends.

Letting herself in Quinn's front door as she had her own key, Eve popped in and out of his life at her leisure, sometimes without warning and sometimes announced. Anything went with Quinn, he was happy to have her visit anytime she felt like it, that was the main attraction for Eve, she could call him on a Friday morning from France when she was feeling lonely or board and be in London for dinner. It didn't matter, Quinn let Eve be, he let her do what she had to do, she even had a room in his house all of her own. He was like a big brother who took her on great dates, and never asked her any questions about her past. Poor, sad Eve didn't exist with Quinn.

He really needs a regular cleaner, Eve thought as she walked through the foyer and up the stairs to her bedroom. This visit had purpose, Quinn had a gala dinner on Wednesday evening that required a date, someone he could show off in front of the two hundred guests at the Willow and Spence Foundation annual fundraiser, in which he was a guest speaker. Then on Thursday night was dinner with his family for his mother's birthday, of course he was going with Eve! And Saturday he was surprising Eve and his teenage daughter.

Eve knew to expect the unexpected when arriving at Quinn's home, she was used to finding women's underwear lying about the house, many a random sex toy, days of dishes in the sink, she'd even walked in on two naked nurse handcuffed to his bed posts, while he laid asleep between them. Eve had ended up cooking the nurses dinner that night, it turned into the best dinner party ever. Eve and Quinn had a unique friendship.

Today was nothing out of the normal, in fact it looked like he had tried to clean up. But wait no! As she peeked into Quinn's room there was a condom foil on the floor near his bed with a chewing gum stuck to it, and a pack of pills that looked something like Viagra, on his bedside table. Eve laughed thinking he had probably put it there just for her benefit knowing she was arriving today and snoop in his room.

The Notting Hill house was why kept Eve coming back, she loved the location right in the heart of everything, bars, restaurants, café's, shops, markets. It was like a mini break for her when she visited. A friendship of convenience for both, Quinn got to spend time with a young sexy woman who made him laugh, and who he could have a half decent dinner conversation with. And as for Eve, she loved London and enjoy Quinn's house, and his company and his playful humor that never failed to give her a good old laugh. As one of the best neurosurgeons in Britain and Europe, his home was something else, somewhat a beautiful and mostly messy sanctuary for Eve. Quinn was smart and witty, and fun to be around, he didn't give too many fucks about much in life other than his career. She was a sounding board for him, and over the years there had been plenty to listen to, his strained relationships with his parents, sisters, and daughter, and then there were all the random and weird sexual hook ups, they were always entertaining. Eve however, never discussed her past with Quinn, he already knew everything anyway, he knew all about Evan, the baby they'd had,

Eve's daddy issues, of course from his parents. Quinn was the kind of guy who'd rather talk about himself than Eve anyway, he was basically a narcissist, and he didn't make any apologies for it.

'Thank god you're here…' Quinn dropped his work bag in the middle of the kitchen floor, put two bottles of red on the counter and went straight to Eve and hugged her, she was making a curry for dinner.

'I like your hair,' Eve said as he came to her with open arms. They hadn't seen each other in a while and Quinn had cut his blond curls into a short back and sides with curls on top. He was a handsome manly man, a little quirky, average height, distinguished looking with an edge that she found interesting, but that was all. When she hugged him, she didn't get that special feeling and never had.

'You didn't have to cook; I was going to take you out to dinner; I've got so much I need to tell you… The worlds gone fucking made since I last saw you,' Quinn said comically as he kissed her on the cheek.

'I thought it might be nice to stay in, drink loads of red wine and catch up.' Eve needed to chill, and she didn't feel like having the waitress comment on how cute it was she was out with her father for dinner, it happened all the time when they went out together.

'Well now, that sounds good, I've had a shit of week, I could do with lots of red wine and you,' he chuckled, 'Oh, and I need you to come shopping with me for a suit tomorrow?' Quinn liked Eve around when he needed things done, she was great at getting things done. He didn't need her for sex, although he'd certainly thought about it, she made him feel youthful.

They'd had dinner in the kitchen drinking wine, chatting about Quinn's teenage daughter Clementine and her wild ways. Eve didn't see too much of what Clementine was doing as a big deal, she had done it all too, and it wasn't really that long ago either, Clemy was a good girl with a naughty streak. Eve was fond of her.

The fundraiser was a gala event and luckily Eve had bought one of her favorite full-length gowns with her, a deep red velvet dress, off the shoulder, very

Julia Roberts – Pretty Woman, only shorter. This was English high society, and the snobbery was out of control. Her wild curls freshly washed and flowing about, a new pair of Jimmy's and beautiful nude lips and eyeshadow to compliment her cinnamon skin. Quinn knew he could rely on Eve to turn heads and impress his colleagues, most of all he got to flaunt her to his old university alumni, which he loved to do. They envied him being with a younger woman, they didn't know it was a non-sexual relationship.

The family dinner where Eve was an unofficial non-committal part of the family. Henrietta adored Eve, annoying the rest of the family with the way she enjoyed Eve's company; she had adored Evan and his death had devastated both Clive and Henrietta, it had been such an unlikely friendship, yet a strong one all the same. It pleased them that they still had contact with Eve, they secretly prayed she'd fall in love with their son and make an honest man of him, it was not to be.

Chapter Two

The VIP pass hung around his neck, he had a beer in hand living his best life, the Foo Fighters rocking out Everlong and the cutest girl dancing and wiggling her little arse a few feet in front of him. Life was awesome, surrounded by his mates on the best trip ever. Crazy nights, adventurous days and now they had scored VIP tickets into a famous London music festival. Buzzing from the atmosphere alone, the coldish day felt warm and the girl in front with her friend had his eye, if she would just turn around and he could get her attention that would make his day, there was something about her that was so familiar, and when she eventually turned around his heart stopped.

'Oh. Wow. Hey!' she said as shocked as he was. It wasn't just any girl, those curves had been more than familiar, curves he'd dreamt of for years. Now there she was, right in front of him staring up at him with those beautiful almond eyes.

'Eve Frank!' he gasped as a huge smile grew across his face.

'Marco Rossi,' she gasped holding her breath, jumping up into his open arms, their kiss was more than a peck, it was a long three second peck, evoking every passionate moment they had ever shared. It had been five years since she'd last seen Marco at his parents' house, just after Evan's death, right before she'd left for France.

'What are you doing here, how are you?' Marco asked beaming down at Eve as she looked up at him with her sparkling eyes, he remembered the way she used to look at him, adoringly.

'Um. My friend surprised me with the tickets this morning. What are *you* doing here?' The more Eve stared up into his breathtaking eyes, the more it started to sink in that she was talking to her Marco. Her Marco.

'We've been in Europe holidaying. We won the Grand Final. We're celebrating.' He was excited telling Eve as he gestured to the few other guys he was with.

7

'I know, congratulations.' She left out that she had actually woken up at two am to watch the game from her bed in France and cheered so loud she'd woken the house. *Yep, he was still her Marco. So incredibly handsome and sexy, just as she remembered.*

Eve was mesmerized as she watched Marco's mouth moving. Everything but Marco disappeared as she did so. A tingle ran through her entire body, one she hadn't felt in years.

'How are you doing anyway Evie… I mean, are you alright? Last time I saw you-' he didn't know what to say, he knew from Tessa that Eve had taken a long time to find her feet after the murder of her fiancé. He waited for her response; she took her time. Undoubtably still the cutest little chick he'd ever seen… All that hotness wrapped up in all those fuckable curves. Eve Frank was still gorgeous.

Eve began to breathe again, 'I'm good. I'm great… You look amazing.' *Fuck, too many drinks*, his flattered smile diminished any humiliation. His concern and mention of her past had been confronting for her. But Marco made her feel like no one else ever had. Like a besotted schoolgirl in dreamland. He still took her breath away.

'Evie, I can't believe it's you, and here of all places. I thought we'd run into each other at some stage in New York… I'm there every year to see Tessa and you've either just left or coming right after I leave.' Marco put his hand at her upper arm, he needed to feel her, he remembered her being so soft and smooth.

Eve had been purposely avoiding bumping into him in New York for years. Every year Tessa invited her to spend Christmas and New Year in New York, and every year Eve made up an excuse, so she didn't have to deal with seeing Marco. It was too hard, and she didn't know if she could handle those kinds of feelings again.

'How long are you in London?' she asked, the music was loud, and the atmosphere was hyped, she couldn't hear or see anything but Marco. Her perfect Marco!

'We fly to Portugal tomorrow,' there was regret in his voice and eyes.

'Oh… Have you been there before? I love Portugal. You're have so much fun there.' Her heart sank when he said he was flying out tomorrow, she was flying back to France herself anyway, but she still felt an odd feeling of disappointment.

'Look who I bumped into,' Marco shout as the music was so loud to someone walking by.

'Rory, it's so good to see you,' Eve gasped with surprise, another huge hug, she was more than excited to see Rory who looked the same as she'd remembered. This was evoking feelings and thoughts that she had thought she'd left in Palm Cove all those years ago. Eve found herself misty eyed with emotion.

'What the fuck... Eve.' Rory couldn't believe it, she looked exactly same, only better, hotter. Marco called her *the one that got away.'* 'You live in France, right? What are you doing here?' Rory held her by the arms as he looked her over, taking in every inch of her as she stood beside Marco, he'd forgotten what a cutie she was, he had great memories of that trip to Palm Cove.

'I do live in France; I'm visiting a friend here... I'm freaking out, who else are you here with?' Looking around she could feel Marco's eyes on her, he hadn't taken them off her once, she bit her bottom lip to stop it from trembling as she looked back up to Marco's dreamy smile.

'This is Connor and Trent. There's a few others over there,' Rory said introduced Eve as Marco was clearly too shocked to do so. 'This is Eve, Marco's friend from Sydney who lives in France now. His sister's best friend, Eve.' Rory was very clear and particular with his introduction of Eve, almost like they should know exactly who she was.

'Sweetheart!' Quinn appeared at her side, his hand finding the small of her back as he looked Marco and Rory over, a little territorial. *He never called her sweetheart. WTF!*

A little taken back by sweetheart! she managed to speak, 'This is Marco, my friend Tessa's brother. And his friend Rory,' Eve sounded bubbly and exited as she introduced Quinn.

'Nice to meet you. I'm Quinn. Eve's boyfriend,' Quinn put his hand out to shake hands with them, deciding to be her boyfriend suddenly. She looked at him quickly, wondering what the hell had come over him, was this a jealous streak?

'Nice to meet you... You two are together?' Marco couldn't hide his intrigue as he looked at both Quinn and Eve, wondering just how much older this guy was than Eve.

'No, we are not! We live in different countries,' it was out of her mouth with a strange smile before she could think of what to say. Denying it point blank!

Quinn laughed like Eve was crazy, he seemed amused by Eve's answer, he knew he had thrown her with the boyfriend label, *fuck he had thrown himself.* She had four strapping young Aussie guys surrounding her and Quinn felt a strange feeling he'd never felt before.

'What are you doing tonight?' Marco asked Eve, ignoring Quinn.

Then Quinn interrupted, 'I was coming to find you; we're heading back to our seats now.'

'Give me a minute and I'll be right there,' Eve smiled holding an impatient finger up to Quinn who she thought was acting a tad odd!

'Good to meet you lads,' said Quinn before he turned to Eve, 'We'll be waiting.'

Eve waited until Quinn turned away, she didn't say a word until he had taken several steps from her and then she sighed heavily before her smile crept back to her face.

'I'm so glad I ran into you Marco,' she said loving the sound of his name leaving her lips, her eyelashes battered up at him lustfully, he was so tall, still a dream… So absurdly manly and handsome, her heart was fluttering with a billion butterflies.

'We should catch up,' he was breathless at the thought.

'I can't tonight, we've got dinner plans, and you leave tomorrow, so do I. I'm heading back to France.'

'If you're ever in Melbourne Eve Frank, give me a call, I'd love to take you to dinner again.' Marco's eyes fixed to Eve with a huge smile, he thought about Palm Cove, taking her virginity, and kissing every inch of her body. Reaching down, he hugged her in again one last time.

'Of course, I'd love to do dinner with you again,' she said with a smile that had been missing for years, 'You take care and enjoy Portugal… It was so good to see you Marco.' Their eyes lingered. Her smile faded as she leaned into yet another goodbye hug, squeezing him in close to her body, breathing him in.

'Great seeing you Eve Frank.' Marco couldn't take his eyes off her as he released her from his arms, she was breathtaking. He watched her say goodbye to Rory and the other boys. Eve was still so gorgeous and kind, cute and dainty, she hadn't changed at all. She was still as sexy as hell too.

Arriving at the airport an hour earlier than needed for her flight back to France. Eve had been thinking about Marco all night long and all morning. *What were the chances of running into him again today at the airport?* She had no idea what time he flew out, or even if he was leaving from the same airport. Seeing him at the festival yesterday had tipped her upside down.

She'd gone to dinner with Quinn, Clementine, and some of their friends after the festival last night, Eve barely spoke as she sipped on the same glass of wine the entire dinner. All she could think about was Marco and how she had felt seeing him after everything, and all the time that had passed. She still felt exactly the same as she had felt when she was ten years old, the sight of him made her weak at the knees, her heart raced, her body broke out in a nervous sweat, and she so desperately wanted to kiss him.

Sitting in a bar after clearing customs, Eve couldn't believe what had happened, seeing Marco had been a freaky, she'd touched him, hugged him, kissed him hello and she realized then, she was still that young wishful girl who used to pinch his clothing and dream about one day being his. Even after everything.

Bursting in the front door of the chateaux, Eve dropped her bags and hurriedly walked around in search of her grandmother, she'd been on a euphoric buzz since yesterday. 'Mamie, I'm home, where are you?' she called out. Flinging the terrace door open she found Vivienne sitting with Louis and a bottle of wine, both smoking and laughing as they did every evening together.

'Here she is, how was your trip belle fille?' Louis asked as Eve kissed them both enthusiastically on both cheeks and flung herself down into a seat at the table like she had something exiting to tell them.

'My trip was great.' She was glowing.

Vivienne took a moment, Eve's enchanted mood was good to see, 'How was Quinn?'

'He's fine.'

Vivienne paused with a curious look on her face. 'You look so happy.'

'I am happy... what's been happening here?' Eve hadn't stop smiling and her cheer was intriguing both Vivienne and Louis.

'I hired Lisabeth to help you,' Louis told her. This was music to Eve's ears, Lisabeth was the daughter of a neighbouring family, she helped with the vine picking in season and did odd jobs for some pocket money, Eve had suggested to Louis that perhaps Lisabeth could be of help to her with the wedding preparations.

'That's fantastic, I'm so excited, was she excited?' Eves exuberant response was joyous.

'Of course, she looks up to you,' said Louis.

'How did everything go in London?' Vivienne wanted to delve a little farther.

'Good, fantastic,' another bubbly answer that gave nothing away, she was in such good spirits, Vivienne knew there was more to it, she'd find out eventually.

For days Eve floated around on heavenly air, humming in such a merry mood, it was eating at Vivienne, who had tried to pry into the London trip a little more each day. She knew Quinn wasn't the reason for the sudden delightful and uplifting mood her granddaughter embodied... Well, she hoped not! No, Quinn and Eve had this bizarre friendship slash relationship that Vivienne couldn't get her head around.

Tessa had been more excited about Eve seeing Marco in London, than Eve. She'd made such a big deal out of it, adding Zoe into a phone conversation while they both interrogated Eve about Marco, squeezing every little detail out of her.... they left no stone unturned. The two best friends had waited years for this moment in time, the fact that they hadn't played a part in it all, meant that it was divine intervention.

'So how did it feel to see Marco, I hope you were nice to him?' Zoe said very matter of fact.

'Of course... it was nice to see him after all this time. I just wish Quinn hadn't been there, he told Marco he was my boyfriend! Can you believe him?'

'Fucker!' Tessa hissed; she didn't like the idea of Quinn and Eve's friendship.

This random meeting with Marco had sparked something in Eve, the girls had always trodden so very carefully around her and the whole Marco situation, especially after Evan's death. She'd thought it was a secret the way she had avoided Marco for all these years, but Tessa and Zoe were so onto her, they knew Eve had issues with coming face to face with Marco.

Then the strangest thing happened, just as Eve had stopped thinking about her chance meeting with Marco day and night, she'd received a message on her phone from him. She sat at her desk staring at his name on her screen. Then she began to read.

Eve Frank,

It was so good seeing you in London, you haven't changed a bit. Still beautiful!

Rory said he thought you seemed taller! I told him it was those black boots you were wearing!

We spent a week in Portugal, you were right, we had a lot of fun. Then two days in Dubai before heading home. I'm back at training and trying to lose the weight I've put on over the off season. I went to LA before Europe, and LA tried to kill me, way too much partying.

I'm glad you're doing okay Evie.. I know you've had it tough, I always asked Tessa and mum how you're doing. I really hope you're happy, you deserve to be.

I saw your mum when I went back home to Sydney for a few days, she coming to New York this Christmas, our mums are now inseparable according to my dad. You should come to New York too!

Tessa was talking about coming to live back in Australia next year, I'm sure she's told you. She is thinking of auditioning in Melbourne to do a show here. Maybe that was supposed to be a secret now I think about it.

I just wanted to touch base with you and say hi after London.

Take care, and remember if you're in Melbourne, call me.

Marco

He'd remembered she was wearing boots at the festival. Marco seemed so very grown up now. Eve felt her cheeks blush, she literally broke out in a sweat whilst reading his message. It was without doubt a modern-day love letter. *What did she do, did she write back to him, or did she call?*

Jumping up from her desk, Eve went outside into the fresh air, she sat on the garden seat that looked out over the vineyard, the rows had fascinated her from a child, she found them calming, perfect for contemplating her next move, unable to think straight as peaceful as it was. This was Marco, her Marco, and as she sat looking out over the rolling hills, Eve wondered how her life would have been different, had he had wanted her after Palm Cove. It was like a stab to the chest every time she allowed herself to go there, and then another to the neck as the knife twisted. All the pain surged back with vengeance, her clammy hands gripped the seat, her knuckles going white as she thought how she hated herself for go there again, and it wasn't just Marco and his baby. It was her parents, Evan, and Rafael. It was everything that had happened to her after Marco Rossi. Part of her was angry at him, she'd partially blamed Marco for all her anguish, because the hurt had started with him, his rejection was the first heartbreak and it just seemed to snowball after him.

'It's cold, I thought you might like tea.' Vivienne sat down next to Eve on the bench seat and handed her a cup of hot herbal tea.

'Thank you.'

'Something is on your mind?' Vivienne trying not to sound to interested. Eve didn't answer her grandmother, that meant she most certainly did have something on her mind, she just didn't know how to articulate it, Vivienne would have to work harder. 'You've been so happy since London, is it Quinn?'

'No!'

'Tell me who has made you so happy. I should have known it was not Quinn,' Vivienne said unable to hid her sarcasm.

'You're a harsh woman sometimes Mamie, he's a nice man,' a giggle in Eve's voice. She had known from the start that her grandmother didn't like Quinn. He was too old and too English for Vivienne's liking.

'Tell me, I hate suspense.' Vivienne was like a dog with a bone. She needed to know, she lived for romantic suspense and tales, especially Eve's.

'I ran into Tessa brother,' Eve was hesitant to tell her grandmother.

'And…'

Eve laughed at her grandmother's persistence, 'I saw Marco. My Marco.'

'The Marco?'

'Yes. My Marco. Marco Rossi,' saying his name made her smile. Explaining everything about the chance meeting at the music festival, and the recent love letter. Her grandmother listened with great interest as she watched Eve's emotion, bright and radiant as she talked of this Marco. Vivienne new his parents well, they had stayed at the chateaux twice whilst travelling through France. Vivienne liked Tessa a lot, she was a true friend to Eve, the Rossi family had Vivienne's approval.

'Are you going to write back?' She wanted to know everything, she amused herself by living vicariously through her darling granddaughter, having Eve around kept Vivienne young.

'I really want to, but I'm scared. He was my first lover,' she paused getting serious, 'I can't just be friends with him Mamie.' Eve had a longing lust like look on her face that was breathtaking. This was a happy Eveline Vivienne was seeing, if only this young man could see how beautiful her face was right now! She wanted her granddaughter to embrace life, start living again and move forward. It felt like even though Eve was holding herself back from her own future.

'It's better to have tried and failed, than to have not try at all. You don't want to die wondering. You must write back at once,' Vivienne told her granddaughter.

Eve re read the message several times over the next day before she replied. She was guarded, she couldn't read into it too much. Her writing back was just one friend to another, it had to be nothing more for her own sake, the slightest rejection from Marco would set her back and she knew it. Before she started to doubt herself and the meaning of Marco's letter, she started to type.

Hi Marco,

Yes, it was nice catching up in London. Rory was exactly the same as I remembered him. Can you tell him, that I said he looked older, and it wasn't what he was wearing either.

I knew you would love Portugal, LA sounded like fun too! Anything else planned, besides New York at for Christmas? I'm going to Vienna for Christmas

with friends. I can't believe my mum is spending Christmas in New York, she
doesn't even like cold weather.
Take care.
Eve

The next day she received a response, Marco must have been testing the waters
with his first message. What did it mean that he'd replied straight away?

Hey Eve Frank,
You actually wrote back to me! I wasn't sure you would.
What do you do to pass the time over there?
> *London was a nice surprise, you looked like you wanted to run away for a*
minute there, I feel like you've been trying to avoid me since Palm Cove. I know
Tessa's invites you to New York every Christmas, and you never come. You
always seem to visit her just after or before me, it's not a coincidence is it? When
I asked Tessa why you never come to Christmas, she always says it's because of
me. Just so you know, I don't regret a minute of what happened between us.
How's that boyfriend of yours anyway?
Oh, and while I'm at it, Zoe is coming to New York for Christmas too. You should
seriously think about it Eve Frank, we'd all love you there.
Marco

Eve rapidly taping her pen on the desk as she read the message over and over.
Louis looking up over his glasses at her from his.

'We will miss you at the Christmas party this year,' he said, trying to stop the
tapping of the pen.

'I know, but I've promised Clive and Henrietta I'd got to Vienna,' said Eve.

'Oh, so you're going for Clive and Henrietta... not Quinn?' Vivienne had told
him about Marco and the message. They were so protective of Eve; they had seen
her in her darkest hours, and it had been more than a person her age should have to
endure. It had taken such a long time for her to come out of the dark hole. They
worried about Eve, her only friend beside the girls was a man twice her age.

'Of course, I'm not going for Quinn,' she laughed.

'I don't know why you're not going to New York with your mother and your friends,' Louis felt compelled to say so, her life was on hold, and had been for a long time.

'Because I've committed to Vienna,' she said as Louis left the office and Eve thought about her response to Marco's message.

Marco Rossi,

    Does this mean we're pen pals now?

    I don't regret a thing about Palm Cove, it was actually the time of my life, especially the time spent with you.

    For kicks over here, I go to London and Paris when I can and shop. It's an hour to Bordeaux by train then just over another hour to London by plane. I take the train to Paris too. I prefer the train to be honest, at least there is something to look at, or I zone out and read a book. My grandmother has this bookshelf full of sexy old French books, that I can't stop reading as weird as that sounds. Sometimes I get bored at the chateau, so I visit my friend Quinn in London, and yes he is only my friend, not my boyfriend.

    Merry Christmas Marco.

Eve x

Fuck it, she added a single lonely kiss after her name. Debating it for ten minutes before pressing send, Eve felt strangely comfortable with this new messaging affair she was having with Marco. Her Marco.

When Tessa found out that Anna was coming to Christmas in New York, she got on the phone to Eve. 'You have never spent Christmas with me in New York... And you know I can't leave here because of this fucking show that's slowly killing me.' Tessa was in a dramatic mood. 'Don't you want to come and have Christmas with us?' She was taking Eve's absence to heart. 'You're not falling for fucking Quinn are you E? I hope you're not fucking him. And why are you spending Christmas with him!' Tessa got on her high horse.

'It's more about Clive and Henrietta.' Eve felt the pressure, Tessa knew exactly how to get under her skin.

'Fuck them... What about me? This might be my last Christmas in New York. You're my best friend and it would mean so much if you could just come and be with us. Your mum and Zoe are going to be here E!'

'You're just mentioning this festive get together to me now, after I've already made plans. Stop trying to make me feel guilty.' Eve acted innocent.

'Are you telling me, Marco never mentioned coming to New York for Christmas to you. I'm sure he said he invited you and I don't have to ask you to come, it's an open invitation every fucking year.' Tessa called her out.

'Stop being unreasonable, you're putting a lot of pressure on me. I'm not coming just because Marco asked me too.' Eve got her back up.

'Yeah, whatever. You should be here with us, not with Quinn the creep.'

'I don't really care what you think Tessa, and I can't believe you just said that to me.' Eve was defensive, 'What do you suggest I do exactly? Wait for your brother until the end of time, or cry over Evan for the rest of my life.' Eve ended the call there. She was flustered and furious. It had been a long day and she was tired. She was upset with Tessa; she knew how hard these past years had been for her, and she knew Quinn was only a friend, not a solution. Eve had been to New York to stay with Tessa several times, they spoke on the phone every few days. Moving on after Evan's death had been a roller coaster of emotional torment. She still missed him more than she ever thought possible, and the trauma of losing Evan in the way she had, was hard to forget. Eve dreamt about Evan and Rafael almost every night, and she still felt guilty about his death, even though the police had confirmed it was more than likely the Chinese who had killed Evan and nothing to do with Sonny Smith. She'd try to move on in her own way... Not a single day had been easy. Her friendship with Quinn did seem strange from the outside, she knew that, but it gave her something to do instead of feeling sorry for herself and he wasn't a bad man, just selfish perhaps.

Ferez, Kellie, Jo, and Tia where the only people that Eve still had contact with from her old life. Ferez was a better friend to Evan than she had ever realized. He called her at least once a month for the past five years to see how she was doing, and always asked if there was anything she needed from him. There was no ulterior motive other than he was a good guy, who had known and respected how much Eve meant to Evan. Ferez wasn't involved in any business dealing with Evan, it was purely friendship, unlike Marcello who relied on Evan and his father for his livelihood. Marcello was a career criminal who now answered to Evan's father Martin. Once Evan had gone, Marcello and Sarah and the others had completely wiped her, just as they had done with Jo. That was more than fine with Eve, she didn't want them in her life either.

Jo and Tia had been constants. They had been over to stay with her in France twice and they spoke regularly. Eve had a bond with them that would never die. She loved Tia with all her heart, and always would. As for her friendship with Jo, it went deep although they were unlikely friends.

Chapter Three

Over the next week, Zoe tried to ignore the standoff going on between her two best friends. Tessa was upset that Eve wasn't coming to New York for Christmas, she felt like Eve was choosing Quinn instead of her dear friends and family. Zoe had always been a little more accepting of Eve's relationship with Quinn, and her need to keep clear of Marco. She had been the one who was there when Eve lost that first baby, Marco's baby and she had seen the despair and heartache in Eve's eyes due to her brief romance with gorgeous Marco. Whereas Tessa just wanted Eve and Marco to see each other and fall for each other again, like a fairytale.

Zoe tutted her disappointment to Eve over the phone. 'It's usually you saying this to us. You know Tessa's coming from a good place, she just wants you to spend Christmas with us.' Being the meat in the sandwich was always difficult in the friendship triangle.

'I don't want to talk about this anymore,' Eve told Zoe who had rang her with a last-ditch effort to persuade Eve to come to New York.

'Evie,' Zoe huffed down the phone, 'I wish you were coming; we would have so much fun the three of us in New York, can you imagine? But I also understand why you're not, so enjoy Vienna,' Zoe sounded sad. She had decided to call Eve one last time before it was too late, it just seemed like such a shame for Eve to miss out all because of Marco, and Zoe knew that was the only reason behind her friends stubbornness.

'I love you Zo,' Eve said with a terrible ache in the pit of her stomach, FOMO had a grip on her!

'I know you do. I love you too.' Zoe had a heavy heart, this was the first time the girls had had an international standoff, it was foreign to all of them, it wasn't how they rolled at all.

As Eve packed her two large suite cases meticulously, she heard her phone beep on the edge of her bedside table. She'd become accustomed to knowing who was messaging her by the time of the day. She received her mother's messages early in the morning, the girls always messaged her late at night and of late Marco's was messaging around the middle of the day, which was usually after dinner for him. Since she and Marco had started to message back and forth, almost on a day-to-day basis, Eve found she had become a slave to her phone, checking it regularly for his messages. Before she would be lucky to look at it once a day.

Opening Marco's message, he was at LAX, there was a photo attached before his actual message, it was of the side of his face, he had a huge graze on his cheek bone. It looked sore, he still looked so devilishly handsome she couldn't help but smile.

Merry Christmas Eve Frank,

This is what happens when you face plant at training. We had our last training session before the Christmas break. There's usually a little too much mucking around and well, look at me. I know you're wondering, yes it hurts.

My mum says that your mum is devo you won't be coming to New York for Christmas. So am I.

It's not too late to change your mind. You know where to find us.

Safe travels Evie.

Marco x

He knew exactly how to hit her right in the heart. Using her mum was a good start, but then to add that he was devastated! And the one kiss after his name! Marco only compounded her conflicting feelings.

Eve had started to doubt everything, her friendship with Quinn, her behavior toward Tessa, and her life in general. She had never doubted the way she felt about Marco though, and for that reason alone she had to act with caution. Under no circumstances was she putting herself at risk of heartbreak.

Her train trip had been a different one, she usually enjoyed the chance to relax and read either a book or a glossy mag. But today, she had stared out the window in her comfy first-class seat thinking about how lonely she was, how she felt like she was her own worst enemy and how she just couldn't seem to get out of her own way no matter what she did. When Eve let the smallest thought of Evan into her head, it was all over. Discretely wiping her tears as she imagined him holding her, comforting her as he did when she needed him. Today she was thinking about Evan a lot. If there was a higher power, an afterlife, then surely Evan might guide her and set her on the right path. She needed some divine intervention. She began to over process her situation and her life. There were two missed calls from her father over the past day. It was Christmas so he was probably calling to wish her a Merry Christmas. Her relationship with James had been distant to say the least over the years, she had caught up with him just once in London while he was there on business. It was a dinner that made her so anxious in the lead up. Eve debated telling her father that she knew, Sam was her birth mother, the burden of the secret sometimes weighed heavily on her, she'd never told a single soul that her birth mother was actually her father's current girlfriend. She never asked her father about his other family... Her twin sisters would be at least seven years old by now. If she acknowledged them or Sam in any way, then they became a part of her life, and she didn't know if she was ready for that, or even if she would ever be.

Missing Evan and Tia at Christmas was a ritual for Eve, she was conflicted between happy memories and sad feelings. The three of them had spent only one Christmas together, but she'd never forget it. Although she spoke to Tia every few weeks still to this day, she missed her hugs and watching her grow up. Time was passing by and Eve's heartache for Evan always lingering, even with her newfound communication with Marco, she still thought about Evan every day.

Quinn was meeting Eve in Paris at eight that evening. They were flying to Vienna together early the next morning to join his family for Christmas. She sat in the hotel bar on her own as she waited for him. Her sadness had passed from earlier in the day, now she was just somber, wondering what all these people who sat at the bar with her, were doing with their lives. A man sat alone like she, in his sixties or possibly seventies, holding a champagne flute as he looked around the hotel bar just as Eve did. His steely grey hair and neat mustache accentuated his olive skin and fading good looks. *What was such a man doing in a hotel bar on his own two nights before Christmas?* Eve wondered.

'Hello beautiful!' Quinn whispered to her ear, putting his hands at her waste from behind, kissing her neck... Eve spun around on the bar stool. Very touchy feely and a tad intimate for Quinn, she thought!

'Well, hello.' Her sparkling smile was full of Christmas cheer. As to exactly why she was pleased to see Quinn, Eve wasn't really sure. She'd spent the last hour pondering the situation of Vienna v New York, her future and what she wanted out of life. All of which seemed to not include Quinn.

'How was your day? How was your trip into Paris?' he asked as he sat on the bar stool beside her ordering a drink, clearly he'd been drinking already, he was rosy cheeked. Quinn was handsome and sexy in an older guy way; his short sandy greying curls pushed back off his face, nice blue eyes.

'My day was fine, what about you, how was your day?' Her smile hid her manic mind.

'Surgery this morning went very well, thankfully for my patient. I had lunch with Clemy and her mother, who was painfully fucked as you can imagine. Not Clemy, her mother,' Quinn laughed drinking his whiskey fast as he told Eve all about his lunch with Sabrina his ex and his daughter Clemy, Eve listened to him, as she always did. Well, one ear was listening whilst her mind was elsewhere.

'Did you have sex with Sabrina today?' Her smile was questioning. Quinn secretly had sex with Sabrina and had been doing so for the past fifteen years even when though they were never really together. Eve could never quite figure out why Quinn had sex with Sabrina, they hated each other.

'Well, no. Clemy came to lunch... Why do you ask?' He asked her curiously.

'Um... I'm just asking. I'm being polite and engaging in your story,' Eve said very flippant.

Quinn sniffed as he looked to be thinking, staring right into Eve's eyes, 'Why do you think it is, we've never had sex? You and I.' He seemed to be quite serious which threw Eve.

'Because we're friends.' It was simple.

'I'm not even friends with Sabrina and I fuck her all the time, and I don't even like her. But you're my friend, who I adore, and we've never had sex.'

Eve bit her bottom lip, 'I think we're supposed to be friends without benefits.' Not that she'd never thought of having sex with Quinn, she had.

'You know after seeing you with your ridiculously talk dark and handsome Aussie friends at the music festival, seeing his eyes literally undressing you and fuck you as you stood in front of him, I've been thinking about us Eve,' Quinn took a breath. 'Do you think we should have sex, get it out the way?'

'He didn't fuck me with his eyes, we're old friends!' Eve laughed, 'And no, I don't think we should have sex.'

That part she was didn't laugh about; she was crystal clear.

'You mean to tell me all this time, you've never wanted to sleep with me.'

'No.' Eve said. They'd never had this kind of conversation, not about the two of them anyway. Suddenly for some reason she became extremely anxious, short of breath. 'I don't want to have sex with you.' Unsure if she should leave. 'Why after years of being friends, are you talking about having sex,' Eve asked, her face rather confused, her heart now pounding.

'Come on Eve, I know who you are, I know you love sex. Admit it.'

'I haven't had sex for over five years,' she couldn't keep the emotion from her voice.

'What!' Quinn looked shocked. He knew that meant she'd not had sex since she'd left Australia. He'd had no idea. 'You're kidding me, right?'

'Why would I do that?'

He could see her eyes filling with tears, she wasn't enjoying the conversation at all, it wasn't a lighthearted chat for her at all. 'Eve!' Quinn's smile went, he looked at her with concern. 'I didn't know.' Like it was astonishing and terribly sad, he put his hand on hers at the bar. 'You're a little onion, layer by layer.' He smiled, bringing a smile to her face.

'Do you think it's weird.' She the tears fall, smiling.

'You my girl have simply been taking your time, healing.' He smiled; he really did care for Eve.

Eve smiled. 'That very tall dark and handsome Aussie was my first love you know.' Her eyes cheekily sparkling as she spoke of Marco.

'Oh, that's him! I knew it, I knew he'd fucked you. Lover boy number one,' gushed Quinn.

'Don't say it like that, Marco's special., Eve said with passion in her voice, her eyes shining bright, her smile as wide across her face.

Quinn smiled at her, she was such a gorgeous girl, 'So you didn't hook up with him after you saw him at the festival?'

'No, I had dinner with you and Clemy. Then I went back to France the next day.'

'Eve, sweetheart, you need to take your opportunities otherwise you'll be sexless for the rest of your life.'

'He messaged me when he got back to Australia, and he's going to be in New York with my mum and Tessa and Zoe for Christmas.' She was so matter of fact.

'What the hell are you doing coming to Vienna with me?' Quinn screwed his face up. 'You should be going to New York and getting your rocks off with tall dark and handsome.'

Of course, Eve bit on her bottom lip in thought.

'Don't bite your beautiful lip, change your fucking flight,' Quinn said with an element of urgency.

'I'm not sure I'm ready, there's a bit of history with that one too.' She was speaking of Marco.

'You can't keep your walls up forever darling.'

'Yes I can,' Eve said, feeling a lot calmer now, her heart rate has slowed right down.

When Eve went to her room later that night in the palatial two-bedroom suite she was sharing with Quinn for the night, she couldn't sleep. After she and Quinn had eaten dinner, drank too much wine and laughed a lot, she phoned down to reception for a packet of cigarettes and another bottle of red wine to help her think. Her life felt like it was floating between what was and what could be. Sitting on the balcony wrapped in the plush bath robe with a scarf, socks, and hotel slippers on, in the freezing cold, she gazed across the rooftops of Paris, processing her past and her future and everything in between. It was a sliding door moment for her as she stared down at her phone reading the message that had plunged her into the depths of her reality.

E, I'm sorry for being a complete bitch face.
I just really wanted to see you; I miss you.
Have a wonderful Christmas in Vienna my
beautiful friend.
Forever and ever your friend Tessa xoxo
P.S Zoe, Nick and Marco say hi!

When Quinn woke it was still dark outside, a bedside lamp lit his room and Eve was sitting in a chair at the end of his bed, fully dressed, her coat on, staring at him. He glanced at her two oversized suitcases by the door. He didn't even have to ask what was going on, he knew. 'Lucky I'm used to waking up to strange women in my bedroom.'

Eve laughed, she watched him sit up in bed and wake himself up, 'You snore incredibly loud.'

'Henny and Clive are going to be devastated. They love you.' Quinn smiled at her.

'I need to be somewhere else,' she paused, 'Thank you for being my friend without benefits, I appreciate it more than you will ever know Doctor Portman.' Eve stood and went to the bedside. Quinn took her hands as he got up.

'It's been my absolute pleasure. You are a wonderful young woman, with so much life to live Eve. Promise me you will go and take life by the balls. Don't settle for anything less than everything.' Quinn's emotions snuck up on him as he farewelled his young friend.

'I most certainly will. Wish everyone a Merry Christmas for me.' Eve squeezed Quinn's hands. They hugged, and it was over. She walked out the room confident with where she was going next.

Making the flight to New York by the skin of her teeth, Eve had rushed to check in on time, then had an hour and a half to wait until the flight left. She took the opportunity to do some duty-free Christmas shopping, mostly gifts for herself. *Bless duty free!* Waiting at the gate, waiting for the first-class passengers to be called up, she decided now was a better time than any to call her father. It was always uncomfortable, she always feared Sam or one of her sisters would answer her father's phone.

'Eveline, I called you two days ago. Where are you?' Since Evan's death James had treated Eve like the adult that she was, he'd accepted she was now a young woman, who could run her own life.

'I'm in Paris. I'm just about to get on a flight to New York to spend Christmas with mum and the Rossi's.' She still wanted to love her dad, even though she would never forgive him.

'That sound wonderful sweetheart, I'm sure you'll have a great time,' he was chirpy.

'Are you in Sydney?'

'We are, I can't leave the country, I've got a big trial at the moment,' said James sounding as important as ever. Eve had her father summed up, yes he was smart, successful, egotistic man. As per usual, they did the small talk and wound the phone call up quickly.

'I'm about to board my flight Dad, I have to go.' Sometimes it felt like if she talked to him for too long, she might tell him just how much she really missed him. She just wanted to love him.

'You have a great Christmas darling. I love you.'

'I love you too Dad. Merry Christmas.' And just like that, another Christmas phone call to her father was over. They'd probably call each other again in a week or so, to wish a happy New Year and touch base, then James would call her for her birthday in late January, and then again at Easter to check in on her. At least they were being civil to one another. Their relationship was strained, but they were in contact with each other.

By the time Eve boarded her flight, she was exhausted. After travelling to Paris, staying up all night contemplating her decision to go to New York, then booking a flight and trying to get a room at the Forty West Hotel on Bryant Park, were her mother, Zoe and the Rossi's were all staying. It had been a huge twenty-four hours.

Tessa was staying in her parents suite, so they could all be together, her apartment was only a few blocks away, but it was very small. Zoe had her own hotel room, as did Marco, Nick, and Thomas the eldest Rossi son, who was with his English girlfriend Emma. Of course, Anna had bought Nigel along, and they had their own suite too. The hotel was fully booked when Eve called ahead from Paris, she put her name down for a cancelation and could only hope by the time she touched down in New York around dinner time on Christmas Eve, she would have a room. Worst case she was sure she could stay in Zoe's room. It was Christmas after all, and the Forty West Hotel was famous for its New York elegance and luxury at this time of year.

After eating a lite breakfast and drinking a pot of tea on the plane, Eve closed the curtain in her first-class pod and laid in her remarkably comfortable pod bed. The second her eyes closed; she was asleep for the next six hours.

To her own surprise she was excited to be landing in New York. Anna and Jackie would be happy to see her, Tessa and Zoe would be ecstatic. She could feel her anxiety kicking in at the thought of seeing Marco though… Seeing him face to face again, she had no expectations when it came to Marco, Eve knew she had to be careful though. The key was to not fall for him, don't get seduced and certainly don't allow false hope to cloud her judgement. Eve went over her survival techniques again and again in her head. If Jackie got an inkling that she had feelings for Marco, that would be disastrous. It was important to Eve that she didn't out Marco, and that her secret, remained her secret. Jackie would be devastated if she found out they'd had sex in Palm Cove, first and foremost. She'd be mad at Eve for lying about who the baby's father was in the first place, Eve had said Evan was the father. She never wanted to tell Marco he had fathered a baby with a seventeen-year-old, it always made her feel stupid and even a touch dirty. Eve couldn't help how she felt, it had been a confusing and terrible time in her life, one she had done her best to block out and push down where she kept all the other heartbreak in her life.

Standing at the hotel reception Eve was sure she was going to be seen before she was actually ready to make an appearance. As she waited patiently for the guy behind the counter to tell her if she had a room or not, she didn't turn her head for fear of seeing someone. Her arrival would be a total surprise to everyone, they all still thought she was on her way to Vienna with Quinn and his family.

'Ms. Frank today is your lucky day,' the tall skinny guy behind the counter nodded his head as he continued to confirm her details. 'We've had a late cancelation, I'm afraid it's only a standard room on the twenty second floor, but it's all yours if you want it.'

'I'll take it,' Eve said smiling.

'Give me a minute to prepare your room key and you'll be good to go,' he said looking at her with his perfectly manicured eyebrows and neatly slicked back hair, so very efficient and proud of himself.

The room was just what Eve needed, she did her usual inspection of the linen, bathroom, and cupboard space, all up to her standards. Cozy and stylish, so New York, navy, white, and black with a pop of red.

By the time she'd showered and dressed, it was well and truly past dinner time. She went down to the bar to have a quiet drink on her own, then she'd call the girls when she was feeling a little more courageous.

Sitting at a hotel bar alone for the second night in a row, Eve made sure she had a full view of who came and went. The bar was situated at the front of the hotel looking out onto the street and beautiful Bryant Park that had been transformed into a winter village. Watching the snow fall lightly through the windows, she felt good about her decision to let Quinn go to Vienna on his own. Her psychologist once suggesting she used Quinn for his fatherly representation, a notion Eve fiercely denied at the time. For the life of her, she couldn't see why she'd willingly befriend a man who represented her father.

Two vodka neat and a few eggnog shots later, Eve was feeling chatty and warm as she sat at the bar. No longer fixated on the door, talking, and joking with two bar tenders and an attractive gay couple who bought her another shot. As she talked and unconsciously flirted with the bar tenders, Eve caught the eye of a passing Nick, he rushed into the bar like she was his long-lost friend.

'Eve!' Nick said going straight to her and hugged her, 'What are you doing here?' He was genuinely happy to see her, and shocked in a good way.

'My plans changed.' Nick was probably the best person she could have run into first.

'Everyone's on their way back here for a drink, we've just had dinner in Korea Town. Your two mates are going to completely freak out when they see you. Did you get Tessa's text last night? We were right here in this bar having drinks when she messaged you. She's been stressing out like you've broken up with her or something.' He was genuinely pleased to see Eve, which was a weird.

'Yes, I got the message, it's kind of why I'm here.'

Then from the door a sound Eve knew immediately. A cross between an exited squeal and a shocked laughed. 'Oh. My. God.' Tessa almost got a run up as she flew toward the bar and flung herself at Eve. 'You came.' Tessa cried with joy holding onto Eve dramatically.

'I got your message last night; it was just what I needed.' Eve hugged Tessa back, squeezing her, trying not to get herself upset.

'Oh, E. I'm sorry for being horrible to you. Zoe told me how upset you were and I just felt terrible about it.' Tessa was on the edge of tears.

'No. I needed to hear it, you were right, I should be here with you guys and not in Vienna.' Eve saw Zoe patiently waiting her turn. She jumped off her bar stool and into Zoe's arms.

'I can't believe you're here,' Zoe gushed as everyone else came into the bar at that moment, and spotted Eve.

'I needed to be here.' She looked at both Tessa and Zoe.

'Eveline. Darling.' Anna was a combination of shocked, surprised, and happy to see her daughter. She had just been divulging her disappointment in her daughter's absence to the table at dinner over several glasses of wine.

'Merry Christmas Mum. What was I thinking not being here with you?' Eve got teary seeing her mother emotional, it had been a while since they'd seen each other and no matter what went on in their lives, they would always be mother and daughter.

'What happened with Quinn?' asked Anna almost too excited.

'Nothing, I just needed to be here.'

'Oh, I'm so happy you changed your mind.' Anna turned to Jackie and Nigel to share her joy.

'What a wonderful surprise, this is absolutely the best Christmas ever.' Jackie was next to pull Eve into her arms.

'I thought you'd be happy,' Eve said with a big, long hug, 'I've missed you.'

'Are you kidding? I'm ecstatic, look at your mother, she's crying.' Jackie pulled Anna into their huddle of joy. It was an emotional welcoming; Eve was feeling the love.

Eve greeted Nigel and Mario, saying hello to Thomas and his lovely girlfriend Emma. Kisses and hugs all round in front of the fireplace as they all stood around together cheerfully catching up in the hotel bar. A couple of flustering minutes passed before Eve realized Marco was the only one not there. Her chest sank with disappointment, her smile subsided for that initial moment, and then there he was, walking through the door, his hair had grown out again, he was in a sweater and jeans, and he was utterly breathtaking. Eve's heart literally stopped at the sight of him, she only had a second to convince herself it was going to be okay, that she could do this. *Just don't fall for those beautiful brown eyes the second he looks at you... Too late!*

'Hey, wow!' Marco said almost stopping still a second when saw Eve standing in the middle of everyone, she was so very beautiful, he'd been thinking about her day and night since London. 'Evie, you're here.' His big strong arms scooped her up into his, her feet leaving the ground. This was the best surprise ever!

'Merry Christmas,' Eve gasped softly with caution, wrapping her arms round his neck came naturally, breathing him into her lungs was magnificent... then a kiss. Not just any old peck on the cheek either, this was a kiss on the lips... a pausing kiss that got everyone's attention.

Tessa and Zoe watching on, knowing how it looked and so excited at the reception Marco had given Eve.

'Let's get drinks, this is the best Christmas ever,' Tessa said cheerfully breaking up the embrace of her older brother and her best friend, she'd caught sight of her mother's curious gaze. Eve and Marco looked fucking great together. They belonged together; Tessa had always felt this way. *But would her mother!*

Marco had been like a magnet to Eve's body, they came together with ease, just as they had all those years ago. His lips at hers for those slight seconds warming every part of her just as he had when she was a love-sick innocent teenager. Eve felt Zoe at her side, like she was trying to break the connection, their immediate bond. There was a buzz between Eve and Marco, and Tessa and Zoe were in a spin.

'What happened to Vienna?' Jackie came quickly to Eve as Marco stepped back. She and Anna were excited and curious all that the same time. Jackie interpreting the touching embrace between her favourite son and Eve, as two old friends catching up, nothing more.

'I should have been here all along... What was I thinking?' Eve's eyes looked at the dotting women who surrounded her. Anna and Zoe flanking her at either side, Tessa behind her mother looking extatically wide eyed. Jackie center and front to Eve, wanting to hear all about it.

'I don't know, what were you thinking?' Jackie humored her.

'What about Quinn Darling?' Anna questioned wanting an explanation now.

All eyes were on Eve, she was conscious of Marco standing at the sidelines with Nick listening in.

'We're not together Mum, were just friends,' as she said it, she saw all their faces looking at her puzzled, they'd all expected more of an explanation, something more exiting perhaps, but that was all Eve was offering up.

'Good. Great. You'll have a better time here with us anyway,' Tessa broke the awkward silence.

Then Jackie took hold of Eve's hands, 'I'm sure he was a lovely man Eve, but really, he's old enough to be your father!' Jackie huffed, frowning at Eve.

'We're just friends,' Eve repeated, nobody was listening to her.

'Mum!' Tessa was mortified, even she knew it was too much.

'Oh, god,' Anna gasped in pure horror at the thought of James.

'You know what I meant, Quinn's too old for Eve, she needs someone her own age, she needs a man she can have a family with and enjoy a full life with,' Jackie was now planning Eve's life for her.

'She's attracted to older men though, it's inevitable.' Anna noted forgetting Eve at her side.

'It's not like she was ever in love with Quinn, it was a friendship,' Zoe put her two cents in.

The woman who Eve loved the most, were all having a conversation about her as if she were invisible.

'Right. Well, never mind. She's here now, how amazing is that!' Tessa pointed out happily with an unsuspecting glance in Marco's direction, he was half listening and half talking with Nick.

'There's nowhere else I'd rather be,' Eve said winking at Tessa who came to her for another hug.

As they sat around the burning fireplace, the snow lightly fell outside the windows, Dean Martin Christmas carols filled the packed room as everyone was there to celebrate this wonderful Christmas Eve.

Eve sat wedged between Zoe and Tessa on a big chesterfield, with Nick squashed in next to Tessa. Anna, Jackie, Emma, and Thomas on another sofa, while Marco, Mario, and Nigel stood by the fireplace encompassing the cheerful group.

'What's going on with you, and you know who?' Zoe whispered into Eve's ear from one side during the course of the evening. It was like the whisper went right through Eve's ears, and out the other side to Tessa.

'My brother is very much single at the moment, and so are you. Now's the time E,' a whisper from Tessa into the other ear.

'Who Nick!' Eve joked, she'd switched from vodka to red wine, she was feeling humorous.

Tessa ignored her, 'He told us last night that he's had a thing for you ever since Palm Cove,' Tessa continued to whisper. 'You need to stop pretending he doesn't exist.'

'I always thought Nick hated me.' Eve's tired and wary laugh made her friends smile.

'I'm being serious,' Tessa's voice was louder now.

'I know. I'm just not sure, I need some time,' said Eve taking the sound down again in her soft and now also serious voice, 'I don't want to make it something it's not.'

'Bullshit E. I've thought about it, a lot,' Tessa spoke quietly to Eve and Zoe, everyone else was having their own conversations. 'Marco wants you, I'm sure of it. You've just got to watch out for my mum. You know why, don't you?' she focused in on Eve.

'Oh, God, now you're giving me anxiety,' Eve gasped.

Tessa spoke like she was an FBI spy, 'If my mum finds out anything happened between you two in Palm Cove, she'll know it was him who got you pregnant,' Tessa took a breath, 'She will go fucking nuts E - like you've never seen Jac go nuts before. She'll know we all lied to her.' The situation was far more complicated than just Eve and Marco lying, they'd all lied. Eve and Zoe sat listening intently as Tessa continued. 'I know you two will get together, because I'm making it my festive fucking mission,' said Tessa, 'Don't look at me like that E. You know this is your destiny.'

Eve pulled a face at Tessa, 'Or it'll be my downfall!' It was all very sudden for Eve, Zoe not so much, she had heard it all before, she and Tessa had spoken about Eve and Marco several times.

Tessa continued, 'But you're going to have to tell him what happened at some point, otherwise he will fuck himself up with my mum big time. I know my brother, and he's so open with Jac, he'll tell her everything, and she will kill him.' Tessa looked at Eve suddenly. 'And then she'll kill you. And then me. Even you Zoe.' She gave Zoe a look like it was somehow her fault too.

'Wow! You've really have been thinking this through, haven't you?' Eve was stunned.

'I told you, I'm on a mission.' Tessa was so serious.

An amused Zoe laughed, 'You're scaring her with this mission shit... she'll be gone in the morning, off to Vienna,' Zoe said speaking across Eve to Tessa.

'If you two are going to work, you need to make out like it just happened now, here in New York. Like there was never a past. And Marco needs to know why, so you need to tell my brother the truth,' Tessa said to Eve who all the sudden felt sick to her stomach. This was not what she'd expected on her arrival at all.

'I'm not here for Marco, I'm here for you two and my mum. He's not my destiny. So, can we calm down and enjoy Christmas please,' Eve said feeling uncomfortable.

'Of course, we can.' Zoe kissed Eve's cheek.

'I'm on a mission either way,' Tessa looked at Eve and then Zoe, as if to let them know she wasn't going to be derailed by either of them.

Everyone crammed into the lift in the early hours of the morning. Eve squished up against Jackie and Mario with her mother beside her holding her hand. When they woke up it would be Christmas day.

'Is everyone good for lunch at one tomorrow?' Jackie asked. Everyone came back with a yes. All the official gatherings had been planned and booked by Jackie months ahead, all that had to happen was the addition of Eve to each booking. Jackie had it covered. She loved Eve like a daughter, it was no secret. Even Anna knew Jackie had a weird parental right to Eve. She had been there for Eve at every turn of her life, Anna was very grateful that Eve listened to Jackie and confided in her.

'This is me,' Marco said when the lift stopped at level twenty-two.

'Me too,' Eve said looking up feeling an air of awkwardness. They hadn't spoken all night besides their greeting and now they were looking at each other in a lift full of family.

Tessa cleared her throat, it was miracle, they were on the same floor together. It was a sign!

'Marco, make sure Eve gets to her room safely please... I love you both.' Jackie waved them out the lift.

'Goodnight kids,' Anna happily added as the doors closed.

Now it was just the two of them standing face to face in the hallway. Eve was smaller than he had remembered, the top of her head was at his mid chest. A quick flash of the first time he'd bed her, passed through his mind. He'd been terrified of hurting her, she'd been so delicate and sweet, he'd never forget how he felt.

Eve was tired, jetlagged and after several drinks, weary on her feet, she stood looking up into Marco's eyes. His long lashes melting her heart as they always had.

'I'm glad you decided to come to New York Eve Frank,' Marco said smiling down at her, taken by her beauty and her mass of long unruly curls. She was slightly drunk and ever so cute.

'Me too.'

'Merry Christmas Evie. It's officially Christmas Day.' He looked at his watch, his hair falling into his eyes.

Oh, heavenly gorgeous man. She was mesmerized by him.

'It is,' her smile faded. 'Merry Christmas and good night Marco Rossi. I'll see you at lunch tomorrow.' Reaching out and touching his arm, she took a step back. *Don't fall into his magnificent charm.*

'Good night.' Marco watched her walk to her door and disappear into her room.

Chapter Four

Breakfast was a quiet affair with just her mother and Nigel at a table in the hotel restaurant. Eve and Anna had so much to catch up on, so once breakfast was over, they went for a walk out in the snow lined streets. Small flakes of snow fell from the sky as Nigel walked with the ladies. He was a nice man, a good man and Eve definitely approved. He wasn't her mothers' type though, she didn't judge, Eve just wanted her mother to be happy.

Mother and daughter did some window shopping as they walked with arms linked along Fifth Avenue, it was the one thing Eve and Anna did together so well, shop. Their morning was unexpected and wonderful, Anna so in need of this time with her daughter, this Christmas holiday was exceeding all her expectations. Her heart was full, she had a wonderful friend in Jackie, a loyal partner in Nigel and now her precious Eveline was here.

Arriving back at the hotel, the instant warmth of the lobby was welcoming, Christmas cheer was in the air and all around. Lunch was at The Plaza, Jackie liked to do things right, there was no skimping when it came to making memories with her family. The Plaza was her favorite place to visit in the city and she had made the reservation a year in advance, so not to miss out.

Eve spent the best part of an hour getting ready for Christmas lunch. Brushing her long curls over and over so they were soft like silk waves. Her makeup was light and natural against her cinnamon skin with the brightest of red lipsticks channeling her Christmas spirit. Stylish in a sexy Valentino outfit, fitted black silk pants, a nude sheer shirt open to the third button, revealing just a peek of her voluptuous cleavage. Her faithful black Jimmy Choo stilettos accompanied by her favorite black woolen coat finished her look off.

The Plaza was a buzz with people celebrating Christmas day with friends and loved ones. Jackie had managed to add Eve to the table at such short notice. Tessa ushered Eve into her place at the table, conveniently right next to Marco, while she sat opposite so she could see and hear everything they did and said. Beside Tessa was Nick and Zoe, Eve sat between Marco and Emma, who was tall, slender, and blonde, completely opposite to Eve, though she was quiet and reserved, the two would get along famously.

'Where in London do you and Tom live?' Eve started the conversation. They had an in-depth discussion about London and Paris. Emma had a lot of questions for Eve about the chateau, asking what was the best time of year to have a wedding in France. It was an instant friendship, the two finding they had a lot in common.

The table had many conversations underway; champagne was being poured and every time Eve looked at Tessa, she was watching her.

'Is everything alright?' Eve eventually asked Tessa as they ate their extravagant Christmas lunch.

'Amazing, thank you... You?' Tessa said smiling, looking at Eve and then at Marco.

'Well. It has been a long time since we've all sat and eaten a meal together,' Eve said cheerfully to their end of the table which consisted of the younger people.

'We just need Zach and Rory here and it would be the Palm Cove crew,' Tessa's eyes lit up when she said Zach's name, she had been so infatuated with him on their Palm Cove holiday.

'Oh, and Nick isn't being such a dick like he was in Palm Cove that summer,' Tessa nudged her brother.

'You were a bitch if I remember right, just for something different,' he couldn't help himself, he had to bite back at Tessa, it wouldn't be the same unless there was bit of Nick v Tessa banter.

'You were definitely a dick on that holiday,' Eve gave him a friendly but sarcastic smirk across the table, realizing as the words left her mouth, that Jackie was tuned in to their conversation.

'Yeah, especially to Eve,' Marco added.

Jackie's eyes followed everyone as they spoke, her radar was sharp as a tack.

'Did I miss something?' Tessa had no idea what was going on.

'I knew you'd say that.' Nick gave Eve an apologetic look.

'It's okay, I forgive you all these years later.' She raised her eyebrows, letting him know she was all good with it now. They had a good talk last night by the fireplace in the bar and Nick seemed to have grown up and matured into a half decent guy, Eve wasn't one to hold a grudge even though she would never forgive his treatment of Zoe.

'You always gets away with being an asshole. That was some of your worst behavior,' Marco said keeping it going. Eve glanced again at Jackie who was pretending not to listen, but Eve knew she was.

'What! What about what you all did that summer? Yeah. I thought so...' It was the worst thing Nick could have said, Jackie was definitely zoning in.

Oh no, Eve thought as Nick defended himself to his older brother, he still had a bit of shit in him and couldn't be trusted. He looked at all of them, knowing he could expose them all for their behaviour.

'People in glass houses, shouldn't throw stones Nicholas,' Zoe warned him with an icy glare. She could see that this was getting out of hand, and Nick had been the one who had definitely behaved the worst in her opinion.

Just as Eve was starting to panic, Tom stood from his seat and tapped his dessert spoon on his glass of champagne, commanding everyone's attention. Eve didn't know Tom very well; he was an older more serious and sophisticated version of Marco... She didn't think as good looking though!

'Merry Christmas everyone. It's not often I get all my siblings on the one continent along with Mum and Dad. So, I think now is a good time to let you all know, Emma and I have decided to get married, there's no date yet.'

A few seconds of gasps and gushes of happiness as everyone started to congratulate the happy couple.

'These are tears of happiness. I'm just so happy. I love, love,' Jackie told the table as she settled back into her seat and the tempo of the table hit a high with more champagne and the story of how Tom had proposed to Emma while they skated at the Rockefeller Centre only yesterday.

With excitement in the air and everyone enjoying what had turned out to be a wonderful lunch, Marco casually slipped his arm around the back of Eve's chair.

Tessa smiling like she had accomplished something, but it meant nothing other than the fact he was a big guy who needed to stretch out.

'I'm going to cry of happiness next,' Tessa teased Eve, making a crying face, partly mocking her mum, but mostly just stirring Eve up. Clearly, Tessa had had a few champers and was feeling silly.

'Stop it,' Eve said trying not to laugh whilst Marco was oblivious, he was in talks with Zoe and Nick.

'I'm on a mission E,' Tessa teased with a giggle.

'Are you drunk?' Eve used the same tone as Tessa had.

'No, I'm not. Now, come with me to the bathroom.' She stood up and gave Eve a look, a bossy like look. Slipping off through the tables with her arm hooked into Eve's, Tessa looked like a Hollywood starlet in her tight white dress, her dark blonde locks up in a big round bun on her head. Her eyeliner was very Amy Winehouse, she towered over Eve in her white heels. In the privacy of the bathroom Tessa and Eve looked in the mirror fixing their makeup and checking themselves out.

'You're acting creepy. Please don't set us up,' Eve told Tessa regarding her and Marco. Her matchmaking ways where in her blood, she was just like Jackie, always out to set up someone or change a situation.

'Do you not want him anymore?' it was a ridiculous question, and Tessa only asked it to get Eve to admit she did for clarification.

'You know the answer to that, but I'm,' Eve sighed.

'I don't want to hear your bullshit, he's mad about you E, can't you tell?'

'Who's mad about E?' Jackie appeared like a Jeanie out of nowhere.

'I said he's mad *at* her, not about her. You shouldn't sneak up on people Mother Dearest, we might have been talking about you,' Tessa hissed at her mother, pissed that she had followed them.

'Oh, really.' Jackie didn't believe them; she knew what she had heard. Her daughter could be such a bitch at times, no respect! She'd heard the comments going back and forth between Nick and Eve, she was now convinced they had been together in Palm Cove... When Eve conceived the baby! Jackie had paid particular notice to Marco's comments, he seemed upset with Nick's behavior in Palm Cove. *He was keeping something from her!*

Lunch rolled into drinks at their hotel bar again. While Jackie and Mario along with Anna and Nigel went off to have a lite dinner at a restaurant nearby, the younger ones ordered tapas from the hotel bar.

'I should never have treated you the way I did in Palm Cove. I wish I could take it all back Eve,' Nick said as they sat together on a sofa for two by the front window of the hotel bar.

'I wish you had treated Zoe better that summer.' Eve stared him straight in the eye. He knew he got under Eve's skin; he knew she didn't think much of him and that bothered him, and he should have guessed she knew what had gone down between he and Zoe that summer.

'The worst thing about it, is that I really like Zoe… As a friend I mean,' making himself clear.

'Well, you're full of surprises, aren't you Nick Rossi? You're not such a dick after all.' Eve gave him a friendly smile, there was no point taking Nick to task over something that happened years ago.

Nick narrowed his eyes to Eve, 'What's going on with you and the big fella? You're sleeping with him aren't you?'

'What! No.' Surprised Nick would go there.

'I've been wondering why he was talking about you so much when we first arrived in New York, he grilled Tessa asking her why you didn't want to come and asking about you and that old guy you're seeing.' Nick scrunched his face, 'And then you sit next to him at the table today. I'm not stupid Eve, I see the way you look at each other.'

'I never said you were stupid, just very annoying… I'm not sleeping with your brother. And I'm not with the old guy either.' Eve took drink from her martini glass battering her eyes at Nick to correct him.

Marco came and squeezed in on the other side of Eve, so she was sandwiched between the two brothers, an innocent move on Marco's behalf, but it fueled Nick's suspicions further.

'Can I have a minute with Eve, would you mind?' Marco said to Nick.

'You two kids… I'm onto you,' he said getting up off the sofa with a smile.

Eve moved herself back into the space Nick had left. Marco moved with her, so he could talk to her one on one and privately. They sat sideways, face to face.

'Has anything ever happened with you and my brother... You know, romantically? Or not romantically?' Marco asked as he thought how pretty Eve was, particularly today.

'Are you seriously asking me if I've been with Nick?' she couldn't help her reaction. *Was he for real?*

Marco put his hand on Eve's knee that was bent up on the sofa. 'You can be straight with me Evie.' He was serious. He thought there had been something between Eve and Nick, his mother had sparked the thought a few times now over the years, almost like she knew something.

Staring at him for a second dumb founded, Eve was breathless, a bit devastated. The day was getting to her, she'd tried her best to be upbeat, over the years she'd struggled with Christmas day and the loss of Evan. Having Marco around had been a distraction until now, now she felt flooded with her past.

'Nothing has ever happened between us; besides him irritating me immensely.'

'It's just my mum said something to me today. I get the feeling she's really upset with Nick for something he's done to you. It didn't make sense to me, maybe she had too many champagnes at lunch.' Marco laughed to make lite of things.

Oh, Fuck! Now Eve was really breathless. To make matters worse she could see Tessa over Marco's shoulder trying to listen in. 'I've never been with your brother. I think your mum would like to believe there's something between Nick and I,' she huffed. She could tell by Marco's face he didn't like the thought of that.

Over his shoulder Eve saw Tessa mouthed the words *'Tell him,'* her stormy eyes warned Tessa off. Eve was more than annoyed with her best friend, she threw Tessa an intolerant frown. Immediately she excused herself and went up to her room, claiming to be tired and needing a nap before they hit the town later in the evening. It may be a mission for Tessa, but it was far more to Eve. She'd been living in her little sheltered bubble in France for a long time, she was extremely private and wanted to keep things that way.

It was nearly midnight when Zoe and Nick showed up at Eve's door to collect her, they had decided on a nearby spot not far away in Hell's kitchen. It was an old theatre that had been turned into a club and it was one of Tessa's regular hang outs. Every corner they turned Tessa had a hang out in New York.

Tom and Emma came along, they weren't really into clubs as such, but they still felt like celebrating, it was Christmas and they were engaged, everyone was very merry with the excitement of a New York club.

Eve had showered and changed into a suit, she had packed three suits for Vienna, they were her going out attire, her go to cold weather choice of clothing, she looked stylish and sexy, especially when she wore only a lace bra underneath her jacket and her abundance of cleavage was on display for all, it made her feel particularly feminine. This suit was lipstick pink, she paired it with black Jimmy Choo stilettos. Her hair out and unruly as always, not a lot of makeup, nude lips and her dainty E rose gold necklace hanging at her chest, she never took it off.

The bar was strangely packed to the brim, who would have thought that so many people wanted to go out and party on Christmas night! Tessa said it was like this every night. She was a regular so no queuing – of course. They had a booth right next to the bar, a few of Tessa's cast mates were there too, one of their boyfriends owned the club. Zoe and Eve stood at the bar with Marco and Nick while Tom and Emma went off to danced, Eve hadn't picked them to be dancers, but they were, and they seemed to be having a lot of fun.

Nick was being his usual entertaining self, mainly concentrating on Zoe, doing his very best to make her laugh and impress her. Not missed by Eve's eye, it was interesting to say the least!

Marco took the opportunity to speak with Eve, he leaned down to her ear, 'Are you upset with me because I asked you about Nick earlier?' he leaned down to her ear pushing back her thick curls as she tingled to his touch.

She shrugged; she had been taken back by Marco's earlier comments.

He held an intimate gaze with Eve as she looked up at him with a troubled expression, still trying to get used to being in presence so often.

'Evie, I hope I didn't offend you? You know my mum; she's always looking for something.'

Eve knew Jackie all right, and she wished she would just leave it alone. The truth would near kill her if she found out her precious Marco was the one.

Come to think of it... It did really pissed Eve off that Marco would even question her about Nick. *Really, Nick!*

'Like I said, I've never been with Nick. Not even a kiss.' Unintentionally her warm breath to the side of his ear in the noisy club was seductive as always. 'I'm a little offended you would think that I would do anything with your brother,' she paused, 'It's always been you Marco.' Eve stood back from him, surprising herself at what she'd just admitted to Marco Rossi, she looked up at him with an innocent adoration.

'Really... Me!' Curiosity got the better of him. '

'Always,' she confirmed, not taking her eyes off his for a moment.

'E. I need you to come to the ladies with me!' Tessa was between them; she completely ruined the moment in her semi drunk way.

'You're interrupting.' Marco gave her a long blink of his eyes in annoyance, of all times for his sister to but in, she had absolutely no idea how to read a situation.

'You will thank me later,' Tessa told him and took Eve off to the bathroom.

Eve was baffled... On one hand Tessa had always wanted Eve to be with Marco. Then finally after a painstaking seven years apart, she'd just told Marco it had always been him; they were staring into each other's eyes and boom! Tessa interrupted rudely. Eve couldn't believe it; honestly, she didn't like Tessa and Jackie being so in her business when it came to her private life. She was not used to this interference in her life, she lived in a world where her grandmother respected her boundaries and gave her privacy.

Eve had craved Marco with all her being from the minute she first saw him as a gawky fifteen-year-old boy on the school bus. She'd had him; she had given her innocents to him, and it had ended in utter heartbreak and pain for her. Now she had the chance to heal some of those wounds and Tessa was fucking around.

'What are you doing, I'm confused,' Eve huffed as they stood by the basins in the bathrooms.

'You need to tell him upfront about the baby and all that stuff,' Tessa was slurring her words slightly; she had been drinking since lunch time.

'Are you insane?' Eve was annoyed at this bizarre behavior, 'You need to mind your own business and give me some space, I'm just getting to know Marco again after all these years... besides, I don't want to tell him. And I don't want to talk about it, not with him and not with you. It's not some exciting gossip Tessa. This is my life.' Eve was angry and Tessa was drunk, not a great combo.

'He is my brother. I think he should know he got you pregnant, especially if… '

'No!' Eve cut her off, 'This is nothing to do with you. It's my very private and personal life and I say who I tell and when I tell them,' Eve raised her voice. She turned around and Emma came out of a cubical, she stopped and looked at them both.

'Ignore me, I never heard a thing,' Emma said washing her hands.

'Great.' Eve pushed passed them both and stormed out of the bathroom.

Eve headed straight for the stairs and down to the exit, she grabbed her jacket from the cloak room by the door and went out onto the cold street where people were still lined up to get in. Her feet froze as she stepped out into the slosh of cold snow, angry that it would probably ruining her beautiful shoes.

What did you think would happen when you came to New York? Did you really think you and Marco would fall in love and live happily ever after! And that Jackie and Tessa would just leave you be! Eve knew that was a load of bullshit, there was never a happy ever after and her dear friends just couldn't help themselves.

'E. Where are you going?' Tessa rushed out onto the sidewalk. She had gone back to the bar to find Eve had gone, realising she'd stepped way over the friendship line.

Eve stopped in her tracks, 'I'm going home,' she said without turning around; her voice was depleted like she had a sore throat.

'You're right - it's none my business. I'm so sorry,' Eve didn't turn around to Tessa as she spoke, 'I just think you and Marco would be so great together, and I think it would be better if you were honest with him, he'll be upset if he finds out down the track, that's all,' Tessa was desperate.

As Eve turned to look at Tessa, she saw Marco standing right behind his sister. By the look on his face, he'd heard everything Tessa had said.

Tessa swung around to see what Eve was looking at. She stared at her brother in horror, then turned to Eve whose eyes were full of tears. Tessa couldn't take it back, there was nothing she could say to fix this even though she hadn't actually said anything about the baby.

'I'll walk you back to the hotel Evie,' Marco spoke calmly from the edge of the curb. He looked as gorgeous as ever, the cold air fogging as he spoke, he was so tall and handsome, it actually hurt Eve's heart to look at him.

Tessa had apologetic eyes; she didn't say a word as she headed back into the club. She knew she had fucked up big time. She knew better than anyone how much Marco meant to Eve, this secret little crush from schoolgirl to womanhood had never wavered, not even when Evan had been in her life. And Marco had always held a flame for Eve too. All Tessa wanted was for them to be together and to have no secrets between them.

They walked in complete silence the entire way back to the hotel. Eve stared straight ahead realising the shit, had well and truly hit the fan. All she'd wanted to was to just get to know Marco a little.

He followed Eve into the lift and to her hotel room door, 'Can we talk?'

'Come in, I'll order us some coffee,' Eve said opening the door and letting him in.

'It's so hot in here, what have you got the heating on?' Marco raised his eyebrows and pulled the front of his shirt out from his chest nervously; he stood in the hallway of her room.

'I didn't want to come back to a cold room,' she said taking her coat off, realising just how hot it was, 'I'm going to order coffee and carrot cake; would you like some?'

'Only if you turn the heating down.' He was still on edge, an uncertain look on his face, playing with his top like he was melting.

'I'll turn it down.' She sensed he was a little tense.

Marco was unsure of what was about to go down… Of what Eve had to tell him. He walked in past the bags on the floor and stood in the center of the small space. He looked around anxiously.

Eve watched him. 'Is it the same as your room?'

'Exactly. My beds not a king size bed like yours though, my beds a queen.' He hit the end of the bed with his hand as he looked back at her, she kicked her shoes off.

'Queens too short for you?' They began to banter back and forth with pointless conversation.

'Yep.' He wandered over to the window and checked out the view of the park. 'I don't have this view either, I'm looking at a brick wall.' Marco was agitated, it was in his tone.

'How do you have your coffee?' Eve sat on the bed and picked up the phone beside her bed ready to call room service.

As he said it, room service picked up, she ordered and then hung the phone up and put her knee up on the bed turning to face Marco who was now sitting in the chair. It was weird, she couldn't help but think how strange it was to be in a hotel room with *her* Marco. After all these years it still felt like a dream to be in his presence, she knew it was stupid, but she still got butterflies and was completely intimidated by his handsome good looks.

A bit of small talk and chit chat, avoiding the inevitable conversation they would eventually have. Room service arrived, and Eve tipped the attendant as he left after placing the tray of coffee and cake down on the table near were Marco sat. After she shut the door and came back placing Marco's coffee and cake near him on the table, she took her coffee and plate of cake back to the edge of the bed where she sat and took a big gulp of coffee.

'I'm really sorry for everything you've had going on in your life, Eve.' He surprised her with his words.

Where was this coming from? She looked at him hating his pity, she didn't need it and she certainly didn't know what to say, she froze, her throat felt like it was closing over with a lumps of emotion.

'Thank you,' she managed. What else was there to say.

'I'm glad to see your doing okay, are you doing okay?' Marco had decided to go about this with Eve the best way he knew, open and honestly with care, they were in uncharted waters right now.

'I'm fine. Thank you Marco.' Oh, God, she just had to go with it. And she was grateful he cared; she had always known he was that kind of guy. Eve knew he had called several times after Evan had passed away to see how she was doing; Tessa had told her. His messages in the past few weeks had been kind and thoughtful, just like him.

'What's going on Eve?' he needed an answer.

For a moment she thought he might have forgotten what Tessa said outside the club. 'Um... err. I don't know.' She was stumbling, so she stood up.

'Did something happen between you and Nick? Just tell me if it did.'

'No, it really didn't.' She tried to be sincere but was now offended all over again. 'I wish you would stop asking me that.'

'What does Tessa and my mum know that I don't Eve?' he paused with a strained look on his face, 'Does my mum know about Palm Cove, is it something to do with that stupid morning after pill Zoe gave you. I've always felt bad about that by the way. I'm sorry.' And he went on as Eve felt the bile in her stomach rise to her throat. 'That should never have happened, especially on your first time. I should have used protection. That was a mistake and if I could change it, I would.' Marco was going to keep asking questions as long as Eve was avoiding them, and if she didn't stop him soon, she was going to explode and possible combust into a million little fucking fucked up pieces.

Her survival mechanisms kicked in and she decided to shut down. She didn't answer his question, she froze and looked everywhere but at him.

'Evie, I feel like something happened?' his voice a touch louder, still gentle and calm as always.

She glanced at him briefly as he sat on his chair, she looked down at his hands clenched between his knees, his knuckles were white, he was waiting for her to fess up to him. *Did he know already, and he wanted her to confess to his face?* Eve's mind was in meltdown mode.

'Whatever it is, you can tell me.'

Oh, God, shut up. Stop!

'Your mum knew I was heartbroken after Palm Cove,' she paused, 'I don't know, she must think it was Nick I was pining for, I never told her it was you.' It was only partially the truth, and mostly a lie.

Marco sighed like he was relieved, 'I'm sorry your heart was broken.' He rolled his lips concerningly, like he was in the depth of thought.

'Everyone gets their heart broken once or twice, my first time just happened to be by you.' Eve lifted the mood with a cute smile.

'It was bad timing. You were young, and I probably should have known better than to do what I did with you.' Marco smiled back at her.

'But you just couldn't resist me?' her smile widened; humour was her go to whenever things got tough.

'How could I resist you Eve Frank? You're beautiful inside and out.' Taking in every inch of her perfect face, Marco wondered if she still felt something for him, the way he did for her.

'You got anything better than that!' laughing at his attempt to flatter her.

'What would you rather hear, that I just wanted to get into your pants, because you're incredibly sexy.'

'Ha. If that was the truth, then yes.' She was overwhelmed, it was almost too hard to hide her teary relief at how she'd managed to avoid telling him about the baby.

'I liked what we had in Palm Cove.' He was a gentleman.

'Me too.' Eve felt the moment getting deep again, it was like waves of intense depth and then light romantic humour, she was beading with sweat under her clothes.

They sat sipping on coffee and eating carrot cake for an hour, talking about Palm Cove, and snorkeling and what Eve did at the chateau with her grandmother and Louis. They talked about Zach and his wife Brooke and how Marco was happy to live with them forever, they were like his family. The night got away from them as they chatted catching up on what was then, and what was now. Both so comfortable sitting in each other's company that it almost felt weird. Marco asked how she'd coped with Evan's death, and how she was now with it all. It was this questions that made Eve shut down instantly.

Her stormy eyes pulled Marco into her soul with their intensity. 'I don't talk about it; it's just how I need to do things?' Eve stood up from her seat, Marco got up too. 'I'm really tired, it's been a big day,' she said as she walked to the door.

'It has,' Marco followed her to the door, a little taken by her sudden change in demeanor. He stepped forward to her and put a hand around the back of her neck, then he leaned down to Eve, he knew it probably wasn't the right time, but he was willing to take the risk. He took a breath before he kissed her on the mouth. A small lingering peck goodbye, all of five seconds, nothing more. Eve moved her lips to his ever so slightly, it was the briefest moment of bliss, then she broke away.

'I'm sorry I broke your heart Eve Frank,' Marco said touching her face as she stood with the door open for him to leave.

'I'm not.' Her eyes sparkled up at him. 'It was the best broken heart I ever had.'

Reaching out and putting his pointer finger on her nose gently, giving her a smile as she stood close to him.

'Tomorrow's a new day,' he said melting her heart with an extremely sexy wink.

'Goodnight Marco.' Eve slowly closed the door behind him.

Chapter Five

Eve woke to the loud banging on the door, she'd barely slept, scrambling into the robe she made her way to the door, 'Who is it?' she asked as she reached up to look through peep hole.

'It's us,' Zoe said as she stood at the door with Tessa.

Eve let them in, Tessa looking around as she entered like she was looking for something… or someone.

'Have you seen Marco this morning? I thought he might have still been here with you.' Tessa didn't know what to expect from Eve after last night.

'He didn't stay here,' her tone a little off.

'No. I didn't mean it to sound like that. He didn't come to breakfast, he's not in his room. I just thought you might know where he was,' Tessa said, she didn't want to get on the wrong side of Eve again, things had gone pear shaped between them last night and she was feeling terrible.

'I don't know where your brother is. Maybe he went for a run,' Eve had tone pulling her hands through her hair. The bath robe gapped open revealing her curvy naked body.

Tessa's eyes lowered to her friends morish body, 'Well, was he okay last night? Did you tell him?' Tessa asked afraid of the answer, in the light of day, she knew she shouldn't have pushed Eve last night.

'I didn't get to tell him.' Eve's eyes went right through Tessa who slumped down on the bed.

'I just think...' Tessa gasped, devastated that *she might* had ruined it for Eve and Marco.

'Tessa. Don't do that to me again. I've told you; I will decide who and when I tell someone the private details of my life.' Eve was still angry, and Tessa knew it. Zoe looked on from the sidelines holding her breath.

'I'm sorry E,' Tessa said slowly, 'But he's my brother, and I'm as protective of him, as I am of you. I love you both so much.'

Eve accepted the apology, 'I know.' Both girls had always known were they stood with each other, it was just that sometimes that line got blurred with emotions and loyalties.

The girls talked Eve into going shopping, which consumed the rest of their day, they did all the big stores, it was a shopping bonanza. Eve decided to buy herself the Jimmy Choo boots she had been thinking about for weeks, just by chance they had her size. It was meant to be. Her arms were full of bags, clothing, cosmetics, sunglasses, and handbags. The day had turned out to be a fun with her two best friends on the loose in New York City.

Whilst Tessa was in the bathroom midway through their Bloomingdale raid, Zoe and Eve got a few things straight about the Rossi brothers, minus the Rossi sister.

'Would you seriously go there again with Nick?' Eve asked curiously as she watched out for Tessa.

'You know I'm the queen of repeat bad boy sex,' Zoe giggled proudly.

'Yes, you are,' smiling at how forgiving her friend was of the guy who used and abused her all those years ago when she was merely a teenager.

'We've all had one bad boy get under our skin Evie. Nick is mine.'

'I think you've let a few bad boys get under your skin, or on, or in... I don't know,' joked Eve pulling a funny face that made Zoe burst out laughing.

'I don't think I want a bad boy anymore. I want a good man. Bad is not good.' Zoe showed a flash of seriousness. She'd grown, her career was great, she was independent more so than ever, she was strong and smart, Eve admired the woman Zoe had become.

'No. Bad is not good,' Eve agreed, she lost her smile, her friends words hit her in the pit of her stomach.

Zoe saw Eve's face change. 'You know what I mean Evie,' she said hoping she hadn't hurt her friends feelings, 'Oh, Evie, babe, I just want someone to love me. I've never had a man fall in love with me.'

'I love you.' Eve pulled Zoe into her arms and hugged her in like she wanted her to feel her love. 'I've been in love with you from the minute I met you.' Both smiling, feeling the love.

'What's going on!' Tessa was at their side, scowling at them like they were doing something wrong.

'We're loving each other.' Zoe laughed as they set off to finish their perfect day of shopping.

The cab pulled up out the front of the hotel, just in time for Tessa to get herself to the theatre for showtime. When the cab driver opened the boot, the bags literally sprang out at the girls, they had to laugh.

'Do you need a hand?' Emma and Tom happened to be walking by at the same time. Tom took Tessa's bags as she ran off, they had cut it really fine, and she didn't have the time to hang around fussing over her shopping. Emma helped Eve to her room with all her bags, she'd really been excessive. Eve liked Emma, she seemed genuine, earthy, and kind.

As they dropped the bags on the floor of Eve's hotel, Emma lingered.

'Um, Eve, about last night in the bathroom at the club... I don't really know you that well, and I don't know your history with Marco,' Emma stalled, 'But I can't unhear what I heard.' Her face was wary as she looked at Eve.

'I can only imagine what you're thinking,' Eve said awkwardly.

'I'm not thinking anything. There's no judgement from me Eve, and I haven't told anyone what I heard, not even Tom. I promise you.'

'I really appreciate that Emma. I know it sounds terrible, like I'm keeping secrets from everyone, but I have my reasons.' Eve didn't feel the need to elaborate any further with Emma, she trusted Emma for some reason. She was a good person, a girl's girl from Eve could tell.

'You have my word.'

'Thank you Emma.' Eve watched as Emma went to the lift, her chest felt heavy.

Sitting at the bar in a tight black sweater and black cropped pants, and her new boots, Eve started with a tequila shot, followed by a neat Vodka. She sat with her own thoughts, a dangerous pastime. Sometimes she felt like she had lived a lifetime already, and Tessa and Zoe still hadn't had a real love in their life, and Eve had had two that she would never completely get over.

'How did I know I'd find you in here?' In a cloud of magical glittering sparkle, Marco sat down beside her.

'I like sitting in hotel bars on my own talking with random people, it's strangely therapeutic,' Eve smiled back at him, to her surprise, there was no ill feeling or thick air between them, it was instant pleasure.

'Am I interrupting,' Marco asked eyeing the hovering bartender.

'Not at all… I'm glad you're here.' *Oh, was that too eager, too much?*

'What, he's not that talkative?' gesturing to the guy behind the bar.

'Not really,' she chuckled at his observation.

Marco nudged into her with his arm without saying a word, he had so much he wanted to say to Eve, but didn't know how to say it, or even where to start. He ordered a drink and another for Eve as they sat in a familiar silence for quite some time, just enjoying the presence of the other, as they did.

'Tell me more about where you live, what do you do for fun there?' he smiled, and the world was good again. Just like that, Marco made her feel so spectacularly special. Taken by his interest in her life, Eve now found herself lost in his dreamy eyes and those long lashes, his imperfect nose, and the slight gap in his front teeth. The tiny freckle under his eye always distracted her. Marco was handsome in a manly way, not flawless, but that was what made him so perfect to Eve. He was masculine and big with an ever-present glint in his eye and a smile she found comfortingly irresistible. She was still awestruck by Marco after all this time.

Quickly remembering he'd asked her about her home. 'It's really beautiful. Very quiet except for when there's a wedding and there's music and dancing and people. I don't really go out much, fun for me is enjoying the serenity, being with my grandmother.' Eve spoke softly and so very feminine, her pink lips moved in a pouty love heart shape, her words were mesmerizing… It was everything that Marco had fallen for all those years ago in Palm Cove. Her way. That and her undeniably sexiness, which oozed from her so effortlessly. Eve Frank from up the hill had shocked the hell out of him that summer.

'Do you enjoy what you do there. The weddings and all?' He was relaxed and genuinely interested in her life.

She gasped with enthusiasm. 'I really do. I love the flowers and setting the tables. I should have been a florist... I love flowers, all the colours and the textures. That's the reason I love my job.' Eve beamed as she spoke. Marco leaned an elbow on the bar and watched her as she lit up with every detail. He found her intriguing; he couldn't get enough of her natural radiance. He'd known Eve was special all those years ago back in Palm Cove. She had something that attracted him with such a force he'd not forgotten a minute of their time together.

'Are you even listening to me?' Eve frowned at Marco as her knees seem to find their way between his as they faced each other on their bar stools. Their eyes stilled to one another.

'I'm listening. You love the flowers.' A grin coming to his face, he'd been one hundred percent lost in the memory of being naked with Eve in his parent's bed in Palm Cove.

'Do you feel like an ice cream Sunday, even though it's minus twenty million degrees outside?' Eve had a blank expression on her face.

'I always feel like ice cream.'

'Can I have a chocolate ice cream Sunday please,' Eve asked the bartender. He nodded to her request.

'I'm supposed to be eating clean. You're a bad influence Eve Frank.' Marco would do anything she wanted, he knew right there and then, Eve Frank was his weakness.

'A little ice cream never hurt anyone.' Her eyes tempting him to kiss her. 'You can run it off tomorrow.'

'I can.' He returned the seductive eyes and put his hand went to her knee, he looked intently at them and then up into her eyes. A connection that neither could deny another second. Now as they sat face to face, it was right there in front of them again after seven years, and it was becoming hard to ignore. Marco looked down to Eve's awaiting lips, it felt like a blessing that they had found their way back to each other.

'I thought you said you were coming alone!' Tessa was right there, looking at Eve then to Marco.

'Excuse me,' he narrowed his eyes to his sister.

She long blinked him, 'I didn't know you would be here.' Tessa had mild attitude after just finishing her show and thinking she was meeting Eve alone for a night cap at the hotel bar, it was nearly midnight.

'Well, I'm sorry, but I'm here,' Marco huffed.

'It's fine, I just expected E to be alone, that's all.' Tessa definitely seemed put out by him being there. 'Did you avoid me today because it felt like you did?' She said to her big brother.

'Do you want a drink or something because you seem a little wound up?' Marco asked his sister as the chocolate Sunday was put on the bar between he and Eve.

'No, thank you. I'll leave you two alone to eat your Sunday... I'm so tired, I need to go up to bed.' Tessa was desperate for a drink with Eve but pleased to see she was with Marco. 'By the way, unless you're both okay with everyone finding out about this little rendezvous, you might want to take it up to your room.' She oozed sass as she walked off out the bar, thinking she was using reverse psychology by planting the seed in their heads that someone might be seen in the bar, really just in the hope they'd go upstairs and spend the night together and then fall madly in love. It was wishful thinking by Tessa, but she could only hope!

'What do you think?' Eve looked at Marco who had let his sister irritate him.

'We better get out of here,' Marco said with a gentle smile, automatically leaning into Eve, giving her a soft peck on her perfect love heart lips. 'If you want to, that is. No pressure,' he added with a teasing whisper of suggestion.

The lift door closed, and Marco and Eve stared at each other in wonder. The tension was most definitely there, they'd barely made it halfway through the chocolate Sunday before leaving the bar, now Eve was in a state, all she could hear was her own heartbeat. She bit down on her bottom lip, it was just the two of them in the lift going up to their floor, deep breaths, Marco broke the stare and looked up at the lift light and watched as they came to level twenty-two.

'Would you like a coffee in my room?' Eve took a breath as the lift doors opened.

Marco let her exit first. 'Coffee!' he said raising his brows trying to seem casual.

'Mm Hm.' Not letting him rattle her she turned toward her room. 'Or I can order up a bottle of wine.'

'If you'd prefer wine, I'm good with wine.' Marco was as anxious as Eve.

She fumbled with her door card nervously as he stood to her side.

A voice came from down the hall. 'I've been looking for you.' It was Nick, all dressed up with a coat on and a hint of adventure in his eye. 'Tommo and Ando... SoHo. They're waiting for us.' Nick had come to collect Marco; they had made plans the previous day to have drinks with two of Marco's teammates and their girlfriends who were in New York too for a short break.

'Fuck... I forgot.' Marco looked at Eve who stood at her door watching on.

Before he could say anything else, she said. 'I'm going to bed anyway. You should go.'

'Why don't you come with us to SoHo?' he wanted to be with Eve, but he'd made these plans and Nick was waiting for him, he couldn't get out of it.

'No. You go,' she reassured him it was fine with a beautiful smile, 'I'll see you tomorrow.' She was low key devastated. *It was a sign!* Eve thought, she needed to take things slower.

A back-to-back shopping trip was always dangerous. Today it was Anna, Jackie and the girls, Emma included. Tessa took them to her favorite bargain shopping destination, Century 21. It only took a few minutes for Anna and Jackie to switch into bargain hunter mode. The minute they found the four-hundred-dollar rack of Valentino handbags... They were like kids in a candy store, scouring every floor for designer bargains.

Lunch was an hour of sandwiches and soup in what was more a cafeteria than a restaurant, nothing flash, but they didn't have time to leave the building, there was still more shopping to be done!

Eve was texting at the table, Marco was apologizing for bailing on her last night, she was telling him it was all good, and how she was looking forward to seeing him tonight, a little emoji smile face with heart eyes.

'Who is making you smile like that Miss Frank?' Jackie interrupted Eve's thoughts. Looking up surprised, she put her phone straight in her handbag.

'I bet I know who,' Tessa teased with a naughty grin over the table for all to hear and see.

'It's not Quinn is it?' Anna asked, she would be disappointed if it was.

'No, it's not Quinn,' Eve scoffed, flabbergasted that her mother would suggest it was Quinn.

'Well, you're smiling, whoever it is,' Jackie made the comment. Eve chose not to answer, not to say a word was the safest thing she could do. Tessa, Zoe, and Emma all knew who it was. 'Did I see you and Marco in the hotel bar last night?' Jackie added, she was amazing, the woman always had something up her sleeve.

Eve blushed, it felt like a lot of pressure, 'Marco was waiting for Nick; they went and met some friends of Marco's for drinks in SoHo. And I was waiting for Tessa to get back.' Eve was becoming a terrific liar; Jackie wasn't giving her much choice.

'Oh, that's nice.' Jackie gave her a look, an unsettling look. Because Eve had so much to hide, she was paranoid every time Jackie said something to her.

The ladies made it back to the hotel right on dinner time, nothing had been planned for a change, and everyone was doing their own thing. Tessa had to rush off to her evening show, so Zoe and Eve were doing dinner together down in the hotel restaurant, inviting Emma as they were completely drained from the day of shopping and couldn't be bothered leaving the hotel. In turn, Emma told Tom, who mentioned it to his brothers. So now they were all in the hotel restaurant having dinner together.

Things with Zoe and Nick were weird, they were super friendly, and they'd been enjoying a friendship without sex, and according to Zoe, it was working. Nick was a changed man, very mature and only interested in her. Another odd occurrence was that Nick was still getting over his last girlfriend apparently, and he'd told Zoe the breakup wasn't his doing and that he was having a hard time understanding why on earth she'd left him, because all he'd done was worship this young woman! So here Nick was, a changed man because of heartbreak, not pressing Zoe for sex and enjoying spending time with her outside of the bed. It was a watch this space situation!

Eve sat between Marco and Emma, they were having a pre-dinner drink, as you do. Light snow falling outside as Zoe watched across the table thinking how wonderfully perfect Eve and Marco looked together. Eve had confided in Zoe earlier in the day, that she was scared of letting herself open up to Marco, scared of telling him the truth and scared of getting hurt again, she was simply down right scared all together. All of which Zoe understood, she got her friends apprehensions.

Dinner was like a rom-com full of suggestive looks, a lot of smiling and twinkling eyes, plenty of drinks and laughter too. Once dinner was over they all sat enjoying one another's company back in the hotel bar. The fireplace was keeping them warm; it was a romantic and cosy atmosphere.

'My dad told me he thought you and I were very chatty at Christmas lunch,' Marco smiled.

Eve paused a long hard minute, 'I don't think we should do this again.' Her heart didn't want to say it, but her head was telling her it had to be done. She's spun into instant panic mode. Nothing had happened between them at all, and yet it felt like it had. Her Marco dream was never meant to become her reality.

'Evie.' Marco watched her face as she looked straight ahead, knowing it wasn't how she really felt. She put all her walls up immediately to protect herself. Marco could feel it, she was shutting him out, cutting him off as she stood up from the table.

'I'm heading up to bed. I'm feeling a little unwell, my head hurts. Goodnight everyone,' Eve said innocently enough and with enough convincing that nobody questioned her.

'You know what! I'm just going to walk you up to your room, make sure you're okay.' Marco stood up and looked down at her shocked face, 'It's fine, I'm happy to, I'm heading to bed too.' Making out like she was protesting his good will.

Eve couldn't catch her breath, she needed to escape, she needed to be alone with her thoughts. It was such an automatic response to just run from anything that potentially posed a threat to her sanctuary of inner peace and security, she'd been doing it for years. Marco was being charming, and she was running. 'I can go alone,' Eve said looking up at him.

'I'll go with you.' Marco smiled at his brothers, moving along beside her.

'I'll come up and check on you soon babe, are you alright?' Zoe could read Eve like a book. She could tell by her body language, that her friend wasn't okay.

'I'm fine, I'm just over tired,' Eve said as she left the table.

They stood at the lift waiting for the lift in silence, things had gone south so fast. One minute they were enjoying a beautiful night, now this.

'Well, hello you two. What are you up to?' Mario said unassumingly, Jackie linking arms with him. Their faces as shocked as Eve's and Marco's.

Fuck! Eve couldn't believe her luck. *Could things get any worse!* Jackie's smile questioning, or so her paranoia thought as she held her breath, her anxiety choking her.

'We're just popping out for a romantic late-night stroll,' Jackie said to Marco who did his best to disguise his own discomfort in front of his parents.

'I'm walking Eve up to her room, she's not feeling well.' He went for the innocent favorite son smile.

'Oh, what's wrong darling?' Jackie put her hand to Eve's shoulder.

'I'm tired, that's all,' she managed a smile.

'Oh. Well Marco, why don't you take Eve upstairs and then come for a walk with us?' said Jackie.

'Go for a walk with your mum and dad, I can take care of myself.' Eve looked at Marco as she stepped into the lift. 'Goodnight, enjoy your walk,' she said as the doors closed.

Marco spent the next few days trying to bump into Eve at any chance he got, she was avoiding him big time, spending most of her time with her mother and Nigel or out with Tessa and Zoe. He had questioned the connection he'd felt with Eve, he was sure it was there, and he was sure she felt exactly the same. It was like suddenly she switched off and he was left wondering what the hell had gone wrong. He'd gone to Tessa and Zoe for answers, they'd told him she'd never been the same after losing Evan, that it had changed her. Eve was no longer the sweet young innocent girl that Marco had been with in Palm Cove. They'd explained she was cautiously protective of her own feelings; that she'd fallen for him before, so he was behind the eight-ball right off the bat. *He'd just have to try harder to win her over.*

Chapter Six

It was New Year's Eve, and Eve had shut herself off, pushed back, avoiding Marco at all costs. It had been days now since they'd had a conversation. She'd become the master of sabotaging her own happiness, fearing her secrets and the impact they'd have on her relationships with the people she loved. Not even Tessa and Zoe could make her see sense. All the while she put on a brave face for her friends, yet suffering tremendously on the inside, crying herself to sleep at night alone in her hotel room, coming to New York had been a mistake.

New Year's Eve had the hotel was in a festive buzz, and the only place besides her room for peace and quiet was in the window of the hotel library. The view was distracting, looking out over the beautiful Bryant Park, Eve found herself gazing out the window more than she read the book on Jackie Kennedy Onassis that she'd picked off the shelf, this woman's life had taken Eve's interest over the past few years, and what better place to read about her than in New York. Reading a good book was better than sitting in her room feeling sorry for herself. She had tonight's party sorted anyway, one of her knew dresses and a simple plat down her back, a light brush of bronzer with a flick of mascara would do it. She didn't see the point in spending hours preparing. She really wasn't sure if she actually wanted to go, seeing Marco on New Year's Eve would be torture.

'Evie… I've been looking everywhere for you.' Zoe came in the library with her sweatpants and joggers on, a puffer vest over a long-sleeved T. So very unlike Zoe, she was puffing and panting like she'd run the New York marathon.

'You've been exercising in this weather!' Eve said, it was snowing lightly.

'Yes. It's very calming, you should try it sometime.' Like she was the fitness queen just because she had exercised this once in her life.

'If I were any calmer my heart would stop. I don't need to exercise... Have you actually been exercising?' Eve could hardly believe it.

'Oh. God. Marco made me go for a run with him,' gasped for air, still catching her breath, 'You know he's freaking out over you right?'

'Mmm. You're not usually a runner.' Eve remained cool even though a slight tingle made her feel a spark of happiness in her somber state.

The girls knew Eve was avoiding Marco like the plague, and they knew why. Last night she had dinner with her mum and Nigel and then went straight to her room. Today she'd ventured out into Manhattan on her own, spending most of the day at the New York library nearby. When Eve was like this, the girls knew they needed to give her space, she was in thinking mode, but seeing her ruin her chances with Marco was hard for them to stand by and watch.

Zoe stood catching her breath for a moment, she'd sheltered Eve from many storms, so she was definitely the best one to say what needed to be said. 'You my friend, need to snap out of this bubble shit you've been living in for the past five years,' Zoe managed, she'd always nurtured Eve, but enough was enough.

'What!' Appalled instantly. Offended too! Eve could see the body language Zoe had going on, it was like she was going to burst out crying. Dramatic as she huffed and puffed for breath.

'I get the whole protecting yourself thing. You don't let anyone into your Eve bubble... and I get it, I really do. But it's not living and because I love you, I need to tell you.' Zoe made finger quotations when she said Eve bubble, which annoyed Eve. 'Marco knows exactly why you're avoiding him,' she took a few breaths, 'He's onto you, he knows you're protecting yourself from him in case he breaks your heart again. He's trying to connect with you, and you're running away.' Zoe was still panting, she needed to refill her lungs with air. 'Would you rather hang out with an old man like Quinn? Or fuck a hot and sexy man like Marco Rossi?' Zoe gasped determinedly as only she could, throwing her hands in the air in frustration. She had to be careful what she said next to her best friend, she loved Eve so much and it was okay to offend her, but she didn't want to hurt her. 'Marco Rossi adores you Evie; he always has. Give him a chance, give yourself a chance at being happy, with someone who is genuinely good and kind and thinks you're totally amazing.' Zoe was getting emotional and upset. 'Stop punishing yourself... I'm over it!' She had more to say, she just couldn't get there in the one breath, she was nearly passing out from lack of oxygen, but it had to be said, and she knew her friend was about to come swinging back at her. 'Let yourself love Marco. He wants you.'

Eve listened, knowing Zoe was right about everything, and she wanted more than anything to be brave and strong and let her walls down. 'I do love Marco, you know I do,' she said in a reasonable soft voice. It must look so straight forward to her friends, but it wasn't. 'I've been thinking about this a lot, all day actually. And I'm not right for Marco.' *Oh, fuck that killed her to say out loud!* 'He needs a good wholesome woman who is as untarnished and perfect as him. Someone without my past. Someone who will be a good wife and the mother to his children,' Eve signed, 'That's not me Zo.'

Zoe screwed her face up, pissed off beyond belief at her stupid, idiot friend, 'Crap! That' just such fucking crap and you know it,' pouting and huffing, Zoe was getting less and less tolerant of Eve's sob story bullshit, 'Marco doesn't give a fuck about your past. He knows your fiancé was murdered the day before your wedding, he knows you and Evan lost a child. You have nothing to be ashamed of... It's not a cross you have to bear for the rest of your life.' Tears fell from Zoe's eyes. 'Are you saying you won't be a wife or mother ever, for real?' Zoe was showing a rare emotional side, she felt terrible for brining Evan and Rafael up, she knew Eve didn't like them being mentioned, but enough was enough.

Sitting there a little stunned, yet absorbing Zoe's barrage of truths, Eve remained calm, 'I don't really want to be a wife or a mother,' Eve lied so matter of fact. This subject was taboo, and Zoe knew it. Eve was a little taken back at her best friends boldness to broach the subjects.

'Well, I don't believe you. And you're getting way ahead of yourself. How do you know what Marco wants or expects from you anyway, he might not want to get married and he might hate kids for all you know!'

Eve just looked at Zoe, she had no come back. Deep in her heart, she would love to be both a wife and a mother one day, more than anything in the whole entire world. But the past still hurt so much that she was so scared to move forward when real feelings were involved. Even with her Marco!

'It's time to take a chance on yourself,' Zoe now spoke in her gorgeous sympathetic *best friend ever* way, that Eve cherished so much. 'My Evie deserves another go at being happy, and I think she knows she does.' Zoe had gone full circle emotionally.

'I love my bubble; I feel safe in here.' Eve's lips curled with a surrendering and emotional smile.

'I know, but I just popped your damn bubble, so go up to your room, and make sure you don't come to the party, until you look super-fucking-extra-hot.' Smiling at Eve with her arms out as Eve slumped into her hug. 'I just love you so much, I want you to be happy, and I know Marco makes you happy.' Zoe snuggled into Eve as she held her tight.

The ceiling was a cloud of twinkling lights, the floor to ceiling windows looked out over the sparkling city that is New York, a band played, and the room was glamorous. The cozy winter terrace was a buzz with smoking party goers. Impeccable waiters roamed with trays of fancy cocktails with gold flakes in them. Everyone was dressed in their best, designer suits and beautiful gowns, it was like festive fashion week up in the clouds of New York City.

Zoe had a silver and diamanté Happy New Year tiara atop her silky blonde bob. Her silver satin dress hung from her slender body; she looked glamorous in an old Hollywood way.

Now, Tessa was considered a local, she definitely looked the part. She wore a stylish canary yellow dress that had a skirt full of ruffles and layers of fabric, it was like something you'd wear to the Met Gala. The full length of her sleek long leg peeped through the skirt as she walked, her abundance of honey colored hair pulled up in a big round bun atop of her head, her makeup, cat like. Tessa looked like a New Yorker in full bloom.

Eve stood in the lift with her mother and Nigel, ready to make her entrance, nervous about seeing Marco. She was confidently at peace with herself, more so than she had been in days, all her anxieties that clouded her head, had been washed away in the hour-long bath she had taken after her chat with Zoe in the library. The woman Eve had become was far from the girl who had lost her virginity to Marco in Palm

Cove. She missed the innocent Eve of years ago, now she had to embrace the woman she had become and accept all that she'd been through to become who she was today, because it was time. Tonight, was her night, and Eve felt an air of excitement.

Like always, her entrance commanded attention. She was exotic and sensual, oozing with style and refinement as she looked around for her girls. Standing beside her proud mother Eve was a vision of beauty, her sleek pulled back hair was shining in a long plait all the way down to her waste. The new black Dior dress was simple and elegant, on Eve it looked sultry and almost mildly provocative with her cinnamon cleavage peeking through. A splash of mascara, clear lip gloss, she didn't need much, her best look was natural. The old faithful Jimmy Choo black stilettos made everything look good.

'Absolutely stunning, as usual,' Jackie gasped to Eve, welcoming her to the party with a kiss to both cheeks. People stood around in gatherings enjoying the view and celebrating the New Year's arrival. The atmosphere of the party was magical with everyone enjoying the festivities. Eve spotted Marco immediately, he was so tall, it wasn't hard to find him. An instant flush rushed of heat through her body at the sight of him. He was talking with his father over by the windows, Eve was utterly and completely in love with him, just like she always had been. Dark waves of hair pushed back off his face. His eyes sparkling at her across the room when he saw her. Her heart fluttered in her chest as they held each other's gaze. She knew in this very moment, more than ever before, that Marco was, and always would be, the love of her life.

'Wow, that's one hell of a long plait.' Tessa stood in front of Eve, she was all smiles and so very beautiful.

'You look amazingly magnificent; I'm lost for words!' Eve said as she admired Tessa's look. Zoe rushed over, also astounding Eve with her beauty and style. 'Oh, my God. Look at you, you're gorgeous Zo.'

'Evie! Where's your necklace?' Zoe was alarmed; Tessa eyes went to Eve's neck... Eve without her E necklace was unfathomable. For the past seven years, not once had it come off her neck, not since the night Evan had given it to her.

'It's somewhere safe,' she smiled as Zoe reached out and touched her arm in support.

'Good for you,' Tessa sighed, 'If you're lucky you can replace it with a warm pearl necklace later tonight.' She couldn't help herself; she didn't take things too seriously and she loved that Eve had turned a personal corner, letting part of her past go. It was a huge step forward, hopefully towards her brother.

'I can just see it, dripping down her sexy bronzed skin into that canyon of a cleavage.' Zoe's grin was full of hope. Dirty, funny, silly hope. Nothing like softening a serious moment with a bit of gutter talk from your besties.

'I love you both. What would I do without you?' Taking a champagne from a passing tray, Eve held her glass up to the girls and they toasted to whatever it was that they were. Beautiful, loyal, and unconditional friends. They would never need anything more or accept anything less from each other. Their bond was eternal.

'What do you think of the waiter with the man bun over there?' Tessa pointed.

'It's a yes from me,' Eve said, he was so Tessa's type, rugged and blonde.

'Oh, is there another one of those for me.' Zoe laughed looking around in search.

'E, you need to find someone at this party for Zoe. I've got dibs on the manbun,' said Tessa.

'Well, what about Nick. He's available, and you two have been getting along so well,' Eve suggested testing the waters with Tessa. Both Zoe and Tessa looked at her like she was an alien with two heads and forty eyes, or like she'd suggested Zoe test fuck everyone in the room.

'My brother Nick!' Tessa pulled a face.

'Yes,' Eve said looking at Tessa, then to Zoe, 'Why not?'

'Been there, done that, I've evolved.' Zoe forgot herself a moment and she'd only had two drinks.

'You've been there and done that, with my brother?' a wary Tessa asked with an almost amused smile.

Eve cut in, in a bid to save their New Year's Eve, it had just started and was now possible about to end. 'Would it be an issue for you... Let's say if Zoe and Nick where to um, ever hook up?'

Tessa didn't respond to Eve; she was glaring at Zoe. 'Have you fucked my brother! When?' Tessa spoke softly, which was not a good sign. Zoe stared back at her with her mouth open not knowing what to say.

'Are you angry?' Eve squinted moving her head in front of Tessa so she would look at her instead of Zoe.

Tessa sighed, 'Why didn't you tell me. Did this happen the other night after the club, I thought you two seemed a little tight, but...' Suddenly the realization hit Tessa. 'Oh, my, god. You've both slept with my brothers. You're both brother fuckers!' The look on her face was nothing short of pure horror for a split second before she burst out laughing at the notion. 'Tell me now Zoe. Out with it, did you slept with my brother?' Just as Tessa put Zoe on the spot, Marco walked up beside her.

'What?' Marco wasn't sure what he'd heard.

'Not you. Nick. She slept with Nick!' Tessa was mortified, and getting louder and as luck would have it, Nick then appeared between Marco and Zoe, innocently full of cheer until he heard what Tessa had said.

'Who did I sleep with?' Nick asked with pride, his hand at the small of Zoe's slender back, a nervous smile growing by the minute, he had no idea what he had walked in on.

'Did you? Of course, you did you rat!' Tessa still had an unpredictable look on her face.

'Me and Zoe?' Nick questioned.

Marco and Eve glimpsing at each other briefly and then to the others as the story unfolded. Tessa frowning at Nick and Zoe, waiting for the explanation.

'It was a long time ago, in Palm Cove.' Zoe was squirming.

'What!' both Tessa and Marco said in simultaneous shock. Zoe looked like she was about to cry, Marco, Nick and Tessa were all as shocked as each other at Zoe's confession.

'I'm guessing you knew,' Tessa turned to Eve.

'Sort of,' Eve sighed, 'Do you remember how upset you got when Nick and Zoe kissed at Emily Morello's sixteenth birthday party?' Eve was trying to make Tessa understand why nobody told her. 'Exactly, Zoe was scared to tell you.'

'This is fucking hilarious. It's almost incestual. I never would have thought in a million years, you'd all fuck each other?' Tessa was working herself up into a laughing frenzy in a bid not to freak right out.

'We're not fucking each other,' said Marco pointing at Zoe, 'Not all of us.' He wanted to clear up that it wasn't a free for all Rossi family orgy.

'You should have told me E,' Tessa gave Eve a shake of her finger. 'But I guess it's the same as Zoe and I not telling you we've both fucked Curtis and Emilio. We were scared too.' It was not odd at all for Tessa to be so open in front of her two older brothers about her sex life, they were very used to it.

Eve's jaw dropped. 'Are you serious? Both of you. Curtis and Emilio?' Eve needed to clarify.

'Yeah, we had a foursome. So, I think we're all kind of even, unless there's anything you need to confessions?' Tessa said jovial to Eve. It was the most bizarre conversation ever, Marco and Nick speechless and enthralled. And Eve now the one who'd been kept in the dark, although it didn't surprise her. It would be interesting however, when she later told Zoe and Tessa that all three of them had slept with Curtis... That would be a conversation for later.

'Okay, we are more than even now.' Eve noted.

Tessa smiled, 'And whilst we're being even and fare about things; Tom's probably feeling like the odd brother out right about now... Maybe one of you two should go and get it on with him in the bathrooms!' Tessa said sarcastically to her best friends, by now they seeing the humorous side of things. The situation was bizarre and now ridiculously funny.

'I think it's important to note, that Nick and I are not attracted to each other anymore.' Zoe pointed to Nick and herself. *Mm, really... She was the only one buying it.*

'We're not?' Nick questioned Zoe; she saw something in his eyes. Their confusion was cute. With remarks going back and forward, everyone was part relieved, and part shocked that Tessa hadn't totally blown a fuse. Was she just pretending it was all okay, was she going to flip out tomorrow and never speak to either of them again? Who knew.

Tessa huffed her pain, 'I don't know if I can handle this shit, you two are bad enough, now I've got these two to worry about?' she said to Eve and Marco as Zoe and Nick walked off debating their attraction to each other. Leaving Eve, Tessa, and Marco to talk it out on their own, which was a blessing, Eve and Tessa had a rational

69

adult conversation without too much drama, Tessa admitted she would probably have taken the news of Zoe and Nick initially in Palm Cove, very badly. The attentions of the blonde man bun waiter eventually took Tessa from Eve and Marco, it had been a weird and revealing conversation to kick the night off with, and now it was thankfully over.

'You look beautiful as always Eve Frank,' Marco's voice was slow and measured, now it was just the two of them as they'd recovered from the Nick and Zoe revelation. Gazing down into Eve's eyes as he took a few steps into her space. It was hard to hear over the music. Zoe had told Marco earlier to try harder with Eve, he'd win back eventually, so that was his plan.

'You look very handsome yourself Marco Rossi.' Her hand went to the front of his shirt, her finger sliding into a gap between buttons like they'd been together forever.

'Can we talk out on the terrace, I know it's cold, but it's a little quieter out there?' he asked, still gazing into her big almond eyes.

'If you can get me under one of those heaters, sure thing,' she raised her eyebrows to him, then followed him out to the terrace.

Marco found a spot under a heater, nestled among the smokers and cigar goers, 'Are you worried someone will see us because I'm not.' He noticed Eve looking around.

'I'm looking for a waiter. Why, do I look worried?' Eve asked trying not to shiver.

'You're either really worried or really thirsty.' A touch of humour never hurt anybody Marco thought.

'Oh, I need a drink after what just happened in there,' Eve smiled, she couldn't believe what had just gone down and now here she was out with Marco on the terrace. Alone.

'Aren't you the little secret keeper!' he teased Eve as she took two glasses of champagne off the passing waiters tray, passing one to Marco.

'Yeah, well believe me, it was better kept a secret.' Careful not to say too much, if she told Marco how awful Nick had been to Zoe that summer in Palm Cove, he'd be horrified. 'Zoe and Nick, Tessa, and Zach, you, and me. Your mum would never recover if she ever found out we all hooked up. She can never know what happened on that holiday,' Eve laughed. They all had a secret to keep, but Eve was protecting the biggest secret of all.

'If I upset you the other night somehow, I'm sorry Evie,' Marco had to say it, even though he had no idea what he said to make her so upset in the first place, it had to have been bad for her to avoid him for days.

'No. I'm sorry.' Instant emotion on her face as she looked up into his dreamy eyes. 'You didn't say anything to upset me at all,' she gushed apologetically, 'Really, I'm sorry for how I've been behaving these past few days. I hope you can forgive me.'

'You're forgiven,' Marco said straight away, and Eve was swept up into those gorgeous brown eyes as she had been so many times before.

'Well, thank you, I probably don't deserve your forgiveness,' she said with a sigh, a relieved sigh.

'I have to ask you; do you have feelings for me, or am I misinterpreting things?'

'Feelings!' She laughed and looked up at him, her eyes sparkling… It was now or never. 'I've never stopped having feelings for you. Not for a single day.' Surprising herself at how easily the words fell out of her mouth.

He looked down at her, his heart fluttering at her honesty. 'Oh… Um. Okay. As you know football has always come first in my life. Always.' His face had empathy. 'I never meant to break your heart Evie. I didn't realise how much-'

'Don't be sorry. No more apologies.' She made him smile. Snowflakes started to fall around them.

'When I saw you in London, it hit me. I wanted you like I've never wanted anything in my life before.' Marco regretted letting Eve go all those years ago. He always had.

Unable to speak, she was lost in his words and the sparkle of his eyes. She'd dreamt of this moment since she was a ten-year-old girl, and now here they were on a terrace as the snow fell in New York, all these years later, it was beyond romantic. Eve was savoring every precious second as a stray tear escape the corner of her eye. The tear was for this gorgeous man who she adored standing in front of her, and for the past she was letting go from this moment on.

Marco put his hand to her chin, gently lifting her face to meet his kiss as he bent to her, his tender kiss made Eve feel like she was an angel floating in the clouds high above this amazing city. This was it. The kiss… And the moment that would change everything. The more Marco's soft lips brushed over hers, the more Eve surrendered herself to him. Her hands went up to his neck, his arms wrapped around her body, holding her to him. The kiss was nothing less than magical, absolutely unforgettable in every way.

'What happens now?' Eve asked as their lips parted. It was out there; they'd kissed in full view of the windows; anybody could have seen them.

'We take a chance on each other,' said Marco, 'Come and stay with me in Melbourne?' He'd thought about this for days. Holding Eve tight to his body, the wait had been so worth it, her warm gentle fingers at his face touching him, her eyes melting him from the inside out. 'I wish I could come to you in France, but I can't.' Marco felt guilty asking her to come to him, he knew she had a life of her own in France, and that it always seemed to be about him and what he could and couldn't do because of his career.

Eve was subconsciously wary, she'd done this before, fallen fast into the arms of a man, only this time she wasn't being rescued. Yes, it was sudden, yet it felt unbelievably right. *This is your moment, do it!* she told herself. *Being with Marco Rossi wouldn't be the worst mistake you've ever made!*

'When would I come to Melbourne?' Eve smiled as she devoured his face with her eyes.

'Whenever. Now,' he paused, 'Before March if you can. No pressure… I'll have more time to spend with you if it's before the season starts.' Marco had put a lot of thought into it - Eve coming to stay with him, he'd thought it was a long shot. Apparently not, she was contemplating it.

'I'm sure I could work something out.' She stretched up to him for another kiss.

Jackie and Anna stood side by side watching out the window in a silent state of what could only be described as ultimate shock as Marco and Eve kissed. It wasn't a first kiss either, it was too intense and precise for a first-time kiss. There was a history behind that kiss, and both mothers new it.

'What's going on out there?' Jackie said looking over to Nick, who then turned to look out the window to his brother and Eve.

'It's nothing new mum, they go way back,' Nick sighed with a knowing smile. Zoe stood watching too, this was a very public display, and possibly the opening of a messy and complicated can of worms.

Jackie gave Nick a glare, 'How far back?' she said asked her son, with Anna just out of earshot.

'Palm Cove, that time we all went there together, they were inseparable.' Nick went to the bar for a straight hit of scotch. Zoe was left with her own awkwardness, she'd heard the exchange between Nick and his mother, and she knew what Jackie would be thinking, her mind would be ticking.

Jackie could feel herself going numb, her heart beat strong in her chest as she stood staring out the window at Marco and Eve. Her thoughts were unconceivable.

'This is a surprise isn't it?' Anna said to Jackie as she snapped out of her initial moment of shock.

'It certainly is.' Jackie couldn't help but feel betrayed, hurt and somewhat stupid. 'Excuse me,' she said heading off to the lady's, barely able to contain her emotion a second longer in front of Anna.

Locking herself in a cubical, hyperventilating at the realization it had been Marco who fathered Eve's baby all along. Staying in the cubical until she had thought it through and pulled herself together Jackie needed to center herself, this was more than she could have ever imagined. Deciding tonight wasn't the place or time to have it out with Eve and Marco. When she first saw them kissing, a rush of excitement had raced through her, the thought of Eve and Marco romantically involved was initially overwhelmingly lovely... then Nick's revelation had knocked the wind right out of her sails. All these years, it had been Marco who got Eve pregnant, not Nick. Never in a million years did Jackie suspect it was Marco. Not Marco! She'd blamed Nicholas if anyone. And Eve had protected Marco so staunchly, so had Tessa. They'd all lied to her.

'We need a drink,' Jackie said on her return from the bathrooms, linking her arm through Anna's and leading her to the bar. She wasn't going to make a scene tonight, a matter such as this needed a calm head.

'Was this thing with our kids completely unexpected,' a beat, 'Or is just me?' Anna asked with a little spark of joy in her tone. She really liked the idea of Eve and Marco.

Jackie stood with her friend at the bar, the situation was eating her up, 'You know I love your daughter like she's one of my own. I'd never say or do anything to hurt her,' Jackie began, 'But I think Marco was the father of Eve's baby, I think she covered for him.' She came straight out with it, then skulled her gin in three big gulps.

'What!' a pause of confusion from Anna, 'Evan was the father!'

'The first baby,' Jackie reminded her, 'If I'm right Anna, I'm apologizing in advance for my sons' irresponsible behavior with your then teenage daughter.' She took another drink from a passing waiter. A cocktail this time. 'Marco and Eve were together, perhaps intimately, in Palm Cove that summer that Eve got pregnant,' Jackie sighed, she was gutted. The look on her face was one of shame, hurt and devastation.

'How do you know?' Anna squinted at Jackie; this was so unexpected that she didn't know how to react. *Was she supposed to be angry?*

'Nicholas just told me that Marco and Eve where inseparable on that holiday.' She took a big tearful breath. 'I can't believe Marco would have unprotected sex with anyone, let alone Eve.' Jackie was utterly flustered. 'I'm so sorry Anna.' She knew Anna blamed that pregnancy for the unfortunate path Eve took at that time in her life.

'Jackie, stop. You don't need to apologize for what our children may have done years ago. If there's one thing my daughter has taught me, it's that we as parents have no control over what our kids do, or who they do it with.' Anna rubbed Jackie's arm understandingly.

'I'm more than a little shock, Marco was older, he should have known better,' gasped Jackie.

'Let's keep drinking and try to put this into perspective,' a smile from Anna, 'Another thing I know, is that no matter how hard you try, you can't change the past. And did you see how happy they were in each other's arms just now?' Anna was past her initial shock, she'd had her fair share of shocks when it came to her daughter, finding out Marco was the father of the first baby she'd lost at the tender age of seventeen was a C grade shock in the scheme of things. Unlike Jackie, Anna had realised a long time ago that her child was not perfect. Eve was human and she made mistakes just like everyone else. It didn't matter now; Anna knew Eve was of the purest of hearts and she adored everything about her daughter.

Until now Jackie hadn't been faced with great disappointment as the result of her children. Never. Not like Anna had. Her children had been a joy, good souls, well maybe with the exception of her wild Nicholas. *Oh, Nick!* Jackie's guilt was immense, she'd suspected Nicholas of getting Eve pregnant and leaving her alone to go through her unfortunate ordeal. She had instantly blamed Nicholas, who in the light of day, may have been the only one to not lie to his mother. Through her rose-coloured mother glasses, Jackie saw Thomas as always striving for success, he was fiercely independent. Tessa was head strong and opinionated; she took life by the scruff of the neck and did things her way, she always had... *And she had lied.* They'd all lied accept Nicholas. Marco had been her delight, he was gracious and considerate, everyone loved Marco! Her heart actually hurt from the disappointment. 'They've lied to us the whole time. My son got your teenage daughter pregnant.' Jackie was sad, she was almost in tears. *Why couldn't they just have told her the truth?*

Anna had drunk two glasses of champagne in less than two minutes, 'I'm not comfortable questioning Eve on this tonight. Knowing my daughter, Marco has no idea she was ever pregnant.' Anna's eyes engaged Jackie's. 'We need to keep out of this one. They're adults, let them find their way.' Anna didn't want to get involved, she didn't jump into things headfirst, ever.

'This is why you and I make great friends,' Jackie held her glass up to Anna's, 'You're the voice of reason.'

For the hours in-between their conversation at the bar and the New Year count down, Jackie and Anna danced and laughed with their children, enjoying this memorable moment in New York with their families together. Eve and Marco seemed so natural together, just having genuine fun, no more displays of affection, just enjoyed their time with everyone, laughing and mingling, dancing together as odd as it looked with him so tall and her so small. It was a wonderful night of celebration and togetherness, just as Jackie had planned. The more she drank the less she thought about the betrayal... For tonight anyway!

Tessa had been smoking pot on the fire escape with the man bun waiter, Zoe and Nick decided to see where the night took them... They were so into each other, yet so hesitant to act on their feelings. It was a whole new Zoe and Nick.

On the stroke of midnight, a light shimmer of sparkle fell from the ceiling, snow fell lightly outside, and Frank Sinatra filled the room. Everyone exchanged the traditional kisses and well wishes for the year ahead. Eve, Tessa, and Zoe shared hugs and kisses first, then Eve turned to Marco. He lifted her delicately petite feet off the floor, his adoring lips met hers with a blissful kiss. She could taste the alcohol at his lips, feel the warm as his body pressed to hers. Seven years later and here they were again, together on New Year's at the stock of midnight.

'Happy New Year,' Eve's lips said to Marco's.

'Happy New Year Eve Frank. This is the best New Year's I've ever had.' He laughed. 'Well, there was one other I remember that was pretty spectacular too... Mind blowing actually!' His smile melted her. There was no doubt in her mind about how Marco felt about her.

'Can you believe it was seven years ago tonight?' Eve fluttered her eyes lovingly.

'I will never forget that night as long as I live.'

'You were the perfect first lover Marco Rossi,' she gasped to his lingering lips.

'Happy New Year you two!' Jackie said trying not to sound sarcastic as she appeared between them.

'Happy New Year Mum.' Marco only took one hand away from Eve as she stepped back. He put out his arm to his mother to hug her in. She noticed immediately he wasn't letting go of Eve. He wasn't hiding it which immediately led her to believe he had no idea about the baby. Maybe she was being a protective mother again, but maybe she was right.

'Happy New Year Jackie,' Eve said with a smile.

'This is a surprise, the two of you. Well, to me anyway,' Jackie said, 'You're two of my favourite people in the world.' She'd been drinking heavily, switching between Gin and champagne, she looked at Marco, 'You make sure you take care of Eve this time.'

Marco's smile disappeared and the colour drained from Eve's face. She knew exactly what Jackie was talking about. Marco had no idea of the magnitude of his mother's words. He'd just thought perhaps she knew they'd hooked up in Palm Cove years ago, nothing more. 'Mum!' He'd been caught off guard, they all were, even Jackie.

'I love you. Regardless!' She put her hands at Marco's chest, 'I love this girl too, very much. More than you probably realise.' She took an emotional pause, never taking her eyes from him, 'I've been there in her darkest hours. And I never want to see her like that again.'

'Jackie!' Eve said cautiously. She was both touched and wary.

'Oh. My. God. Mum. I hope you're not giving them grief are you.' Tessa slid her body into the triangle just at the right time. *Thank God...* Eve had never been so utterly relieved for Tessa's intrusion.

'Now why would I do that Tessa?' Jackie smiled at her daughter, she removed herself from the circle and moved onto Anna, Nigel and Mario who were standing nearby.

A somewhat stoned Tessa kissed her big brother happy new year and hung her arm around Eve's shoulders.

'This is your thing, New Year's Eve hooking up's,' she said happily with a substance infused cheer.

It became a mash of people kissing and hugging and well wishing. The laughter and the resolutions filling the air as fireworks went off out in the Manhattan night sky. Marco reached for Eve's hand and pulled her in close. There was no need to hide, it was out there for everyone to consume now. Whatever it was between them, it was stronger than either of them, it was happening and there was no stopping it.

It was well into the early hours of the morning when one by one they all called it a night. Nick, Zoe, and Tessa managed to get themselves into the private party down in the hotel bar, the older crew had headed off to bed well before.

Eve and Marco found themselves getting out the lift on level twenty-two. In seconds he had her up against the wall in the hallway, her feet off the floor and her arms wrapped around his neck. Their breaths quick and desperate as they kissed in

77

private for the first tonight, it was with a craving passion. Swinging her legs up around Marco's waist, encompassing him, he lifted her, one hand under her arse, the other hand he held her face to his, Eve was like a little bird in his arms, so effortlessly he held her. Eve pull herself up his body, her fingers entwined in his dark waves of hair, her mouth breathing into his. Every inch of her wanted all of Marco. Eve had clarity; she was taking control of her situation from here on out.

Marco's hand left Eve's face and went to rest at her chest, sliding between the fabric of her stunning Dior dress and her beautiful cinnamon skin, his frantic desire had gone from hot and steamy to now manic. With one arm still holding Eve, Marco managed to move down the hallway towards her room, her legs still around his waist as she clung to him, their mouths never parting as they fumbled and bumped down the hall.

Her clutch bag wrapped around her wrist, Eve scurried through it for her room card, still at Marco's mouth and holding herself to him as she miraculously unlocked the hotel room door… It was an impressive maneuver.

They stumbled through the door, Marco still holding Eve up in his arms, their mouths pressed together as he took her straight to the bed, their bodies hitting the mattress with a thud, Marco landing over the top of Eve's curvaceous body. The softness of her beneath him was so familiar and welcoming.

Eve glanced up at Marco for a momentary gasp. *It was really happening!* She began unbuttoning his shirt, pushing it off his athletic shoulders, she could lost her breath at the sight of his broad shoulders, she'd missed him. Her hands went straight down to his pants, his sensual kisses to her lips were heaven. Unbuttoning him first go, Marco kicked off his shoes and wriggled out of his pants. Moving over her he began to peel her out of the dress he'd admired the entire night. Her underwear a feast for his eyes, sexy luxurious lace, so very Eve Frank.

His warm hands slithered down her body, then her legs, spreading her knees apart and kneeling between them. The gaze of his gentle eyes and his caring touch took Eve back to when she was seventeen, a time in her life when she'd been so carefree, she'd absolutely taken her youth and her innocents for granted. Marco's warm fingers rimmed her lace knickers, Eve lifting her hips hoping to hurry him up, filled with sexual adrenalin. His euphoric gaze caught sight of the white thick white scar that tarnished her perfect cinnamon belly. She saw him looking at it, and without a word she sat up to him and went to her knees, laying him back down to the mattress so she could climb over his body, Eve was now on top.

Marco's want for her went way deeper than his throbbing cock, he looked deep into her eyes with a wanting eye. They took a moment to savor one another. Her thick plaited hair falling to Marco's shoulders, she was the exception to any other woman he'd ever had, so spectacularly beautiful and sexy, special in so many ways. This was his second chance, and he was determined to impress her.

As she stared into the eyes of this exceptionally good man, it felt like she was having the best dream of her life, only it was real and there was a possibility she may never wake up from her ultimate happiness this time. A surge of lust and emotion powered through Eve's veins, she began kissing Marco like they had only seconds to live, devouring him with emotion filled huffs and puffs, rubbing her hands through his hair and down over his chest and shoulders, lusting for him, wanting him like she'd never wanted before.

She did want him, as much as he wanted her! Marco realised, rolling Eve onto her back, and coming up to her side, he continued to kiss her soft pink lips, he tussled with her knickers again, this time pulling them down her legs, flicking them across the bed. His broad shoulders at her face as he put his hand between her legs, two gentle fingers immediate rubbing at her sensitive moist flesh, as he looked over her womanly curves. Exquisite lace still holding her large voluptuous boobs... *There was still more to come, Eve was insatiable.*

She let her legs fall apart, sighing with anticipation. Marco bent to her, kissing her like only he could. The touch of his fingers at her pulsing clit was mesmerizing, sensual and intimate. Instantly she was there... Short breaths of overwhelming want. Eve remembered his caring touch, the way it made her feel so special, the powerful sexual chemistry they'd shared all those years ago was still alive and stronger than ever.

'You're exactly how I remember you Eve Frank,' a breathy beat, 'Soft and so sexy.' Marco's hot breath in her ear as she turned her head away from him taking big deep sensual gasps of air, her pulsing pussy begging his fingers to go deep inside her. She felt her wetness at his hand as he thumbed over her neat folds, making her squeeze his hand between her wet thighs, for want of explode with of sheer pleasure.

'I can't believe this is happening again,' Eve's moans sounded like she was delirious, and she was. After everything she'd been through these past seven years, nothing ever felt quite as right, as Marco Rossi.

Was this how it was meant to be, had she come full circle?

'I've wanted to do this to you from the moment I saw you in London,' his hand moved away from Eve and his body went to her. Marco wasn't easily flustered, although Eve Frank definitely flustered him. He moved over her, their bodies sliding together effortlessly, like they knew each other well.

'I never thought this would ever happen again,' she gasped as Marco's large, smooth cock touched at her folds, taking the air from her lungs as she remembered what she was in for!

He relished in Eve's dreamy words, he rubbed himself over her moist flesh, trying to keep his initial excitement to himself. Her silk like flesh licking at the tip of his cock had him wanting to cum. Everything about the gorgeous Eve Frank was exactly as he remembered. Her tenderness, her smell, it was overwhelming sensuality that he'd never forgotten.

She arched her body to Marco's; in awe of the man, she had loved for more than half her life, she unclipped her bra and let herself pillow to Marco's body, skin to skin.

'I hope I can make it worth the wait.' He took her hand and kissed her fingers.

'You can, or have you forgotten us?' Eve asked.

'I could never forget being the first to make love to you Eve Frank,' Marco stopped still for a few seconds and looked down at her, she pulsed at the tip of his cock. *Did she really think he could forget!* 'I could never forget us, you were my very own virgin,' Marco breathed his words to her lips, 'Little Eve Frank from up the hill.' Leaning down to her as the slow pressure of his hardness began to open Eve's delicate pussy. His pure girth widened her hips. Marco knew Eve wasn't that innocent little virgin girl anymore when he felt the erotic roll of her hips meeting his as he gently pressed inside of her… He wanting to cum in a literal second!

'Am I still your only virgin?' she kissed his chest as she accepted all of Marco inside her, he went a little deeper with each god sent thrust. It was all coming back to her… Everything about Marco was large, and after all this time of no penetration with an actual human, it was burning like it had the very first time!

'Like I said, you're my very own virgin. Still to this day.' He took one of her knees in his hand and pushed it out wide, her body tightening at his cock, not that Eve wasn't tight, she was very tight, just as he had remembered. Tight was good... *Eve's tight was great*! Marco loved a wet tight pussy, and that Eve, and with just the right amount of friction between them, they began made love.

'Do you ever regret Palm Cove?' Eve asked in her erotic daze, she was a sex talker, she loved to talk while making love. Marco's sex was like a drug, big and hard right up inside her stomach.

'Never... you?' Marco said ramping up his thrusts, it was raw sexual adrenaline because he was with Eve again, loving her again and filling her with his pleasure was mind-blowing.

'Palm Cove was the best week of my life, a moment in time, I'll never get back.' She felt her life had changed soon after that blissful holiday, she was no longer a child, she'd grown up fast.

There was something about her words that Marco knew to be true. He knew her life had been complicated; she'd been through a lot since they'd last been together. 'The best week of your life! That's a big call,' he said needed a little more clarify. He believed her, he just wanted to hear it again.

'It really was.' Eve ran her palms over his shoulders and his magnificent masculine chest. Taking a deep breath to settle herself, the combination of Marco inside her and emotional reminiscing were a lethal combination. She felt like she was on the edge ready to burst into tears of jumbled joy, heartbreak, and carnal ecstasy.

Marco would think she was a complete basket case and he'd be right. She needed to concentrate on the amazing sex they were having... but don't let it get too intimate and personal just yet... too late!

They were already making love, their bodies rolling harmoniously in rhythm together like time had never come between them.

Marco's urges were getting the better of him, Eve's confession had made him want all of her.

The best week of her life!!!

This overload of desire took him way back to Palm Cove, back to the pleasure he'd experienced when discovering this beautiful woman for the very first time.

Without a second thought, he spread both her knees back to mattress as she laid beneath him, his body meshing to hers. He was so deep inside her; he was hitting into the wall of her uterus with every intense thrusts. Marco was deep inside Eve as far as he could physically go. Her small hands rubbing over his body, devouring, and savoring every inch of him. Marco knew her desperate moans that bordered on cries were for pleasure and pain. 'I'm making love to a woman now. A beautiful woman,' Marco's eyes in a sexual trance as he felt himself hitting his peak, ready to cum. 'I never meant to hurt you Evie,' he had an apologetic tone to his climatic groan, 'Evie I'm...' His face scrunched up in pleasurable agony.

'Ssshhh.' Her hand reached up to his lips. 'You don't need to say anything else.'

Wanting him, loving him, her body oozing to him. Thoughts and memories swirled in her head; inside she was crying at the sheer magnificence of having Marco Rossi again... finally, they were together as adults. Eve had cum in with an emotional and sensitive orgasm, her whole body trembled as she felt Marco throbbing inside her.

With Eve's sweetness at his thighs, all Marco could think was how lucky he was to have found her again. The feeling of cumming inside her was just as he'd remembered it. Eve did something to him that he couldn't describe, she made him feel complete. Yes, Eve made him feel like everything was how it was meant to be. She had no hidden agenda, other than she wanted him... Marco could feel it, he had felt it the very first time he'd ever kissed her. She knew him, she knew who he really was, and she adored him.

'Why did we ever stop doing this?' Marco caught his breath. He must have been out of his fucking mind to ever let her go the first time.

'Someone had a career, remember,' she joked with a smile, but not really. It had been very clear in Eve's mind that Marco had chosen his football career over her, and she was just a teenager. It had stuck with her for all these years, she'd felt insignificant to Marco back then.

He sensed the hurt in her words. 'And before I knew it you were getting married.' As the words left his mouth, he felt bad. They'd never talked about that part of her life.

Were they really doing this now? Eve thought to herself. Marco was still inside her; they'd just made perfect love... now was not the time. She ignored his comment, she put a finger to his lips to silence him with a calming sigh. For Eve it was such a sensitive and personally complexed time in her life, nothing that happened in her life after the Marco's heartbreak, would ever dull the impact he'd had on her life. She'd be scarred by Marco forever, literally, and he had no idea. For years Eve couldn't bear to say Marco's name out loud or hear it, because the pain was just too damn much. Eve did what she did best in that moment. She pushed her painful memories deep down.

Eve had been awake for a good twenty minutes, just watching Marco as he slept beside her. It was beyond surreal to wake up next to him again. Her eyes devouring every inch of him as she tried to find something she would change about him, there was absolutely nothing. Everything about this gentle giant of a man, she adored, and she always had. *Try harder... make today the day you find something about Marco Rossi that you don't like!* Eve told herself. If she had something she didn't like about him, then it would make leaving him at the end of this holiday a hell of a lot easier.

Her eyes stilled at his face, his imperfect nose, the freckle just under his eye, those long dark eyelashes. Eve wanted to touch him, feel him, Marco was perfect to her, and she didn't know if she would ever love another human being as much as she did Marco Rossi. She loved everything about him, absolutely everything! Even that he was so big compared to her and that sometimes it limited them physically, Eve could only kiss Marco's chest in the missionary position, *all the more reason for her to be on top. Bonus!* It didn't bother her that she had to be on tippy toes to kiss and hug him. To Eve it didn't matter that they looked miss matched as they walked down the street together, and it didn't matter that he was career minded and she was not. Eve didn't care, she loved Marco exactly how he was. She loved his way, his heart, and who he was, unconditionally.

She rolled over, still feeling like it was all a dream... Marco was in her bed. Reality was setting in though. *What was last night, a one nighter? What was supposed to happen now?* Her mind was racing off into a state of catastrophizing as it most often did when things got too real in Eve life.

'What are you thinking about?' Marco had woken to see her stared up to the ceiling in deep thought. His voice was sleepy, barely awake he smiled.

What happened now? What did she say to him? And what about the secret?

Back to catastrophizing… Suddenly, she wasn't feeling so great about things. She'd let her protective walls down for a mere second and she was anxious.

'You want to tell me what's on your mind. I know somethings bothering you,' Marco asked.

'How can you tell?'

'I have special superpowers when it comes to you Eve Frank,' he said making her smile.

'Yes, you do,' she bit her bottom lip. 'What happened last night?'

'I spent the night with you, and I can tell you, I'm never sleeping in that queen size bed again,' Marco said avoiding her actual question.

'It is a very big bed; I'm willing to share it with you.'

'I was hoping you would be,' he said sounding pleased with the bed negotiations.

And just like that, they'd both avoided the awkward conversation and yet somehow agreed to sleep in the same bed again. Eve took this as a positive.

The blinds were open as she laid in pure bliss in Marco's arms, watching the snow fall ever so lightly out the window. The touch of his hand in her hair and at her scalp was soothing and comforting, she nearly fell asleep.

'How soon can you come to Melbourne?' His mind was going around and around, all he could think about was getting Eve to Melbourne before anything distracted her.

'You really want me to come to Melbourne?' She asked like she didn't believe him.

'I really do.' He was serious.

She rolled her lips and bit down on the bottom one in thought again. 'Why do you want me to come and stay with you?' *Was it the night of sex they'd just had, or was it her? Was he serious? Did he really want her?* It was hard not to be her own worst enemy… *Why couldn't she just accept the invitation and go for crying out loud!*

'I want to spend time with you, not on holidays with our families… Just you and I.'

She stared at Marco contemplated the notion. 'I have to go back to France first.' She tickled his arm that rest across her body.

'Are you thinking before March?' he couldn't help but ask, the feeling of going home without her was not good, especially after last night.

'I'm thinking soon.' She couldn't give him any more than that at this point. She had been in a similar position before, dropping everything to be with a man! Only this time it was a little different, it was Marco, and what if by some ridiculous chance of bad luck, he went back to Melbourne and met the girl of his dream girl next week... Eve would never forgive herself.

'What do you think your grandmother will say when you tell her you're going to Melbourne to see a guy?' Marco had been told Eve's grandmother had a huge influence over her, and that she was very protective.

'Mamie knows everything about you,' Eve chuckled softly, and Vivienne did know everything, she loved knowing all the details when it came to her granddaughters love life.

'Everything. What does that mean?' his voice pepped up with interest.

'She knows you were my first love, lover, and heartbreak,' a cheeky smile came over her face.

'Oh, so she's that kind of grandmother?' again, Marco was surprised.

Eve knew how much Vivienne would love this latest update. 'Mamie lives for love stories.'

Marco nodded, getting the picture, 'So, she probably doesn't like me then I'm guessing?' he didn't like his chances, he'd broken Eve's innocent teenage heart.

'She knows how I feel about you; she knows you're special.' She rubbed his arm assuring him.

Marco signed, 'I have to deal with my mum today, she knows about Palm Cove, did you hear her last night. She's going to interrogate me like I'm an evil villain. My mum loves you more than she loves me, you know that right!' Marco kissed the top of Eve's head.

The thought of Marco speaking with Jackie, before she got to Jackie, sent Eve into a panic!

Chapter Seven

Showering and dressing in record time, Eve had something to do. Marco had left her room to go to his own room for a shower and then a run. She needed to get to Jackie, with no idea what she was going to say, or how Jackie was feeling today, all Eve knew was that they needed to talk.

The knock at the door startled Eve, she didn't need any distractions now, she needed to find Jackie... But as it turned out, Jackie had found her first. They stood at the door in an awkward space, Eve and Jackie eyeing each other with the weight of the situation upon them. They were face to face and alone; this was it.

'Are you angry with me?' Eve had to know straight up. Jackie was one of her best friends, her confidant who she cherished and had always looked up to, and it was a massive thing to have come between them.

Jackie walked past Eve and into her room without saying a word, she looked around, taking a few moments to observe the unmade bed and survey the room, she could tell her son had stayed the night. There were coffee cups, a half-eaten bowl of chips, a can of diet coke... She knew for a fact Eve didn't drink diet coke, and that Marco did. The room was comfortably disheveled, which was most unlike Eve!

'Where's Marco this morning?' Jackie's calmness frightened Eve.

'He went for a run.' Eve held her breath.

Jackie looked around the hotel room some more, she needed a moment. 'Eve, was Marco the father of your baby?' No beating around the bush, she needed confirmation.

'Yes,' said Eve with her heart beating like a drum in her chest.

'I see. So, you lied to me.' The hurt was evident. 'And I thought we were friends; you could have just told me the truth.' She was pissed off in a deep way, although remaining calm.

Eve began to gasp for her breaths. 'We knew it was wrong to be together in Palm Cove, and I didn't want him to get into any trouble. I knew you'd be angry with us.'

'I asked you to your face at the time, who was the father of that baby... And you lied to me. All these years you've kept this from me.' They stood in the middle of the hotel room, face to face. 'I gave you no reason to not trust me Eve, I've been there for you with every mistake you've ever made.'

That hurt. *Every mistake!* The anxiety building in Eve was overwhelming. She was losing Jackie and the thought was unbearable. She could barely breath, yet now she also a little pissed herself... *Every mistake!*

'And now what, the two of you are playing bed friends again,' Jackie was losing her cool. 'I hope you're using protection this time.'

It felt like Eve had been punched in the chest and then her stomach. Against her will, tears fell from her eyes, she hadn't been prepared for this kind of anger from Jackie. 'I need to explain to you how it was. How it is.'

'Well, yes, maybe you do.' Jackie decided to sit on the end of the bed that looked like it'd been ransacked, it was the bed her son and Eve had spent the night in obviously, it felt weird to say the least and yet it there was something rather lovely about it... She'd let her feelings be known, and now Jackie had to be the older woman here, poor Eve was on the edge of hyperventilation, she was obviously very emotional after Jackie's harsh words.

Eve felt the sudden shift in Jackie's demeanor and sat on the bed beside her giving her eyes a quick wipe.

'I'm all ears if you'd like to tell me now,' said Jackie reaching for Eve's hand. This was her olive branch, because this young woman meant the world to her on any other day. The fact that she'd rattled Eve emotionally, disturbed Jackie. Now all she wanted to do was comfort her.

'From the day I first saw Marco on the school bus, when I was ten years old, I've been abnormally besotted with him.' Eve took a deep breath to center herself. 'I used to take his T shirts and sweaters from his room, and you'd think he'd lost them at school.' Eve glanced at Jackie with tears rolling down her cheeks as she let it all out. 'They're all in my draw at Mum's by the way.' *That was one confession out of the way.*

'Right!' This was all news to Jackie, she lived for this shit normally, and it had happened right under her nose, and she hadn't even known.

'Nobody knew how I felt about him, not even Tessa and Zoe, until we went to Palm Cove,' Eve began to breathe as she continued with her confessions, 'Marco was my first crush,' she whispered softly, 'And he was my first lover.'

Jackie was the one now holding her breath. 'I see,' was all she could manage.

'And before you go thinking it was wrong, I want you to know it wasn't,' Eve wasn't going to feel bad about it another day of her life, 'It wasn't something dirty or promiscuous between Marco and I, it was special.' Eve could feel her emotions getting the better of her again as she continued. 'That baby,' Eve found her courage as she turned to Jackie, 'Was made from goodness. And the fact that it was Marco's baby, broke my heart.' She sighed with angst. 'I didn't tell you because I wanted to protect him,' she gushed through her tears. 'And one more thing, it was my body and my baby, and I did what I thought was right,' Eve found her strength.

'Okay, well what can I say to that,' Jackie said softly hugging Eve into her side, 'You always manage to see the best in people Eve.' Jackie was numb, she was humbled that Eve had cared for her son so much she'd protected him to her own detriment. 'You know I love you and the last thing I want is for this to come between you and I.' Jackie paused, 'Marco is my son, but men are strange creatures, I know I don't have to tell you that.' Jackie found herself smiling. 'I am so sorry my son did that to you, I'm sorry he wasn't there for you, I tried to raise him to be a better man than that.'

Eve panicked, 'Marco doesn't know about the baby.'

The look on Jackie's face was nothing short of horror! 'He doesn't know you were pregnant and that you lost his baby!' she repeated, again shocked by Eve.

Oh fuck! Eve felt her teeth tingle, her anxiety was like a violent storm invading her body.

'Oh my god, Eve,' a long pause, 'How do you manage to get yourself into these situations?'

Again, condescending, and downright nasty, Eve was gutted that Jackie would say such a thing, whether it was right or wrong, she was taking offence even though she knew Jackie was in total shock.

Eve sniffed, 'I was seventeen,' her voice was dead calm, although she was on the defense, 'I didn't want to be a burden on Marco's life or career. And I've stayed away from Marco all these years because I've never stopped loving him, not for one single day, which nearly half killed me by the way,' a pause, 'Oh, and just so it's clear, your son didn't want me after Palm Cove.' Now that was Eve's truth for Jackie.

It was awful for a mother to hear these revelations and to see Eve upset, Jackie knew her so well. This was a person she loved, a young woman she knew was genuine and honest, for the most part! She wanted to wrap Eve up in her arms and save her once again. Her son had hurt her and now everything was starting to make sense, as awful and confronting as it was.

'Eve,' Jackie took a second, 'As wonderful as I'd like to think my son is, he's hurt you before, I don't want that to happen again.'

Eve looked at Jackie, knowing it wasn't easy for her to say that about her beloved Marco. 'I'm going to Melbourne to visit him.' Eve bit down on her bottom lip wondering how Jackie was going to feel about that. *Was she for or against her being involved with Marco?*

'Oh!' It dawned on Jackie; they were grownups now.

'He asked me to visit so we could spend some time together alone, and I'm going to.'

'Well. You should go and visit then, clearly these feelings are strong.'

'I'm just going to ask you because I need to know,' Eve began, knowing it might be the end of everything. 'Would you prefer I didn't go and see Marco?'

'Why would you ask that?' Jackie squinted; she wondered what Eve's angle was.

'Because it's me. Because of whom I am. Because of Evan,.' Eve blinked away from Jackie in shame.

'I'm disappointed that you would even ask me that.' Jackie was serious.

'I've got baggage, and if there's one thing I know for sure, I can't change my past,' Eve sounded sure of herself for the first time in the conversation.

'You don't need to change anything about yourself. You shouldn't be ashamed of your past; our pasts are what make us good strong women. I've got a past believe or not.' Jackie laughed flippantly.

Eve was wide eyed. 'Really!'

'I met Mario at a time in my life when I was a little reckless, it was just good timing he came along when he did, and I fell madly in love with him. Needless to say, Mario's mother didn't approve of me, I was from the wrong side of town, I didn't speak or dress like I do now. His mother still doesn't like me if we're being honest.' Jackie nudged into Eve.

'Why?' asked Eve, 'I thought Nona Nina loved you.' Eve referred to Tessa's grandmother who had always seemed such a cute and lovely old Italian lady.

'No, no. Nona Nina doesn't love me. I will never do to Emma or any of the women in my sons lives, what Nona Nina has done to me.' Jackie shook her head.

'What has she done?'

'I've never told anyone this. But when Mario asked me to marry him, his mother asked me to my face if I was a virgin. I said I was of course, even though I was sleeping with Mario every chance I could.' Jackie laughed again. 'I don't think Nona Nina believe me, and she's never let me forget it,' Jackie sighed at how ridiculous it was. 'And while I'm being completely honest with you, I should probably tell you I was devastated when you were marrying Evan – But only because I always wanted you to marry Nicholas,' Jackie scoffed, 'Boy did I get that all wrong?' Laughing loudly and then leaning to hug Eve again. Evan and the wedding was a super sensitive subject for Eve and Jackie was about the only person who could get away with saying such a thing to her. She truly did love Eve like a daughter, she admired the young woman she had become and was secretly thrilled about her and Marco hooking up. Jackie would get over the lie in time, she now understood why Eve had kept such a massive secret.

'Jackie I'm sorry I lied to you about Marco.'

'No. No. Don't be. I see in your eyes how much you adore him, and how much he means to you.' Jackie was coming around; she was touched that Eve loved her son so much and had protected him so fiercely.

'I'd like to be the one who tells Marco about the baby if that's okay?' Eve asked of Jackie, 'And I'd like to tell him in my own time.'

'You need to tell him sooner rather than later Eve.' These were words of wisdom.

'Can you please not tell him? This is really important to me Jackie.' Eve was beginning to feel the full force of her secret, Marco was and had always been her main priority when it came to the secret.

'I will be having a chat with him today. I promise I won't tell him about the baby, so long as you do.'

'You know I'm going home tomorrow,' Marco told Eve as they both laid on her bed. It had been a huge, gigantic day for both of them. After Jackie and Eve had their chat, Jackie moved onto Marco in the afternoon, it had been as uncomfortable as expected. His mother's disappointment in him hooking up with Eve when she was just seventeen was brutal. He'd explained he couldn't fight his attraction to Eve, not then, not now, not ever. Jackie had her say and then let it go. How could she deny such a love story!

'I'm flying to Australia with Zoe from here,' Eve said very casually.

'You are?' He was pleased.

'Yep. I've got some people to see in Sydney. Then if it's okay with you I might just pop straight down to you in Melbourne. That's if you don't mind me coming so soon?' She wanted desperately to see Jo and Tia; it had been too long. Maybe a dinner with her father, depending on how she felt when she got to Sydney. She would love to catch up with Kellie and of course see if Ferez was available too. Eve needed a good week or so to do the rounds.

Vivienne and Louis would understand, she had no life in France besides her work and the two of them, she was never going to find her own way in life if she didn't take some chances and make some changes.

'Of course, it's fine with me,' Marco was excited, 'I was thinking I might delay my flight home from here a few days,' Marco didn't know how to tell her he was totally in love with her, 'I don't want this to stop.'

Rolling over so she was facing him, they both laid on the bed fully clothed, exhausted, and completely content with one another's company.

'I might have been just seventeen when we were in Palm Cove, but I thought I was going to die when you left the bedroom that last morning.' Her eyes sparkled with emotion. 'These feelings are all new for you Marco, but it's how I've felt since

I was a little girl,' Eve's soft words mesmerizing Marco, 'Wanting you constantly, a fierce burning inside me every time someone mentioned your name. Wondering why I wasn't enough for you, why you didn't want me the same way I wanted you?' It was hard to say those things to Marco, but maybe this was her chance to tell him about the baby.

'I wanted you in Palm Cove!' He was taken back by Eve's account of events, 'I wanted you the minute you came downstairs in that little bikini - if we're being completely honest here. I tried not to like you; I really did. You were so beautiful and so smart; I couldn't resist being with you.'

Eve watched him get lost in his thoughts of how he felt about her all those years ago. 'I'll take a chance on you Marco Rossi if you'll take one on me,' Eve propositioned him at a whisper.

'I'm in.' His eyes piercing through to her core. He began kissing her lips softly, his body rolling over her as he gave Eve his assurance in a long slow kiss. She took deep breaths so she could absorb every part of him into her soul. The more Marco opened up to her the more she became enthralled in this magnificent man who was every part the man she had ever dreamed he was, and more.

He was sucking at her soft responsive lips as he touched her face with his big gentle hand, Eve wondered if there was anything possibly more comforting in the world... Her mind and body transfixed with his commanding mouth. She finally let the thought into her head that she had been suppressing from the minute she first touched Marco in New York, he made her feel whole, he was the one!

Her softness had him on the edge as it always did, it was a fine line between utter pleasure and blowing his load right there in his pants. That and the sensual way she moved her lips to his, sucking his lip when he sucked hers, licking at his tongue when he touched hers. Breathing to him as he inhaled her. Eve's hands rested at his arms as he stroked her face and held her. They rolled around the hotel bed kissing and feeling each other, and it soon turned into a night of making love like they had never before. This was not there first time at the rodeo with each other, they were familiar and knowing of the others needs and it was intoxicating, yet more excitingly, there was still so much to learn about each other, after all this time, they had both evolved and grown sexually.

Now both fully naked, Marco sat up against the bed head as Eve sat on his lap... she liked this position! Her body against his. His huge hard penetrating muscle of pleasure deep inside her stomach as she slid her wetness over him. They were both adults now, they could make love openly and freely. Eve just had one little secret hanging over her head... She had to tell Marco about the baby as she'd bypassed it earlier. In her head she planned to tell him in Melbourne, she needed to be feeling right though, she needed to be prepared, and right at this moment here in New York, she wasn't ready. Partly because she feared the worst, that Marco would hate her for not telling him all those years ago. Her mind switched back to her erotic reality as Marco pulled her up his body. His knees at her back, she was wedged to him as he cupped a handful of her breast to his mouth and began to suckle at her. His tongue flicked over her nipple and setting off an arousing alarm throughout her. She felt her legs turn to jelly, she had all of him inside her, filling her, loving her. Fingernails scratching at the overpowering sensation flooding her body, Eve's nails dug into his shoulders as she pushed herself up to his mouth as he tantalized her nipples, one to the other, over, and over licking and sucking as she squirmed with pleasure over his cock, still deep inside her.

His arm holding her to him, the softness of Eve all over him was the most sensual feeling he'd ever felt.

No condom, no sex was out the window when it came to Marco, Eve was on the pill, and she trusted!

Eve's hips widening, she let herself pull away from his eager mouth and her body leant back, arching backwards to his legs as she continued to grind over his girth, he held her hips to his as she pressed her chest up, her soft pillows of flesh moved as he pleasured her. Marco grabbed at her, kneading, and groping at her boobs. His other hand forcing Eve's hips down, so all of him was penetrating her warm pussy. It was an overload of erotic sensuality, Eve moaning, her body sweating as she felt her hips locking with her powering orgasm. Marco stiffening as his cum shot into the depths of her body.

How could either of them ever live without this!

Chapter Eight

As a teenager Zoe embedded herself into Tessa's family and household as did Eve, it was always lively and happy at the Rossi's. Then moving to university on the Gold Coast had been a solo adventure. When she finally came back to Sydney she was out on her own pretty much. Her mum had moved on and was living with her new boyfriend, her sister was married. So, Zoe took a job working in a city hotel at nights to pay for her tiny one-bedroom flat, while she did her internship at a fashion magazine. Now the internship had finished, and Zoe was looking for a permanent position in the industry she so loved. Money didn't come as easily to Zoe these days, although her mum helped her out, she still worked hard to support herself and was fiercely independent and proud.

At dinner, everyone came together. Zoe and Nick sat next to each other, after spending so much time together, they were no closer to being anything but friends, they hadn't had sex.

It was just like any other night at dinner, there were several conversations going on at the table, Eve didn't take part in any of them, in fact she felt awkward, even uncomfortable. It was because now her mother, Jackie and Mario knew about Palm Cove, and they all knew Marco had been her baby's father, and Marco didn't. After all these years, it seemed the secret was now as threatening as ever.

Marco sat next to Eve and did everything right as he always did, touching her knee under the table, at one point he had his arm around her, and he talked to her as they ate dinner, her extra quiet demeanor was noticeable.

When Marco announced he was extending his stay in New York by a few days to the table, everyone seemed pleased, even a little surprised. Mario gave Eve a smile across the table, but Jackie had questioned Marco's decision, in which he brushed his mother off. Zoe gave Eve a look, Anna also recognised Eve's distracted mood, she gave her daughter a few sympathetic motherly smiles, they still hadn't discussed the Marco situation, it was still very much new news.

The truth of the matter was Eve felt overwhelmed and a little guilty about how things were progressing with Marco. She felt guilty because he made her feel so happy... *Was she still punishing herself?* Her psychologist said her self-sabotage was just result of Evan's death in which she felt guilt over, based on no factual evidence at all. In other words, Eve blamed herself for Evan's death, still convinced it had something to do with Sonny Smith and what he'd done to her. Therefore, she couldn't move on with someone else. Was she going to sabotage this second chance with Marco too!

Tessa and Zoe sprang out of the lift door, both laughing, drunk, and high on life as Eve and Marco shared a kiss in the hall between their rooms.

'E, you should really come out with us. Come clubbing?' Tessa said ignoring her brother's existence.

'Marco, you can come too,' Zoe had a humorous tone to her words. She had been drinking champagne at dinner and was semi drunk.

He looked at her with a bland smirk. 'Thanks Zoe. But no thanks.'

'You've got the girl. Now you're trying to keep her all to yourself. Not happening lover boy. She was our friend first.' Zoe poked her finger into Marco' chest.

'Where's Nick?' He looked at both Tessa and Zoe, unimpressed with Zoe poke and Tessa's shun of him, it was unlike his sister to ignore him.

'He's getting changed. He is coming out on the town for a night to remember, because he's a fun guy.' It was a hard not to love Zoe, she was cute when she was drunk, funny in an annoying way.

'I'll go change. We can all go together.' Marco turned to Eve who stood in bewilderment at her friends' humor. He knew Eve wanted to go.

'I'll call you soon.' She gave him a smile as he headed down the hall.

Zoe clapped her hands excitedly. 'How weird is it, after everything, it turns out he loves you as much as you love him.'

'Do you think so?' Eve was a little coy.

Tessa scoffed, 'I know so. There's no way on earth my brother would ever miss a minute of fucking football for anyone. He's in love with you E.'

'I've decided to go to Melbourne.' Eve announced.

'Wow! I hope you tell him about the baby before it all gets too serious.' Tessa was putting it out there, this secret of Eve's was making her very nervous.

'Don't pressure me, I'm going to tell him.'

'You deserve all the happiness in the world E, and I think my brother's the one for you. But you need to be honest with him from the start and tell him about his baby.' Tessa was trying her best to say it nicely, in a semi drunk, and possibly high kind of way. She loved her brother and was expecting the baby secret to shake him up.

An hour later Tessa was getting them into a small, crowded bar downtown that was again, one of her hangouts.

Eve leant up against Marco's leg, he sat on a bar stool at the funky crowded bar. Cool looking guys made cocktails and did a little show as they did so. Very cool music and very cool people. Tessa and Zoe were lively and chit chatting to any hot guy who looked their way, Eve watching on wondering where they got their courage from. It was entertaining if nothing else, two sexy girls putting it out there.

'Have a look at those two,' Nick said as he stood with Eve and Marco by the bar.

'They're having fun.' Eve caught something in Nick's tone, 'Are you jealous?' she asked.

'Absolutely not. No way!' He was so jealous he couldn't stand it.

'Am I missing something?' Marco asked, without getting an answer.

Eve moved closer to Nick. 'I know, you like Zoe, and you know it too.' She found it hard to resist teasing him, after all she did owe him big time.

'We're just friends, I don't care what she does.' Total bullshit.

'Mmm, I don't know about that.' Eve managed to get the last word in before the girls danced their way back over to them, which in turn infuriated Nick. That was what drove him nuts about Eve, she always had the last say in her quiet little voice. This thing between his brother and Eve was definitely more than he'd first given them credit for back in Palm Cove, they actually really liked each other.

Zoe wore a tight pair of red leather pants; red was her color. A tiny black little boob tube top, and a red tie around her neck. She was half Sandra D, half sex worker. She'd taken it upon herself to tell Eve what she was wearing out too, Zoe loved dressing Eve. Tonight, was a special occasion, she went all out in a bid to make Marco fret. And fret he did. A pair of nude colour pants from one her suits, sexy nude heals and sheer nude top that required no bra, so Eve's great boobs and cherry nipples commanded the attention they deserved. Marco hung onto her hand every chance he got, it was impossible to not look at Eve in that top, he thought maybe the outfit needed a jacket or a special kind of bra, to keep the impure minds of every other man from wondering.

Tessa had developed a very New York look; she'd become more fashion conscious after her years in the city. She wore a skimpy white silk slip, black stilettos, and a zebra belt to pull it in at her tiny waist, very eighties of her. Her long legs went all the way up to her neck, she looked sensational, with waves of hair flowing around her body like a shampoo model.

As they walked back to the hotel after a fun few hours out on the town, Nick and Zoe were drunk, Marco not so much, Eve was tipsy, and Tessa had secretly done blow in the bathrooms, it was better than having a hangover. They got pizza slices around the corner from their hotel and took it back to Eve's hotel room. Pizza and water for a very drunk Zoe, which didn't really make much of a difference. She refused to eat more than two bites of pizza for fear of calories, which bothered Nick who seemed to be very interested in her analogy of consumption of such food and the way her body reacted to it.

'It makes me feel sick to my stomach to even watch you eat pizza,' Zoe said leaning into his side as they stood in the hotel lift. 'Don't you feel sick? Look at all that oil.' She frowned up to Nick as he ate his second slice.

'If you got some pizza in you, maybe you could hold your drink a little better,' Nick said.

'If I ate pizza, I'd definitely throw up on you,' Zoe laughed, so did everyone else.

'And here I thought you'd changed… You're still a little bitch,' his words spat at her as he put his hand out to stop her getting any closer to him.

Zoe saw red. 'You are a pig. A using fucking pig.' She had gone from happy drunk to bad drunk fast.

'What is going on?' Tessa was now in on it. 'What are you two doing?' she asked as they stepped out the lift.

'Your friends a bitch,' said Nick with a slur, and everyone gasped. Tessa's eyes growing with disgust.

At that moment, Zoe leaped at him, grabbing him by the shirt front. Nick dropped his pizza and grabbed hold of her arms, pushing her back against the hall wall with a thud. It was beyond pent up sexual tension!

'I hate you,' screamed Zoe, she wouldn't let go of him and while everyone stood rooted to the floor in a state of shock, Zoe hit Nick with a closed fist to the face. 'You made me a bitch, you asshole.'

WTF!!! Where was this all coming from, everyone wondered as they watched on.

'You loved fucking me babe... you couldn't get enough,' Nick was spitting evil.

'I hate you,' Zoe began to cry.

'Stop!' Marco raised his voice, stepping forward and pulling Nick away.

'You were a dirty little whore,' Nick said as Marco pushed him to the opposite wall.

Eve holding Zoe back, 'Don't you call her that,' Eve gushed in her most disapproving voice to Nick. Eve hated the word whore unless she was the one using it!

Marco had Nick; it had gone from zero to one hundred in seconds. Then Nick pushed past Marco, Zoe pulled away from Eve, and right there in the hallway they scrambled for each other and began desperately kissing like two possessed lovers.

'Are you two fucking kidding!' Tessa was beside herself and so very confused at the display of utter madness that she could only laugh. Eve and Marco watched on speechless.

'I'm sorry. I'm so sorry,' Nick's words to Zoe's mouth as they kissed, he was emotional and clearly out of his mind.

'I know, I know,' Zoe kissed back as if nobody was watching.

Tessa threw her hands up in confusion, 'What are you sorry for?' she said to Zoe, 'He's an idiot. That's exactly why I didn't want you near him from the start, now look what's happened.' Tessa rolled her red stained lips at Eve. 'How many times did they fuck. I'd like details.' demanded Tessa, 'I know you know,' Tessa looked at Eve.

'Zoe could probably answer that better than me. I'm not quite sure how many times exactly.' Eve couldn't tell if Tessa was going to make this something it didn't need to be. Zoe and Nick took the opportunity to slip back into the lift while the girls squabble in the hall with Marco looking on.

Tessa squinted at Eve. 'You should have told me.'

'Tessa, I didn't think it was my place to tell Zoe's story.' It was like being on trial, an interrogation. *How on earth was she the bad guy here?*

'You always choose her over me,' said Tessa with harshness.

'No, I do not.'

'Yes, you do E. I get that she was there for you with all the Evan shit.'

'Does it really matter girls?' Marco was there like a shag on a rock.

'No Tessa, I don't agree with you,' Eve paused, 'You were the first person I told about my feelings for Marco, because I trusted you. I've always told you everything besides this one thing, which is minor in the scheme of things. And it wasn't about me, so I didn't feel it was my place.' It had hurt Eve that Tessa thought she would choose Zoe over her. It would never happen. She would never choose one over the other, she loved them both like sisters. 'I haven't told anyone how much coke you're actually really using,' Eve said it as payback for bringing up Evan, and Tessa knew it, but in front of Marco, she thought that was super low of Eve.

Tessa coming back at Eve with full force, 'Oh, wow. You're so perfect; and the biggest secret keeper of all fucking time… Who happens to drinks herself to sleep every fucking night and thinks nobody knows.'

The gloves were off!

'Serious Tessa!' Eve frowned with anger, 'I'm sorry if you're upset with me for not telling you exactly how many times our friend fucked your fucking brother.' Eve wasn't taking Tessa's shit any longer. And just like that the great night ended. Tessa went one way; Eve went the other.

The hotel room door shut; Eve pressed Marco against the wall. Deciding to take her frustrations out by fucking him good and proper. It seemed the best way to blow some steam off. Pulling her top over her head and throwing it to the floor and slipping her bra off, then unbuckling his belt and unbuttoning his pants. She wasn't in the best frame of mind before Tessa's outburst, now she was really unraveled.

'What was that all about?' a confused Marco asked as Eve began undressing him in the middle of her room.

'I don't know, she's your sister, he's your brother and they're both crazy... No hands!' Eve tapped his hand as it went to her bare boob, he was into them in a big way, he couldn't keep his hands and mouth off them. 'No touching,' she insisted as she bent down and leaned into his large erection. Hands at the base, mouth ready to take him, first she put her chest forward to him and ran him between her soft boobs.

'Fuck, Eve!' Marco said reaching for her hair, she was complexed on a whole different level.

'I said no touching.' She bent forward slightly and took him straight into her mouth and sucked him harder than she usually would, only for a moment before she started to lick at him, licking all the way from the base to the tip, giving a little suck with her lips every time.

'What am I supposed to do with my hands?' Marco held them out to his sides.

'Put them on your head.' She went straight back to him, sucking and licking at him, catching up on all the years of her sexual deprivation. She'd been waiting to blow Marco for days! With one hand at his base and the other under him, kneading his balls as she sucked, her nipples and fleshy boobs touching his thighs. At that very moment, wondering to herself if it was distasteful to be having sex with her gorgeous Marco, in a bid to numb the guilt and heartbreak of Evan. Tessa had set her off and it was something Eve knew she had to get over, and fast!

'Does Tessa really do a lot of coke?' Marco asked as her tongue swirled around his cock.

Eve shook her head slowly to appease him. *How was she supposed to answer during oral sex?*

'Do you think Nick and Zoe will stay in the same room tonight?' Marco was puzzled, it had been the strangest evening!

Eve couldn't believe he was asking her all these questions while her mouth was full.

'I'm about to cum Evie,' he gasped breathlessly.

She gave him the thumbs up, which made him smile. There was no stopping Eve, she loved a grand finale, she put both hands around the back to his athletic arse and squeezed at him, pulling him to her as she fixated on him cumming in her mouth, this was her specialty, she knew she was good at it!

'Eve Frank!' Marco groaned as she kept sucking him, 'Oh, my fucking... Fuck!' his voice louder on the last fuck. Her blow jobs really left nothing to the imagination, she was the ultimate. Her hair was frizzed out, sucking him like her life depended on it, Eve was like a little sexy pleasure doll on the end of his cock.

Eve came up for air, 'I've never seen Zoe like that. Should I check on her?' her face winced with concern as Marco's hands went to her face and pulled her up to him.

'They're probably making it up to each other by now.' He didn't want Eve to go anywhere but back on his cock as soon as he was ready for action again, Eve was insatiable, he wanted to fuck her every which way as he took her to the bed.

'Mmm. Maybe not.' She sat on his stomach, her hands at his chest.

'I'd rather you stay here with me,' said Marco with the sexiest smile, he didn't have to say it twice.

With that Eve turned herself around and sat on Marco's again hardening cock. The reverse cowboy was something she loved, and Marco would be a challenge because of his sheer size, but she was giving it a go!

A little eyebrow raise from him as she took over again, he laid back in the pillows and watched her move over him. Her long curls touching his stomach as she let her head fall back, she let her body fall down over him, his cock digging deep inside her painfully, which was exactly what she'd needed. Hardcore sex always helped.

Marco liked the semi drunk and pissed off Eve, she moved herself over him looking back at him as she reached out behind her for his hands. Holding his hands into her sides, Eve felt her body break into a chill of sweat, the pain had turned to intense erotic pleasurable pain, her favourite pain of all. Within seconds she was in the grips of a heavy orgasm. Eve willing herself to take it, telling herself that she deserved the painful punishment for still loving Evan and wanting Marco at the same time. *Was she not quite right?* She didn't feel like this was normal.

How could someone so small be so fucking much! Marco thought as he let Eve take over his body. With every moan and every little cry of pleasure, he was taken with another surge of orgasmic sexual pleasure, cumming as Eve came to him, holding her hips down to his pulsing cock as she cried his name. It was powerful.

Chapter Nine

Tessa's lifestyle seemed all glitz and glamour, but it was far from it. Six nights and two afternoon a week she danced her arse off, which was great, most of the time she loved it. Being so far away from her family and friends, not so great! She was lonely more often than not, even though it seemed like she had such a busy social life. Having nobody who knew where you came from or who you truly were, sucked. She'd started to put her feelers out for auditions coming up in Asia and Australia to be closer to home, her experience on Broadway had to count for something.

She'd apologized to Eve for last night, then she'd arranged for a get together in her parent's suite on her night off, snacks and movie with her siblings and Eve and Zoe. All had been forgiven, Jackie and Mario had gone to dinner with Anna and Nigel, it was all of them lounging around just as they had in the Rossi home as kids on a lazy Sunday afternoon after a weekend of parties and shenanigans.

To everyone's dismay, Nick and Zoe had slept in their own beds last night, they'd had their fight, kissed, made up and then decided they wouldn't rush things.

It was obvious, Nick felt something for her, he appreciated her bubbly personality. Zoe was insatiably funny, and she stood up to him when he stepped over the line which most women didn't. Zoe was like a mate he wanted to fuck or had fucked rather.

Pulling her knees up as she felt Marco's hand glide down her stomach and into the top of her pants. Eve felt herself flush at what was going on under the blanket that covered her and Marco on the sofa, she laid at his front, they looked very comfortable. Eve looked around to see if anyone was watching them, but everyone was fixated on the movie that had finally started.

'What are you doing?' she whispered as his hand went further into her pants.

'Nobody can see… Just keep your knees up,' Marco's warm breath at the side of her face as he whispered back, his hand moving into her knickers, he kissed the side of her head.

'I can't believe you are doing this here,' she breathed deeply at a whisper still.

'I can't believe you're letting me do this here,' a slight chuckle to his whisper.

A big, 'Ssshhh,' from Tessa silenced them, their mumbling from the back stalls was annoying her.

Marco's big fingers pressed between Eve's warm folds, she felt the immediate rush of heat through her veins, her heart started to pound, the pulsing of her clit as his finger rubbed over her warm wetness was unbearable.

'You have to stop.' Her head turned into his chest; her legs opened slightly so he had better access to her.

'Stop talking and just enjoy it,' Marco whispered, it was literally enough to make her cum, his arm that was around her body pulled her in a little, his other hand moving slow and pleasantly in her wetness.

'We're going to get caught.' Eve loved the risk of it.

'You're so wet, I want to fuck you Eve Frank,' Marco whispered, plunging a finger inside Eve's pussy.

Tessa turned around to them. 'If you two can't stop talking, you need to go in the other room if it's so important.' Bless her, she gave them the perfect out! Marco removed his hand from Eve's pants, she got up with the throw at her front and she followed Marco into his parents' bedroom.

Falling backward onto the bed, he was on top of her before she could blink, an elbow beside her head holding him over her, his other hand pulling her pants off swiftly. Eve scrambling at his jean. Him pulling them down his thighs. Eve pulling her top up. There was no time for talking or complete nakedness… This had to be a quicky. Only the sound of their breathing and desperation could be heard. Eve running her hands through his tasseled hair as she held Marco's head to her chest, his lips and tongue stimulating her nipples. Her legs wide apart as the pleasures of his fingers over her wet buzzing fold made her throb. It was all so risky; Eve loved the thought that someone could walk in on them at any minute. Rolling her head from side to side, her gasps turned into sighs of arousing madness as Marco pressed two fingers inside her wet flesh again. Eve wanting him to pull and push at her, she was pulsating around his fist. The double stimulation was more than she was able to take in silence, his lips at her nipples with hard sucks as he fingered her intently.

'Marco!' Eve said like he was hurting her, he knew it was pure pleasure, not pain. Raising himself over her he took his fingers from her and sucked them to his mouth so she could see, Eve wrapped her legs to his waist until she could feel his erection at her, pressing, hard and stiff, eager to get inside her.

But then he moved down her body, his mouth kissing over her boobs as he pushed her top up, then he kissed her stomach, then he licked her wetness. Eve lifted her hips to his silky long tongue, always consciously protective of her scar in the light of the room, Marco hadn't mentioned it yet. Everything about him was depriving her of oxygen, overloading her sexual senses so she couldn't see or hear, she dug the side of her head into the bed and clenched the covers with her fists, trying to be as quiet as possible. 'Don't stop, never stop,' she begged, her heart thudding inside her chest as she lifted a leg up to Marco's shoulder, he was above her now, with his big athletic cock stretching her pussy open as far as it could, plunging inside her with one hell of a thrust. He was taking her to a place she'd been before, Eve was struggling with thoughts of Evan... rushing, Marco was being rough by his standards, yet she trusted him completely with her body. Marco would never hurt her, not in that way.

With joy in his voice as he pounded away at Eve on his parents bed, Maroc said, 'I never want this to end. I want to do this for the rest of my life. Imagine if all we did was this, everyday forever, we'd have so many kids, we'd have a football team,' said Marco innocently with that sexy 'I'm about to cum' look on his face, the one Eve so loved... until now!

His hand resting at her side, his thumb touching Eve's belly, brushing over her scar and suddenly she felt herself tense up, like a clam snapping closed to protect herself. Marco sensed it immediately; her body felt different. 'What's wrong?' he asked like he might have been hurting her. Her body stopped moving with his. Marco bent to her and kissed her forehead as he stopped still just for a brief moment, he was inside her, moving gently in and out of her still body.

'I'm good,' Eve assured him with her mouth reaching up to his, she rolled with the motions and did her part, how could she not? She had to follow through, her focus was on making Marco cum, that was the job at hand.

She'd discussed having children in her future with her psychologist many times, having babies and motherhood was a bone of contention. Eve didn't want to be pregnant or give birth ever again, she was so frightened it would happen again.

Why did Marco have to ruin their extraordinary sex on his parents bed by talking about kids? The thought of being a mother terrified Eve almost as much as the pregnancy did. Besides all that could go wrong with the pregnancy, what if she gave birth and didn't feel a connection to her baby, what if she didn't love it or just didn't want it. *What if she was just like Sam and didn't want her baby?*

Marco came in record breaking time, they raced to the finish line, it had been over almost before it had begun, Eve didn't have her usual passion and Marco felt something went wrong along the way.

Eve pulled her pants back on and smoothed the bed covers on Jackie and Mario's bed as Marco cleaned himself up in the bathroom, then they returned to the others, like nothing had happened.

Later in the night back in Eve's hotel room, after Marco had showered and they lay side by side in bed, she wondered if she could maybe somehow find it within herself to want the family Marco clearly wanted.

Was this a deal breaker for him? One minute she would do anything to be with him, anything, and the next she was checking out because he had mentioned kids. The thought of getting pregnant made her feel ill, sick like she was going to throw up. She was catastrophizing… *It was too good to be true right from the start. Marco was always going to be too good for her. He deserved the normal life he wanted; she couldn't give him normal… She wasn't normal!*

Laying with her back to Marco, Eve was still, pretending to be asleep as hot stinging tears rolled to her pillow, the lump in her throat was choking her. In her catastrophizing mind, it felt like it was over between them, her heart ached with the pain. She'd opened herself up again, only to have it fuck her over… Again.

Marco was gone when Eve woke up, daylight peeking through the gap in the drapes. Eve remembered the night before, she leaped out of bed as there was a knock at her door, wrapping the fluffy white robe around her body, she rushed to open the door.

Zoe was all smiles. 'Good morning sleepy head. We've got a great day ahead of us. Tessa's gone to the gym with Marco… Have you had breakfast?' Zoe was bubbly as she scoped Eve out, her hair was crazy as it always was first thing in the morning, she had obviously just woken up.

'I need a coffee. What about you?' asked Eve as she walked to the phone at her bedside.

'I ate an apple already. I've been up for hours, we're in New York Evie!' Zoe was very upbeat.

'Are you okay, did you drop acid this morning?' she asked Zoe, they hadn't really had any time alone.

'I'm great. We watched the rest of the movie after you guys left last night, then we talked until late.' She was even excited about that.

'Sorry we ditched the movie.'

'Evie, I understand, you're making the most of your time with Marco, you don't have to explain yourself to me, you know that.' Zoe was a romantic at heart and she loved this reunion between Eve and Marco, everyone did now the dust had settled. It was if they were falling back into their Palm Cove grove.

'Any idea where my mum is?' Eve asked.

'I don't know, she's probably with Nigel or Jackie somewhere. Why?' There was definitely something going on with Eve, Zoe just knew it. Eve was texting on her phone; she didn't sit down, and she still had that look on her face like she was bothered. 'It's snowing outside, we thought we could go build a snowman or woman over in the park,' Eve didn't give her a response, 'Can you hear me babe, what's wrong with you?'

'I'm sorry.' Eve put her phone down.

'Hey, what's going on!'

'I'm fine.' She didn't want to get into it with Zoe. They left it at that.

Zoe left and Eve showered, she dressed in black pants, her new boots and a new black woolen wrap, Eve put her hair in a side plait and was ready to face the day as confused about Marco as ever. She'd called her mum who was in her suite, and went to see her, she needed to touch base with her mum.

Eve was pleased to find Anna alone; Nigel was out which gave her a chance to talk openly about the state of mind she was in, she trusted her mother and desperately needed her advice.

'I don't think this thing with Marco, and I is working out,' Eve took a deep breath.

Anna closed her laptop at the desk and starred over the top of her black rimmed glasses.

'What's happened?' It didn't surprise Anna they were having this conversation. As good as Eve seemed to be doing, Anna had expected she would have issues with a relationship situation after her ordeal with Evan. Her daughter had never been the same since his death, it had been a long road back to some kind of normal for Eve, and now Marco was putting her to the test.

'I got ahead of myself,' Eve told her mum as she settled into the chair by the window.

'It's been all of five minutes Eveline, what are you talking about?' Anna knew how to open Eve up; she could tell she was going to have to work her with key questions. It was the lawyer in her.

'Marco wants me to go to Melbourne.'

'And that's a problem, why?' Anna was ready to go.

'We want different things in life.' Saying it out loud sounded silly to Eve, she wanted the same things deep down in her cautious heart of hearts, she just didn't know if she could live up to his expectations. Also, well aware she may well be talking herself out of being with Marco, because maybe it was easier that way.

'Well, don't go if you don't want to.' Anna was good, Eve wasn't giving much away.

'I'd like to go. It's just I think he wants a family. I don't think I can do that.' Eve made it sound casual.

'Oh, I see.' Anna took a moment as she thought about how to go about this one with Eve, it was a tender subject that needed careful words. 'Why don't you just take it a little slower darling, you're not even dating yet, technically. Did he mention it in passing or did he say he wants you specifically to be the mother of his children right now?' Anna tried to make light of it, but Eve just stared at her. 'Have you told him what happened after Palm Cove yet?' She needed to help her take a step back. Anna could see Eve packing her bags in her head, going to the airport, and flying back to France. Anna new the drill!

Eve glared at her mother; she was going to ignore the Palm Cove comment. 'I know he will eventually expect a family, and I don't think I can do it. So maybe I won't go to Melbourne.' She was trying to convince herself, sabotaging her happiness.

'I can't answer this one for you Eveline,' Anna said knowing that wasn't going to be enough, she needed to give her daughter more than that. 'Sometimes when you love someone, you compromise on things within the relationship, it's what people do when they love each other. They compromise on things like finances, where they want to live, what kind of car to buy, the colour of the carpet and having children,' Anna took a breath, 'But all that is way off for you guys, don't you think?' Anna smiled, she knew Eve was a thinker and she suspected she might be over processing and thinking too far ahead of herself.

'I don't think it's fair to stop someone from having what they really want in life. So maybe it's better to just remove myself now.' Eve wasn't seeing Anna's point.

'If you love Marco, then why not give this a chance, don't run away just yet?' her voice was gentle.

'I'm not running away,' Eve hated the suggestion she was a runner, even though her track record said she was indeed a runner! 'I do love Marco. I've always loved Marco; I've never not loved Marco.' Eve began to get upset. She hadn't really had a good talk with Anna about her feelings towards him, or about the baby. Jackie had been the one to fill Anna in on the finer details.

'He's frightened you with the family thing?'

'Hmm.' Eve knew her mother understood, she didn't want children with James, and yet she ended up raising his child to a whore. *Compromising was a bitch!*

'I understand how you feel. But in time you might have a change of heart. Maybe you should give Marco the benefit of the doubt. I think you should tell him what you've been through, be honest with him and maybe he'll understand.' Talking to

Eve wasn't like talking to a regular young woman, she knew all about how difficult life could be, and then some.

Eve's eyes were full of unnecessary worry. 'I don't want to tell him about his baby Mum. He might hate me. And what if it happened again, and I lost another baby?' Eve shook her head. The anguish in her eyes was enormous and Anna didn't know how to help her.

'Darling, it may happen again, it may not. Don't live your life in fear of what if! That's what I think.' How clearer and direct could Anna be, she was a straight shooter, and she wasn't going to beat around the bush with her own daughter any longer. 'You need to live your life and take some risks again Eveline. Make sure you tell Marco about the baby, make it a priority.'

Eve nodded her head like she understood what Anna was telling her, like she knew what she needed to do.

The girls went for lunch a few doors down from the hotel at a funky little cafe, just the three of them. The air between Eve and Tessa this morning was thick.

'I have to say this because Marco's my brother and he's not as tough as you think he is E. He has fallen for you big time.' Tessa began the best way she knew how.

'And you're telling me this because?' Eve was her calm self.

'He wants you; he really wants you.' Tessa couldn't help her tone, Eve didn't respond. 'You know him E, he's a good guy, a kind guy who wants you as much as you want him. I hope you're not going to freak out on him and run back to France for the rest of your life. Because if you do…'

'What!' Still calm, Eve didn't raise her voice, she wasn't going to.

'I know how you operate. You finally get the guy of your dreams, the only decent guy you've ever had in your life, and you're going to lose him if you keep playing these stupid mind games with him. You're shit scared because you've got this huge fucking baby secret… Just tell him about the baby already!' Tessa had pulled the trigger and she knew she was on the money by Eve's face.

'That's a little harsh,' Zoe huffed at Tessa.

'We're fine,' Tessa disagreed.

'Eve. What about you, are you fine?' Zoe said compassionately. She didn't like her friends arguing. Eve didn't say a word, she couldn't, if she did, she would explode into tears of rage. At this point she felt a little betrayed, Tessa had never put Evan down before, and Eve didn't like it, it hurt.

'You know what, it's okay Zo. I'm fine.' Finally, Eve spoke, glaring at Tessa with disappointed eyes.

'I'm sorry. I didn't mean to speak ill of Evan,' snapped Tessa to Eve across the table, knowing exactly what she'd done.

'Save it. I don't want your apology,' Eve said calmly dismissing her.

Tessa liked the last word, 'Can't you see how stupid you are being. Throwing away what could possibly be the love of your life... All because you're scared to move on.' Tessa turned to Zoe. 'I know she will regret it for the rest of her life. Fuck. It's like she's scared of being fucking happy!' frustration was now boiling over, 'She's going to run back to France after sucking my brother into her little sexy dark world again, leaving him wondering what the fuck he did wrong, and all the while, I'll have to keep her secret. It's fucking ridiculous.' Tessa was being so assertive and loud that people in the café were actually looking over.

'Tessa,' Zoe gasped in a bid to stop her.

Eve sat back in her chair and sighed. 'It's okay Zo,' Eve looked at her and then at Tessa, 'You're right, I'm scared of having the most beautiful man I've ever known, love me. And yes, I have loads of issues, I'm very aware.... it pisses me off more than it pisses you off, believe me,' Eve's voice quivering, 'It's not what you say Tessa, it's how you say it,' she took a breath, 'I know how much you love your brother. But you're my best friend and yet you seem to get off on saying hurtful things to me, and I don't know why.' Still calm, still not crying. 'I don't want to hurt Marco, I love him, but I can't give him kids, and ultimately he wants a fucking football team, that's what he told me.' A beat. 'So, I'm allowed to be scared and unsure if I want to be Tessa, and I think you should shut the fuck up if you don't have anything constructive or supportive to say to me.'

For three seconds nobody spoke, they had listened to Eve's slow and measured response to Tessa's heartless assault, Eve had a way of commanding undivided attention when she needed to.

'Don't push him away E. I think you should tell him about the baby. That's all. For your own sake. I think it would make your life a hell of lot easier,' said Tessa looking at her friend with now apologetic eyes, that was the closest she was getting to an apology.

Eve wasn't going to hold a grudge, she couldn't, even though Tessa had hurt her feelings and been an awful bitch. She wondered what Marco had said to his sister this morning. *Was he always going to run to his sister every time they had a problem? Probably.*

'Marco knows somethings is wrong with you,' Tessa said like she had just sold her brother out, which she was, he'd come to her in confidence.

Tessa just wouldn't stop, and Eve was over it, big time. 'He better not make an official complaint to you every time things get tough.' Eve narrowed her eyes to Tessa.

'E, Marco's new to deep feelings. All he's ever done is dated randoms here and there.' When it came to her big brother, Tessa would go in batting for him every time, she would also do whatever it took to make Eve and Marco work.

'You're making it sound like he's a virgin or something. He's a grown man,' Eve couldn't help her sarcasm.

'Oh, he's had plenty of pussy, but he's never been in love.' Tessa was now being delicate as she spoke about her big brother's personal affairs.

'Oh. My. God. Stop.' Eve was half laughing, half dying. 'I don't want to hear about how much pussy he's had.' Thankfully, the vibe changed here between the two girls who loved Marco Rossi with all their heart.

'I do. Tell me.' Zoe was serious. *Of course, she was!*

'He's been a player, not a lover. Please be careful with his heart E, I think he loves you.' Tessa's whole demeanor was changing. This was important to Marco, so it was important to Tessa.

Eve new it was coming from Tessa's heart, she idolized Marco. 'Thank you for your constructive support, I appreciate it,' Eve smiled to Tessa, then she turned to Zoe. 'And I don't know why you need to know about Marco's sex life.'

It was always the same, when tensions boil over, they soon calmed back down, Tessa was always at the center of everything, she was the turbulent one. Eve and Zoe rarely crossed words, but they both did with Tessa, it was just the way it had always been. Tessa didn't have a filter and she spoke before thinking most of the time. It wasn't long before she said her goodbyes, she had to leave for her evening performance on Broadway.

Jackie had arranged a private dinner up on the terrace level, everyone was going.

'Have fun at dinner with my fam bitches,' Tessa smiled as she got up from the table.

Eve and Zoe thought she was getting over her bustling New York lifestyle, the energy she usually had didn't seem to be as electric as it used to be.

'We'll wait up for you,' Eve said letting her best friend know all was okay between them. They got over things as fast they got into them. Tessa blew Eve and Zoe a kiss as she left them.

Marco arrived back at the hotel an hour before dinner. He had gone for a run with his dad in Central Park just after lunch and they'd only just got back. He was freezing like an ice cube, yet hot - stripping off his top layers the minute he came in the door. He'd moved his suitcase into Eve's room yesterday, and today had started to wonder if it was the right move, she'd been weird since last night.

'Your cheeks are red; you look cold,' she said, eyes full of swirling emotional as she looked up at him. 'This is how people get sick you know. You should take a warm shower.'

Marco stood apprehensively like he didn't know what mood Eve was in. Looking at each other for a long moment before she reached up, brushing her thumb over his lips. All her heart ache, pain and grief had stood in her way for too long. Her surrendering eyes sparkled up at him, her heart had been battered and bruised, and now in this very moment, all she wanted him to do was kiss it better. Marco was the only one who could heal her. Leaning into him, she ran her loving warm hand over his cold face and chest.

He could see it in her eyes, she'd turned the corner, she was his again, and his cock was hardening at the very thought. 'Have a shower with me.' His icy face touched hers as his lips kissed her.

'I just had one,' Eve stood in her robe ready to get dressed.

'Have another one.' His cold hands went into her robe and touched her warm skin, there was no possible way Eve could say no, he stood smiling down at her with those gorgeous brown eyes and long lashes. She shrugged her robe off and followed him into the shower.

'We've got dinner with everyone in less than an hour.' Eve stood naked; her warm womanly body against Marco's freezing cold skin. They stood arm in arm kissing under the water, she was tiny compared to his tall athletic body, somehow they found a common ground that worked for them physically. Eve reaching all the way up to him, the cold and the warm between them as the steaming water run over them. Lifting her feet from the floor, embracing her with caring arms. Eve was in a better place than she had been last night.

'You've got to talk to me Eve Frank, tell me how you're feeling,' said Marco, his hand cupping her boob gently. She loved that he didn't do anything fast, like he was savoring every moment. The way she did. And most of all she loved that he came back to her.

'I'm not like you Rossi's, I'm not a good communicator,' Eve smiled, 'Sometimes you might need to dig for the dirt.'

Marco pressing her to the cold tiled wall. 'We can work on that.' He took her small and delicate hand and put it to his very hard and erect cock, she started to gently slide her hand up and down cock. 'Put your foot up on the shelf.' Marco tapped his other hand gently on her hip. Lifting her foot to the shelf; she was now spread open in front of him, her grip on him intensified, his fingers went to her open pink pussy, fingers flicking vigorously over her folds, then Eve put her own hand over his.

'Put your fingers inside me,' her breathless whisper sexy. Marco leaned in, his mouth moving to Eve's as she still had him in her other hand, squeezing and tugging at him, she wanted him. Marco's kisses went down her neck to her shoulders, his fingers finding hers, meshing with them as he pressed into her warm silky hole. Marco guiding her finger further into her depths, plunging inside her as his thumb tweaked across her sensitive clit.

'You look beautiful when you touch yourself Eve Frank,' he smiled. Lifting her, pinning her abruptly up to the wall. As erotic and mildly rough as it was, it was intensely intimate. Before Eve knew it they were making love, Marco was thrusting her into the shower wall relentlessly. Eve lapsed into an excruciating pleasurable coma. Everything Marco did to her, took her breath away… It always had. If there was perfect love making, this was it! Marco's mouth kissed hers passionately, their lips melting with steamy desire as Eve felt her entire body ease to his, cumming, she went to jelly, limp in his arms as he buried his head into her neck and came.

It was a miracle they were only twenty minutes late to dinner. Walking out of the lift with a skip in their step, hand in hand, they were an undeniably attractive couple. Gliding across the room smiling like they'd been together forever. Eve in a long black knit dress that had a deep plunging v neckline way into her cinnamon cleavage with a gold Gucci chain belt, a sparkling diamond droplet necklace, a birthday gift from her father last year with matching earrings. Another new pair of Jimmy Choo's and her hair plaited down her back, still damp from her second shower! A distinctive glow to Eve that was the envy of every woman in the room.

Jackie recognised the look immediately… It was the look of a woman who'd just had exceptional sex. It was hard to miss, as mortifying as it was for Jackie to think of. She was quietly thrilled and delighted at the union. As Marco's mother, she hoped her son wouldn't break Eve's heart again. Marco had never made a real commitment to a woman in his life. And Eve, well, Jackie could only hope she'd come out the other side of what had been a terrible streak of bad luck in her personal life.

Marco's smile content on his face, Jackie knew her son was in a good place, he held Eve's hand proudly and walked tall, he was happy, and it was all a mother could want. *But there was still the secret!*

'I'm so glad the two of you could make it,' she said with a champagne induced smile as Eve and Marco went to the only two seats left at the table.

'Sorry!' Eve mouthed apologetically to Jackie as she settled at the table. When Mario had arrived back late from his run with Marco, he'd explained the run was a marathon and that Marco just needed to talk and get some fatherly advice regarding his love life.

Dinner was a degustation; everything serve that came out was minuscule and the Rossi's were big men who ate a lot, Marco kept huffing and puffing beside Eve at the sight of every plate. The conversations along the table were plentiful, Jackie and Nigel talked about the prices of Sydney real estate and how out of control it was getting. Eve, Anna, and Mario discussed wine and cheese and everything French. Marco and Emma where whispering, clearly a private conversation… Eve hoped she could trust Emma… She did know her secret! Nick and Tom had been entertaining Zoe with their take on glossy fashion magazines. The conversations evolved as they went around the table, the laughter got louder as the night went on.

'That's a very beautiful necklace Eve, is it new?' Jackie asked Eve, she'd now made her way up the table and was moving in on Eve and Marco.

'My dad gave it to me,' she said touching her hand to the necklace. Eve hadn't worn her signature rose gold E since New Year's Eve and it hadn't gone unnoticed.

'Wow. Fancy!' Jackie said coming in for a closer look.

'You know my dad and his statement gifts,' Eve sighed, she secretly loved every gift James ever gave her, or rather every gift his personal assistant chose for her. She missed her dad. Never mind the fact that he was in a relationship with her secret biological mother, and they had twin daughters... and this was somehow supposed to be okay with her. In Eve's mind, she thought that if she kept her knowledge of Sam being her birth mother all to herself, then somehow it wasn't real. It was just an awful dirty secret that only she, her father and Sam all knew… And possibly Anna too.

'What did he get you for Christmas?' Jackie asked as they chatted between themselves.

Eve held up her evening bag that had arrived at the chateaux two weeks before Christmas. Chanel. Nothing but the best from James. Eve often wondered if Sam ever had anything to do with her father's gifts, she'd always been under the impression his assistant did all his shopping. For a fleeting moment Eve thought of Evan and how he was so much like her father when it came to gift giving, they never got it wrong because they always went all out. Her hand went to Marco's upper thigh as she took a deep breath to clear her head. Turning to him to wash away the moment of tender memories she didn't need in her head right now, they only made her sad and she didn't want to be sad sitting next him. With Marco right there by her side, his big warm hand went to her thigh like he knew what she needed in this very moment... Eve had everything she had ever wanted sitting right next to her.

The talk of James had jolted her memory, her father had called her three times since New Year's Day, it would be only to wish her a happy new year and see what she was up to more than likely, he was an odd man, he left her alone most of the time, but then there were times when he was simply determined to make contact with her.

Marco had just tuned into the conversation. 'Wait, when is your birthday again?' he asked remembering it was coming up soon.

'The twenty third of January,' Eve smiled blissfully, making Jackie do an eyebrow raise to her sons thoughtfulness.

'So, could possibly be in Melbourne for your birthday?' his seemed almost excited.

'Very possibly. Yes.' Eve's admiration for Marco was in her eyes, every time she spoke to him.

'How lovely,' gasped Jackie, they both looked at her, they'd forgotten she was there. 'That will be nice to spend your birthday with Marco.' It was weird, Jackie had never seen Marco quite as smitten as this, nor Eve for that matter, she just hoped Eve's secret wouldn't derail their connection.

'I think it's so sweet.' Now Zoe was in on the conversation from her side of the table, she looked at Marco. 'You can take Evie out on a real date and do something super romantic for her birthday.'

Marco looked at Zoe like she was crazy, 'Of course, we'll be doing something romantic,' he said like she was having a go at him, like he didn't know how to romance a woman!

Eve just looked at him with dreamy eyes, her heart full as she squeezed his hand under hers. The thought of what the future held was exciting now she was over her angst, now she had decided to really move forward with Marco... Although, she was still keeping a huge secret from him!

After what felt like course twenty-nine, Nick and Jackie swapped seats, he wanted to speak with Zoe. The dynamics had changed in the last twenty-four hours. The things they actually had in common were bizarre, they had made plans to catch up when they got home to Sydney, just to hang out of course, they even planed a trip to Melbourne for a weekend to watch Marco play football in March. Their fleeting little confrontation and kiss the other night had done something wonderful to their relationship, and it wasn't sexual.

Eve had forgiven Nick for his horrid behavior to herself, and for the way he had treated Zoe in Palm Cove. He was making a real effort to be nice this trip… Well trying, Nick was maturing into a man.

Everyone laughed and talked all night, Anna telling the story of how she'd found a draw in Eve's bedroom with boy's T-shirts and jumpers, of which now she knew were all Marco's after Eve had informed her only days ago. Nick shared the fact that Eve and Marco had hooked up in Palm Cove again.

'Oh yeah. It wasn't just us from memory was it now. Don't you have a confession Nick.' Marco wasn't letting his little brother get away with it. 'Not that any of us knew at the time accept for Eve… Nick and Zoe have been hooking up for years.'

'I wouldn't call it hooking up,' Zoe couldn't believe Marco's form, outing them too.

'So, if everyone was hooking up, who did your sister end up with?' Jackie asked seemingly surprised at the Nick and Zoe revelation.

Marco felt it was his obligation. 'She hooked up with Zach.' He still didn't seem okay with it.

'What did you expect mum. Teenage girls and young guys!' Nick teased his mother as her jaw dropped open.

'We expected you all to behave, that's what we expected,' Mario said looking at his two sons who he'd felt had been the main offenders of abusing his trust.

'I don't think I'd change it,' Marco said to Eve, his mother and father taking note.

'None of it was intentional,' Eve said defending her lover, 'It all just happened. Didn't it?' she leaned into Marco looking up at him with admiring eyes.

'It sounds like it was a holiday of uncontrollable hormones quite frankly,' Anna added with a thought as to how it had ended up for her daughter. *Not so great!* It was clear how Eve and Marco felt for each other, Anna wondered what might have been, what could have been avoided in the years to follow for her daughter, had they kept their holiday romance going.

By the time Tessa arrived back at the hotel after her show, she was starting to feel the weight of everyone leaving and going home in the coming days, and her being left in New York on her own.

Tessa sat on the edge of the bathtub in the bathroom of Eve's hotel room, watching Eve wash her face, she found herself overwhelmed with what had been bothering her for some time.

'I want to come home E,' she confessed to Eve, it was just the two of them. 'I've put some feelers out for shows in Sydney and Melbourne. There might be one in Melbourne I can audition for soon.' She sounded desperate and depleted, abnormal for Tessa.

'You've had enough haven't you?' Eve said, she and Zoe had talked about it, they both knew Tessa was over New York, it had been seven long years. Somehow, she didn't really have any money behind her or any strong relationships with friends besides the cast members, all she could take away from New York was her experience. Maybe it was time Tessa came home.

'I don't know how much longer I can do it,' she started to cry, 'I just want to go home.'

'Then go home,' said Eve, 'Imagine if we end up home again together,' Eve smiled, handing Tessa a tissue.

'Would you really go home for good E, or are just saying that?'

'In a heartbeat if it meant being with Marco.' There was a serene calmness to Eve that Tessa hadn't seen a very long time and it gave her a little buzz to think she'd get to spend more time with Eve and Zoe.

'Fuck!' Tessa finally smiled; she couldn't believe it, 'I find out soon if I'm going to audition in Melbourne. You can't tell my mum though, or anyone for that matter, except for Zoe of course. Promise me E. Not even Marco, even though he kind already knows, I don't want him to get excited.' It was very cute the way she knew her brother would react to her coming home. He was very much a family man and Eve loved that he adored his sister.

'I won't say a word, I promise.' Eve hugged her; Tessa needed a little love and care.

'Imagine I get the Melbourne show, I'll need to crash with Marco for a while. You and I could be roomies.' Tessa laughed at the thought.

'Stranger things have happened right!' Eve took a moment as she comprehended it. 'If this thing between your brother don't work out, I swear I will never get over it. I know you doubt me because I'm problematic,' Eve smiled, 'But nothing has ever felt so right in my life as Marco… I would love it if we could both be in Melbourne for each other.' Eve had drunk several red wines, so she was opening up, talking about the future with confidence for the very first time in such a long time.

Tessa looked at her friend with love in her eyes, 'You are not problematic E. Don't say that. I know exactly who you are Eve Frank,' a teary smile came over Tessa's face, 'I don't doubt who you are, I fucking love you. I've always thought you were perfect for my brother.'

Chapter Ten

Marco and Eve had one night left together in New York. Tom and Emma had flown home to London already. Nick had gone back to Sydney after forging a new respectful friendship with Zoe. They would definitely be catching up when she got home.

After several lengthy phone conversations with her grandmother and Louis, Eve now felt okay with not returning to France straight away. They had repeatedly given their blessing for Eve to explore this newfound relationship with Marco. Vivienne giving Eve the talk about how she would never hold her back from finding love or following her heart. Louis insisted things would go on without her. Eve promising to keep in touch and keep them updated. Most of all Eve had to convince her herself it was okay not to return to France. Louis and Vivienne's unique and wonderful view on life made Eve feel very lucky to have them in her corner with their unwavering support.

Jackie and Mario had been supportive of Eve and Marco from a distance, as hard as it was for Jackie, she was doing well by keeping out of their business these last few days and keeping Eve's secret. Anna had gone over the pros and cons with Eve in private, that was just how she did things, it was her way of convincing herself that her daughter was ready to move forward with Marco. It worried Anna that Eve was returning to Sydney. While Zoe and Tessa were over the moon with the whole Marco and Eve union, they'd orchestrated it in the first place, and now it had come together just as they had planned.

Holding hands as they walked around Bryant Park as it lightly snowed, Marco and Eve talked through their plan to catch up in Melbourne. She would go to Sydney with Zoe and spent a week there. Her schedule was already fully booked with social catch ups, now including her father after she'd eventually called him back. A meeting with a real estate agent regarding Villa Rosado had been booked in, Eve thought maybe it was time to sell. It was her past after all.

Marco squeezed Eve's hand in his as they wondered through the park, 'You can come to Melbourne whenever you like, any day or time, just let me know and I'll pick you up from the airport. Zach and Brooke live with me, it's getting close to them moving out. At least this way you will get to know Brooke, you'll love her I know it,' Marco said, fog coming out his mouth with every word, it was so cold.

'I'm really looking forward to seeing where you live, and to spending time with you in your home,' Eve said as they weaved their way through the winter village of glass house stalls, selling everything from food to jewelry. The atmosphere was wintery and very romantic.

'This is really happening – me and you,' Marco looked down to her.

'Are you okay with it, it's kind of happening fast?'

'I'm more than good with it. I want you to be good with it.' Marco let go of her hand as she picked up a ring at the front of one of the stalls. A little silver ring that was in the letter T... T for Tia.

'I'm good with it. I feel like I'm actually in the best place I've been for a long time,' she told Marco as she decided to buy the ring for Tia, she would be seeing her next week and thought it would be great to add to the other gifts she had bought for her while in New York. Eve had a habit of spoiling Tia.

'Are you really Eve Frank? Because I want you to be a hundred percent good with it. With me.' Marco's eyes locked to Eve's as she turned to him waiting for the ring to be wrapped.

'I'm more than one hundred percent good with you Marco Rossi. I've been good with it since I was ten,' she said happily, 'You're the one with the career. I don't want my visit to be a distraction to you.' Her smile faded as she got serious.

'Me staying in New York with you, means I want this more than anything.' He took her hand as they continued to walk.

'I have so much to learn about you, don't I.' Her face had a slight grin, her hand squeezed at his. 'I know you love to eat, all the time. I know you need to run almost every day, rain, hail, or snow... I hate to exercise, I won't lie,' Eve laughed.

He loved everything about Eve. Her way. Her personality. Her smile and even her complexities. Particularly Marco loved the depth of their sexual connection, it was like they had been making love to each other for the past seven years every night, she knew him better than anyone else ever had.

Then Eve got serious for a second, 'You've always been very special to me, you know that... at every turn of my life that came after Palm Cove, even the worst imaginable times, I thought about you. You were this strange comfort to me when I wasn't myself.' Eve let the emotion well in her eyes.

'Evie!' Marco was humbled by her words. He put his cold fingers to her cheek, he wiped a tear as it fell.

'Sorry.' Her face began to cry with happiness as she apologized for her tears.

'Don't be sorry.' And with that, he lovingly kissed her lips with tender short kisses as the light snow fell from above.

Zoe and Tessa arranged dinner at Tao Uptown, Tessa had taken the night off again, she was hoping the production company would fire her truthfully. It was a tactical move she had derived, her mental health depended on it. She was so anxious about everyone leaving New York, that the last thing she needed to do, was the darn show. Her mind wasn't on the job. When she'd called to cancel, the production manager wasn't thrilled, she had just had two nights off for personal reasons and now another night because she said she wasn't in a good place mentally. Which she wasn't! She'd was hiding out in Zoe's hotel room, the minute her parents found out she had missed another night of the show, they would know something was up and intervene. Tessa needed to do this herself, she needed to let her own fate play out and work things out on her own.

They were like the four musketeers walking up Fifth Avenue to Fifty Eighth Street, Marco with Eve linked into one arm and Tessa on the other, with Zoe holding Tessa's hand as they laughed and talked their way in the freezing cold to Tao, trying not to slip as they slushed through the soft snow.

Standing at the bar ordering a drink and defrosting as they waited for their table, Marco looked like he was the luckiest guy in the place... surrounded by the three best looking girls. Tessa was in a very rebellious mood, and it showed when she flicked off her coat to a doorman as they entered, he got more than he bargained for as her coat came off, everyone did. The barely there black dress she was wearing didn't leave much to the imagination, straps winding up her body revealing a hell of a lot of flesh.

A slightly more reserved Zoe had a green jumpsuit on, it wouldn't be Zoe if she didn't have a matching purse. Marco was getting an education on just how these girls operated... Eve had left the hotel looking her usual stylish self in a conservative woolen trench coat. When the coat came off and Marco was gob smacked to watch her pull her scrunched up black dress out of the sides of her underwear, letting it fall to the floor. The neckline plunging deep down to her stomach. Of course, a dress like that didn't permit a bra, and there was literally cleavage for all to see, and he wasn't sure he liked it... Until she pulled at the ball of hair on top of her head, letting her long sexy curls fall down around her body. As Eve shook her head, it was like slow motion porn for every man in the room, all eyes were on Eve. It all happened in a matter of seconds, she transformed from stylish librarian to exotic babe. Marco decided he liked it; the crazy hair distracted a little from the abundance of luscious cinnamon cleavage.

The bar played a cool funky jazz sound, and the vibe was just what they needed.

'Has anyone noticed, I always attract the barman?' Tessa asked as the hot barman gave her the eye.

Marco leaned over to Tessa, 'Christopher Cox is standing right behind you. Turn around now and talk to him, or I will never forgive you,' he whispered to his sister, he was in basketball heaven, he loved basketball and Christopher Cox was one of the best basketballers going around. Both Zoe and Eve did the sneaky eye to Mr. Christopher Cox, who Tessa still had her back to.

Tessa screwed her face up at her brother. 'Who? Cox. I don't think so. It's a name I just can't do. I've always had a thing about names like Cox and Dick.' It was so Tessa to say something like that.

'Um... You might want to turn around and take a look for yourself.' Zoe sipped on her cocktail straw; Christopher Cox was a statement of a man.

'No Cox. I don't do Cox,' Tessa fluttered her eyes at Zoe like she had asked her to eat a shit sandwich.

'Tessa!' Marco was freaking out, ready to just talk to Christopher Cox himself.

'Turn around,' Eve said smiling. Mr. Cox was one of the most splendid black men she had ever seen.

Reluctantly Tessa turned around slowly to see this Cox guy. He had her attention immediately. Standing there towering over her was the most breathtaking man she had ever set eyes on… Leaving her breathless.

Taller than Marco, he had to be over two meters tall. Looking down at Tessa with sexy fuck me eyes, melting that skimpy dress right off her gorgeous body. She quickly turned back around.

'Hi, I'm Marco.' Reaching his arm out over the top of Eve and in front of Tessa, Marco wasn't letting the moment pass him by. He was fan boying it big time!

'Australian right?' The huge Cox put his hand out and shook Marco's hand.

'I'm Tessa.' She turned back around with one of her best smiles, she was back in action. 'This is my brother; he's visiting me from Australia. He's an AFL footballer.' She was hooked instantly.

'Who do you play for man?' Mr. Cox embedded himself conveniently against Tessa at the bar so he could talk to Marco and be closer to this super-hot sister with the long fine legs.

While the guys talked basketball and football, the girls talked quietly amongst themselves briefly. Tessa had maneuvered her way around so she and Eve could face Zoe, she could still feel Mr. Cox against her body.

'My. God. What do you do with a man like that?' Tessa smirked, taken by his size and suaveness.

'I know what I'd do,' Eve laughed, she was on her second cocktail, feeling great with Marco's hand around her waist at her hip as he talked to Mr. Cox.

'Snap the fuck out of it,' Zoe hissed to Tessa; she couldn't believe what she was hearing, 'You know exactly what to do.'

'I think I can feel his cock at my back.' As Tessa leaned to the girls whispering, she felt a huge hand on her shoulder. Mr. Cox was just resting it there as he leaned over her to get closer to Marco. Both Eve and Zoe trying to contain themselves, trying not to make it obvious they were all in awe of this impressive man.

'This is Christopher Cox,' Marco said to the girls, he was pumped, the girls could tell he was fanning big time. 'My sister Tessa. Zoe and Eve.' He introduced them all.

'Well, hello ladies.' Giving them all a flashy smiles, all of them going weak at the knees.

'Hello,' all three said in sync with smiles of delight.

'You live here in New York?' Mr. Cox asked leaning down on the bar to Tessa. Her long caramel hair in waves as it fell down around her arms. Zoe and Eve watching as she did her thing, Tessa looked sassy and stylish, she was naturally blessed with all aspects of the female body. The girls could only watch on as she laughed and smiled with Mr. Cox. She'd had a bad run with guys in New York, it was her harsh schedule that didn't allow her to lead a normal dating life. With one night a week off from her show, there was never enough time to relax and have a life, it made things difficult.

After talking with Tessa briefly, Mr. Cox insisted on having them join him and his friends at their VIP table for dinner. Marco was in immediately, with all of the girls in agreeance, especially Tessa who had by now warmed right up to Mr. Cox. Tessa loved this Cox, the name, the man, and the size of it!

The conversations around the table entertaining the entire night, Christopher's two friends enjoying the company as much as everyone else. John Henry the teammate and Phillip the friend, both good looking and both really nice welcoming guys. Phillip the friend was very chatty with Zoe, who was her gorgeous flirty self.

Marco was close beside Eve, he'd noticed John Henry, Phillip, and Christopher all admiring Eve's deluxe cleavage. It was hard not to look, so he didn't blame them.

The guys had just come out for a dinner, they weren't up for a big night, so once dinner was over Christopher and Tessa swapped numbers with an invitation to come to his game tomorrow night at Madison Square Garden, with courtside seats. Marco was freaking out; there was no possible way he could stay the extra night for the game, he had to get home to training. Zoe and Eve were in town for another few nights, they would go and tell Marco all about it, they'd promised him.

After a great night at dinner, it was time for Eve and Marco to have their last night together in New York, his flight was at six the following evening. Eve filled the bathtub, she loved a hot bath with bubbles, even more so when she had Marco in it with her. She stood in her long black dress with her cleavage out and shoes off waiting for the bath to fill while Marco went over the entire night with Christopher Cox, he was star struck beyond belief.

'What's the most valuable possession you have with you?' he asked Eve out of the blue as she turned the water off, the bath was full. He stood looking at her from the doorway. 'I want to take it home with me.'

'Umm. I'm not sure.' Eve looked around the bathroom. The first thing that came to mind was her rose gold E necklace; she couldn't say that. Then there were her Chanel boots, a gift from Evan. Yeah, she kind of couldn't say those either. The next thing that came to mind was her favorite diamond earrings... Evan also! Then she put her finger up to Marco like she had it, wanting him to wait while she got it. Eve quickly left the bathroom and returned a second later with a bracelet in her hand. She wondered why she hadn't thought of this straight away, it was one of her dearest possessions, so much so, she hardly wore it for fear of losing it, it was more like a lucky charm. It wasn't expensive, just sentimental, she carried it in her purse at all times.

'My grandmother made this for me when I first went to live in France.' Eve looked at Marco and then revealed the fine white leather braided friendship bracelet in her hand. Her eyes welled with tears. 'She's very, very, special to me,' Eve sighed, 'This is very special to me.'

'I know she'd special to you.' Marco put his hand out to Eve's face and rubbed away her tear with his thumb, he loved Eve's eyes and how they showed every emotion she felt, always.

'So, this is my most valuable possession.' She lowered her head.

'I know how important this is to you, so I'll settle for a T-shirt or a piece of underwear.' He grinned as Eve put the bracelet in his hand. 'I'll keep it safe until you come to Melbourne.'

'I'll give you a G string too if you really want them... Don't wear them though!' Smiling she took her dress off over her head. 'Put it somewhere safe, and then it's bath time.'

Sitting with her back to Marco's stomach in the bath, his long legs encompassing her. Eve let him run the bath cloth over her chest washing away the bubbles, he did love her boobs. They didn't speak much, they just relaxed in the warm water, it was sensual and romantic in a lazy kind of way. Her arms resting at his hips as he happily went about bathing Eve.

Then out of nowhere... 'I'm not rushing you am I. I mean after everything that happened with Evan?' It was innocent, yet he felt Eve stiffen at his touch.

'Umm,' she pondered her answer.

He dripped warm water over her shoulders with the cloth. 'You don't have to answer. I shouldn't have even asked you that. Eve, I'm sorry.'

There was a long silence, Eve never spoke about Evan very often.

'I didn't mean to bring up Evan.' Marco knew he'd overstepped the mark; his mum and Tessa had told him Eve was a vault when it came to Evan. He regretted asking her instantly.

'It's okay,' she sighed with hesitation, not knowing if taken her by surprise. She didn't know how to answer, or even if she could. It took her a moment or two to get it, she didn't want to be offended by what Marco had.

it was right or wrong to talk to Marco about Evan.

'You don't have to answer.' Marco could feel her discomfort as she lay in his arms.

'No, it's okay. It's taken a long time to be able to move forward. I mean, you're the first person I've been with in five years.' She gave a little hint of laugh at her own thought process.

'Really!' Macro took a breath. 'You don't talk about Evan do you?'

'No.' She ran her had along Marco's arm. 'It's not because I can't move past that part of my life, because I have. For you.' Eve took the face washer from Marco and began to wash his legs and his arms, he listened to her, just letting her talk. 'After Palm Cove, I had the worst two years of my life, I felt like I was cursed. I had a lot of issues with my parents. I found out Anna wasn't my biological mum, I took off to France, then when I came back, everything changed. My parents hated Evan and I was living with him.' It was a bathtub therapy session for Eve and Marco was all ears as she went beyond his initial question. 'I was happy for a while. Then I found out my dad had a new family... he has twin daughters you know!' she laughed-huffed like she knew it was ridiculous. 'I saw them once, by accident,' she paused at the thought, 'Then I got pregnant, and we moved to Rose Bay, that was our home. I loved that house.' It was flowing out of her mouth, soft slow words. 'I was happy again, we were having a baby and getting married, then everything changed... There was no baby,' she paused for several seconds, 'We decided to get married anyway, I'm sure it was Evan's way of getting my mind off Rafael, that was what we named him.' Talking to Marco wasn't like talking with anyone else. 'Then everything ended and that's when I went to France.' That was it, she had told him everything in her own words even though he hadn't asked for everything.

'I'm sorry that happened to you. I'm sorry you lost your baby and Evan,' the magnitude of what Eve had endured was suddenly upon him, Marco took a minute to comprehend it all. 'Do you know anything about your biological mother?'

'I do. But that will have to wait for another bath confession session Marco Rossi,' Eve smiled, she had to. It was smile or cry. 'I want you to know I have always wanted you. Before Palm Cove and every day after.' Eve dropped the cloth and put her head back to rest at his chest, she just needed Marco to know how she felt about him after speaking of Evan.

'Have you really?' It was deep and serious; he was like a soft marshmallow that she wanted to eat.

'For as long as I can remember. I feel like I've been waiting for you.' Eve turned her head up to him. Marco's lips came down to hers, they sat in the warm bath, they kissed slowly. For Eve it was almost like Marco's kiss had healing powers, she felt like a weight had been lifted from her shoulders, even though she still had a big secret to tell him.

Marco appreciated Eve's openness and understood how difficult it must have been for her to tell him all she had, he only had one response for Eve. He was sad for her and flattered at the same time. He didn't know how to express the feelings her words made him feel. He'd known in Palm Cove that Eve adored him, nobody had ever looked at him the way she did. If he had his time again, he would have done things differently perhaps. Things would have been different for Eve. It was Marco's regret.

His hands moved over her body slowly, over her stomach and up to her boobs that felt like soft pillows of silk in the warm water. Their lips still at each other as she took his hand and moved it down her stomach and in between her legs, his growing erection in her back. Like their attraction to each other, their love making had stood the test of time too. Eve lifted herself forward and up, sitting herself down on Marco's hard-strong cock. He kissed the back of her neck as she felt her blood warming, pumping through every part of her body. Moving herself over him so she could feel him deep inside her, his hands guiding her hips as she held the sides of the tub. By far this was Eve's favorite position with Marco, his body at her back, his arms wrapped around her tight as he filled her with pleasurable passion, her head tilted back to his kiss. Satisfaction escaping her mouth as she groaned with Marco pressing deep into her body, filling her as she let herself fall down over him until she could take no more, giving in to her climax, just as Marco clenched at her hips and made his own expressive moan.

'I never want this to end.' Eve laid back in his arms.

'I promise it won't,' Marco's hot breath in Eve's ear assuring her of forever.

They wanted each other, this almost fairytale-like romance that had snuck up on them again was now in full swing. Eve knew promises were easily broken though; she wasn't taking her guard completely down; she wasn't that naive! It was on her mind, that Marco still hadn't mentioned the scar on her stomach, and she wondered why, but then again, she still hadn't mentioned how she'd got the scar!

The next day Marco's departure was less emotional than expected, everyone was down in the lobby to see him off, they waited for his car to arrive to take him to the airport. Tessa hugged her brother goodbye, whispering an emotional plea to her brother to make things work with Eve.

For Jackie it was bittersweet, she had seen her family reunite in New York all together and now she was saying goodbye to them one by one, luckily for her it was the child she saw regularly, she and Mario still made the trek to Melbourne most weekends to watch Marco's football games.

Eve knew it would only be a matter of a week before she was in Melbourne with Marco. Her life was once again taking her on an adventure of love, and she was on top of the world. Still, the departure of Marco didn't come easy for her. Once again she was used to him being in her bed every night. Today felt different, she didn't feel like he was abandoning her this time.

'It's not goodbye Eve Frank. I'll see you before you know it. Don't have too much fun tonight at the game,' Marco said with jealousy in his voice, referring to the basketball game the girls were going to be special guest at. He couldn't believe the girls were going to the game as guest of Christopher Cox and he wasn't.

'I'll be thinking of you every minute while I'm sitting courtside,' Eve teased with a smile.

'I'll be thinking of you while I'm sitting in business class.' His smile made her weak at the knees.

'Look after my bracelet Marco Rossi.' Her eyes sparkling up at him. 'Oh, and I put a pair of lacy G's in your luggage.'

'You're so thoughtful and very cute Eve Frank. Don't fall in love with a basketballer tonight.' Marco kissed her mouth with his soft lips and savored every last bit of her.

'Not a chance... I'm taken,' she said, her grin adoring.

'Don't take too long getting down to Melbourne, I'm already missing you.'

An embrace and a memorable final kiss as the car waited, Eve breathed Marco deep into her lungs for one last time, then watched the car until it disappeared down the end of the street.

'Have you told him yet?' Jackie asked Eve as they stood at the curb together.

'Not yet,' Eve said with a breath in, unimpressed that Jackie was keeping tabs on the situation.

Chapter Eleven

'I say the red shirt makes you look sophisticated and stylish, ready for anything. Black, it's boring,' Zoe gave Tessa her two cents as they got ready for the basketball game.

'But I'm not sophisticated. I don't wear shirts and I like the black,' protested Tessa with bitch in her tone.

'Do you want Big Cox to think your boring, or fun?' Zoe had been referring to Christopher Cox the basketballer as Big Cox for most of the day, and it was pissing Tessa off, along with her so called honestly about what she was wearing now.

'E, what would you wear?' Tessa asked.

'The red. I think Big Cox is a colours man, he'll like the red. Men like red,' Eve explained.

'Would you two stop calling him Big Cox, we don't know if he has a big cock or not,' said Tessa with a huff, 'And I don't particularly care how men want me to dress. I dress for me.'

Zoe squinted her eyes, 'That's a bad attitude… put the red shirt on and stop your bitching.' Zoe snapped.

'Stop bossing me around and move your arse. I'll be getting nothing if we don't hurry up,' Tessa complained.

'I'm wearing black, so you cannot,' Zoe told Tessa, 'Why can't you just be like Eve and wear what I tell you to.'

Eve gave a little laugh, 'If you'd both stop bickering, we could be in a cab by now.' Standing back and watched her two besties go at it. it was just like old times.

Courtside was full of gorgeous and important people. The three Aussie girls didn't look out of place at all, in fact they looked very much a part of the whole courtside circus. Zoe was having a field day with all the paparazzi that were scooping the sidelines for famous faces. She sat in-between Eve and Tessa in her black conservative silk top, torn denim jeans and black ankle boots. Conservative it may have been, but Zoe never looked dull, or god forbid boring. Her platinum hair, the trademark bob, and her slender frame, she looked like a New York super model sitting between two naughty Victoria Secret models. Tessa wore the red shirt that gathered in all the right places, with skintight black leather pants and high heeled stud ankle boots, she looked stylish with down low sexiness going on. Eve went with the grey mohair wrap top, hugging her boobs in tight to her body, black cropped pants and her Chanel boots and soft leather shearling jacket for edginess. Her mop of unruly curls hanging to her waste. She was content with the positive departure of Marco. All they had to do now, was make it work.

The dancers entertained with some super vigorous dance moves that impressed the girls, Zoe and Eve had never seen this kind of sporting entertainment before, the arena was loud and over the top.

'Tessie, you should be a dancer like these girls.' Zoe laughed in awe of the energy these dancers had.

'I'm a classically trained dancer Zo, not a cheerleader.' Tessa seemed offended.

Zoe turned to Eve and pulled a face as they tried not to let Tessa see them laughing.

'Do you think the players sleep with the dancers?' asked Zoe, thinking the dance moves might indicate yes. It was a very provocative routine.

'Who wouldn't sleep with these dancers, look at them, they are exceptionally sexy woman.' Eve was fascinated; the dance routine was like a workout on acid and the women were gorgeous.

'I don't think I would fuck any of them, personally.' Tessa was still serious, which once again made Eve and Zoe laugh, they both appreciated a sexy woman, but Tessa wasn't having any part of it tonight.

'I like them. I'm even a little turned on right now, I could easily be bisexual,' said Eve casually.

Zoe got it, but Tessa didn't get it at all. That was Eve though.

'I like that Latino looking one with the long dark hair,' Zoe said to Eve as they rated the dancers.

'I do too. Oh, and that all-American girl with the biggish hips, I like her too,' Eve said enthusiastically.

'Listen to you two. Do you realize if you were men, what you're saying would be so inappropriate?' Tessa flicked her long caramel waves in disapproval.

'But we're not men, we're appreciating how gorgeous these women are. Aren't we Eve?' Zoe sat back.

'I'm so glad I'm a woman, our bodies really are so sensual.' Eve was mesmerized with the dancers, it was the whole atmosphere, the music, and they were so close to it all.

'Maybe you're bisexual E!' Tessa stated.

'Maybe I am,' she answered honestly.

The game was an experience in itself, the girls cheered from the sidelines like they were hardcore fans, Zoe was supporting both teams, and confusing everyone around her. Tessa had one player in her sights though.

The postgame room was full of people and very crowded, the girls hung out with Phillip who they'd met the night prior, and a group of friends who were either hangers on or actual friends of Christopher and John Henry. There was a special quartered off area for player guests, and they were in it! It wasn't long before the players filtered into the room, it took a few minutes for Christopher to make his way to the group where the girls were. Tessa playing it cool as he made his way over. He was tall, there were a lot of tall guys who towered over the other normal human beings. Eve felt like she was amongst giants, she thought Marco had been tall, he was nothing compared to some of these guys.

'Would you come to dinner with me?' Christopher asked Tessa, all smiles. All three girls beaming smiles back at him. He was very charismatic and charming; and beyond sexy!

The next thing, the girls were waving Tessa goodbye from the front of the hotel after she and Christopher dropped them off in his swanky town car on their way to dinner.

The doorbell startled Eve out of her pleasant sleep, she had been dreaming about Evan again. It wasn't a bad dream this time. *Who was at the door?* Eve dragged herself out of bed and shuffled to the door with hair frizzing out in a ball to the side of her head, a hotel robe wrapped around her. 'Jackie.' She opened the door, still half asleep wrapped in her fluffy white hotel robe.

'Do you think you and I can catch up for a coffee this morning, just the two of us?' Jackie had that smile on her face that wouldn't take no for answer.

'I would love that.' *What did she want? What was going on?* Eve was fine with coffee.

'Great, give me a buzz when you're ready.'

Eve closed the door and her mind wandered to the dream that she had been woken from, then it went straight to Marco. She wanted to message him and tell him she missed him, and that the basketball game was amazing.

Back to her dream about Evan, *she had been standing in his arms and they were somewhere special, it was a celebration. They were both dressed nicely, Eve knew he was happy with something she'd done, he was softly holding her face and telling her what a good job she had done... At what she didn't know!*

Eve had no idea what she had done in the dream, she was sitting still half asleep with her hands to her face as she slumped back in her bed. A confused emotional rush, she hurt inside her heart. Eve didn't know whether to be angry at herself, or angry at Evan for the dream. She wanted to be angry at someone, or something. Sometimes in her dreams Evan was snarling at her with gritted teeth while he held a hunk of her hair in his fist, or he was covering her mouth as he made love to her. Eve could never make sense of the dreams, and this one had been totally different; he was happy.

'Come in.' Eve let Zoe in as she checked her phone, Jackie was wondering where she had got to.

'Are you crying Evie, what's wrong?' It was like Zoe knew her friend wasn't great!

'I'm fine, really.' Sitting forward she stretched. This was what happened when she let herself go to that place, the place where she still loved Evan and she still wanted him, she still mourned him, and she still missed him. Eve dreamt of making love to him, she still remembered how smooth and creamy his skin was, how he smelt and how good he made her feel. She pulled her hair back out of her face, she couldn't think about Evan, she needed to block him out for a while until she got some clarity on her reality, it was the only way. Eve immediate turned her focus to Tessa not being back. 'Have you heard from Tessa?'

'She's having breakfast with Big Cox.' Zoe confirmed.

'So, you've spoken to her?' Eve asked.

'Yes. She's holding out on all the details, apparently she needs to tell us in person.'

'Interesting,' Eve smiled, 'While she's out gathering stories to amuse us, Jackie wants me to have coffee with me this morning.'

'Are you okay? You don't seem okay babe.' Zoe looked at Eve knowingly.

'You'll probably think this is stupid.' Her face vulnerable. 'I've been dreaming about Evan... I'm awful.' Eve felt ridiculously sad and silly.

'Not at all.' Zoe smiled. 'Evie, you will always love Evan. It's not just going to turn off because Marco's around again.'

'I love Marco, I really do, I'm not messing him around.'

'You don't need to explain a thing to me. You can be in love with Marco and still love Evan.' Zoe was making sense. 'You're allowed to, nobody can stop you.'

'I was in love with Evan, and I always loved Marco, the whole time.' She was surprised at herself.

'Now you're in love with Marco, and you still love Evan. Same. Same,' Zoe said with gentle loving care.

'I guess so.' Eve took a breath and felt better. She knew she was desperately in love with Marco, she didn't just love him, she was madly in love with him. In just a few words Zoe had made Eve see things clearer.

Coffee with Jackie was just like one of their usual catch ups, until Jackie took it down the serious path, regarding Marco and their newfound relationship. Surprise, surprise! 'You know he's popular with the ladies. Football players have fans that live and breathe football and footballers my darling. Don't let any of it intimidate you go to Melbourne Eve,' Jackie said bringing it to her attention, Eve was oblivious to it.

Eating a large slice of carrot cake with her coffee for brunch, Eve didn't get it, 'Why would I be intimidated?' She was clueless to Marco's environment.

'You know what some women are like, they want what they can't have.' Jackie gave her a funny frown.

'Oh!' Eve bit down on her bottom lip, Jackie was making her nervous, she'd been there, don't that with jealous woman before, with Evan.

'Be prepared.' Jackie knew Eve would turn heads herself, she was stunning even on her off days.

'I don't want to jump ahead of things just yet. Marco and I are just friends.'

'Darling. I've watched the two of you with each other. He looks at you like you're a goddess. You're going halfway around the world to see him. I just want you to know, how it is.' Jackie addressed the doubt she heard in Eve's voice.

What did that mean? Eve was confused in a way but wasn't going to ask.

'You really do love him, don't you?' asked Jackie smiling... Eve was so confused... *Wasn't it obvious!*

'I do. I'm surprised you never noticed,' she said like it had been so obvious.

'Now that I've had time to process it, I think it's wonderful, the two of you. I just wish I had had known back when...' Jackie hesitated, 'Well, you know when.'

'I don't think it would have changed much. He wasn't ready my problems; I was too young.'

'You weren't too young to be with Evan.' Jackie knew she shouldn't have said it, but if anyone could, it was she. Evan was older than Marco.

Eve's soft voice and tearful eyes reacted immediately, 'I don't regret anything with Evan, I never will. Regardless of what it looked like from the outside; it was real.'

'I know you loved Evan very much. You were just a baby though and I probably just wish Marco had done the right thing by you, that's all.' Jackie couldn't help the way she felt. 'Tell me. Did anything ever happen between you two before Palm Cove?'

'God no,' Eve laughed at the notion.

'What about when you stayed at my house after Evan died. You left because of Marco didn't you? Did anything happen then?'

Eve didn't know why Jackie wanted to know, or why it was her business. 'I left your house that night because I just couldn't be around him. It was too much being near Marco at that time. I was devastated by my loss,' said Eve with a heavy heart thinking back to the state of her mind back then.

'I thought I knew my son so well; I hope he was kind to you Eve… you know the first time and all.' Jackie had a knack of saying risky things and getting away with it, especially with Eve and their very open relationship.

'He was a perfect gentleman.'

'Did it happen in the house?' she just couldn't help herself; she winced knowing how intrusive her questions were.

'Yes, it happened in the house.' Eve continued to laugh as Jackie smiled.

'Was it in a bed? Please tell me it wasn't in the spa!' Why not go for gold, she had come this far. Jackie liked details; she liked the full story.

'Do you want me to tell you the gods honest truth?' Eve had no reservations about it, she could tell Jackie anything, especially now that everything was out in the open. Well, most of it.

'I don't know… Yes.'

Eve frowned as if to prepare Jackie. 'It was in your bed. I stayed in your room with Marco most nights.' Eve watched the look of horror on Jacki e's face. 'Please don't ask me to tell you how good it was, because that would be going too far.' Eve added that as Jackie covered her face.

'Oh, no I wouldn't ask you that... you've gone back for more, so let's leave it at that.' Her hands still covering her face as she looked between her fingers at Eve now smiling. They were like two girlfriends trading tales.

'I love him Jackie, I need you to know that. I'm not some fan girl. I really, really love Marco with all my heart.' Eve had misty eyes.

'I know you do sweetheart. And there's no one I would rather him be with, I need you to know that.' Jackie was full of warmth and understanding. 'You know I've always loved you and I always will. You and me, we go way back.' She meant every word too. Jackie knew who Eve was within her core; she was a pure and gentle soul who only wanted someone she could love and to love her in return. God knows it was deserved after everything the poor kid had been *through*. Jackie adored Eve.

'You need to be honest with my son though. You need to tell him about the baby.' *And there it was again!*

It made Eve feel anxious because she wasn't ready to tell Marco. She'd tell him when she was ready and not before. It was her very personal secret and she owned it… nobody was going to rush her, not even Jackie.

Tessa was taking herself down an unknown path, skipping the show and spending the night with a random guy she had just met. Nothing new admittedly, but it wasn't the right way to be doing things, however, it was the way she needed to do things to get what she needed. Right now, Tessa needed to go home, and she would do whatever it took to get there, even losing her job. In Tessa's mind it seemed the only way, or at least the easiest way. *Giving up because she was home sick, just wasn't as exciting as having her contract terminated because she was partying too hard!*

'What a night. What a man!' Tessa was on a high, she had returned to the hotel on cloud nine. Eve and Zoe were exited to hear all about it. 'Christopher is so confident and manly; he lives like a fucking king.' Tessa gushed as she sat on the corner of Eve's bed.

'Wow. So, you had a good night?' Eve managed wondering if Tessa was high on coke, she certainly seemed to be.

'Good… It was fucking sensational. He wined and dined me like I was his queen!' Tessa gushed.

Zoe was as curious as Eve. 'So, Big Cox lived up to your expectations then?' Zoe never minced her words.

'Don't call him that. Although, his cock was massive, and I never slept a wink. We're having dinner on Sunday since it's my only night off.'

'Well, that should be fun,' Eve teased as she watched Tessa; she was odd. 'You're very chirpy for someone who didn't get a wink of sleep.' It had just been a hunch, but Eve had been right, she knew a coke high when she saw one.

'Okay, I did a little coke to get me through,' confessed Tessa.

'A little…When?' Zoe asked.

'Last night, this morning, today. Whatever,' Tessa said ready to take Zoe and Eve both on. She had been doing coke regularly for months, years actually, it helped her get through her day.

'That's the most ridiculous thing I've ever heard,' Zoe didn't like it, she knew this was habitual for use for Tessa, 'For someone who is so into her body and keeping fit. I think you're being really stupid. What's going on with you?' getting right to the point, Zoe put Tessa on the spot.

'This is what I do Zoe.' Tessa glared at her. 'I do coke. It gets me by.'

Eve was sitting back on the sofa taking it all in, she knew them both well enough to know this was going to end nasty and she'd have to intervene.

'No, you don't,' Zoe really didn't like what she was hearing from her best friend.

'Fuck me! Yes I do. What are you, my mother?' A big sniff as she got up to walk away.

But no, Zoe wasn't finished. 'Are you for real? How are we supposed to leave you here when you're behaving like this?' Zoe huffed; she was getting angry with every word that came out of Tessa's mouth.

'You know what Zoe. I've done this shit here for fucking years on my own. I don't need you two here to keep me in line. Besides, it was you who wanted me to go home with Christopher last night. Thanks for ruining my buzz too.'

'Don't blame me.' Zoe looked at her.

'Hey!' Eve felt it was time to step in.

'No,' Tessa protested to Eve holding her hand up. 'This is how I live. I don't need you both judging me.' Tessa raised her voice, upset that Zoe was getting in her shit. It was in Tessa's nature to turn this around on Zoe and Eve, only because she didn't know what else to do.

Eve tried to settle things, 'Nobody is judging you. But you seem a little unhinged right now. And we're your friends, we're allowed to ask the question. Are you okay, can we help you?' Eve spoke in her usual soft slow voice which at times like this, pissed both her friends off. She was always the calming voice of reason.

'Oh, fuck me… I'm under a lot of stress living here E. It's okay for you,' Tessa paused, 'Everything is roses for you two, fucking yourselves stupid with my brothers like two little bitches!'

A few stunned seconds passed.

'Are you unwell?' a slight chuckle of disbelief from Eve, 'Would you rather we didn't care about you?' Tessa was spiraling towards nastiness that couldn't be taken back, and Eve had to get her under control. 'I know you know this, but I will remind you again anyway... Zoe is your friend, and she cares about you... I care about you. Tell us what's stressing you out exactly? And stop being reactive.' Sometimes it took bluntness to get through Tessa's stubborn head.

'It's my whole fucking life E, that's what is stressing me the fuck out,' shouted Tessa, 'Can't you tell?' She'd gone from being happy and high on life, to down and out.

'Work with us, not against us, let us help you.' It was then that the girls both laughed at Eve, both with tears.

'You've really been in therapy way too long Evie,' Zoe sniffled as she laughed.

'I have, haven't I,' Eve agreed with a smile, 'We know you better than anyone Tessa. We know you're not happy here anymore. Just tell us what we can do to help?' Eve had her at confession point, at least the tension had come down a notch.

'I want to come home. I want to get out of here.' Tessa was now in tears, and the first person to go to her was Zoe, it was always the way. Fighting one minute, friends the next.

'Then come home.' Zoe put her arms around Tessa and comforted her.

'I need to get fired first. I can't just leave; I've got a contract.'

'Wouldn't it be better to come home because you've had enough rather than because got fired?' Eve asked.

Zoe rubbed Tessa's back in support. 'If you get fired, you've failed. If you have had enough, you've simply just had enough, there's no shame in that.'

'I don't know. You two are like these super women of the world with careers and life experience... I'm a dancer, that's my entire fucking life, it's all I've ever done,' cried Tessa.

'Is that a joke!' Eve scoffed, 'You are amazingly independent, you've lived in this big city on your own since you were seventeen and you're not just a dancer, you're a brilliant dancer,' Eve paused, 'My life is nothing to aspire to. I've lived like a nun for five years and now I'm about to fly halfway around the world for your brother, knowing my luck, I'll end up heartbroken again.' She made it sound comedic.

'I love that you've got this thing with Marco, I really do,' Tessa smiled, 'Take my word for it E, he won't break your heart again. I'm sorry for being such a bitch. And Zoe, I love you. I'm so sorry for being awful to you. I don't love that you fucked my other brother, and kept it a secret, but I'll get over it,' Tessa did a laugh cry.

'That's okay, I don't think I'm going to do it again any time soon,' Zoe smiled.

'What would I do without you two.' Tessa got herself together.

'I think we've all been apart too long. You both need to come home.' Zoe said.

Tessa took a big breath. 'Yep. I'm done. I love New York, but it's time. I can't do this shit anymore.' She was still high but felt clearer in her direction. Tessa was going home, she just needed to figure out how to do it.

'What if you don't get a show back home, will you still move back?' asked Eve.

'You have to. I can get you a job painting nails or waxing vaginas in my mum's salon,' joked Zoe.

'I can barely shave my legs,' Tessa laughed feeling better with life again.

'This is going to be awesome. All of us back home again.' Zoe clapped her hands.

'Don't get excited Zo. Marco and I might not work out, I might not come home for good.' Eve was just putting it out there, she didn't want anyone holding her to anything she couldn't promise.

'If you two don't work out now, no one will ever work out. I'll be alone forever because it means true love is a bunch of bullshit.' Zoe had never been sold on love, she thought love was way overrated, she had never been in love, and she couldn't see it ever happening. She wasn't the loving type, according to herself.

'How much do you love Marco?' Tessa asked Eve, now sitting snug next to Zoe.

Eve just smiled, she thought for a minute before she answered. 'More than I ever have.'

'Then you need to be with him, I know he loves you; I can tell. I'm his sister.' Tessa was so meaningful that she almost made herself cry again.

'Okay, don't go getting all creepy on me,' Eve's shoulders rose up. The fact that Marco was her best friends brother came with complications. More than she perhaps ever realised.

'Marry him and be my sister-in-law. Become a Rossi. Make me an aunty,' Tessa got carried away with her joke, knowing it would freak Eve out, Zoe laughing at them.

'Oh. My. God. You are just like your mum,' Eve gasped, it was so Tessa, she went from zero to one hundred in a minute.

'Don't you laugh,' Tessa gave Zoe a nudge, 'You're next. Sleeping with Nick and thinking I would let you off Scott free. Oh no, I don't think so Miss Brother Fucker... We're all going to be related. I can feel it in my bones,' Tessa laughed like she had a plan.

'Now I know you're fucked up. Get off the coke and go get some sleep,' Zoe scrunched her face up.

'It's my absolute dream, my two best friends become my sister in laws,' Tessa chuckled.

'You're dreaming. It's never going to happen, not me anyway,' Zoe exaggerated her words.

Chapter Twelve

Touching down in Sydney for the first time in five years had Eve on edge and ill to say the least. The car ride to her mother's house after dropping Zoe at her place was strange, she looked out the window as the car drove through Rose Bay, her eyes gazing over to the house on the harbour she once shared with Evan. Technically still her house, of which she would never step foot in again as long as she lived.

The refuge of her beautiful bedroom at her mother's house was not what she had expected, it didn't have the same magic it used to have. Nothing in Sydney did. Now, her childhood bedroom memories consisted of the few nights she had spent with Evan in her bed. The first night with him was a sexual blur, the next was full of his kindness and care as she recovered from losing Marco's baby! Evan had been the one who kept her afloat at the awful time in her life.

Julie the housekeeper still worked for Eve's mother, and she still despised her; she'd betrayed Eve by telling her mother about Evan. She didn't want Julie in her room at all, not even to collect her laundry, not even to make her bed, and Eve had told her so in the first few minutes of being home. Even though her stay was going to be a short one, Julie was not welcome within Eve's private quarters, not for a second. She wasn't even sure she even wanted to eat Julie's food!

Opening the draw that she'd kept Marco's clothes in for years, Eve took one of his high school sweaters out and held it up to her face, it no longer smelt of him. She called Marco as she sat on her bed with his sweater in her hands. His voicemail. Eve's heart sank, she was tired and missing him terribly. 'I'm at my mum's house and I wanted to hear your voice.' Was all she said before hitting the red button. He was probably at football training. Marco had told her it was the hardest part of the year for him, getting back into routine and getting his fitness up to scratch. She just needed to hear his voice as she sat alone in her room, feeling out of place, not knowing what to do with herself. Everything had a memory or a meaning, if it wasn't of her father it was of Evan and it bought up feelings she didn't want to deal with, feelings she thought she had ignored for years.

Ferez was someone Eve really wanted to see. He had always respected her and treated her well when Evan was alive and after, they'd kept in touch on a regular basis. Besides Kellie and Jo and of course Tia, Eve had no desire to see anyone from that part of her life. Not even Sarah or Bec, and especially not Martin or Marcello. They'd never liked her if the truth be told, and she'd never liked them.

She sat watching the boats on the harbour, it soothed her as it had since she was a little girl. The view from her terrace had always been a comfort. It was her thinking place, it helped her relax until her phone interrupted her thoughts. It was okay, the minute she saw Marco's name a smile came to her face, 'Well, hello.' She couldn't keep her excitement to herself. It was instant pleasure.

'Hello yourself Eve Frank. How's Australia treating you?' Marco's happy voice asked, it immediately made all her angst about being home in Sydney nonexistent.

'I miss your voice,' Eve's eyes watched over the harbour as she held the phone with two hands.

'I don't think it's been twenty-four hours since we last spoke,' his chuckle was affectionate.

She took a few moments, her eyes filling with tears of longing. 'I haven't touched you for four days.' All Eve wanted was to have Marco in her arms, to feel him and to be with him.

'When will you be in Melbourne?' he couldn't help but sound needy.

'I need a week here. I've got a few things to do first.'

'I miss you.' Marco missed everything about her.

'Not as much as I miss you.' And she did miss him, more than she ever had.

Anna and Nigel were an odd couple in Eve's opinion, Nigel still lived in his apartment and her mother at the house. Eve didn't fully understand the dynamics of her mother's relationship, but she did respect it and Nigel. His mild manner and intelligence intrigued Eve… She just wasn't sure he was the one for her mother long term.

Tonight, it was just Eve and Anna for dinner, Eve had made dinner and set the living room table for two. It was like old times, the two of them chatting over dinner. For the first time in a long time, they were just mother and daughter enjoying their own company, there were no pressures, no agendas and Eve hoped, no more secrets. But she couldn't be sure!

Eve had plans to see Jo and Tia the next day, she couldn't wait to see them both, to see how Tia had grown and to catch up with Jo, it had been a while. The following day she was lunching with Kellie, then having dinner with Ferez, they had both promised to keep her stay in Sydney on the down low, Eve didn't want anyone knowing she was home if she could help it. She'd fled the country young and naïve, grieving her murdered fiancé and returned a much wiser and mature young woman who was trying to moving on with her life the best she could. Eve was afraid that someone from her past would try to contact her, for what reason, she wasn't quite sure. Almost everything from that time in her life was now behind her, and she wanted to keep it that way.

Excited to see Jo and Tia again, over the past five years they'd seen each other twice when they'd come to the Chateaux to visit, their phone conversations and emails were regular. They had shared so much of Evan's last years together, Eve would always love and cherish Tia, she was a very special girl.

When Jo opened the front door, she looked the same as always. Her hair was still long, the tattoos and the cheeky smile bought tears to Eve eyes, they hugged for what felt like a long time at the doorstep before going inside. It was an emotional embrace, it always was.

'You're still as fucking beautiful as ever Easy E.' Jo looked her friend over.

'And you look really great, so healthy and happy,' Eve said. Jo wore a Ramones T-shirt, torn jeans with converse, she was still cute and funky, she looked like she had more tattoos and she'd pierced her lip.

'Come in and tell me everything, you look like you've got a lot to tell me, am I right?' Jo pulled a face, 'Tia won't be home for a little while,' Jo said leading Eve into the house by hand.

They talked about everything, Eve meeting Marco again and her possible return to Australia. Jo was ecstatic that Eve had finally had someone who might possible be serious about her. They talked about Evan briefly, then Eve got upset, they'd both loved him in their own way, they both missed him in their own way, and it was something they would share forever.

Jo told Eve about how she never heard from Martin and Caroline, which Eve thought was a shame considering they were the closest living relatives on Evan's side for Tia. Kim, Evan's mother was basically nonexistent in Tia's life also. 'Tia's really looking forward to seeing you Easy. You're her connection to her dad, not me. She misses her dad a lot, especially now she's getting older, and it's hard for me to tell her about him,' Jo explained, 'Until you came into his life, I loved to hate his fucking guts,' Jo smiled lovingly.

'You and Tia are my connection too. Who would ever have guessed that out of everyone, you and I would still be friends?' Eve got sentimental with Jo as they remembered.

'If you hadn't come into Evan's life, I would have lost Tia for good, he would have taken her from me,' said Jo taking a big breath like the thought hurt her heart.

'No, he wouldn't have cut you out,' Eve objected.

'Oh, yes he would have. He hated me until he had you. When I went into rehab, he would have taken Tia and I would never have seen her again... but you... you took care of her and bought her to see me. I will never forget what you did for me Easy E, ever.' Jo smiled gratefully.

'And look at you now; you're a guidance counselor for crying out loud, that's amazing. You should be so proud of yourself. I'm proud of you,' Eve glowed as she praised Jo, 'Tell me more about Nathan, what happened with you two, I thought you guys were solid,' she asked getting back to where Jo left off with her separation from her longtime boyfriend Nathan, who Eve and Evan had both liked for his easy going and level headedness.

'It just didn't work out, what can I say. He wanted to travel the world, and I have Tia and my new job.' Jo looked upset momentarily. The whole thing had come as a surprise to Eve, she thought they had been so well suited, and Nathan had kept Jo on the straight and narrow, he grounded her.

'Well, Zoe say it's character building to be single,' Eve gave a little cheeky grin and tried to keep it upbeat.

'There is this one new guy, although it's probably not where I should be picking up guys. I met him at my meetings, he's an addict too, so maybe it's not such a good thing,' Jo laughed.

'Maybe not.' Eve had that instant warning sign feeling… red flag… but she had to trust Jo.

'Maybe not. He's Chinese too, sexy kind of, so I should definitely stay away,' Jo laughed.

'Mmm hmm, stay right away,' agreed Eve with a smile.

'I knew you'd say that.'

'Sexy hey, that makes it really tough,' laughed Eve, 'Unless it's too late.' She gave Jo a look, getting the distinct feeling Jo may have already dabbled with the sexy Chinese addict.

'He's sampled this little Chinese dumpling more than once already,' Jo winced her confession.

'Ohm' gushed Eve right as Tia came bounding through the kitchen door.

'Eve,' Tia said jumping straight into Eve's arms, wrapped herself around her. Tia was so grown up, yet still so tiny and sweet.

Eve squeezed her in tight, every part of her wanted to cry as she reminded her so much of Evan that it took her breath away. Her smell, her touch, her embrace, it was all Evan. 'Oh, my gosh. Look at you, you're a young lady,' She tried to keep her emotions in check, stroking Tia's long ponytail all the way down her back. She was adorable, Eve loved her so much it actually hurt seeing her grow up.

'Are you staying for dinner?' asked Tia as she looked over Eve's face like she was remembering all of her.

'Of course, I am. How would you like to come and stay at my mum's house with me on Saturday night, it will be like old times, we can watch a movie in bed and eat pizza and ice cream?' Eve smiled happily at the gorgeous little girl who was maturing before her eyes.

'I would love that. Can I mum, please?' She beamed with happiness as Eve held her in next to her.

'I already told Easy E it's okay,' Jo said as she watched her daughter sparkle with delight. Tia adored Eve like nobody else, she always had, they had a bond that warmed Jo's heart in the best of ways.

The three girls spent dinner together, Jo loved showing Eve how to cook Chinese food, so they had cooked up a storm. The conversation was about Tia going off to boarding school, boys, which Tia still thought were totally gross. She still had her best friend Mini who had loads of little brothers and sisters, so Tia loved to spend time at Mini's house, just as Eve had loved being at the Rossi's. Only Mini wasn't going to boarding school and Eve could see the sadness in Tia's eyes.

After dinner they walked to the local ice-cream shop and had dessert and walked home again. After Tia had gone off to bed Eve left, she was seeing them both again on Saturday so the departure wasn't as sad as it may have been otherwise. Eve felt like she'd had a fix of soul replenishing love after her visit with Jo and Tia, it was funny how someone who could have been her worst enemy, had turned out to mean so much to her.

The next day before heading off to lunch with Kellie, Eve spoke with Marco, it was Friday and he was having lunch at the club, he thought he would check in with Eve to see how she was doing. Marco worried that Eve being in Sydney may unsettle things somehow for them. He knew he was being oversensitive about Eve being in Sydney for the first time since Evan's death, but he couldn't help it even though the guy was dead.

'How's your day going?' she sounded pleased to hear from him which immediately put him at ease.

'I've been in the gym all morning burning off all the carrot cake you made me eat in New York,' he teased.

'What's your favorite cake?' she asked.

'Chocolate. I love chocolate anything.'

Eve could hear his smile through the phone. 'I'll make you a chocolate cake when I get to Melbourne,' a sexy glint in her tone.

'I can't wait, even though I'm on a strict diet,' Marco said, she always excited him.

'I'm thinking I might come to Melbourne on Tuesday if that's good for you?'

'Any day is fine with me, just hurry up. I miss you,' Marco huffed with frustration.

'Do you miss me, or do you miss what you do with me when you've got me all to yourself?'

'I miss everything,' he sounded like a little boy who couldn't get his way.

'I miss you too, all of you.' Eve looked up to the ceiling of her bathroom as she got ready for her lunch date.

'Hey, I have to go. Have a good day Eve Frank,' Marco said, wishing she was there already.

'You too Marco Rossi. I can't wait to see you.'

Kellie was already at the harbour-side café waiting with two glasses of champagne on the table when Eve arrived, she looked well and her happy self as she stood from her seat to greet Eve. Her blonde hair was tied up in a ponytail high on her head and she wore a little red dress while Eve had jeans and a white shirt, both looking summery as the harbour twinkled behind them.

Over a long lunch, Kellie filled Eve on what she'd been up to, how little Jessie was doing, showing Eve endless pictures of the bubbly little girl. Eve couldn't help but think how proud of Kellie, Evan would have been. She'd taken charge of her life, but she was still that same old wholesome girl. Evan had a soft spot for Kellie and Jessie, and he had looked after them out of kindness and the goodness of his heart. They talked about how Kellie was now out of the adult entertainment industry, her new job working in admin was less stressful than stripping. Marco was on the agenda too… Eve told Kellie the whole saga, which Kellie found totally enthralling.

'I need to meet this guy. How come you never told me about him before now?' Kellie asked, her bright blue eyes full of life, Eve loved Kellie's energy.

'Well, you were Evan's friend for one, and it just never came up,' Eve answered simply.

'I'm really happy for you Eve. I'll be even happier if he can keep you in the country, I've missed you.'

It was a lighthearted catch up with no secrets or strings attached. Kellie had always been one of those friends Eve could rely on and trust for a good chat. Her input was always open minded and respectful, and never judgmental. She was just what Eve needed.

Going straight from lunch to dinner with Ferez, cabbing it around town after sharing two bottle of champagne with Kellie. Eve arrived at the restaurant only ten minutes late, it was nothing unusual to be late in Sydney due to the traffic situation on any given day. Ferez himself had been half an hour late, so Eve found herself happily half intoxicated by the time he arrived. Seeing Ferez was painful for a mere second... all the memories with Evan, they had been exceptional friends.

'Look at you. You're absolutely gorgeous. If it's at all possible, I think you're looking better than when I last saw you.' Ferez squeezed Eve tight, he knew exactly how to make a girl feel great. They'd last seen each other on Ibiza eighteen months ago, Eve had met Ferez for a short break. They both loved Ibiza.

Never letting his image down for a moment, Ferez was his handsome dashing self in pants and a shirt and a blazer, great shoes, a big gold Rolex, and so clean cut he almost shone... that was Ferez! He had always been such a little spunk with so much charisma; he was a genuine person; someone Eve would always have time for and trust with her life.

'I've missed you,' she said touched his arms, they had become good friends. People looking on as they hugged and greeted each other. Ferez was somewhat of a celebrity in Sydney, he was always in the news for one reason or another, mostly making the gossip pages in the daily papers with pretty models and actresses by his side.

With a million questions for Eve, Ferez had wanted to visit her there, but his busy schedule hadn't allowed the time of late, they'd managed to have to have the one catch up in Iviza a while back.

Nothing was that new with him, he was still running his clubs and now had little contact with most of Evan's old crew, he was never part of Martin Li's crew. Of course, they had a lot of mutual friends who he saw on occasion.

'Your dads my lawyer now, you know that right?' Ferez had been close with James over the past few months due to a legal issue he had found himself in.

'He told me,' Eve smiled like it was a cross to bear.

'Things are a little strained with you two still I take it?'

'It's complicated.'

'Your old man's given you a hard time over the years, and I know why.' Ferez held Eve's look, she wondered what exactly he knew, how much did he know and how did he know.

'Tell me what you think you know about my dad, then we'll see how smart you really are,' she said, with a nervous smile, she didn't know what he was going to say. One thing about Ferez, he liked to be in the now, even when it was none of this business. Evan had once told her Ferez knows everything about everyone in Sydney.

Looking at her like he was going to outsmart her, 'Sam's your real mum.'

Fuck! 'Wow, you know your shit,' Eve paused, 'Who told you?' Eve needed to know if her father told him or if Evan had told him, it could only have been one of them.

'Evan. I helped him get your birth certificate. I know he left it in the yellow envelope for you. I know you've got the envelope' Ferez said, he didn't feel good about knowing her inner private secrets.

'Who else knows?' Eve wasn't happy about it.

'Nobody. Just me.' he said with confidence.

'I've never told anyone about the yellow envelope.' She was a little taken back that Ferez would even bring up the envelope.

'That's okay.' He understood. 'I just needed you to know, that I know. In case you ever need anything.'

She was silent for a moment. 'I don't want to talk about it, it's extremely private for me. I need to know you haven't told anyone.' A defensive demeanor came over her.

'Eve, I swear I haven't told anyone. I won't.' Ferez realized the enormity of the situation.

'Have you spoken with my dad about this. Does he know I've got the birth certificate?' Eve was curious.

'Not in so many words,' a beat, 'You know your dad, where do you think you get your need for privacy from,' Ferez gave a little smile. He narrowed his eyes as if to show her he was sorry for being in her business, he felt like he had betrayed Eve.

Eve was mortified and embarrassed and didn't know what she was thinking. 'Does he know, I know?'

'I don't think so, not that I could tell.' Ferez watched as her face darkened, her eyes looked down at the table and she bit her bottom lip to stop it from quivering.

'Eve.' Ferez was now wishing he never bought it up, tears fell down her face. She was visibly upset; her life was such a web of secrets, just as her fathers was.

Taking a deep breath in and regained her composure. 'I've had a lot on my plate, and to be honest, the truth is a hard pill to swallow at times.' Her lips curled into a sad smile. 'Not to mention Sam and Evan … They had sex you know, and a lot of it… You probably know all about that,' Eve said soft and somewhat devastated. She had never discussed this with anyone before.

Ferez huffed his regret, 'Evan knew it would break your heart, he didn't know how to tell you Eve, honestly he didn't. He tried.' Her devastated face was paining Ferez, he didn't want to lose her trust as a friend, that was the purpose of telling her he knew. 'Eve listen to me, I talked with Evan a lot about this, he was so torn between lying to you and telling you. He wanted to tell you before he asked you to marry him, then he wanted to tell you after the baby, then he was hell bent about it before the wedding… And well.' He stopped and trailed off like he had more to say but just couldn't. He wasn't sure Eve needed to hear everything he knew!

'I've never spoken to anyone about this Ferez, you have to understand how personal this all is for me.'

'Talk to me about it. I'm a great listener.' He smiled so she would feel a little at ease.

'This is the woman my dad shares his life with; they have two little girls together, who I've never met. They're my actual sisters and I've never met them. Not to mention she's my birth mother, and she had a sexual relationship with Evan… It' a lot to comprehend.' Eve was emotional and trying to keep her cool.

'I know it must have been a real shock.' He was sympathetic to her.

'It was. I read the birth certificate the night before Evan's funeral... I've felt like my skin's been turned inside out ever since that night,' she paused at the thought, 'Do you know about the house too?' Eve reluctantly asked the question.

'I do. I'd keep that one very quiet if I were you. Martin and Marcello are greedy and ruthless Eve, especially when it comes to money.' Ferez had a distaste in his tone.

'And all along I thought Marcello was the one he confided in. But it was you.' Her teary eyes looked at Ferez warmly, she knew she'd always liked him for a reason, and it was because he was the one person Evan had truly trusted.

'Evan and I had a few secrets between us. He was a good friend to me, and I think he trusted me because I was outside the circle.' Ferez put his hand out over the table and placed it on Eve's. 'I know he really loved you Eve. He wanted that house to be yours more than anything.'

'It's just so much money and such a burden at the same time.' Her voice was apprehensive.

'I will always help you; you know that. You and I are mates, I will always look out for you. Your dad would do anything for you too, never underestimate him Eve.'

'Why doesn't he talk to me about things,' Eve was forever questioning her father; he was a hard nut to crack.

'I don't think he wants to hurt you. Like I said, he would do anything for you. Anything.' Ferez was intense.

'Well, that's fucked. Completely fucked,' Eve laughed, 'Everyone is always keeping the truth from me because they don't want to hurt me. Yet, they don't realise that the secrets, are the worst hurt of all.' She took a deep breath and looked around. 'Have you met Sam?' Eve needed to know how much Ferez knew.

'I've met her once or twice. She's not a bad person... you might actually like her.' Ferez had actually known Sam for many years.

'The day of Evan's funeral I saw her outside the church, and I swear she knew, I knew exactly who she was. She's never tried to contact me, not ever. For fucks sake, she gave me away when I was three weeks old. Clearly she doesn't want to know me,' Eve raised her voice, an expression of her frustration.

'You should talk to your dad about this... Make him talk Eve.'

'I can't.' She held her breath, it was too much to comprehend.

'You can,' making it sound so simple.

'Don't you have shit in your family? It's not easy to talk about secrets.' Eve took a big drink of her wine and raised her hand for the waiter to come back over.

'I have shit in my family, huge shit,' Ferez smiled, 'Of course I do. Shit you wouldn't believe. But we talk about it in my family, it's all out in the open.' Ferez thought that part of Eve's charm was her deep sense of privacy. 'But big secrets like this rot the soul young lady, so talk to your dad about Sam and about the house.' He hoped she would take his advice; all the secrecy was grating on her, he could tell.

Eve was planning on calling her dad tomorrow to see if he could do dinner on Sunday or Monday before she left town.

'Now tell me about this new guy. Who is he, and will I approve?' Ferez changed the subject and moved on with their conversation. He liked Eve a lot and not in any other way, than she was a good girl who he wanted to look out for. The sun had risen and set with Eve for Evan, his longtime friend had gone to great lengths for this young woman, he'd gone to France and wooed her home, committed the ultimate sin in her honor, and wanted to marry her. Evan was no push over when it came to women, so Ferez knew when his friend said he wanted Eve, she was special. And for that reason, he would always have time for her. Besides he liked being around her, she was exotically beautiful, had this calming effect on him, and she was sensually sophisticated. Yes, Eve held her cards close, but she was solid when it came to loyalty and friendship. Ferez knew Eve had no idea, just how much like her mother Sam, she was.

Dinner went late into the night and Ferez then insisted that Eve accompany him to one of his nightspots.

'I'm not really dressed for clubbing,' she said to Ferez as his silver Porsche 911 GT3 pulled into the curb right out front of the bar, very special indeed.

'You could wear a garbage bag and you'd look great,' he said getting out of the car going around and opened Eve's door for her.

She sighed, 'Am I going to run into anyone I don't particularly want to see? Cause you know, I've been drinking since lunch time, and I don't feel like being polite or nice just for the sake of it.' Eve smiled as Ferez took her hand and they walked up the front steps in front of the que that went way down the street.

'I wouldn't do that to you. I will however throw you out if you start a fight though,' he joked.

Heads turned as Ferez a man in his forties, who was known to have a different girl on his arm most nights, walked in with Eve Frank. There were always eyes on him, he was a celebrity in his own right.

Everyone knew her face... Who was she?

Eve and the handsome Ferez strolled to the bar, her long hair floating about her body as she held onto his hand. The bar was full of Friday night patrons out for a good night, dancing, drinking, and enjoying life, the vibe was great. They enjoyed a few drinks and some small talk that made her laugh like crazy to the point of nearly wetting her pants. Ferez gave her all of his time; it was a unique friendship that they each treasured.

He walked her out to the front and got a driver to take her home, he was always a gentleman.

Eve took Ferez's hand in hers, 'I might be moving to Melbourne. I'll let you know how it goes... you might need to meet me in Ibiza if it doesn't work out.' She raised her brows. 'We can have one of those crazy parties again.' She'd been drinking nonstop and was feeling the buzz.

He clenched both her hands in his. 'You're one special little lady Eve. Let me know if it doesn't work out with Mr. Perfect... And I'm all yours.' He laughed at how cute she was.

'Wouldn't that be interesting,' Eve chuckled as she leaned into Ferez and kissed him on the cheek, a few seconds longer than a friendly kiss goodbye, but it was nothing more than that.

'Oh, it would be very interesting.' He smiled still holding her hand. 'Take care pretty girl and talk to your dad.'

She pulled away towards the waiting curbside car. 'I'll think about it... Thank you.'

Chapter Thirteen

Driving with Tia in the car felt just like old times, they talked about girl stuff, clothes, friends, and her dad.

It was the first time they'd been alone in a very long time, and she knew Tia was itching to talk about Evan, she loved him so much. Eve had to tread carefully though; she knew Tia wasn't a little girl anymore, she needed to be spoken to like she was a young lady, that was what she was becoming after all, right before everyone's eyes.

'Did you know you were only a few years older than me when you met my dad?' Tia said as they drove in Anna's sleek white Jag through the traffic to Watsons Bay.

'Er, I was much older than you,' Eve looked at her with a grin in the passenger's seat beside her.

'You were seventeen or something like that, I did the math,' Tia was joking around, she was still as cute as a button and as sharp as ever.

'It was just a kiss when I was seventeen,' laughed Eve as she stopped in the Saturday afternoon traffic.

'My dad was too old for you at seventeen. He was a grown man... A dad.'

'Well, to be fair, he didn't know I was seventeen when we first kissed,' Eve said, 'We actually got together when I was eighteen if that makes a difference to you. Fifty years ago, people were married with kids at eighteen. And by the way, your dad wasn't too old for me, I was very grown up at eighteen,' Eve tried to make it sound better, she tried to help Tia understand.

'I don't care how old you were, I love that my dad found you.' She had a smile as big as the harbour bridge.

'I love that he found me too,' Eve sighed feeling a little overwhelmed at the thought.

'My mum says you have a new boyfriend. Is that true?' There was no judgement in Tia's voice.

'Um,' Eve stalled a second, 'It's not really official or anything, we're good friends right now.'

'What's his name?' Tia was pleased Eve had a love interest.

'Marco. He's one of Tessa's big brothers,' Eve said pulling up to the house.

'Did you know my mum is dating someone?' and just like that they'd had their talk.

After ordering a large pizza and garlic bread, Eve rang Marco, it went straight to his message bank.

'I'm just calling to say hello. I hope you had a great day. I miss you.' She hung up wondering what he was doing on a Saturday evening in Melbourne. She missed him so she flicked through her photos on her phone so she could look at him, his brownish hair with the sun lightened ends in waves, that olive skin, those plump lips and imperfect nose, she loved everything about Marco, smiling just thinking of him.

Tia loved Eve's bedroom, they ate ice cream and sat in bed under the lush puffy linen watching Mulan for the millionth time together for old time sakes. It was their movie... Tia in her pug pajamas and Eve an oversized T shirt, they laid close to one another like they used to. After Mulan they watched The Grinch, another one of Tia's favorites, the Christmas she had with Eve and her dad was the best Christmas she ever had, she'd spent the whole school holidays with Eve at the beach and hanging out.

It was late when Tia fell asleep, Eve messaged Marco red hearts since he had not called her back all day. She needed some sort of contact. Then after she sent the two red hearts, she thought perhaps he was already in bed asleep, she had no idea what his routine was, all she knew was that she needed to hear from him so she could go to sleep peacefully.

Lying with her phone on the bedside table, Eve laid with her lamp on watching Tia as she slept, a flood of memories with this gorgeous little princess made her heart hurt. She was sad that Evan wasn't here to see how amazingly beautiful his daughter was. Sad that life could be so unfair to all of them, and sad that all of a sudden she herself felt so fucking lonely. Sometimes life and all it had dealt Eve, snuck up on her and it hurt like hell. Everything in her life was going well now, she felt guilty for feeling sad. Then the guilt subsided, she understood... This was why they call them memories, they were moments in life you couldn't and shouldn't ever forget, no matter how painful or how beautiful.

In the early hours of the morning Eve woke to a buzz of her phone, instantly waking to see Marco's message. But it had been Zoe messaging her, she was unable to sleep and wondering if she could do lunch tomorrow. Disappointed it wasn't Marco, Eve's heart sank, and she messaged Zoe back, of course she'd have lunch with her, she had to make time for Zoe before she flew down to Marco on Tuesday.

Pancakes had always been a favorite of Tia's, so Eve stood in the kitchen at the cook top making pancakes and topping them with ice cream, strawberries, and chocolate sauce. She didn't want to say goodbye to Tia, it was always the way, they'd given each other so much comfort, but they knew it had to come to an end. On her way to lunch with Zoe, she dropped Tia back at Jo's house. She wasn't looking forward to the goodbye. They'd had a night like they used to have all the time, the two of them doing girl things and enjoying one another's company. For Tia, Eve was a little normality, away from Jo, who had always kept her safe and fed, the only difference was, Eve never made her feel anxious like her mother did. Poor Tia was always expecting something with her mother, the unknown! Since her father had died and Nathan had left, it was like she lived day to day waiting for something else to go wrong. Tia may have been a little girl when Jo went into rehab and her father was murdered, she remembered how it felt and she lived in fear something would happen to her mother. So, spending time with Eve was like respite for Tia.

'I need to run something by you Easy E,' Jo said, she was dressed in little shorts and a crop top, her doll like body of artful tattoos on display, Eve barely noticed them anymore.

Jo wanted to sell Evan's Bondi Beach apartment, which was left for Tia. Evan made sure the payment for the Bondi Beach apartment and Villa Rosado could never be traced to him, it was his way of keeping his girls financially safe should anything ever happen to him.

Somehow, Jo thought she could sell the apartment. What concerned Eve more, was the reason Jo wanted to sell the apartment. She'd given Eve the obvious reasoning of needing money to pay Tia's school fees, which was fair enough, but concerning because Eve was pretty sure Martin had been paying Tia's school fees. Then Jo said she was also thinking of moving, and that she wanted to do some travelling. None of it sounded legit, but it wasn't her business what Jo did with her life. Eve knew Jo owned her house, it was part of her settlement from Evan, she had a job, so there was money. It just all sounded random.

Eve had a cup of coffee with Jo and hung around another half hour, making sure before leaving, she got a moment alone with Tia so she could take the opportunity to have a quick word to her in private.

'You know you can call me whenever you need me, about anything,' Eve pushed Tia's hair behind her ear. 'If you're worried about anything or you need something, or even just someone to talk to, you just call me, and I'll always be there for you.' She looked into Tia's concerned eyes. It was as if they were reading each other's minds and didn't have to say the exact words. Eve could only hope that Tia would come to her.

Zoe sat across from Eve in the hip café close to Zoe's apartment. She looked thinner than ever and yet she seemed her usually determined happy go lucky self.

'I'm trying to get a real job, with a good magazine. All I've been doing is studying for two days straight to finish this module. I'm so sick of studying and working all the time. I need some reward for all this fucking study,' Zoe sounded stressed, 'I need to get serious about this career of mine Evie,' Zoe smiled still looking stressed and worn out.

'Well, that's good, you should be trying your best and striving for a career, you're so passionate about it,' said Eve who was basically on an indefinite hiatus from her own career at the chateau.

'What about you Evie, what are you doing with your life?' Drinking a tall glass of water and orange juice at the same time, Zoe wondered what her best friends' plans were.

'I don't know Zo; I need to try this thing with Marco. Not that he's returning my calls or messages, which is a bit odd.' She was on the edge a little about it, she hadn't heard from him since Friday.

'It's the weekend and he's busy unless there's something else?' Zoe questioned.

'What else could there be?' Eve twitched her fingers as she thought about it.

'I'm sure there's good reason, he'll call you.' Dismissing it without a second thought, Zoe knew Marco was as head over heels with Eve as she was with him, it was nothing. Eve didn't go on about it, although it was all she could think about all lunch.

Eve had left a message days ago for her father, she mentioned she was in Sydney until Tuesday, asking if he wanted to catch up with her and she'd missed him calling her back, when he called her back again she was on her way home from her lunch with Zoe late in the afternoon.

'I've called you five times in two days Eveline,' James didn't sound impressed that she hadn't prioritized him.

'Can you do dinner or not?' Eve wasn't in the mood for her father's bullshit, all she could think about was why Marco hadn't returned her calls or messages.

'It'll have to be tonight. I'm going to Hong Kong tomorrow.' He sounded like she was seriously inconveniencing him… Some things never change.

'If you're too busy we can do it another time,' she sighed.

'No. Tonight. Meet me at Quay at seven,' his voice blunt as he gave her the hurry up.

'Really? I'm driving home, I've just been…'

'Quay at seven.' James cut her off.

'What's with the attitude! Maybe dinners a bad idea.' Her back went up, who did he think he was talking to. James hadn't given such attitude since her days of defying him with Evan. James knew not to push her too far, she could easily cancel him, and he wouldn't hear from her for another six months.

'I'll see you at seven,' he said trying to be polite but still sounding shitty, she could hear a whole lot of noise in the background, like he was somewhere busy.

'Seven.' And she hung up pissed at her father and screeching into her mother's driveway in the white Jaguar.

She sat in the car in the garage for a while thinking about how to handle the situation with her dad. There was so much they needed to talk about, they could possibly be at dinner literally for days.

James had never got over the whole Evan and Eve relationship, he'd been mortified right from the start and there were so many little twists and turns, like Sam's relationship with Evan, the fact that she was also Eve's biological mother infuriated James beyond rationality. To think Evan had been with Sam and his daughter... they were mother and daughter... he simply would never get over it or forgive Evan. *Even if he was dead!*

Hurrying upstairs and getting ready to head back into town, Eve flicked through her cases that she had not unpacked for the simple reason she would be leaving again in a day or two. She plucked out a saucy white dress which was sedate enough for her father to not be too critical of. Her hair was good, all curled out and unruly, she left it be. There was just one thing she needed to do before she left, call Marco again.

'Hey, it's me. Is everything all right? I'm getting worried... Can you call me please,' her voice was soft, calm, and pleasant as it ever was. She didn't want to catastrophize, but she couldn't help thinking of all the awful things that could have happened. Then again, if something had happened to Marco, she would have heard from Jackie or Tessa by now, if he was sick, he would at least messaged her back, maybe. Her mind wouldn't rest. *Maybe he'd changed his mind and he didn't want her anymore!*

A black clutch, black Jimmy choo heels and her relatively non provocative white dress... Boobs slightly peeking out the top. Eve looked like someone famous walking across the restaurant towards her father with a little strut in her step. James watched her approach, it had been a while since he'd seen her, she was a stunning young woman. He couldn't help but smile as she arrived at the table, he rose and gave her a kiss on both cheeks. His daughter was breathtaking... So very much like her mother. Sam.

'Wow. You know how to make an entrance my darling,' James greeted her.

'Why, what did I do wrong?' She asked as the waiter pulled her seat out and her father waited for her to be seated.

'Absolutely nothing, you look beautiful, that's all,' he smiled.

'Thank you,' she said settled herself into her seat and pushed her hair back out of her face with a nervous shake of her head, placing her phone by her water glass, she didn't want to miss Marco's call if he rang.

'Drink?' James asked his eyes firmly fixed on his daughter.

'Vodka. Neat,' she said taking in the breathtaking view of the harbour bridge.

They got the formalities and the New York low down out the way, Eve didn't elaborate on the Marco situation, she kept it basic, she never showed all her cards to her father. Not straight up anyway.

'What about you, what did you do for New Years?' Eve asked, it seemed like a starting point.

'We stayed home, the girls love the fireworks,' James said gulping at his scotch.

'How are the girls? They must be getting big now.' Eve sighed, narrowing her inquisitive eyes to her father. This was the first time she had mentioned them in what felt like forever.

'They're eight years old now. Growing up too fast, as you did.' He kept it brief.

'You're pretty old to have eight-year-old kids.' It wasn't supposed to sound bitchy; it just did. James smiled at her like he was expecting it. 'What are their names again?' Eve knew their names, it sounded awful, and she knew it, but couldn't take it back once it had come off her bitter tongue.

'Your sisters names are Zara and Arla,' James said pursed lipped and matter of fact.

'Mmm,' she said with sarcasm, 'How did you name me, by the way?'

'Anna was reading a book with a character named Eveline.' If he thought that was going to get him off the hook, he was wrong.

'Really? I like Eveline; but then there's always Juliette Amanda to revert back to.' She held her fathers stunned eyes to hers, not letting him escape. Juliette Amanda was her given name on the birth certificate Evan had left for her. James was speechless, he was motionless, clearly rattled. None of what Eve was saying was planned, it was just spilling out her mouth like hot lava. 'That's what I was named at birth.' She was talking with a sharp tone.

'What did Evan tell you?' James broke his silence as he glared at Eve across the table.

'Everything,' she lied and took a sip of her vodka; very cool even though her heart was beating a million to one.

'I didn't know he knew everything,' objected James uncomfortably.

'Oh, come on,' Eve smiled, 'Evan used to sleep with her, you know that, surely.' A slight twinge of jealousy in her tone. It couldn't be helped whether she liked it or not.

'You're referring to Sam I gather?' James felt his blood pressure rise to the occasion.

'Yes.' It was like Eve had dropped a bomb between them. 'And I know she knows, I know.' She couldn't help the hurt on her face although she tried to keep it together.

James' eyes darkened. 'What makes you think she knows; you know?'

'Because I know,' Eve raised her voice slightly; it was a don't argue voice. He was testing her.

'It's very complicated for Sam.'

'Oh, my god!' Eve let out a little amused chuckle, *was he serious?*

'What did Evan tell you?' James glared at her as his voice spewed Evan's name with venom.

'After that Christmas Eve when we ran into you and Sam at the restaurant, I knew they knew each other. He told me she used to work for Martin years ago when he was kid. He told me they'd had a sexual relationship,' she paused so her father knew Evan's sexual past with Sam didn't matter to her. 'I found my birth certificate in Evan's safe the night before his funeral. He didn't tell me who she really was to my face… he didn't know how to tell me something so fucking awful,' Eve hissed the words.

'Don't use that language Eveline.' James was backed into a corner.

She felt her heart race with emotion. 'I don't know which part is worse. That you and my actual mother Anna, have lied to me my entire life, or the fact that *Sam's* never tried to contact me. Maybe that was because she was your sixteen-year-old whore, and she gave me away... you should be ashamed of yourself Dad... very ashamed.' Eve was going at James with all barrels loaded. Her furious voice still several decimals above her usual soft tone.

'Don't refer to her like that,' warned James with a quiet snarl.

'Well, retired whore then. Is that better?' Eve defied her father with glassy eyes, she was angry about so many things. Hating that her father loved the woman who'd given her up at three weeks old. She despised her father for hating Evan. *Was she going to be an awful mother, just like Sam? Was this why she'd lost Marco's baby... was it why her precious Rafael had died?* The thoughts were excruciating, but she couldn't block them out.

'Anna, kept the truth from you Eveline, not me and certainly not Sam. Anna didn't want you to know the truth about your real mother, she-.'

'My real mother is Anna, she's the only mother I've ever had.' The hatred was unmistakable, hatred Eve didn't realise she had inside of her.

'We had to play by Anna's rules, ask her yourself,' James shot back; it was time.

Eve held her breath at the thought. *Anna had told her everything she knew. Apparently!* Eve chose to ignore his accusations. Anna would not have lied; they had no secrets.

'Sam was a young girl who sold her body. She got pregnant to a married man. She fucked Evan when he was kid!' Eve's anger was building, 'So, excuse me if I don't hold her in very high regard won't you, Dad,' although her voice was not obscenely loud, her respect was out the window.

'That's enough,' James said loudly, 'You are never to speak of Sam that way again. You have no reason to be so blatantly disrespectful. You are the heartbreak of her life, and Anna is the reason she has never contacted you. She forbade it, and Sam respected that because she loved you, she wanted the best for you. Always.' James leaned into the table, his eyes a blaze with emotion that Eve had never seen before.

'I hate her... That's my reason for being disrespectful. And you. You're so full of fucking shit. What about all the years you've ignored me. Disrespecting me to be with her and your new family?'

'Anna was the one who didn't want me in your life in the end. She didn't want me in your life if I left the house, not if I lived with Sam. She said the truth was more than you could cope with.' His tone was dramatic.

'Oh. My. God. Really!' Eve shook her head, 'Don't you dare blame this all on Anna. You did this, and you know it.' Tears fell from her eyes as she gasped for breath.

'I wanted to tell you every single day of your life,' James said finally showing a miniscule of remorse to his daughter. 'The day you overheard your mother and I, the day you ran to Evan like a spoilt brat. Anna was the one who kept it from you. Not me,' a pause, 'And while I'm at it, Aria your sister, has a rare form of leukemia and starts chemotherapy tomorrow. So, get off your fucking high horse and stop being so God damn rude. Eveline.' James had reached breaking point. He tried to hold strong as he blurted out what was really clouding his mind and compounding his life.

Eve was shell shocked, she wanted to keep going on about how hard done by she'd been, and how sick and tired she was of her parent blaming each other, and how she despised them all at this point... but now this. Her actual sister was gravely sick! She sat looking at her father not knowing what to say to him. He was visibly upset. She thought for a moment he might even shed a tear. Eve was searching for the next words to come out of her mouth. 'Is there anything I can do to help?' Serenity came over her. Everything changed in that second.

They both took a breath; James was humbled by Eve's instant offer of support. That was the daughter he knew and loved; the angel he had adored from the minute he first saw her. He shook his head in bewilderment. 'Aria starts chemotherapy tomorrow; we have to wait and see how she goes.'

'I'm sorry Aria's sick.' Sympathy and regret flooded Eve.

'Regardless of what you think of Sam, I need you to give her a break. You don't know her,' James sighed.

Eve thought for a moment. 'Maybe you should go home and be with your family, they probably need you tonight more than I do.' She meant it with all the kindness in her heart. Her issues now seemed so irrelevant.

'I'm having dinner with you. I know you don't believe it Eveline, but I love you very much. All I've ever wanted is your happiness. I want you to know that.' James had calmed down and so had Eve, she wanted to so desperately to believe her father.

'What grade are the girls in?' Eve asked her father, deciding to move on, it was what she did best after all. They talked for a while about how the girls were so much like her and about the things they liked and the things they did. James said they reminded him of her, that it was uncanny. It hurt Eve deep inside to hear his voice with so much adoration and love, he seemed so happy as he spoke of his twins. Eve had no idea where she fitted into her father's life, and right now it didn't matter.

On their departure from the restaurant Eve hugged her dad for the first time since Evan's death, she had made a mental note, *funny that!* she loved her dad, that was never in question. Everything he did and said affected her on so many levels, it always had and yet she loved him so much.

'I'll be in touch soon. And stay out of the papers will you – I thought you were smarter than that,' James gave her wink.

'What are you talking about?' Eve was confused.

'You didn't see the Saturday morning papers? You and Ferez... kissing,' James said with a warning of serious proportions.

'What! We didn't kiss. We're friends. Are you saying I was in the paper?' Eve asked still confused, she was oblivious to any picture of her and Ferez in the papers.

'Saturday. Take a look. And try to behave, he's my client... and he's way too old for you Eveline,' James said, a joke in his tone as he stepped out to his awaiting car. He knew Ferez wasn't that stupid to get involved with his daughter, so he didn't need to take it further. They were only friends.

'Bye Dad,' Eve managed. *What picture? Who took a picture of her and Ferez kissing... and what kiss?*

She sat in the car before starting it and googled Ferez and the paper. *The kiss outside the club as she was leaving!* It was the kiss that lasted seconds longer than it should have. The angle of the photo didn't help, nor did the fact that he was holding her hands. Eve couldn't breathe. It looked like it most certainly could have been a kiss of passion. *Fuck! Had Marco seen it? Shit. Shit. Shit. Was this why he wasn't calling back?*

Driving straight to Zoe's apartment in a state of hysteria, hyperventilating and frantically dialing Marco's number over and over. She left multiple messages and he hadn't called her back. *Fuck!!!*

'Marco. Please, pleases call me back. I need to talk to you, now.' Eve was in a panicked, and then he called her back.

'What's up?' he definitely sounded pissed at her.

'Where have you been? I've called you a million times.' She burst out crying. There was no response, he was silent. 'Say something Marco,' she begged him.

'Why are you crying?' His tone was dull, like she was irritating him.

'Because… everything is going wrong,' she tried not to raise her voice or sound like a sook.

'What's so wrong for you Eve?' This was not the Marco Eve was used to.

'That photo of me in Saturday's paper, I'm pretty sure you saw it… I never kissed Ferez like that, I would never!' she took a breath, 'Both my parents are liars, and my little sister has leukemia and I've never even met her. That's what's wrong with me.' It all came spewing out.

A long silence while Marco processed her words, 'Why were you kissing Ferez Ahmad? Let me guess, he is an old friend.' The hollowness was painfully evident in his tone, he wasn't accepting her explanation at all.

'He is an old friend. It was a peck goodbye. Nothing more. I swear,' Eve was over expressive as she continued to freak out in the driver's seat of her mother's Jag. 'The camera angel made it look like more than it was… it was a kiss goodbye, that's all,' she sounded desperate.

'Right!' Marco was not convinced.

'Please believe me.' Eve couldn't comprehend that he didn't believe her, 'Why would I lie to you? Why would I kiss Ferez?' Her lungs wouldn't open for air, it was like someone had punched her in the gut.

'I don't know Eve. How do you expect me to feel… do you kiss all your old friends like that?'

'What!!' *Who was this man on the other end of the phone, it surely wasn't her understanding perfect Marco…* she was in a panic. 'Marco, it was a peck goodbye.

Honestly. That's all it was.' Now it felt the like she was disintegrating from the inside out.

'So, you keep saying.'

'Ferez is my one and only male friend in the world that I keep in contact with. We had dinner and went to his bar. Then I went home, alone,' she felt compelled to explain, although she had already told him it was nothing. Where had her beautiful Marco gone, he sounded cold and bitter.

'Okay,' Marco paused for a moment. 'Maybe you shouldn't worry about coming to Melbourne. I think it's a bad idea.'

The instant pain pierced her chest, nearly killed her. 'No... Marco!' Pleading with him to see things her way. The photo had completely unraveled him, and he was hurt and upset.

Then the line went dead, and he was gone.

'No. No. No.... Fuck!' Eve slammed her fists into the steering wheel and dropped her head to it, so hard it hurt her forehead. Regaining composure, she dialed Marco again, it went straight to his voice mail.

Call the airport, charter a jet to Melbourne NOW. Make him understand face to face. Don't go home, Anna will be there and she's a liar... get a grip. There's a little girl who is your sister, and she's very sick. She about to fight for her life and you're unravelling... Marco! Sitting in the parked car for ten minutes before she decided to call Zoe.

'Hey, you,' Zoe answered the call cheerfully.

'I'm out the front,' Eve sounded vague.

'Why, I mean why didn't you come to the door?' Zoe asked.

'Because I've got a problem.' Eve bit her bottom lip feeling bad she had brought her problems to Zoe.

'Evie are you okay, are you drunk?' Zoe said as she opened the door and looked for Eve.

'Marco told me not to come to Melbourne,' Eve's voice faded out and she walked to Zoe's door.

'What! Why doesn't he want you to go to Melbourne?' Zoe took Eve's hands and pulled her down to sit on the sofa next to her. 'He's not serious... I'll kill him!'

'Didn't you see Saturday's papers? There was a picture of me with Ferez outside one of his clubs. It looked like we were kissing, but it was just a goodbye peck.' Wincing as she flicked on her phone so she could show Zoe.

'Oh, Evie. How did Marco see this?'

'I don't know how. But he did, and he didn't believe me when I tried to tell him it was just a peck.' Eve's face crumbled from pure devastation. 'What do I do? Jackie or Nick probably sent it to him. Oh my god. I'm not meant to have the happily ever after Zo, am I?' Eve bit hard on her bottom lip as she looked through tears at her friend.

'I can't believe he didn't believe you.' Zoe was fuming that Marco was being such a dick, and mad as hell that nobody had shown her the picture in the paper of her best friend. Of course, her friend didn't kiss another man, she was completely in love with Marco.

'He hates me,' cried Eve, her chest was tightening, 'Oh, my god, why did I go to New York,' she was in full catastrophizing motion, 'I knew this would happen. I knew he would do this again.' Eve felt like her world was unravelling all over again.

'Slow down, just take a breath,' Zoe said forcefully, 'Marco has seen the picture and freaked out, that's all. I now I think you need to go to Melbourne straight away and tell him to his face, that it's not what it seems.' Zoe could see how distraught her friend was. This required a massive gesture of love and nothing less.

Chapter Fourteen

Eve flew in the first row on the five pm flight into Melbourne the following day. She wasn't losing Marco without a fight. Every time she thought about living without him, it was like a poisonous spear to her heart. The entire flight she cried, luckily nobody was seated next to her so she could have some kind of privacy as she wiped away stray tears and debated whether to go straight to a hotel or to Marco's house. She'd spent all day with Zoe going over what she would do and say when she saw him. Packing her bags and thrown in a few extra things for good measure, deciding that if Marco didn't see things for what they were, she was heading back to France on the next flight to live out her days as a spinster, with loads of vibrators all named after hot rockstars. She'd live a life of celibacy and never love another man as long as she lived.

Feeling so very hard done by and sorry for herself, Eve thought about the little sister issue she had going on and the birth mother drama! It felt like her life had spun into turmoil again after years of living relatively peaceful in France. Anna had no idea she'd even left Sydney, Eve had conveniently packed her bags and left the house before Anna got home from work, she didn't know how to deal with her mother or what to think just yet. She was well aware that her father was an expert at diverting blame to others, this skill had made him a very wealthy man, so Eve wasn't sure she could really take her father's word. Accusing Anna of lies and secrets while she was edgy about Marco, didn't seem like a wise move. So, she decided to deal with one life issue at a time. Marco was her priority. Anna could wait.

Standing up ready to disembark, looking disheveled with glassy red eyes and bushy hair... her chest fluttering as she sniffing to clear her airways. Filled with anxiety and still unsure of her destination! She managed a smile to the flight crew who had kindly left her alone for most of the flight, tears welling in her eyes as she made her way to the lounge gate. Right now, as she walked off the plane, she was exhausted and depleted.

The first person off the plane was Eve, somber and over emotional as she entered the arrival lounge and looked up. Standing there at the end of the seats, with a huge bouquet of red roses in his arms, was Marco. His unruly hair in waves around his face, wearing jeans, and a white T-shirt, and looking straight at her.

Eve stopped and looked at him, her face crumbled with pain and relief. They took a few steps towards each other. She dropped her bags to the floor and reached up to him. Marco's arms wrapping around her body, the roses tangling in the back of her hair as he lifted her feet from the floor in his engulfing hug. Their mouths met and kissed slowly; the moment was theirs. Eve's hands rubbing up into the back of his hair as she let a soft sob escape her lips at the sheer relief.

'I'm so sorry Evie,' Marco pushed her hair back from her face.

And her Marco was back, she didn't care about anything other than her being in his arms.

'I needed to look you in the eye and tell you that I would never lie to you. That I never kissed Ferez how it looked in that picture.' Her heart was aching for him, in every sense of the word.

'I know, I know... I hope you can forgive me?' Marco pursed his lips with a smile so sexy and irresistible, if they hadn't been in the airport it would have been on, right there and then. *Eve knew exactly how she wanted to forgive him!*

As Marco drove his very black masculine SUV down the freeway, Eve sat sideways staring at him, watching him. She wanted to pinch herself to make sure she wasn't dreaming. They didn't do much talking on the car ride, the silence was strangely comforting. Just being in his company was enough, the past twenty-four hours had been quite an ordeal. Eve understood completely how Marco must have been feeling, and he understood how confused she was not knowing why he was avoiding her, by the time they got to the car, it was all said and done, the Ferez kiss was over. In the end, they were in each other's arms again, and all was forgiven.

The entire way to Marco's house, Eve felt like she was having an outer body experience, she was so very tired. She'd imagined the worst scenario in her head all day. Loving Marco for so long, and then finally getting him back, only to lose him all over again… and now here he was, in front of her in the flesh. He was still nothing short of perfect in Eve's eyes, it was like a dream come true again.

'This is it. This is my house.' Marco pulled into the curb on a street lined with cars and big trees, it was dark.

'Your home!' Her pretty gaze was everything he needed and more. Eve looked pleasantly surprised as she peered out the windscreen up at his white Victorian terrace house. It was dark, but it looked beautiful to Eve.

'Yep. My home. And Zach and Brooke's home for now too, they've been here for years, literally. They normally go to bed early, but I think they might have waited up to see you… You'll get to say hello before I take you up to my bedroom and help you start forgiving me,' Marco smiled at her, 'You are going to love my bed by the way, it's the best bed in the world.'

'I'm sure it is.' Eve could hardly wait as her beautiful grin reminded Marco exactly why he had fallen so hard for Eve Frank from up the hill. She was different in the best way imaginable.

Eve's love for Marco had never wavered, not for a second, not ever! He was her destiny, he had to be. If he wasn't, it was the cruelest of paths she was on.

She took her carryon bag as Marco swung a Louis Vuitton duffle bag over his shoulder and carried her two oversized Louis Vuitton cases. He was the epitome of manliness and strength… which was a massive turn on for Eve; she was buzzing deep inside at the thought of making love to him at the first possible chance she could.

Looking up at Marco's house as she stopped at the front gate, Eve took a big breath in. It looked beautiful in the middle of the row of white houses. It looked homely and warm as they walked up the little path to the front door. Marco stood back with her luggage to let Eve inside.

'Paddy boy,' he gushed with affection, leaving the luggage in the hallway to reach down to the dark grey and white mid-size dog who turned in excited circles at his feet, itching for his attention. 'This is Pat, my dog.'

'Pat the dog, or Pat my dog?' Eve didn't know if he was serious or not, she laughed.

Marco laughed, 'It's just Pat… as in Patty Mills, you can call him Patty. He answers to both, don't ya buddy.' Marco scuffed up Pat's short fluffy hair on his head. Pat the dog wiggled still happy to see his owner, wondering to Eve legs and smelling around her.

'Nice to meet you Patty,' Eve said touching the dogs head, she had no idea who Patty Mills was… but the dog seemed friendly enough.

'Well, well, well, look who's all grown up and finally in Melbourne.' Zach was barefoot, in a T-shirt and shorts, he went straight to Eve for a hug hello as she walked down the hallway and into the living space. It had been a long time since they had seen each other. The truth was they didn't really know each other all that well, but Marco had talked about them so much that they actually felt like they knew one another rather well. And let's not forget, Zach had slept with Tessa.

'It's so good to see you,' Eve said hugging him back.

'Wow. You look the same. You look good.' He held her shoulders.

'So, do you. How weird does this feel,' Eve laughed genuinely happy to see Zach again, 'It feels like a lifetime ago we were all in Palm Cove.' The memories were great ones.

'Eve this is Brooke, Zach's wife and my favorite housemate ever,' Marco said making the introduction.

Eve smiled and took Brooke's unique beauty in, naturally blonde, sharp features, olive skin.

'Hello, it's lovely to meet you.' Eve put her arms out and she and Brooke had a welcome huge.

'Oh, Eve it's great to finally meet you too. Marco hasn't stopped talking about you. I almost feel like we're friends already,' she gushed still holding onto Eve who just smiled looking over Brooke's shoulder to Marco who watched on, Pat the dog was at her side sitting up against her leg. She had never had a dog and never really been around dogs. so, she wasn't sure what Pat was doing. She hoped it meant the dog liked her. Brooke stood back next to Zach. 'You're all he's talked about since he came home from London last year.'

Eve raised her eyebrows and gave Marco a cute smile before she looked back to Brooke. 'Well, I hope it's all been good,' she said playfully to Brooke who took it as her opportunity to take Eve into the living room leaving Marco and Zach in the kitchen. Brooke was sweetly forceful with Eve, making her sit beside her on the L shaped sofa in the middle of the room, settling herself back into the cushy sofa, her smile bigger than Texas as she unconsciously looked Eve over, checking her out. Brooke was attractive and bubbly almost to the point of fake and a little overpowering, Eve was going to allow herself to get to know her before she made gave a verdict.

'I can see why our big guy has fallen for you, you must be super special, he literally hasn't stopped talking about you.' Brooke lounged back into the sofa, Eve could tell she was sizing her up, analyzing everything she did.

'What exactly has Marco said?' Eve smiled curiously as Pat the dog laid up against her leg again.

'He says you're very feminine and lady like, a little quiet, but very smart,' Brooke still had the big smile, 'I think it's so cute how you two have loved each other since you were kids.'

Eve was surprised, she nodded her head, 'Marco said that?'

'Oh yeah, he said he's always had a soft spot for you, since you were kids.' The two women looked at each other with odd smiles for a few seconds. There was something about Brooke that Eve wasn't sold on just yet. There was no bullshit about her, so it seemed, which was a positive. She did talk a lot, that was one of Eve's first observations, Brooke continued on about how all their friends couldn't wait to meet Eve, and about some camping trip on the weekend, which alarmed Eve, although she didn't show it. The truth be known, she just wanted to be alone with Marco. As Brooke kept talking, Eve's eyes kept wandering to Marco. Thankfully, it wasn't long before Brooke and Zach headed off to bed, then Marco gave Eve the house tour room by room, holding her hand leading her through the seemingly long and unassumingly large house. It was a beautiful home, Eve was impressed, it was stylish and tasteful in a way she hadn't expected, homely too. Brooke and Jackie must have been responsible, it was really, really cosy, and comfortable. Rather cozy.

Marco took Eve to his room last, and again, not what she had imagined. Not as manly and stark as she had expected. The room looked out over the street below. She stood at the big French windows for a moment, observing the peacefulness of the dark street. Biting down on her bottom lip, she looked around the interestingly large warm white room. It felt weird that this was Marco's actual bedroom, that this was his house, that she was even there. The past day had been a missive test and stressful to say the least. Eve looked at the fireplace, it was in working order with a beautiful black mantle, art above it and very high and decorative ceiling. She loved Marco's bedroom. Looking at the bed as Pat the dog nudged against it, getting ready to jump on it and snuggle up for the night. The bed was big, king size, Eve couldn't help noticing it had man linen. Nice linen... but man linen! Navy and grey with three pillows. Maybe she could do something about that situation... all in good time, she knew how much Marco loved his bed, he'd talked about it in New York, it was his dream bed, but it most certainly needed Eve's touch, he'd absolutely love it more once she'd bought him new linen, new *white* linen asap.

Reaching up into the top cupboard, Marco pulled out another pillow, Eve could see his revealing skin between his jeans and his t shirt as he stretched up, and while his back was turned, Pat the dog jumped up on the bed and plonked himself down at one side, Eve presumed it was his side most nights.

'Patty, off,' Marco said sternly when he turned around, like the dog had broken a rule. Marco pointed to the door like it was punishment, quickly letting Patty out and closing the door again.

'He sleeps on the bed with you, doesn't he?' Eve gave Marco a little grin.

'Yes, he does,' he tried to keep a straight face, 'But he knows when he needs to keep out, he's fine with that... and the sheets are clean by the way, I changed them before I pick you up.'

'It sounds like Patty has to keep out a lot then,' Eve said curiously still grinning.

Marco smiled, 'Not as often as you'd probably think Eve Frank.' Hugging the pillow into his front. He wasn't the kind of guy who had chicks sleep over all the time, Marco never picked up during the football season... well, hardly ever... it was only if he was seeing someone and they spent the odd night over, and even then, it wasn't often.

'Did you really tell Brooke that we've loved each other since we were kids?' It hadn't left her.

Marco turned around from the bed and looked at her. 'Yeah, I did... I told her that before I saw the picture in the paper of course,' he joked, 'too soon?'

'Yep,' Eve said smiling, as charmed as she was, it was too soon for her.

Marco threw the pillow on the bed and move closer to Eve. 'I told you in New York, that I think I've always had a thing for you.'

'When I was like ten, and you were fifteen!' She shook her head and winced in disbelief.

'When you were ten, I thought you were the cutest little thing. You were always my favorite… don't tell Zoe.' Marco melted her heart as she reached out to the waist band of his jeans, pulling him to her.

'Did you even notice me before Palm Cove?' Eve still didn't believe him, she looked up at him as she spoke in a soft seductive voice.

'I noticed you, just not all of you.' His hands went to her arms and rubbed them up and down. 'You were always so quiet and a little mysterious. The one with the gorgeous eyes and the beautiful long hair.' Marco bent down and put his soft full lips to Eve's, pulling her up into his magnificent body.

Eve had never heard anyone describe her as a kid that way, it was heartfelt, she loved it, it felt really nice to hear after her shitty few days. Gently as they kissed, Eve lifted the front of Marco's T-shirt up to his chest and ran her hands over his warm skin and those tantalizing ab's. He laid her down to his bed and rolled over her gently, taking command, holding himself over Eve, staring down at her with his long-lashed eyes.

Eve spoke in a whisper. 'Was I really cute? Because I always felt like the short hairy friend who was invisible to all the hot boys that circled around my friends.' Her soft croaky voice had a tired and sexy tone.

'You were never invisible, not to me. But then again, I wasn't one of the hot boys.' He smiled and felt a little bad that Eve had felt invisible at all. Marco hadn't been a great looking teenager in the scheme of things, just average in his own opinion, he'd never been anything more than average, and yet Eve Frank thought he was more than average… which made him feel like a king of sorts.

'You were very hot to me,' Eve smiled and closed her eyes, kissing him in her slow gentle way, which Marco adored so much. She pulled his T-shirt over his head, his hair pulling with it as he rolled to his back. She climbed onto his thighs, leaning forward, her eyes at his while she covered his chest with little kisses, her hands tucked in at his sides. She could feel the soft touch of his palms creeping up under her top, he slid it over her shoulders. The lace of her bra scraped against his stomach as she continued to devour him with her tender kisses.

'I've fallen for you Eve Frank,' Marco whispered, his hands fumbling to undo her bra and set her bountiful boobs free as her ticklish kisses adorned his neck with a ticklish pleasure. She looked up at him for a moment and felt the most gratifying feeling she had ever, ever felt. *Marco Rossi had fallen for her!*

'I've falling for you right back.' And she put her mouth back to his sweet tasting skin and meandered down his chest, continued her way down his athletic body with sensual, passionate kisses as her hands worked on his button and zipper. Eve needed Marco physically, all of him. Her want to please him, to show him her loyalty and commitment to him was all that mattered. For her it was the way she gave her all to the man she loved. It had started with Marco and then been Evan and now she had come full circle, right back to Marco.

'Is this part of you forgiving me?' he asked letting her take over.

'Mmm, hmm,' she murmured, lowered her lips to his big hard erect and ever so perfect cock. It was always a pleasure to see Marco's cock... as big as it was, it was overwhelmingly inspiring. He was completely perfect in absolutely every way a man could be... *even when he thought she had kissed Ferez!* Little nips of lips at the end of him as she gently gripped his base, her pillowing boobs pressing to his thighs as she pulled his jeans lower. This was going to be the best blow job Marco Rossi had ever received. It was a gift of love, even though Eve wasn't the one who was asking for forgiveness, *he'd better have something remarkable in store for her.*

Marco groaned as Eve did her very best sucking and tongue rolling, he was fighting his urge to cum from the second she unzipped his jeans. Her erotic overload was unbearable, his big hands clenching at her arms at his sides. He didn't want to cum before he got a chance to be inside of her, it had been an emotional few days for him too, and now he was just glad that they were together, Marco wanted to spoil her between the sheets, he was insistent on making it up to her. 'You need to stop Evie.' He lightly pushed at her shoulders back, he had to get her off him, he was in a sexual incoherent state of no control, one more suck and he'd blow! Eve's magic mouth was more than he could take.

'What's wrong?' she asked sounding unsure and moving to his side.

'Nothing, it's great,' he was huffing, 'I just want to be with you, and you're going to make me cum,' Marco sighed looking at her serene face. 'Take your pants off.' Now he was doing things his way.

Fine by Eve. The gentle way he went about moving her body, it was one of her favorite things about being with him, he didn't need to throw her around or hurt her to make himself feel like a man, Marco was always caring and so, so very sensual. Eve watched his broad shoulders as they rose above her head, she was already ready. Their vertical challenge was evident in the missionary position, his pecks at her face, she kissed his nipple softly and felt every ripple of his chest with the softness of her fingertips as he slid inside her juicy wet pussy.

Did he have any idea how hot he was, or how much she loved him? No, Eve assumed not. The sheer size of his perfect cock tingled and stimulating her like it was the first time she's had sex in years... it seemed to slide inside her forever. Pulling and stretching her tightness to its girth so tenderly. Eve touched Marco, his arms, and shoulders as he took his time making sure she knew exactly why she should forgive him. Digging her nails into his skin, her orgasm began to build like a burbling volcano of stimulation.

'I missed you,' Eve whispered as Marco began to thrust deeper and harder inside her. Pressing his hardness into her body. Immediately she was pulsing around his strong hardness, his hips moving in slow circular motions as she felt all of him deep inside her depths. Marco was one hell of big man, his sheer size and power was sexually overwhelming for Eve, but in such a pleasurable way.

'You've got me now, I'm all yours Evie,' he breathed as he held his thrust at an intense depth, so she could feel her orgasm deep in the pit of her belly as she came around his cock.

'I would rather die than cheat on you Marco... I need you to know that,' she gasped emotionally, arching her back as a warm tear rolled down the side of her face, then her body went into a cumming numbness.

'Evie, Evie, Evie. Don't cry,' Marco breathed, pushing inside her with one last hard thrust, holding his hips to her, pinning her to the mattress. Eve's body tensing at his force, he was like solid rock, cumming inside her, flooding her with sexual emotion. Marco fell to her, their misted bodies meshed together, her legs wrapping around his waist. 'I know you wouldn't cheat Eve Frank, and I don't ever want you to have to justify yourself to me again,' he tried to catch his breath, 'What can I say, I got jealous.' Marco's body relaxed to hers.

'Well, now you're forgiven.' She wiped her tears with the back of her hand. 'And you need to sleep. I don't want to keep you awake; do you have training in the morning?' Eve studied his face as he rolled to her side.

'I do. I'm going to take a shower, and then I'm holding you in my arms until you fall asleep.' Marco got up out of bed and went to the adjoining bathroom, closing the door behind him.

Eve sat up in bed, the covers up under her arm pits as she reached for tissues on the side table, she looked around the room... her secret entered her mind for just a second. Her phone was flashing, she wondered if it was her father. She had been thinking about Aria starting chemotherapy all day. It wasn't her father, it was Vivienne, her grandmother.

'Mame,' she said so happy to hear her grandmother's voice, that she was crying. Eve missed Vivienne already; it had been almost a month that she had been away, and she was feeling guilty for not returning to the chateau.

Vivienne was elated that Eve was in Melbourne, she just wanted her granddaughter's heart to heal. For Vivienne, Marco seemed to be that man who could do that, not that she knew him. They chatted for some time as Eve laid in Marco's bed, then just as they were about to hang up, Eve came out with it. She had to ask.

'Mame, have you told me everything you know about my birth mother? You wouldn't keep anything from me would you?' Eve spoke quietly as she heard the water of the shower turn off in the bathroom.

'I have told you everything Anna has told me. Has something happened Eveline?' Vivienne questioned knowing her granddaughter was testing her.

'How do you think mum would feel about me finding my birth mother?' Eve bit down on her bottom lip, sometimes you needed to make shit up to get to the bottom of things, she thought of it as harmless manipulation.

Vivienne hesitated, 'You need to have that conversation with your mother.' This was no surprise to Vivienne. 'Or maybe your father could help you, I'm sure he knows how to find her.'

Eve wishing she'd never asked. 'I love you Mamie.' She felt awful for putting her grandmother on the spot.

'I love you too my precious girl.' The phone call ended, and Eve sat up in bed and smiled as Marco came out of the bathroom. She didn't want Marco knowing about her parents and her biological mother just yet, so she smiled and pretended all was swell in her complexed life.

'Who were you talking to?' Marco asked towel drying his hair, nude at the side of the bed.

'My grandmother.' Her eyes followed him, he threw the wet towel on the end of the bed and got in next to Eve. It wasn't a big deal, but she'd noticed Marco's wasn't a neat freak like she was!

'Everything all right?' His head turned to her.

'Yep.' They both knew it wasn't, but she was a closed book if she didn't want to talk about something, Marco knew that much for sure. 'I'm just going to the bathroom quickly, I'll be back,' Eve said with a smile, getting up and grabbing his wet towel off the end of the bed, taking it with her.

When she returned, he was waiting. 'Come here.' Tapping his lap as Eve got in bed, straddling him. His hand at her arms, rubbing her sensually.

'You just had a showered, shouldn't you be going to sleep?' suggested Eve.

'We're only talking,' he said looking totally irresistible with his damp wavey hair.

Eve wanted to make love to him again. Her hands went to his chest, her fingertips touching him. 'What are we talking about?' She tilted her head to the side. Her hair hung over her shoulder.

'You. Us.' He kept rubbing her arms.

'Are we okay… us.' she sensed his seriousness.

Marco looked deep into Eve's eyes, 'We're more than okay Eve Frank.' He moved one hand from her arm to her boob and ran a gentle finger over her skin down to her nipple. 'I'm glad you accepted my apology make up sex so graciously.' A smile curled his lips, his words immediately put her at ease. 'But I'm not finished.'

'You need to get to sleep. It's late Marco.'

'I need you more.' Sex with Eve made him sleep better. Marco kissed her lips as his hands ran down her neck to her shoulders. Eve leaned into him and took a deep breath of him into her lungs, sucking at his bottom lip, letting him know it was on. She touched his face as his hands trailed down her body. She felt him hardening under her again.

'I'm really sorry that picture upset you,' Eve kissed to his mouth as she let her body fall down over his, feeling him slide to her depths once again. This time felt more intense than the last time if it was at all possible.

'I'm really sorry I got upset over it,' he huffed, his hands went to her hips and pulled her over him.

'I forgive you; you're forgiven,' her lusting breathy words were a relief. 'Ahh, Marco Rossi!'

He knew he'd overreacted to the photo without knowing all the facts. 'Do you like my bed? I told you my bed was the best.' Reaching to her back, he ran his fingers down her spine therapeutically.

'Yes… but you do know I'm a bedlinen freak right?' The words huffed quickly out her mouth as she felt Marco pull her down to him harder this time.

'I'm not offended at all that you don't like my bedlinen,' his chuckle turned to a slight groan.

'I'll get you sheets you'll never be able to sleep without.' Eve squished her hands into his chest, she was grinding down over him, feeling his depth hard as he stretched her glorious folds wide open. Wanting more and more, losing herself again to the magnitude of Marco's perfect cock.

'I see the way you diverted a potential serious conversation about us to bedlinen Eve Frank.' Marco took her face and brought her to his mouth again. Their gasping kisses sexually intense and passionate, all the woes of the past few days between them was now long gone.

'No more talking.' Eve put her finger to Marco's mouth, she could feel her climax building fast, narrowing her eyes, they watched each other cum simultaneously in record breaking time.

Waking the next morning to Marco spooning her, hair pinned under his shoulder and his heavy leg and arm resting over her. Life was bliss! There was an alarm going off and the birds were chirping. Her chest expanded out as she lay in the safe haven of Marco's bed, she did love his bed. The deep sense of comforting ease and safety she felt with Marco, was unlike anything Eve had ever had in her life before. Then there was the secret, for a split second in the back of her mind.

Eve's hands ran up and down his arms. De ja vu from a long time ago, he was heavy over her body, but she would not move, not an inch, not whilst in this beautiful moment. *Could anything spoil this, like her secret or her past. There was a lot that could go wrong if she really thought about it. So, for now she wouldn't think about it!*

Marco moved at her back then took his heavy leg off her, he nuzzled into the back of her hair, breathing her in. Just having him touch her was stimulating, it was like a dream, it was so the ultimate dream!

In his sleepy voice Marco said, 'I want to wake up like this every morning.'

Eve smiled letting herself back into Marco land, where everything was perfect. He moved a little so he could cuddle her in closer. There was something about the softness of Eve's body and the smell of her hair that utterly evoked every ounce of pleasure within him.

She closed her eyes in a daze of pure sweaty morning bliss, if she could have this forever it would be heaven on earth as it was known. Their bodies sticking together in a warm sensual closeness.

'I really want to stay in bed Evie, but I have to get up, I'll be back around three. Will you be okay if I leave you my car? I can go with Zach. You can explore until I get home,' his soft toned voice said as he moved some more and got out of bed.

'I'll be fine.' Smiling looking up at him as he watched her move into his spot. She looked beautiful in his bed.

'The keys are here,' he tapped his fingers on the bed side table, 'There's house keys too. When I get back, I want to take you to my favorite coffee shop around the corner, I'm pretty sure they do a great carrot cake.'

'I can't wait.' Eve ignored her urge to pull him back into bed.

'You'll be in the house alone with Patty, Brooke leaves for work around eight thirty. Are you sure you'll be okay?' Marco questioned with concern, he felt bad for having to leave Eve on her first day in town.

'Pat the dog and I will be fine together. Don't worry about us.' She pushed the covers down to her waist and sat up, her urges got the better of her and she thought it was worth one last effort to get him back in bed.

'I'm jumping in the shower,' Marco said turning and going through to the bathroom. Eve got out of bed and put his T-shirt on, following him into the bathroom. He was getting into the shower; her eyes looked him over and it was another pinch moment. Marco had very tanned legs and white feet, she hadn't noticed this in New York, it took her a moment to realise he had a sock tan.

'Is there anything I can get you while I'm out on my adventures today... Where am I, by the way?' Sitting herself on the bathtub and watching him.

'You're in Albert Park,' a beat, 'And crotchless underwear – you can get me a pair of those,' Marco joked turning the water off and reached for his towel, sexy smile, and all.

'What size are you?' She liked his morning humor, he never failed to make her feel warm and fuzzy.

'You're funny Eve Frank.' He rubbed at his hair with the towel.

'I try my best Marco Rossi.'

At nine thirty Eve headed off on foot down the street, Brooke had pointed her in the right direction over breakfast. As much as she felt guilty leaving Pat the dog behind, she wasn't sure she wanted to take him on her very first adventure out and about, he'd been following her around the house all morning.

The sun was out, and it was a comfortable twenty-six-degree day in Melbourne. Eve swung her bag and happily strolled to the end of Marco's street where she found a shopping strip. She walking the entire street absorbing every store, boutique, and café there was, Eve was in her element! The cosy street curved around the tram lines. Down the very end was a florist, which was heaven for Eve. She bought hydrangeas and Iris's, then she stopped into a café for a coffee and drank it at the curbside table – so very Melbourne of her, she thought. The day was delightful, and Eve took a moment to call Zoe while she enjoyed the great coffee and the lovely street.

'Oh, my god. Evie. You said you would call and tell me what happened straight away. What's going on?' Zoe answered the call, she'd been waiting for Eve to call since last night.

'I'm fine. Marco was waiting at the airport with roses, thanks to you calling him twenty times apparently to tell him my flight details... I love you Zo.' Eve was more than grateful that Zoe had sorted it out in the way only Zoe could, she'd left message after message on Marco's phone with Eve's side of the story and her flight details.

'Good! It told him to pull his shit together and get over himself, or you'd be gone forever,' Zoe sounded bossy and also triumphant.

'Thank you Zo,' Eve smiled, there was nobody quite like Zoe, she was a good egg without a doubt.

'Evie, I told you it would all be okay, just to get on that plane.'

'I know, you know everything, you're always right,' a beamed with a happy smile.

'You bet I am,' joked Zoe just pleased she could be of help to her friend.

'I think I might be going camping,' Eve said hesitantly.

'We don't camp!' Zoe was horrified.

'Well, I can't say I'm not going, I'm a guest here. It must be something they do here.'

'I hope Marco isn't going to take you camping for your birthday next weekend!' Zoe puffed her disapproval down the phone, 'Surely he doesn't think camping is romantic... It sounds like I need to make another phone call.' There was only one Zoe, she wasn't letting this thing between Eve and Marco fail. 'Have you told him yet, about the baby. How did he take it?'

And there it was. *Why was everyone so fucking interested in her secret... Fuck!* 'No, I haven't told him yet,' sighing at the thought.

'Don't leave it too long, I have a feeling he's falling in love with you Evie.'

Oh, God. was Zoe always right; Eve knew she needed to pull her finger out and tell Marco before someone else did. Someone like his mother or sister, which would just be awful.

Finishing up her coffee and her call with Zoe, Eve continued back down the street. It had everything she could possibly want and need – a makeup store, florist, cafes, boutiques, nail and hair salons, a bookstore and then, there it was like a savor at the end of the street, Country Road... her go to store. Eve bought white bed linen and rushed back to Marco's to wash and dry them so she could have the room set up by the time he got home at three. She fussed around with Pat the dog following her up and down the stairs all day, Pat was hot on her trail. By the afternoon, Eve was flicking through a magazine on the sofa when Marco walked through the door. Zach had dropped him off and gone out. Marco was wearing short tight black skins and a black T-shirt, his joggers, and his sports bag over his shoulder, all cheery and sexy looking, Eve would never get tired of this man.

'How did your exploring go?' he asked dropping his bag in the middle of the floor, which was noted by Eve.

'Really good, I went to the end of the street. Pat and I were just relaxing. How was your day?'

'My day was excellent. Better now I'm home with you.' Always positive and enthusiastic, Marco pulled her up by the hands off the sofa and into his arms, planting a big smoochy kiss on her.

Eve's arms going straight up around his neck, with Pat the dog wagging his tail at her side, he'd stuck to her like glue all day while she washed the sheets, made the bed, tidy a little, and arranged flowers in small vases in Marco's bedroom and bathroom and the kitchen.

'I've been waiting to do this all day.' She kissed him back and breathed his smell deep into her lungs. She could feel a stirring inside, needing him, wanting him, running her hands down his arms that wrapped around her, sliding her hands up the front of his T-shirt. 'I've been thinking about this all day too.' Her fingers hooking into the waist of his shorts.

Marco picked her up, his arms under hers, walking over to the kitchen, placing her down on the bench top and stood between her spread legs, still holding her, still kissing her.

Eve lifted his T-shirt over his head, Marco against her, he pulled her dress off and tossed it to the floor. He went straight for the clip on her bra letting her magnificent boobs fall to him as she reached up around his neck again, making him hard instantly. Kissing like they had longed to kiss each other all day, their lips sucking at each other, their hands exploring their bare skin as their hearts raced. Marco's hands finding Eve's knickers, peeling them down under her arse, then down her slender legs. Before she could reach for his pants, he was pulling them down his thighs, their mouths still connected and their hands still exploring each other. He pulled her hips to his, Eve halting for a moment, her eyes in a sexual daze.

'Patty's watching,' Eve said breathy.

'It's okay, he won't tell anyone we had sex on the kitchen bench,' Marco's soft moist lips mouthed to hers as he cupped her large soft pillowing boobs. His hands held one each as he gently thumbed over her nipples back and forth driving her crazy. His cock once again eager for her wet pussy, she was pulsing for him to be inside her. Eve craved Marco inside her all the time, it was like having a sexual illness where all she could think about, was the magnificent sensation of him stretching her pussy open wide.

Clinging to his body as he pressed inside her, Eve gasped. Still sitting on the edge of the stone benchtop. Marco's hardness entering her warm flesh, taking her breath away on entry. Their bodies so different in size and yet it worked so well... it felt so right and so good, that neither ever acknowledged the vertical challenge whilst having sex.

Marco lifted Eve off the bench and held her in his arms, still inside her, he walked to the small hallway that connected the kitchen to the laundry room. Pressing Eve high up against the wall he thrusted into her, ravishing her, pumping frantically, getting as much of her as he possibly could. Eve was like an addicted, the more he fucked her, the more he wanted her tight dripping pussy around his throbbing cock.

Pushing back on the door frame with her foot, the traction was giving Marco a better angel, pinning her hard and strong with every thrust, her back slid up and down the wall as she hung onto his strong shoulders.

Eve Frank was the most beautiful woman he'd ever been with; her beauty and sweetness was undeniably out there for the world to see. She was breathtaking. 'I love fucking you Evie.' Marco groaned as he pounded her.

'Don't stop. Don't drop me,' Eve begged taking his powerful penetration. Long dark curls jolting about her body as he watched her face wince with ecstasy, she was nearly there, and he wasn't letting her go lightly, he was fucking her hard, right to the end.

Eve had one arm around Marco's shoulders and the other his neck, his cock alone was more than enough to keep her pined to the wall. It was like waves of peaking sexual emotions flooding through her veins. Fucking Marco was always a challenge due his large appendage, she loved that one minute she was on the edge of cumming, the next she was in the most pleasurable erotic pain of her life… all the while Pat the dog laid in the doorway watching on.

Marco took one of Eve's hands in his and held it at to the side of her head, she rolled her head from one side to the other moaning, almost whimpering. Eve was orgasming hard, and he could feel the tightening pulses, he knew she was in the thick of things. But he couldn't help but dig deeper inside her belly until he felt a surge of cum shoot out into her. Nailing her, squeezed her hand and pressed his body to Eve's as they both came.

'Marco!' she managed to gasp his name in her sexual euphoric coma.

'Eve Frank, I've missed you.' He nuzzled into the side of her head.

'I've missed you more.' She let herself enjoy this perfect moment.

'You're still the same gorgeous, beautiful Evie.' Marco was having his own moment. He wrapped her in his safe arms and placed her down to the floor so she could stand up, her legs like jelly.

Marco got tissues from the kitchen to clean themselves up with, Eve retrieved her dress, bra, and knickers from the kitchen floor. 'Don't you think it's freaky we found each other again?' Eve asked him.

'Very!' said Marco with a smile.

Eve watching him, feeling an overwhelming surge of gratefulness. Not only did she adore him for the extraordinary man he was and always had been, but their sex was always nothing short of mind blowing, it was natural sex, neither had to try too hard, the magic simply just happened. Eve picked up Marco's shorts and his T-shirt for him, she'd noticed he wasn't overly tidy, she could let it go… after all it was Marco.

He stood comfortably naked on the other side of the island bench from her. Taking his time, he looked down at the girl from up the hill, he'd let her go once, and here she was again in his life, it really was freaky. Marco had watched Eve from a distance all these years, regretfully. 'I'm in love with you Eve Frank,' he just came out and said it as they stood on opposite sides of the bench.

She looked at him, no smile. He was serious. *Did she hear him correctly... was she dreaming?* The world stood still as his words settled with her. After all these years, he finally loved her!

'I've always been in love with you Marco Rossi,' Eve told him in their perfect moment.

They'd taken a shower together and made love again, before heading off on their walk. Slowly walking along the shaded street hand in hand, Pat the dog on the lead, with Marco not displaying great leadsman-ship, and Pat constantly walking to Eve's side as they enjoyed the afternoon. The coffee shop Marco wanted to take Eve to was a corner shop hidden down a street not too far away, it had tables and chairs outside with umbrellas and pots of flowers... a little French, Eve thought. A nice quiet serene feel that instantly relaxed her.

'Hi Marco,' said the cute little blonde waitress from the door as he and Eve sat at an outside table. 'I'll be right with you.'

'Thanks Josie,' Marco replied politely, then he reached for Eve's hands across the table. 'I really hope you like the carrot cake here because this is my favourite coffee shop, I'm here nearly every day.'

He'd had rosy cheeks and a glow from their sex, he was so goddamn handsome, Eve thought as she stared across at him, her heart was full. Looking into his gentle eyes, she knew right then, it was always meant to be Marco... he appreciated how much she loved her carrot cake; and to Eve it was the simple little things that meant the most... oh, and the fact that he'd just taken her to another level sexually. The intimate sexual connection she'd just experienced with him, was something knew, deeper, stronger, it was nothing short of spectacular.

Marco ordered Eve a big slice of cake and two coffees. The café was full of people out enjoying the sunny afternoon, every table had a dog under it, and Marco was clearly a regular, every second person went out of their way to hello and pat him on the back as they passed like they all knew him well... even Pat the dog seemed popular with the locals, pats coming his way left right and center. The whole vibe was rather fascinating for Eve. Marco and Pat were low-key celebrities, Eve was seeing things in different light here in him Melbourne. *Was it a football thing or a neighbourhood thing?* It was like this strange little community of friendly coffee and dog loving people. Everyone was vibrant and happy, Eve understood why this was Marco's favorite coffee shop. It felt welcoming and comfortable, and it was called Old Friends, which seemed just perfect for the two of them.

If there was an award for fantastic carrot cake, this was it. Eve went as far as saying it was possibly the best carrot cake she had ever eaten. They sat in the afternoon sun for a long time, talking about their families and how they functioned or misfunctioned. Whilst Eve's family was very difunctional on a massive scale, Marco's was normal and very together, besides Nick of course. They had two parents who loved each other, four siblings who were good people, besides Nick being a little crazy... but even he was a loving brother and son most of the time, and he had begun to mature and change his ways, so it seemed.

'I'd like a big family like mine someday, how about you, how many kids do you want Eve Frank?'

That one snuck up on her, she wasn't ready! 'Um, I don't know.' Quick to brush it off, slightly flustered.

'What, two, three – four?' Marco took it all in his stride, leaning back in his seat, very relaxed. Still glowing.

Did he really want an answer from her? Eve felt her heart start racing. 'I don't have a particular number in mind,' she thought a smile would cover her distress.

As they got ready to go out to dinner, Eve looked Marco straight in the eye. 'I've got to tell you something.' She shocked herself with her sudden confession. Since their declarations of love earlier in the day, she hadn't stopped feeling guilty about her secret. Now was the time, it had to be done. But courage failed her... 'It's about my dad really, not me.' A last-minute changed of course. 'There's only one other person in the world who knows what I'm about to tell you, besides my dad.' She took a deep breath of relief. 'You're probably not going to like who it is, but I need you to know I didn't tell him, Evan did, so technically I had nothing to do with him finding out.'

Oh, fuck, she was going from bad to worse rapidly and she felt like she was rambling on, but she needed to get this secret off her chest too. Marco stopped getting dressed and looked at her. 'It's personal and I've kept it to myself for a long time.' Rattled by her blundering she bit down on her lip. 'Evan knew this information before I did, but he didn't know how to tell me, so he told Ferez.' Eve almost cowered just mentioning his name, but she had to continue. 'Ferez is the only person who knows.' She repeated, waiting for Marco's reaction.

'Okay, so Ferez knows. Are you going to tell me?' Marco was trying to follow, he didn't know why he was so jealous of Ferez, he didn't even know the guy. It must have been the kiss and the photo still fresh in his mind.

'Not even the girls know. Nobody knows.' Slightly offended that Marco wasn't getting the magnitude of it.

'Accept your dad, Ferez and Evan,' he frowned sarcastically, 'That's not really a secret Eve Frank.' He had no idea what Eve was on about, she was unpredictable at the best of times, this could be anything, Marco thought.

'It's not really a joke,' she wanting him to take her seriously.

'I'm sorry,' he sighed, trying to keep it jovial.

'My birth mother was a sixteen-year-old prostitute.' *Did it sound worse than it actually was?* Eve waited for his reaction. Marco just stood there looking a little shocked. 'She worked for Evan's dad at one of his brothels. And Evan lost his virginity to her.' *What a fucking debacle of a story!* But if she was going to tell it, she had to tell it in its entirety. 'Are you okay?' Eve asked nervously as she ran her hands down Marco's arms like she was talking about his family. He looked confused, yet he didn't batter an eyelid. She knew it was a lot to take in, especially right before they were going out.

'Fuck!' He managed. Not sure if he had heard right.

'It gets a bit worse.'

'Really? How can it get worse? Your dad slept with a sixteen-year-old prostitute who is apparently your mum, and Evan slept with her too if I understood right… how did you find all this out?' Marco had the story right but sounded confused still. Very confused.

'My birth certificate was in Evan's safe, I found it after he died,' she sounded regretful for saying his name, like she'd done something wrong. 'Among other things. You see, it turns out my birth mother, is also my dad's current girlfriend. His mistress. The woman he left my mum Anna for. She's the mother of my twin sisters too.'

'How did you find out she was a prostitute and that she slept with Evan?' Marco was trying to take it all in, as horrified as he was, he moved closer to Eve and put a gentle hand to her side.

'Evan and I ran into my dad and his then mistress, Sam, in a restaurant. She said hello to Evan, and I questioned him. I wanted to know how he knew her, I wanted to know who she was – because she was with my dad and these two little girls,' emotion from the reflecting memory apparent in Eve's tone. 'Evan told me about his past with Sam and how he knew her. Which all made sense... it explained why my dad hated him so much.' Eve had spent a lot of money on therapy, comprehending it all. 'After that night, Evan obviously did a little investigation of his own, I guess he suspected something, because he knew the past my dad had with this woman, and he knew I'd found out that Anna wasn't my biological mother. He put two and two together and go my birth certificate somehow.' She stood still blinking at Marco as he consumed her every word, she'd told him about the entire saga in a under two minutes, it was everything she knew.

A knock at the bedroom door startled them as they dressed. 'Are you two going to be ready for dinner soon?' it was Zach on the other side of the door.

'Yeah. We'll be down soon,' Marco dismissed him. 'Fuck Evie. That's some big shit to keep all to yourself.' He put his hand to her chin, his eyes sympathetic.

She sighed, 'One of my sisters is sick. She's just been diagnosed with leukemia.'

Marco's face lost its curiosity and seemed somber. 'I'm sorry, that's awful.' He was still comprehending everything Eve had told him. 'So, you're telling me you've only seen your sisters once. What about the mistress girlfriend, slash biological mother?'

'I saw her at Evan's funeral from a distance. My dad and I only ever meet alone, we don't talk about his other family,' Eve referred to them as her fathers' other family, she'd unconsciously removed herself as family.

'What do you know about her?' Marco asked now very curious.

'Her name is Sam. Short for Samandra. She's Sri Lankan and she was basically a young sex worker who had me when she was sixteen… and she named me Amanda.'

'Amanda!' Marco was bewildered, 'How did you end up with your dad and Anna?' he was enthralled. 'I can cancel dinner with Zach and Brooke.' Marco wanted to give this the time it warranted.

'No, I want to go to dinner,' Eve smiled. It was like a ton of bricks had been lifted from her just talking to Marco about her real family situation.

'Okay, so you ended up with your dad and Anna?' Marco immediate went back to the story.

'Apparently my dad gave her money to sort it out… you know to have an abortion, but she didn't … and well here I am,' Eve said very matter of fact, 'She gave me to my dad when I was three weeks old.' An awkward smile adorned Eve's face, Marco could see right through her, he could see the hurt in her eyes. 'Anna doesn't know that I know about Sam, and for now I'd like to keep that way,' Eve said. Since finding out her sister was sick, it had been on her mind a lot, she needed to tell someone, and she trusted Marco.

'Fuck!' he sighed understandingly, 'You're a tough little thing, aren't you Eve Frank?' He stroked her hair out of her face and looked deep into her eyes. He felt hurt for Eve. That must have been a horrible thing to learn about yourself, and to hold it in all this time. To Marco it seemed so scandalous and inappropriately provocative, it had the making of a good book he thought, he was rather perplexed by it all. 'Thank you for telling me. And your secret is safe with me.'

The two couples sat at a table with a quaint little table lamp, the kind you find in New York or Paris, Eve loved them. They were tucked away in the corner of a small local restaurant. Zach and Brooke tried not to bombard Eve with questions before turning to tales of Marco and his famous routines and house rules… all of which Eve found amusing, some she had heard before, like the no sleepovers the night before a game. There was absolutely no breaking of the routine or rules, never. Which made her wonder what he'd do with her if they continued this thing of theirs into his footy season. Playing down the extent of his rules and regs, Marco did his best to assure Eve that his house mates were over exaggerating. All the while he sat close to her, his chair butted up against hers, his arm around her as to keep her safe.

He felt particularly protective now that he knew her secret. He had no idea there was more to come!

Chapter Fifteen

Eve got through the next two days with Marco at training by adventuring and getting out and about, she loved that the beach was a short walk away. The beach particularly made her feel good. The sea was like a meditation tool, she sat alone for a long time on Thursday afternoon just soaking it all in on the bluestone wall that ran along the beach. She chatted on the phone to Jackie as she sat, she was now back home in Sydney and eager to see how Eve and Marco were progressing. Jackie stressed to Eve again that she needed to tell Marco about the baby. Pointing out that the longer she let it go, the worse it would be for Marco. Now the pressure was on, her trust that Jackie wouldn't say anything was dwindling. They talked about Marco's house and Jackie and her upcoming dinner party, how Anna was attending, how Tessa was doing. Jackie questioned Eve on Nick and Zoe, nothing got past her... she knew something was going on and of course Eve didn't have anything to tell.

Strolling home from the beach, feeling concerned about telling Marco her next big secret; she couldn't help feeling angst about his reaction, wondering if she'd be heading back to France sooner than she thought.

Would he understand, or would he be hurt that she hadn't told him her biggest secret of all!

Arrived back at Marco's house, he was in the living room with Zach planning the weekend of camping, something Eve wasn't looking forward to, but would gladly do just to be with Marco.

'We're leaving around three tomorrow,' Marco told Eve with a tad of excitement, 'So, you'll need to pack a bag for the weekend, nothing fancy, we're camping in the bush remember... it's rugged, there's no toilet, but you'll love it.' He smiled like it was going to be fun.

All Eve heard was no toilet, she was still in a daydream over telling Marco about the secret.

'Or you'll hate it,' Zach teased, seeing the horror on Eve's face.

That was more like it! she thought to herself. With the pressure mounting, Eve couldn't see how she was going to enjoy anything until she told Marco about their baby. Camping was making her anxious, she had to tell him before she threw up.

'We love a camp virgin,' Zach continued to stir Eve up, 'You can expect a lot of practical jokes coming your way, fake spiders in your sleeping bag, bad food, bush showers.' He was enjoying it, there was something about having Eve around that he liked. Perhaps it was the memories they'd made up in Palm Cove that year when they'd all got to know each other so well.

Taking it upon herself to cook dinner for Marco, Zach and Brooke, Eve watched as they each marveled at her cooking. Three big plates with food in the center of the dining table. One with fresh green vegetables cooked the way her grandmother taught her with garlic and butter, another with roasted potatoes and pumpkin, and another with her homemade beef wellington from scratch... which was the most impressive part of the meal, Eve had excelled.

'Where on earth did you learn to cook like this?' Brooke asked with a mouth full of baked potatoes. She wasn't any good at cooking and didn't really care for it.

'I took cooking classes in Sydney years ago instead of going to Uni,' Eve smiled humorously, 'And then in France my grandmother and I cooked all the time together.' It was a combination of influences for Eve.

'Well, you can cook for us anytime, morning, noon, or night. Good food is always welcome in this house,' Zach said piling his plate with food.

'Oh, my god, Marco. You definitely need to keep her,' Brooke said with a mouth full of food, looking at Marco as they all kept eating. He winked at Eve who he could tell was happy, although she had been a little quiet.

'I'm trying.' His gaze across the table to Eve. She wanted to take him upstairs and make passionate insane love to him. Most of the time all it took was a look from Marco to stir her juices.

Eve went back to the shops at the end of street early Friday morning after the boys headed off to a morning training session. Brooke had the day off, so she join Eve on her shop for camp clothing. Eve had nothing whatsoever she wanted to wear on a camping weekend, she didn't do camping. Brooke mentioned that all her things would come home smelling of campfire. No, no, no… Eve definitely didn't have that sort of clothing. A quick shop at Country Road for some basic camp wear was needed.

Five T-shirts, three jumpers, jeans, track pants, two shorts, two casual shoes and a dress later, and Eve was all set. Swimwear apparently would be needed according to Brooke, there was a lake and that involved boating and swimming, which kind of sounded like fun to Eve. Not the camping though!

Brooke watched on as Eve picked up item after item without even looking at the price tags, clearly Country Road was Eve's Kmart! Everything Brook had seen Eve wear to this point had been designer, so this shouldn't have been a surprise, Eve clearly wasn't your average gal!

'You do know we're only going for two nights, right?' Brooke said as Eve's pile of clothing and accessories grew on the counter by the minute.

'Yes,' Eve rolled her lips in thought, 'I'm an over packer by nature.'

'I can see that,' Brooke laughed looking on in amazement at the girl who had turned up at their house with Louis Vuitton luggage and a jet setter reputation. Brooke tried to take Eve on face value despite her excessive and somewhat thoughtless shopping spree… she had clearly pussy whipped Marco beyond belief and in saying that Brooke like Eve very much so far, she was lovely and cute, her cooking was out of this world, and she had fabulous clothes!

The cars were packed, and they were on their way for a weekend of camping. Eve had packed two extra-large Louis Vuitton overnight bags which made the others laugh. The weekend was going to be good weather; Brooke had warned her the evenings got cold, that was where the confusion set in and Eve over did the camp shopping, she needed to have all bases covered, she also liked to have options.

The three- and a half-hour drive east of Melbourne to the camp destination was underway and Eve was comfortable with Pat the dog in the back seat and Marco behind the wheel of his four-wheel drive. Brooke and Zach were driving up with

Trent and Jules, another footballer, and his partner. Then there was another two couple's and two more guys from Marco's team also joining them.

Not from a nasty place, but Eve was glad to be free of Brooke and Zach for the drive, she was glad it was just her and Marco. Maybe she would pluck up the courage to tell him. *Maybe she wouldn't!*

'I was going to string you out, but I think it's best I put you out of your misery now,' said Marco smiling as he glanced at Eve, 'You're anxious about camping I can tell, you're very quiet and I know you're not a camper Eve Frank,' he said about an hour into the drive down the freeway.

'How can you tell?' she joked with a smile.

'So, the place we are going to is private property on Lake Glenmaggie.' That was how he started.

'What kind of private property?'

'I'm hoping you love it… right on the lake, there's a lot of trees and privacy.'

'Whose property is it, are we allowed to camp there?' Eve was curious.

'It belongs to me and Zach, we bought the land a few years ago.' He looked quickly at Eve to get her reaction.

'Wow. I can't wait to get there.' Now she had no choice but to sound enthusiastic.

'It's our own little piece of paradise. Somewhere we can get away from things and have privacy and good times without worrying about anything. The best part is that there's a little shack on the property, you're not actually camping, and there's a toilet,' Marco laughed; he had a spark in his voice like he really loved this place. 'We're only ten minutes from a supermarket… and there's even a pub.' That seemed to be the clincher for Marco.

'Sound great,' Eve wasn't sure she'd be up for a shack either, but it was better than a tent.

Two hours later and after several conversation, Marco turned onto a dirt road; He drove slowly as they continued down a winding road, she could see the lake beyond the trees. It was sunset as Marco pulled off the dirt road and into the property. The car pulled up and Marco looked at Eve.

'This is it, we're here,' he said with such pride as Pat the dog jumped around; he knew where he was. Marco got straight out of the car and let Pat out the back seat.

Eve emerged slowly from the car and stood looking at the long house that ran parallel to the lake. It was stylish and modern, very Hollywood Hills sixties type of thing… and most certainly not a shack! A low roof line, elongated, bold stone and cement walls. The house blew Eve away, it was very architectural with modern elements yet so very lake house-ish as it sat among the gum trees beside the lake.

'Wow, this is really amazing!' her soft surprised voice had a slight chuckle as she stood realising there was really no camping. The house was awesome. Thank goodness.

Winking at her, 'You can still sleep in a tent if you want. I, however, will be sleeping in my very comfy bed, with great bed linen, I think you'll approve,' he joked wrapping his arm around her shoulders and pulling her into his embrace.

'You had me thinking I was camping for days. That was a terrible trick,' gushed Eve.

'It was Zach's idea,' Marco blamed Zach who had thought it was great to see Eve fretting about sleeping out in the bush, worrying about bugs and how she would go to the toilet. 'Come on, we don't have much time before everyone arrives, I want to show you around without the circus here.' That left her wondering as Marco called out to Pat who had raced off into the trees. *Who was the circus!*

'This place is really beautiful Marco Rossi,' Eve said as she followed him around the back of the house to the lake, a huge deck ran the length of the house. It looked out over the lake, and had lounges and tables, a built-in fire pit and even a big BBQ kitchen. The orange sun lit up the lake as she looked across the water to see a boat slowly skimming over the water and houses in the distant, very remote, very secluded.

'I want to show you something.' He took her hand and lead her down to the jetty to a shed over the water, a boat inside. Eve wasn't a boat expert, but it looked good. Marco began to take the cover off as she watched on from the jetty at the side. He was like a child with a toy, a very sexy grown-up man child. Before she knew it, he was in the boat with his hand out to her.

'Come in.' Literally, he pulled her into his embrace and began kissing her with a surprise of passion. The panicked scramble to pull Marco's pants down to his thighs was feverish and desperate on Eve's behalf. No time for blow jobs, it was a ten second luscious suck at the end of his cock, before he had her pants off. In the fading light of day, they clung to each other… Marco sitting on the bench seat at the back of the boat as Eve straddled him, rubbed her hips to his super ready cock. It was a race to the finish line, a sudden sexual frenzy of sorts.

'That's it.. oh, baby,' he was panting, 'Fuck me, I love this fuckin boat.' With a scrunched-up face, Marco was cumming, it was hard, fast, and excruciatingly awesome. His hands pulled Eve's shoulders down to him so she would feel him throbbing as he came inside her. Hoping she could feel how much he loved fucking her, so she could feel what she did to him. Marco had cum in record time, it was literally no more than a minute of grinding sex and he'd cum.

Eve's mouth open, she felt the warm tingle of her blood rushing to her clit. Her orgasm met Marco's, breathy, yet silent as she let the sexual rush take her. It felt like nothing was off limits, sexually that was, they were getting closer and closer, all that was between them now, was the secret!

'When I said I loved you yesterday, I meant it Evie,' Marco said laying his cards on the table, knowing Eve was serious and genuine about being with him. Not like some of the girls from his past who had perhaps had other intentions, and they had nothing to do with his heart… only his status. His nice-guy persona wasn't always what women had expected of him, he wasn't the hard rugged guy deep down who treated women mean to keep them keen, it felt like that was what most women wanted from him. They wanted him to be an asshole, which lead him to believe he was hooking up with the wrong kind of women over and over. Until now.

No reply from Eve, she sat on Marco, him still inside her body, she rubbed herself over what was left of his hard on, getting one last rush as her climax came to an end. Something stupid went through her head… *what if this was the last time he made her feel this way? What if she told him about the baby, and it was all over?*

'You are by far the most seductive and sexiest woman I've ever known. You always have been.' Marco kissed her. 'I bet you've heard that before.'

'No.' *Liar…* she had heard it a million times before, but she preferred to not think about how Evan had whispered it to her as they made love. *Block it out, NOW!*

'I know that's not true.' Marco kissed her mouth gently, still recovering from his orgasm.

Just accept the compliment! Eve told herself as a mound of emotion flooded her.

Marco saw her emotion and gave her a small soft kiss to her lips. 'It wasn't supposed to upset you, I'm sorry.'

'I'm not upset,' she lied to his beautiful face... *God, she felt like the luckiest girl in the world.* 'It's just the fact that you said it, that makes it very special,' her emotional smile eased him. Marco melted her from the inside out. *How could she ever risk losing him?*

The house had been built around a year ago, inside it was very Scandi which made for a great lake house. A lot of thought had been put into the layout and styling. A large L shaped sofa, a long light timber dining table with bench seats, a sleek fireplace, and a huge galley kitchen that Eve couldn't wait to cook in... all looking out over the deck and the lake. To either side of the main living area, two master bedrooms with private bathrooms, one side for Brooke and Zach and one for Marco. To the back of the house were more bedrooms and another two bathroom. The house was the perfect getaway to share with all their friends who were starting to arrive.

Trent, who Eve had briefly met in London at the music festival, came with his girlfriend Jules, they'd driven to the lake with Zach and Brooke. Jules was a smallish blonde, very attractive, skin and bones with possible fake boobs and lips... she seemed nice at this point, regardless, Eve thought on their introduction. Trent on the other hand was a man mountain, solid and tall, dark, and handsome... he towered over Jules. Full of life when he wasn't being bossed around by Jules... funny enough! They were a glamour couple from what Eve could tell.

'The girl from London... it's good to see you. How are you?' Trent said giving Eve the once over in a blink of an eye, Marco watching him with a grin on his face.

'I'm good. Nice to see you again too,' she said as he gave her a kiss on both cheeks, then promptly went about complaining how Jules was pissing him off already, she quickly snapped him into line ordering him to take their bags to their room.

'I'm snagging the room with the view of the lake,' Jules said gathering her things and following Trent.

'Is Louise coming with Tommo? Are they even back together?' Zack said as they all stood around.

'They're coming together. I don't know how together they are though, and it's not really out business,' Brooke answered with a concerned look on her face. Literally a second later in came a group of people, and for Eve, a very welcomed familiar face. Rory, who made a beeline straight for her, making a big commotion as he bear hugged her and lifted her feet off the floor like they were long lost siblings.

'Here she is, finally!' Rory swing Eve around. 'I bet the big guys happy now that you're here.'

'I sure hope so, I've come halfway around the world to see him.' Eve hugged him back, it was a mutual joy, it felt like no time had passed at all, the connection was instant. The others all looked on waiting for their introductions while Rory and Eve reacquainted.

Marco stepped in putting an arm at Eve's waist in a territorial fashion, 'Eve, this is Tommo and Louise, Jack, and his wife Ro. And these two troublemakers are Taylor and Joel, or Pooja and Nuts.' Eve shook hands with everyone. 'Rory wasn't actually invited; he just came because he wanted to see you,' Marco teased.

'I'm glad, I need all the familiar faces I can get,' she said gravitating closer to Rory again.

'It's great to meet you Eve,' Louise said stepping forward, a taller brunette with blonde streaks... Eve liked her on site, she looked non-confrontational and organic although apparently she was amidst a marriage crisis.

'I'm Ro.' This one definitely looked confrontational. Eve was going to be cautious, purely on first impressions alone. Her eyes pierced right through Eve as she introduced herself with what seemed like a snide fake smile.

Eve reminded herself to not judge a book by its cover! 'Hi, it's really nice to meet you both.' She was her usual polite and friendly self.

The girls seemed all very consumed with Marco's new female friend. The rumors were rife!

Within half an hour they were barbequing on the deck, as Zach cooked the barbeque, they all sat around the large outdoor table drinking enjoying life. It was obvious everyone was checking Eve out, the guys asking her the obvious questions, whilst the girls were conducting an unofficial interrogation of sorts. Brooke listening intently, she knew all about Eve, Zach hadn't left many details out… so she felt a little protective. Marco was at Eve's side also keeping watch on the Q and A session that was in session, he knew how these girls operated, and he didn't want anyone getting to personal or stepping over the line.

Ro was the one who Eve could feel watching her intently, she hadn't taken her eyes off her since arriving. Eve wasn't sure how to take her, Ro seemed tough, in a hot way, almost captivatingly scary… alarm bells for Eve.

'You're so small to compared to Marco,' was Ro's first comment to Eve, getting off on the wrong foot immediately. *Rude!* It rubbed Eve up the wrong way right there and then. 'Exactly how long have you two known each other?' Ro questioned both Eve and Marco as everyone listened in.

Marco stepped straight in, 'Eve's my sisters' best friend. I've known her since she was ten,' he felt it was his place to answer. Ro was a piranha waiting to tear Eve apart, Marco could see it coming.

'So how old where you back then Marco?' Ro seemed overly interested in their past. *Still Rude.*

'I don't know, fifteen,' he said coolly.

'So then, how old were you when you two got together Eve, like sexually? Twelve!' Ro laughed.

Eve just stared at her, letting her know just how fucking rude she really thought she was. This awful person was annoyingly curious. Eve could see Zach out of the corner of her eye, he wasn't laughing either.

Again, Marco answered, 'I was twenty-two, Eve was seventeen if you need the details Ro!' He knew exactly what she was doing, everyone did.

Ro's eyes widened as she looked at him, 'Marco, that was probably illegal,' she sighed dramatically, only getting a small crowd reaction.

'It wasn't illegal Ro,' he dismissed her whilst Eve was dumb founded at the boldness of this nasty girl.

'Why don't we leave them alone,' Brooke said loudly, seeing Marco was a little pissed and she felt sorry for Eve, who had been under the microscope from the minute everyone arrived. She was new and the interest was avid, everyone wanted to know who this exotic little chick was, and what her deal was.

The truce didn't last long though, after being quiet for a sometime and disappearing inside for some time, Ro came back out armed with ammunition this time.

'Have you been married before Eve?' Ro asked like she was genuinely interested in Eve.

'Rowena!' her husband Jack huffed; she had stepped over the line again. Another moment of silence.

What the fuck! Eve could feel Marco tense beside her. She watched Zach pull a face at Ro, like she was an idiot. Eve was instantly guarded.

'Fuck Ro. Do you want to know her menstrual cycle too... Eve can you tell her the last time you bled please,' Brooke snapped giving Ro a filthy look intended as a warning to lay off Eve.

'I thought I heard somewhere that you were married to some-'

Eve cut Ro off, it was time she defended herself, 'No. I've never been married,' she said with her own warning in her tone. She wondered who the fuck this person was, and why was she so interested in her. She had the strangest feeling that Ro had just been inside googling her, she felt her heart begin to race.

Marco was furious, he and Ro had never seen eye to eye, not from day dot. She was a player before she got her hooks into his teammate Jack. The fact that Ro was so inquisitive towards Eve pissed him off big time. *Who the hell did she think she was?*

'I thought you were married to some underworld guy that's all,' Ro couldn't help herself.

'That's enough Ro,' Marco snapped, his voice non-threatening although he wanted to slap her face. At the same time, he didn't want to make out like Eve had something to hide either.

Being the bigger person, Eve let Ro's behavior slide although she didn't appreciate the questions.

Once the difficult dinner was over, Marco took Eve aside into the bedroom in private, so he could touch base with her. He was conscious that Eve had kept to herself most of the night, she'd been really quiet just listening in, this environment was foreign to her although he was very accustomed to it.

'I'm fine,' Eve looked up at him, the minute she spoke, she felt the emotion rush through her body.

'I'm sorry Ro is such a bitch. She's not my favorite person... can you tell?' Marco smiled.

'She's not the first mean girl I've ever had to deal with.' Eve didn't want it to become a thing for Marco. She managed to keep her emotions in check, convincing him she was fine, when actually she was an anxious mess who just wanted to be alone. All she could think was how out of place she felt here with these people, and how she needed to tell Marco about their baby.

Later out by the fire, Eve sat on Marco's lap as they circled the fire talking and laughing in one big group. The boys had their own little conversation going on to one side and the girls to the other. Marco and Eve seemed so at ease with one another, so natural and comfortable, it was hard not to notice.

'Eve I'm really sorry if I offended you before,' Ro decided she would give Eve an attempted apology. Rory, Brooke, and Zach had told her how out of line she had been, and how furious Marco would be with her.

'That's fine.' Eve said, not giving Ro much, not even looking at her.

'I knew I had heard something about you, I didn't realise,' Ro said as Jules and Brooke looked on.

In her slow and quiet tone, Eve turned to Ro, 'You didn't realize what? How do you even know who I am?' Narrowing her eyes; she wasn't letting Ro get away with it again. Ro clearly had something to say, it was better if she did it now so they both knew were they stood, Eve felt.

'I didn't realise your fiancé was murdered,' Ro tried to fake sympathy, 'My apologies. You seem so sweet to be involved with such brutality.'

Who was with this fucking bitch! thought Eve, not really knowing what she should do or say next.

Marco's ears pricked up; he had been trying to listen to two conversations.

'Oh, fuck it, Ro. Give her a break will you, let it go.' Brooke beat Marco to it, she was well aware that Ro would have made it her business to know who Eve was, so in effect she was asking questions she knew would press Eve's buttons, she was testing Eve.

'I'm just interested,' Ro scoffed like she was being persecuted.

Then Marco butted in out of sheer temper, 'Well don't be Ro,' he snapped loudly with anger in his eyes looking straight at Ro and then to Jack. Eve at his lap as his arms went out to the handles like he was going to jump up. Because this outburst was way out of character for Marco, it had everyone's attention. Eve rubbing her hands at the sides of his thighs to ease him. Zach could tell Eve was rattled, and he could tell Marco was livid.

The night went on into the early hours of the morning, the tension with Ro had subsided and everyone was telling stories and jokes, with Eve and Marco ignoring Ro. Eve was learning a lot about how the groups dynamics functioned, all these people were overwhelming but interesting. Zach was the football clubs vice-captain under Marco. Tommy and Jack were both regarded as senior players. The very quiet, and somewhat intriguing looking Taylor was a younger player in the team while Rory and Joel played for a different team all together, she thought that was how it went anyway. Brooke was the designated DJ and played a lot of random music that Eve wasn't familiar with. Eve stayed with Marco while the other girls had stints of dancing and disappearing inside. She wasn't there yet, she needed to observe, to take it all in, and figure out who was who.

Eve and Marco had called it a night first, not surprisingly, and as they got ready to get into bed, they heard a knock at the door. Marco opened the door in his underwear, it was Brooke and Zach.

'We just wanted to make sure you were okay,' Brooke said to Eve who stood with her toothbrush in her mouth in a T-shirt and undies. Brooke didn't know Eve that well, but she knew she'd had a rough night.

Brooke was growing on Eve; she'd had her back tonight, and it held a lot of weight with Eve. 'I'm fine, thank you.' Her toothpaste smile was cute. *'I'm fine'* was her go to answer.

Brooke was relieved, 'Good. Ro can be a stupid fucking mole sometimes. I'm sorry she targeted you, but I did kind of expect it. She always harasses new people,' she spoke at a whisper.

'She's lucky I didn't pay out on her, and Jack too,' Marco wasn't whispering.

'She'll behave herself now.' Brooke knew Ro well enough to know how she operated. Deep down she wasn't an overly bad person, however she did have a bad habit of getting all up in Marco's grill at any given chance.

'She better or she can go home,' he said with a gruff.

'Okay… we just wanted to make sure you were all right Evie, good night guys,' Zach went to the door.

'Good night Eve, I'm glad you're okay,' Brooke said giving Eve a hug.

'Thank you, Brooke,' Eve hugged her back. She'd dealt with jealous sex workers and strippers fucking Evan, Ro was going to be a walk in the park.

Standing outside the shower, Eve undressed as Marco stood with the hot water running over his head watching her, his arms crossed, his eyes inspected every part of her voluptuous body, she was small and petite unlike any of his past girlfriends, curvy though, with femininity he found captivating. Eve was the real deal and that was what had been up Ro's nose, Eve didn't have to try to be kind, sexy or good looking, she was naturally all of those things.

It puzzled Eve that Marco hadn't asked about the scar on her stomach, not once. Tonight, she was feeling particularly tender and didn't think it would be the right time to tell him about the baby even though it was making everything totally worse. Ro's treatment had her in a silent spin, every insecurity had come to the surface. Not only did she have the baby secret, but she also had a past that had been documented publicly on TV, in newspapers and on the internet, and it was out there for anyone who wanted to delve into her past.

Was she worthy of Marco? Doubt consumed Eve as she stepped into the shower, immediately greeted by Marco's open arms pulling her into his protective embrace. Her face at his chest, her lips touching his precious warm skin as she breathed him into her soul. Tenderly her hands roamed his body as she felt his growing hardness at her stomach. Looking up as Marco gently gripped her hair at the back of her head, they kissed.

'Are you really okay Eve Frank? They're a tough crowd to crack I know.'

'It'll get better.' She didn't want to sound like a sook.

Lifting her to his body Marco kissed her again. His tongue began to passionately explored hers, with growing enthusiasm as he pressed her against the cold tiles, she gasped and slid down the wall until his knee held her firmly in position, her legs parted, her hands at his chest.

'Well, you were a hit with the guys,' he smiled cheekily, thinking it was amusing.

'Great. Just what I need, the guys to like me, while the girls hate me.'

'Ro's the only mean girl, the rest are great, you'll see,' assuring her, taking his time kissing her and stroking her wet hair away from her face as his knee between her leg moved at her with just enough pressure to make her aroused to his touch.

Eve felt super sensitive as he rubbed against her tenderness, the sensation of his leg between hers was enough to make her want more. Marco's hardness at her stomach, large and warm. Taking her hands in his, he pressed them to the tiled wall at her sides, spreading her arms out as he moved his knee away, bending forward, kissing a trail down her neck and shoulders, then her chest until his lips found her nipple. With strong tantalizing suckling he moved from one to the other as he held her arms out, her legs parted. Invigorating her senses and desires, slowly he moved Eve's hand down between her legs. Marco was bending forward, sucking at her nipples with almost a biting sensation as his sexual intent gained momentum, his fingers guiding hers inside her opening, with a slight forcefulness. Her breaths became a needy whimper as Marco rubbed her hand, her fingers moving inside herself, he touched her clit, stimulating her, coaxing her into a heavy erotic daze. Eve felt the kind of sexual daze that back in the day, was usually the result of a lot of alcohol and drugs... Marco had that effect on her.

Closing her eyes, she let him turn her around, now her palms were flat to the cold tiled wall, her face and chest pressed to it. He was behind her towering over her, the touch of his body close to hers. Marco spread his legs and lowered to her, worked himself softly between her arse checks, then into her tightness. Eve's heart pounding as he lifted one of her legs to him, pulling her body up onto his cock. Her hands holding her weight to the wall as he held her hips. His legs spread wider as so he could enter her arse at the right height. The intensity of anal penetration took her breath away, her body tingling with a strange energy as she accepted Marco into the unfamiliar territory. It had been a long time since Eve had had anal sex! A whimper, the pain of him going deeper inside her was erotic in the oddest of ways. Pulling Eve's hips to him as she tried not to hold her breath at every thrust. How could she deny Marco even though her own enjoyment wasn't quite there... his moans of pleasure and satisfaction willing her on as he fucked her arse like a man on a mission. It seemed men loved arse. Anal sex would always been a mystery to Eve.

As Marco began to move her up and down his large firm manhood, Eve subsided to the pain, relaxing to his penetration. The more she relaxed, the easier it became. The more groaning and moaning, the more intimate it became. Marco moved one hand to Eve's front, his fingers brushing quickly back and forth over her sensitive clit as his other hand continued to push and pull her, and yet somehow Eve managed to stay midair pinned against the wall by Marco's large strong cock. Her panting became a whimper as she felt every inch of Marco sliding in and out. It had turned into an erotic overload of sex... him loving her desperately, in a way that only Marco could, and Eve taking him, as only she could.

Feelings of guilt powered Marco, he felt terrible for what Ro had put Eve through earlier, was an understatement. He'd felt a protectiveness with Eve, that he'd never had for a woman before, he was in love with Eve, no doubt. He had two fingers imbedded inside her cumming pussy, pressing into her so her arse still slid up and down his hard cock. His free hand holding her to him, finding himself completely lost in Eve's sexual intoxication. The water gushing over them as Eve's whimpers became louder cries of sheer pleasure. Something so foreign had become such a sensual act of love between them, connecting them even deeper if possible. Marco's cum shot into her as she hit her own orgasmic peak... hiss fast finger work now dominated her clit. Eve completely resting her body to the cold wall, too weak to hold herself up.

'Come here.' He slid out and adjusted his footing. Turning her around to him, his feet still wide apart, hugging her to his body, Eve wrapping her arms around him in return.

Chapter Sixteen

The scene was almost too much! Eve had stopped breathing just thinking about how much Zoe would love to be here. A buffet of hot male athletic bodies. All topless, only wearing shorts, and all on the deck sweaty and stretching out after a lengthy morning run. They'd made an impressive effort to outdo one another, all were completely exhausted, it was the most steamy and sexiest vision a woman could ask for first thing in the morning. Eve sat quietly and carefully observing each and every one of them… surely the other girls were doing the same, she thought as she sat with her feet up and her knees tucked into her chest. The girls had staggered out of bed one by one over the past hour. Louise and Brooke were clearly not morning people… thankfully, because Eve was taking some time to come around too. Ro was drinking a green juice; she'd made one for everyone, Jules was chatty, but no one was listening.

'Can you get the bacon and the eggs out of the fridge for me Brooke, please?' Zach asked as he rushed by, the pleasantry was missing from his tone, something was wrong with him.

'No,' she said from under a woolen blanket on the opposite end of the sofa to Eve. It wasn't cold. Brooke didn't look well, she looked like she needed to go back to bed.

Eve and Ro automatically getting up and going to the kitchen, Ro was like a different person this morning, Eve was still on guard though, she didn't trust her. Taking out the food from the fridge, Eve didn't say a word as Ro got utensils and oil and paper towel. She stood still and watched Eve do her thing for a minute.

'Will you accept my apology for last night?'

Eve stood up straight and looked right into Ro's eyes, so her words were clear, 'Of course. I'm a very private person Ro.' Eve held her eyes. 'I don't have anything to hide or to be ashamed of. But parts of my life are extremely personal and off limits. I don't talk about them,' Eve was cool and to the point, she said what she had to say without threat. Very Eve like!

'I understand. Please accept my apology.' Ro might have been sincere, and she seemed remorseful, but Eve didn't know her, so how she could be sure. She was sure however, that Ro sensed the angst in the room between Brooke and Zach too. Choosing not to say anything else, Eve felt it was a better to leave Ro hanging, rather than let her think all was forgiven straight away, because it absolutely was not. Eve was mature enough to not let herself put up with mean girls like Ro anymore, there was no way she would play that game again.

Brooke slumped off and disappeared into the bedroom while Zach seemed to have the shits for a good portion of the morning. This seemed like more than just a tiff. Before lunch Brooke surfaced again, she and Zach went into Hayfield to get rolls and salads to feed the hungry masses again… it was never ending with the food. Eve had never met men who ate so much in her life. They ate a lot at breakfast, then they ate a lot again, and then they had a huge lunch, and then they ate more… eating was a consistent part of their day.

After lunch everyone enjoyed an afternoon of boating and lounging on the deck looking out over the beautiful still lake. It was a casual and relaxing vibe, towels and sunlounges scattered all over the deck, girls sunbathing, the guys talking and joking. The sun was beaming down, the temperature was sky high, it was a feast of bikini clad bodies in and out of the lake cooling off. Eve was tempted to take pictures for Zoe, this was so her scene, she was excited for Zoe, and she wasn't even there.

The afternoon was lazy but interesting, as Eve sat on the edge of Marco's boat that was tied to the jetty, she looked around at the different people, immersing herself into his life and his friendship group wasn't going to be easy. She'd never really had a lot of friends or been overly social, whereas Marco was everyone favourite person. This group seemed to know each other well, and Eve was the newcomer who had to find her way. Besides Ro and her rudeness last night, the others were trying to get to know her the right way. To Ro's credit though, she had been nice today, but she had a long way to go to get into Eve's good books. When Eve compared herself to the other girls… which was never a great idea, it was very hard not to given the situation. Her skin was different, her hair was crazier, she was shorter and curvier. She had never felt more different in her entire life, and it was effecting her. Zoe and Tessa had never been any different to her, even though they were both tall and blonde, *they'd fit in well here!* Sure, there were times when Eve had felt like the short hairy friend, but it was only ever for a second, Zoe and Tessa never made Eve feel different.

Late afternoon and everyone headed to the local pub for a bit to eat and a few drinks. It was a low-key eye opener for Eve, one which she rather enjoyed. Marco and the guys were like superstars at the pub, getting pictures taken with locals, everyone knew Marco and Zach, it was like they were locals themselves. They had a good old chat with the publican, the said a quick hello to a neighbour by the bar, it was all very social and country-ish.

Saturday night was a drinking night for the girls, they'd started with wine at the pub and now they were home, they progressed to shots of Sambuca and a made-up cocktail by Louise, which happen to taste great and was going down well. Eve had a little sneaking suspicion that perhaps Ro and Jules may have been powdering their noses in the bathroom too.

Tommo was the one out of the guys who was really letting his hair down, the other guys not so much. He and Louise were dancing to the music, very intimate and all over each other. It looked like they were definitely back together.

'He's drunk again. She would fuck him off if she had any brains,' Jules snarled to Ro who sat beside Eve, she'd been working on Eve progressively all afternoon.

'He's a serial cheater... he drinks a lot too,' Ro whispered quietly filling Eve in discreetly. 'Watch that one, he tries to fuck everyone's girlfriend, wife, mother, whatever. Poor dumb Lou keeps taking him back, but Tommo's a bad egg.'

Eve didn't know what the right response was to such information, she was shocked that they were having such a conversation only meters from Tommo and Louise, and she felt like she perhaps wasn't entitled to know such information about their personal relationship just yet. Eve really liked Louise, she was probably the nicest one of the lot thus far, and Tommo hadn't seemed such a bad guy either.

Jules turned to Eve, 'This here is a vault. You don't repeat anything we say to Marco, it's girls only,' she warned, letting Eve know how it was.

213

'Got it,' Eve nodded, she kind of wished she wasn't in on this conversation, it felt too soon.

Ro leaned into Eve's side again, 'There's a few to look out for. You'll know who they are when they hit on you… and I'm not joking either,' Ro whispered casually, confident that Eve had a fuck boy radar. Most smart women did.

Eve couldn't help but smile, she was getting an education. The more time she spent with these women the more she learned about how things went down. Ro was becoming rather amusing as the night went on, they all liked to talk about each other, and they seemed to be very judgmental and actively vocal about each other's relationships. Eve could only imagine what they were saying about her and Marco when she was out of earshot. She took note, *don't get too close!*

Eve along with the other girls had gone hard once they got back to the house. Brooke was the only one who didn't seem to loosen up the entire day or night, she had decided to go to bed early, and Eve heard Zach tell Marco he didn't know what he wanted; she didn't know what that meant exactly, but it had sounded serious.

'So, what's going on with you two?' Jules asked Marco and Eve in front of the whole group as they sat around the fire pit.

'What do you mean?' Eve smiled as she settled back on Marco laps. Everyone was in on the conversation.

'Are you like, together?' Rory said frowning curiously, as much as he loved having his single friend around, he loved Eve and thought she was good for Marco.

Marco squeezed Eve into his arms, she felt soft and relaxed, 'We're exploring our options. Is that enough?' He couldn't believe the nosiness of these girls… and Rory. *Oh, yes!* actually he could.

'What are the options, do tell?' Jules asked like she was daring him.

'We don't know yet,' Marco didn't like being put on the spot.

'Are you here to stay Eve?' Rory looked at her, he felt like he needed to know, given he'd been at the conception of the relations many years ago back in Palm Cove.

'I'm visiting,' she said thinking about how it could all go to shit when she eventually told Marco about the baby they'd conceived together all those years ago. The alcohol and the fire were making her feel hot.

Nobody knew really what to say. If Marco and Eve weren't sure about what was going on, how could anyone else be. Marco was a little taken back by Eve's *just visiting* remark.

'Well for what it's worth,' Rory said with a cheerful uplifting smile, 'I've seen you two kids together once before, and I think you should definitely be together now. You both look really happy when you're around each other.'

'I agree,' Ro added, 'I think you're a great couple.' That was a lot coming from the girl who was ready to burn Eve at the stake last night! 'You should definitely be together; you can't keep your hands off each other.' The turnabout was welcomed by Eve tonight... *Who needed enemies!*

Sunday morning Marco was awake first, which was no surprise as Eve had been drunk when they went to bed. Jules, Louise, Ro, and Eve had bonded over drinks and some good old fashion late night girl talk.

Marco watched her sleep peacefully beside him; he watched her chest moving in and out and her lips parted ever so slightly, he wanted to kiss them. She was under the covers naked, the sheet rest just over her chest, tempting him to reach out and touch her. Curls of her dark hair in a tangled mess at the side of her head, she sighed as he watched, his mind drifting to that young girl he saw naked for the first time in Palm Cove all those years ago. Eve had been absolutely mind blowing then, and here she was again, naked in his bed, still blowing his mind. *Was it coincidence or was it their destiny?* His hand crept to her chest and touched her soft warm nipple beneath the sheet. Instantly his cock was firming as he ever so lightly pinched her now hardening nipple. He didn't care if she woke, in fact that was the point. Pulling the sheet below her boobs, running his palm over her nipples, his cock was pounding. She didn't wake... just another sigh! Marco curiously looked at her to see if she was reacting to his efforts, he thought perhaps she was pretending. A little more pressure to his soft pinches and rubs, Eve laid asleep while he did this for some time, until the throbbing of his cock became too much, he had to touch himself to stop his urge to cum. The pressure of his own hand was enough to subdue his cumming urge, he went back to Eve and her luscious tits and nipples, tempting pink and chocolate treats that he just had to have more of. Sucking her nipple gently, his eyes glanced up

215

to see if she'd stirred. Her mouth opened to take a breath, obviously rousing as Marco sucked just a little on her hard cherry nipple, his hand wandered slowly under the sheet and down between her legs. Another breath, Eve's head turned to the side as she exhaled, parting her legs as Marco kept sucking, his fingers finding her moist warm clit, tenderly rubbing over her in circular motions. Watching her rouse from her sleep to his touch was like watching an R rated movie. She was even sexy when she slept... Marco's heart was beginning to beat fast as he slowly but firmly pressed his fingers inside Eve's wet pussy. And then she moved. *Was she asleep or not?* He pressed further inside her wet juicy hole... *surely, she was awake now, she had to be*! Eve sighed and Marco's mouth moved from her nipple up to her mouth, kissing her lips ever so gently, their bodies warm and clammy in the morning heat of his bedroom. Marco needed to fuck her with his morning hard on, she was going to wake up whether she liked it or not, it was becoming a matter of urgency, his cock was throbbing for her.

Eve kept her eyes closed and laid still; she had been awake from the minute he first touched her nipple, but she was enjoying his attention, so much she played along. Her mouth moved to Marco's kiss softly as he slipped another finger inside her, she drew a big breath to let him know she was enjoying herself; she wanted him. Putting a hand to his arm as he tucked into her side, she squeezed his forearm as she felt his fingers, deep and somewhat sensually swirling as she breathed heavier to his motions, his mouth kissing hers as she waved her warm tongue to his lips. He sighed a breath to her mouth and plunged his fingers into her melting pussy... Eve was awake! Rolling into his body she pressed her knee to his overwhelmingly large hardness, her hand roamed at his chest and shoulders as she responded and becoming eager for him. Opening her eyes, she found Marco's gaze on her as they kissed. Taking his hand from between her legs, Eve felt her own wetness at her thighs. In her mind, if she pretended to be asleep, it delayed having to tell Marco her secret! It was ever present.

Rolling over her and moved up her body as she kissed his chest with light soft lips, Marco was over her and inside her in seconds. Thrusting to her. In and out with firm slow strides of heated morning desire. Eve ran her hands over his manly body, feeling his strength and want for her, every thrust plunged deeper and deeper. His elbows holding him above her small frame as their bodies entwined together with increasing heat and sweat.

'Evie. I love fucking you without a condom,' Marco's words startled Eve. She was now wide awake. The warmth left her body.

'Why would you say that?' she moaned as her pleasure built.

'Because it feels so fucking good,' he groaned, 'Remember in Palm Cove, we had sex without a condom, and I swear,' his voice actually had elation to it, 'I will never forget how good you felt... you were my first sex without a condom ever,' he huffed an erotic breath into the top of Eve's head.

Her wide eyes looked up to his broad chest, moving over the top of her. All of a sudden she felt empty.

'Don't you remember baby; it was the best sex I'd ever had!' Marco was beyond intoxicated in her sex as he rammed it on home.

Eve faded into the mattress for a moment in her own thoughts. *And why was he calling her baby? Oh fuck! Block it out and finish having sex with this gorgeous man. Focus!* she told herself.

Eve's guttural groan sounded excruciating as Marco thrust deep within her body, rolling her head back into the pillow as she plunged into an intoxication sexual coma. Marco's body was taking her to a place she hadn't been for so long, forgetting what he'd said a second ago as a free loving, unrestrictive wave flushed through her as she felt her wetness at her jelly thighs as he pushed her to her limits. Every time they had sex, Marco pushed her just that little more towards completeness, where a woman loved a man so much, she would do anything to satisfy him, including taking the pain! In her head, Eve tried to think of something unthinkable that she would do to satisfy Marco sexually. It was a game she used to play in her head a long time ago, when she felt like she wasn't enough for Evan. She usually had these thoughts right when she was on the edge of a mammoth orgasm. To satisfy Evan in her head, Eve always imagined there was an audience watching them as they made love... or fucked. She felt she was never quite enough sexually for Evan. But Marco was a different man, a better man. It hurt Eve to think such a thing, but it was true, Marco was perfection even if his cock was too big for her vaginal. It wasn't such a bad thing; their sex was always a challenge... the thought made her smile. Marco's hand came to her head and pushed her abundance of long curls from her face as she sighed with pleasure. It turned her on and preoccupied her mind to think such erotic and peculiar things about sex with Marco. Thoughts of how much she wanted to please him and show him her love. She had fleeting moment of needing all of him, as much as she could possibly take inside her body util he split her wide open.

Eve pushed at his shoulders as they rolled together, she scrambled to the top position without him leaving her body. She sat filled with his hardness inside her petite body. Letting herself fall over Marco until she could feel him all the way up inside her, until he could go no farther, until the agony of him became an erotic pleasure yet again. This was one thing she would do for Marco for *his* ultimate pleasure, even though it felt like she was going to die. This strange carnal self-punishment actually made her orgasm, it was so powerful that Marco felt her clench around his cock so hard it made him cum instantly. His hands squeezing at her abundance of arse. Eve fell forward onto his stomach, her skin sticking with sweat and cum to his.

A sigh, 'I want to lay like this with you forever,' Marco said in a low exhausted voice. Eve was the woman who kept on giving. Just when he thought he'd hit the ultimate sexual high with her... BANG! she blew his balls to smithereens once again!

'I know, me too,' her voice soft as he rolled her over to her side. His cum spilling to her thighs as he pulled away, trickling to the bed sheets as he moved down nestling into her sumptuous body so he could feel her soft breasts at his chest.

She needed to tell Marco about their baby! It was consuming her.

'How do you feel this morning?' he asked, referring to her big night of drinking.

'I feel great,' she smiled making him curious.

'What are we doing Evie, what's going to happen with us?' He had a serious twinkle in his eye.

'What would you like us to do?' her smile gentle and loving as she gazed up into his eyes.

As they looked at each other with meaningful eyes, a knock at the bedroom door interrupted them. It was early, they really didn't expect anyone else in the house to be awake.

'I'm not looking. Sorry. Are you decent?' Ro whispered opened the door and popped her head in. 'I just wanted to say thank you for having us guys... we're heading home early... Jack's sister's idiot husband is turning fucking forty today!' Ro complained. 'It was lovely to meet you Eve, I had a blast last night and I'm looking forward to getting to know you better.' Ro stood unsure where to look, blowing kisses with her hands as she backed out the door.

Jack came to the door to say his goodbyes. 'See ya later big fella. Nice meeting you Evie, see ya soon,' he said.

'We'll have to catch up for dinner,' Ro said before Jack shut their bedroom door.

Marco looked at Eve as if the events of the weekend with Ro had freaked him out. Eventually, it had come full circle and Ro had redeemed herself.

'You need to answer my question.' Marco was at the stage where he needed to know what was going on. Eve had mentioned by the fire last night that she was just visiting, and he needed to know what her plans were.

'Where would you like things to go between us?' Eve said, feeling her skin getting goose bumps.

'I like having you around, I want you to stay forever.' Putting all his cards on the table so to speak. Knowing it was a risk being so forward.

Eve bit down on her bottom lip, it was everything she wanted to hear and yet it seemed so sudden and serious,

'I've done this kind of thing before - rushed into living with someone.'

Marco could see her mind digressing back to Evan. He could tell when she was thinking of him, by the look on her face. 'I'm not him Eve... without sounding like a prick or disregarding your feelings and what you've been through. You've known me since you were ten years old, we're hardly rushing things.'

The tone in his voice was obvious, she had offended him; and she detected a hint of jealousy.

'I wasn't comparing you Marco.' Eve felt a touch of emotion surging. 'I know you're a good man. You are the most perfect man I've ever known actually,' pausing, trying not to get upset as she felt her heart ache, 'This is about me and you, nobody else.' She was determined to keep a dry eye.

'I don't care about your life with him.' He put his hand on hers. Another knock at the door. 'Not Now!' Marco raised his voice assertively, startling Eve, she jumped and immediately lost her nerve, biting very hard on her lip to avoid her crying. 'Sorry, are you okay?' Marco saw she was rattled.

She wasn't going to cry… she hated crying.

Marco thought her quivering lip was the sweetest thing he'd ever seen; she was so beautiful; he loved her sensitivity and vulnerability. Eve was like a flower opening in spring, each day revealing more of herself to him.

'Marco. The thing I need you to understand is… I can't change my past,' she said shaking her head, 'I'm sorry.' Struggling to keep everything together, thinking it was all too much to be talking about Evan while she lay in bed naked with Marco, it would always be a bone of contention, her thoughts got the better of her. *Marco was being polite. Why would he want her… seriously. She would only tarnish his shining reputation!* Her mind was tormenting her.

'Evie stop; I don't care about your past.' His hand touched her arms as he leant closer to her face, his wavy hair in his eyes. 'All I care about is you. I wish I could change the past too… because I would never have said goodbye to you in Palm Cove,' Marco spoke with heartfelt regret, 'Your life, and everything you've been through, makes you the beautiful woman that I'm absolutely crazy in love with.'

Oh god! How was he so insanely God damn perfect? Eve was totally speechless as she absorbed Marco's words. It was now or never, she needed to tell him about the baby now, she was tired of the secret weighing so heavily on her, plus she loved him more than anything in the world. Even in a moment like this, when she was emotionally charged, Marco still managed to say the exact right thing… loving words that diffused her instantly.

'I'm so in love with you,' the words fell out of her mouth as she leaned into Marco and kissed his beautiful perfect lips. Gasps of anxiousness as he pulled her into his protective arms. A desperate kiss as their lips rolled to each other, the moment took them to a place where it was just the two of them, where the secret didn't exist. The sounds of voices and morning banter coming from the living room vanished. Both knowing what they felt for each other was immensely powerful. Eve had loved Marco for more than half her life, without any doubt she knew that no matter what life had in store for them, she would love him until her last breath on this earth.

Eve's skin atop of Marco's lap, his growing erection pressing to the front of her as his arms embraced her body, pulling her soft cinnamon skin to him. He was never letting her go. Marco had felt their connection when he'd ran into her in London, *she was the one!* Eve Frank from up the hill had always stood out to him, even as a little girl. She had always been a presence in his life, and now he had to find a way to make her his, forever. This was the woman he wanted to spend the rest of his life with, without a single doubt.

The drive back to Melbourne was spent listening to soothing music as Pat the dog rested his head on the center console between Eve and Marco. The day had started off emotional and unpredictable, now they chatted as they drove along, finally it was completely just the two of them… and Patty.

'While Tessa and Zoe begged me to let them come to Palm Cove. You sat at the kitchen bench and never say a word. Was that a tactical move Eve Frank?' Marco remembered exactly how Eve had looked; he hadn't noticed how grown up she had been at that point for some unbelievable reason. It was only days before he'd finally see her in all her bikini glory… as a busty and curvaceous sex bomb.

She smiled, 'I was the brains behind the plan to pressure you. I planted the seed with Tessa and then sold the idea to Zoe, and then I let them do all the hard work talking you into it.' Eve thought about how she had been the one to suggest spending New Years in Palm Cove, and how it would be the greatest girl's trip of all time. She'd been right.

'Look how it ended up. Fuck… Jackie would have had a coronary,' he joked.

'She almost had one in New York, and we're all grown up.' Eve thought Jackie was never going to forgive her for lying to her.

'Jac loves you, you two are solid. I think she actually likes the idea of us being together.' Marco had got off light because he was the favorite child. Eve felt like she'd pay for it forever.

'I don't know about that, she's still weird about it with me.'

'Nah, she's fine. I think my dad was the one who took it the hardest. He wasn't happy about us hooking up in Palm Cove... not at all. He told me I had broken his trust, which kind of got to me more than my mum being angry. My dad's never said that to me, he was really bent out of shape over it.' And Eve knew exactly why!

Marco was close to his father and was the apple of his father's eye. 'However, Mars does think your pretty good, so the fact that it was you made it less of a grilling.'

'Really? What did he say exactly?' Eve was surprised and curious, she had always had a dad crush on Mario, and he knew the baby secret too.

'He wasn't happy because you were young, and the fact you were a virgin probably made it worse.'

'Hold on... What!' she nearly jumped out of her seat. 'He knows I was a virgin... Marco, why would you tell him that?'

'My dad doesn't care.' Marco thought it was funny. 'He said I should have known better... I told him I tried not to be with you, but there was something between us and I couldn't fight it. In the end I think he understood. At least he tried to,' Marco explained as he drove along the freeway back into Melbourne.

'You make it sound like a romcom; I don't know that I like your dad knowing I was a virgin,' Eve scoffed as Pat the dog nudged his head into her side creeping a little further forward.

'It was romantic Eve Frank.' Marco squeezed her hand with one of his gorgeous smiles.

'I'm a little uncomfortable about the virginity and Mario, please never mention your dad and my virginity in the same sentence again.'

'You're uncomfortable with the virgin part?' he laughed in disbelief.

'How did you say it?' she frowned at Marco.

'I said, oh and Eve was a virgin by the way. Bonus for m!.' His laugh was cute as he teased her. 'What about your dad. Does he know why you're even in Melbourne?'

'James knows about you. I don't like to tell him every detail of my life. He can be overbearing even from a distance.' Eve stared out the window thinking how forgiving she was when it came to her father.

'Really. How?' Marco had been given a run down over the years from his mum and Tessa, Eve herself had told him some things, but not a lot, which left him wondering how great of a man the high and mighty James Frank really was. James was rumored to have strong connections with both sides of the law and was apparently untouchable. He'd never lost a case; this was why he was so wealthy... so Marco had read once.

'My dad was furious when he found out I had run off to France at barely eighteen, all because of his doing mind you,' Eve said with a smile, 'Then he didn't approve of my relationship, and we literally didn't speak because he was so disturbed by it. He's still not over it.'

They'd gone from Mario and James, complete polar opposite fathers. They discussed their sexual history; Marco had clearly slept with way more people than Eve. She asked if his number was over twenty, he didn't confirm or deny. His past didn't bother Eve in the slightest, she had her own, pasts were in the past, *or were they?*

They'd had a day of deep conversation but got nowhere in the scheme of things. Marco still didn't know if Eve was going to commit to him in Melbourne or if they had a future together even though they both had declared their love this morning, he sensed some kind of hesitancy from her.

As for Eve, she still hadn't told him her secret, and it was eating her alive.

Arriving home with an ounce of daylight left, Eve needed to speak with Zoe, her trusted confidant who would set her straight on the day's events. She was willing to give him everything, move to Melbourne, to leave her peaceful life in France, she just needed to find the courage to be truthful first.

Waving the dog lead to Marco as he sat at his desk on the phone in the front room, indicating she was taking Patty for a walk, pointing to the beach. Marco gave her a wave accompanied by a strange look of surprise; he was too into his conversation to talk or go with her.

Heading down to the beach on the hot still evening, Eve dialed and redialed Zoe who wasn't answering her phone. She knew the next question from Marco would be regarding their future and what Eve's commitment would be, he'd tried to get an answer from her this morning, and it had led off into a sex romp, it always did.

It seemed like Pat the dog understood Eve's mood, she was somber and at odds with herself and he was by her side with her all the way, looking up at her occasionally with those smiling big brown dog eyes, assuring her all was okay. It was like Patty knew exactly what was on her mind. She sat on the bluestone wall that looked out over the beach with Patty sitting alongside her, waiting for Zoe to call back, thinking about how on earth she would tell Marco their baby secret. She'd left it too long and that would be her downfall now. He'd be angry with her; he wouldn't be able to forgive her for all the time that had gone by. He'd probably feel betrayed by her and his mother and sister… it was an awful situation that she'd ultimately put them all in. Soaking up the beach evening, Patty sitting at her side so calm and peaceful, Eve felt herself delve deeper into despair. In her heart, she just knew Marco would be devastated.

'I found you!' Startling Eve out of deep thought. Marco was out of breath; he'd decided to go for a run to see if he could catch up with Eve and Patty as he was nearly dark.

'You scared me half to death,' Eve put her hand to her chest.

'I don't know that it's a good idea to walk in the dark on your own.'

'It was light when I left.' She watched him put his legs over the bluestone wall to sit beside her, he pulled Patty close to him taking the lead from Eve.

'What's on your mind Evie girl, you're not quite right are you? I've sensed it all weekend?'

Not only the most beautiful man to ever breathe air, but a fucking mind reader too!

Eve had known he was onto her; she had been a little quieter than her usual quiet self, she'd tried really hard to no distance herself, but it had been hard, especially with all the new people and after the situation with Ro.

'Mmm.' Smiling at him, she savoring the last moment between them before it all went to shit.

'I want this to work between us, I really do. But if you feel differently, you just have to tell me Eve, rip the band aid off so to speak.' Marco needed to know, he needed to know where he stood with her.

'There's something I need to tell you, and it's serious.' She couldn't look at him.

'Out with it then,' he said with a grin.

Her phone rang in her hand, she looked at it, Zoe.

'Call her back,' Marco said looking at the caller ID on her phone, not wanting the moment to pass them again, 'Tell me what's going on in that head of yours Eve Frank.' He'd caught his breath and was prepared for Eve's seriousness.

She fluttered her anxious eyes up at Marco before beginning with a big deep sigh. 'I came home from Palm Cove heartbroken after we'd been together.' *Why not start with a statement,* Eve thought putting off the awful confession as long as she could. 'You were just a dream in my head, and then I had you. It was the best ten days of my entire life.' She took a deep breath. 'But when I got home Tessa went to New York, Zoe went off to Queensland and I was all alone. No, you. No friends.' She took another deep breath and continued. 'After a while of feeling sorry for myself, I met Evan. I saw him a few times until I found out who he was, and then I stopped seeing him.' Only managing a sentence at a time between breaths, she hadn't planned how to tell Marco, it was all just coming out. Eve was going about it the long way. 'My mum was away; I was home with Julie the nightmare housekeeper.' She despised Julie to this day. 'I thought I was having a really bad period, there was a lot of blood, and I was in so much pain.' She paused at the pain, the dreadful memory flustering her a moment. 'Evan came over to the house to plead his case to me, and when he saw me, he knew I was unwell, he insisted on taking me to the hospital... which turns out, probably saved my life.' Eve gasped for breath; she had tears welling in her eyes.

'How did he save your life? I don't get it.' Marco was intrenched in her words, his eyes narrowed, his face intently waiting for her answer as they sat at the bluestone wall. He put Patty down on the path so he could focus.

'I more than likely would have bled to death if he hadn't taken me to hospital,' she spoke matter of fact.

'Why were you bleeding?' Marco didn't miss a beat; he was calmly hanging onto every word wondering where it was going.

Emotion flooded Eve against her will, she bit down on her bottom lip hard.

'Eve. Why were you bleeding?' Marco was trying to be patient.

'I had an ectopic pregnancy,' she blurted it out, sniffing deep to center herself, to keep her cool. 'Do you know what that is?' She huffed a sigh looking at Marco, a hint of blame in her tone.

'No.' His eyes glared at her.

'It's when you're pregnant and the baby forms in the fallopian tube instead of making its way to the uterus where it would normally grow,' a beat, 'The baby can't survive in the tube, so, it's a form of miscarriage.' Her head fell to one side as she watched him comprehend her words.

Marco watched her... a look of realization, a look of shock. 'Was it my baby?' he gasped in what seemed like horror to Eve.

'I was ten weeks pregnant. Yes, it was your baby.' Her lungs felt like they'd collapsed.

'And you're telling me this now... all these years later.' His face twitched in disbelief. Marco immediately felt overwhelmingly guilty and angry, he didn't want to come across heartless as he was trying to comprehend what Eve had just told him. It was an overload of fuck knows what! He got up off the wall and stood facing her, in shock, numb at her revelation.

Eve watched him grapple with it, she tried to read his face... *Was he turning on her?* 'Um... I had surgery that night. I was alone and I was scared; my mum called your mum; and Jackie came to the hospital the next day and asked me who the father was.' Eve was now on the defense, and it felt like she was fighting for her life. 'I said it was Evan's so she wouldn't know it was you. I was trying to protect you.' Eve was border line frantic. 'But as I found out in New York, she knew I was lying all along, because ten weeks meant I got pregnant in Palm Cove.' She gulped for air as she said everything that came to mind. 'I should have told you before now; I know, but the secret just got bigger and bigger and I didn't know how to tell you,' struggling to get the words out, her voice jumping with emotion.

'And so let me get this right, my mum knows all about this?' Marco was numb, he couldn't believe his mother was sitting on this and hadn't said a word to him.

'She only found out in New York that you were the father... I'm sorry, I thought I was protecting you. You had your career, and you didn't need some stupid dumb girl telling your mum we'd had unprotected sex.' Shameful tears flowed from her eyes, she let out a gut-wrenching sob as she looked away from him, in fear she had ruined it all. 'I love your mum, you know that. But I couldn't tell her what had happened between us. So, I lied to her, and I never told you... I'm so sorry Marco.'

'So, you let her think you got yourself pregnant to some random you'd just met?' He couldn't bring himself to say Evan's name. Marco took a second to evaluate things in his head. Eve had been basically a kid. They'd made a baby together. She would have been terrified. 'Who else knows besides my mum and obviously Evan?' he said Evan's name with distaste, which hurt Eve all the more.

'Tessa and Zoe knew it was your baby because they knew we'd been together... I made Tessa keep my secret from you and I know how wrong that was, I just... I.' Eve fumbled with her reasoning. 'My mum knew, but not that it was you. My Grandmother knows it was you, she's the only one I could tell.' She fumbled her words with a cough like every word was draining her of life. It was. This was harder than she'd ever imagined.

'Oh, Eve.' The disappointment was evident as Marco sat back down on the bluestone wall beside her.

'Please don't hate me,' she began to sob her words, crying at her dismay, 'I know I should have told you. I should have told you so many times.'

'Then what happened. How did you end up with Evan?' Marco was calm but cold and so curious. His question had taken Eve by surprise, she wasn't sure how to answer him, it was hard for her to speak about all this at the best of times, let alone to Marco's face. But it was out there, she just had to work through it now, regardless of the outcome.

'I found out about Anna not being my mum, I just lost your baby, and I was confused and hurt. I went to France to see my grandmother because I had nowhere else safe to go.' Eve shot Marco a look, it was really how she'd felt at the time. 'Evan came to France. He wanted me when no one else did.' The ache in her heart was pulverizing.

Eve's words cut Marco to the core. A storm of emotion rushed through him. Evan had been there to pick up the pieces of her poor broken heart after she'd miscarried with his baby. Marco was now the devastated one.

How could this have happened, why was he the last to know?

227

'Did you sleep with him while my baby was inside you?' It was a disgusting thought, but he needed to know.

Eve couldn't breathe, 'What!' she gasped; she was stunned at his harshness.

'Well, did you... did you sleep with him while you were pregnant?'

'Why does that even matter?' Now she was majorly defensive.

'It matters to me Eve,' Marco said abruptly, not that he would say it out loud... but he wanted to know if his baby was inside Eve's body when Evan fucked her... it was a horrible thought that he wished he'd never had.

'Stop it!' She was getting visibly upset and crying, her heart was pounding, and every breath was a like her last as she now stood facing Marco who sat on the wall.

'Why, because it makes you uncomfortable?' Marco said quickly as things became tense.

'Because this isn't about Evan, it's about us,' Eve cried unable to keep it together, she was about to break.

Marco sighed as he watched her, realising he'd maybe gone too far. 'Sorry. I'm sorry. I'm just fucking angry that he was there for you, and I wasn't, and everyone knew but me. How do you think I feel?'

Eve stared at him; she was hurt even though she knew she deserved his fury. 'You know it's always been you Marco, since I was ten years old. All I've ever wanted, was you,' she sobbed her teary words in a bid to get air into her lungs. 'I'm not some misfortunate whore who went from guy to guy getting pregnant and losing babies, and yet that's exactly how I feel.' Eve had had enough, she slumped and sat on the wall, she'd shocked herself with her admission of just how she felt. Marco's hand reached out and touched her arm. Looking at her like he was going to cry, his face looked hurt, like he'd been really crushed. Eve looked up to him, offended that he had questioned her about Evan at such a tender moment. She stood up again anxiously, looking at him, her face crumbling again. 'I feel like I've been in love in with you my whole life, wanting you, crying myself to sleep over you, wishing I had you,' pausing to calm herself, 'You have no idea how losing your baby effected my life, how ashamed I felt in the hospital with strangers touching my body, looking at me like I was some promiscuous young girl that had made a mistake and was now paying the price. I was hurt and angry that you weren't there.' She stopped, remembering the fear she'd felt, all the blood, it wouldn't stop, the pain that felt like she was dying. Evan looking at her, watching her. The shame had stuck with her all these years.

Marco's hand reached out to her leg. 'Eve, I didn't even know, I would have been the one with you if I'd known.' He was absolutely freaking out; this situation was deeper than anything he'd ever had to deal with.

'I'm sorry. I sorry I didn't tell you, I'm sorry. I thought I was going crazy in my head, so I blocked you and all of it out for a very long time… and then I turned around at that concert in London, and there you were,' Eve sniffled her sobs. There was a long still silence between them, her worst nightmare was now a reality, they were broken. 'I'm going to go home to France. I'm sorry I never told you. I'm sorry that I made your mum and sister keep my secret from you.'

Just when she had faced her worst nightmare, a big warm hand gripped hers.

'You don't need to say sorry again,' Marco sighed, 'I wish I had been there for you.'

Their eyes held each other, Eve was crying, unable to hold it in as she stood, her face crumbling, Marco still holding her hand lovingly in his.

'All I wanted was you. I was alone and scared, and I thought I was protecting you.' Whipping her cheeks with the back of her hand and wondering if she'd unintentionally self-sabotaged her own life with the ultimate secret.

Without hesitation, Marco pulled her into his arms as he sat on the wall, Eve between his legs. She buried her head into his neck and sobbed. Stroking her hair gently, Marco's head was spinning, but he had to settle things down before they got out of hand. He'd never seen Eve quite so emotional; she was beautiful, open, and raw. He was supposed to be the one who had protected her, but he felt like he'd thrown her to the wolves, and she'd staunchly protected him all this time.

'I'm here now Evie. I don't know what else to say to you.' Marco kissed the side of her head.

For Eve it was like all the sadness she'd harbored with all the painful memories had all come to the surface as she took refuge in the comforting arms of her beautiful Marco on the bluestone wall. Unsure of his thoughts and how he felt, Eve took the moment for what it was and let it all out.

Marco held her tight; he didn't want to let her go. *What the fuck had he done?* *He'd been the catalyst to Eve's life taking the path it did,* he felt sick at the very thought. *How could he have been so fucking selfish, what a stupid selfish prick he'd been. Firstly, for having unsafe sex with someone who was just a girl, all be it a beautiful sexy and irresistible girl! He'd been caught up in how good she felt, how pure she was, even how much she adored him! Secondly, for leaving her in his parent bed in Palm Cove that last morning and going on with his life without her... when every fiber in his body wanted to keep seeing her. Look what had happened! If only he'd been brave enough to follow his heart back then.* Drowning in guilt, Marco kissed the side of Eve's face as he held her.

'I don't want you going anywhere.' He put his hand to her chin and lifted her teary red face to him. 'It's okay, I'm here now. It's okay now,' he whispered gently to her ear.

'Don't feel sorry for me, I'm fine,' Eve said bravely.

'You're not fine Evie,' Marco said softly.

Her chest felt tight, her head actually ached, she felt sick with the fear of losing Marco. Eve put her hands to her face to cover it as she stepped back from Marco, then her fingers pulled at her swollen eyes as Marco watched. Her hands dropped and she looked at him. 'Do you hate me; I get it if you do?' Things were calm, but uncertainty was clouding the air.

Marco smiled and reached out to hug her into his arms again, 'I couldn't never hate you, not even if I tried. From this second on though, it's nothing but the truth between you and I... deal?'

'Deal.' Her lips curled just a touch with crashing relief.

'Good, now let's go home,' Marco said with a cute smile that was never going to be refused. The relief was enormous for both of them, and it was from this moment that things started to change in their relationship. They walked home arm in arm in the dark slowly as Patty sniffed every tree and every post. Both completely drained from the intensity of emotion the weekend had brought their way.

'Do you want to tell me about the surgery, what happened to you?' Marco asked as Patty took another wee on a tree. Marco's thoughts had settled, all he was concerned about now, was Eve.

Eve still had tears falling from her eyes, 'They removed the fallopian tube and an ovary.' She looked up at him with regret as they stood waiting for Patty, the night was balmy and still.

'Can you still have kids; I mean now after everything?'

'I'm not sure how I feel about being pregnant again... I mean it's a big deal for me after everything. What if it happened again? And there's the chance that I might be a crap mother anyway. God works in mysterious ways.' It felt easy for some insane reason to talk with Marco about her deepest feelings and fears.

'Don't say that,' he said tenderly, 'You're going to be a great mum one day; you just wait and see.'

Marco had spoken about the big family he wanted on several occasions. Each time it put Eve on edge. *There was always something, it was never going to be straight forward for them,* Eve thought to herself. Just as things seemed to move forward, here was something else that could potentially break them.

Marco made love to Eve that night... all night, in a way he had never loved her before. So intimately and caring, full of emotions that neither had ever experienced before, it was a spiritual connection. He needed to kiss it better, kiss and love away all the pain that he'd ever cause Eve Frank. Making love to her was Marco's way of beginning to heal her, they both needed to heal, together.

Chapter Seventeen

As the week rolled on, things settled for Marco and Eve. She began to familiarize herself with her surroundings and how Marco lived. He'd worked through his issue with Jackie and the baby secret, and the fact that she'd never told him. He understood, women were wired differently to men, they had each other's backs when it came to things such as this. His mother was not just a friend to Eve, they were so much more, and he loved that about them. As for his sister not telling him... well Eve was her best friend after all, and they had an unbreakable bond that not even he could come between, and he respected that too. There had been a long conversation on the phone with his mother, and in true Jackie style, she made everything okay when it really hadn't been. Marco would always be her golden boy, even though the whole baby saga with Eve had disappointed her, she told him if he ever wronged Eve again, she wouldn't be so understanding. Jackie also told him how much she loved the idea of them being together now, and how they were good for each other. It gave Marco the peace of mind he needed to move forward with Eve, he needed all the important women in his life on the same page, and they were.

Eve walked with Pat the dog literally for hours every day, it was their thing, Patty loved having Eve around. They walked around the lake in the mornings, then down to the beach and all the way to the marina before making their way back through the leafy streets, every day took them on a different adventure as Eve explored. They stopped for coffee and a dog bowl of water at another little hidden strip of shops and Cafes nearby, she loved a new discovery. All of a sudden her world was opening up and she was loving where Marco lived. She could literally walk to everything. Life was calming down; she and Marco had this new deeper connection, but no plans for the future had been made. Eve was still due to go back to France in the coming weeks.

There was a new love in Eve's life... the local market. Both Brooke and Marco told her just how much she would love it, and they weren't wrong. The fact that she could walk there was one thing, but most of all it inspired her love of cooking, something she felt always grounded her. The food at the market blew her mind, wandering around with her own thoughts and no time to keep.

Eve had a lot on her mind besides Marco. There was her dad, her mum Anna, her birth mother, her ill sister, and the fact that she even had two little sisters, she processed it all in her own time as she walked and walked.

There was something about cooking for other people, especially her beautiful Marco, that Eve found very rewarding. She'd cook him dinner, and he'd reward her in the most pleasurable of ways!

As Eve wandered through the market with her hands full of shopping, Marco called to see where she was at, he offered to come and pick her up, which she wasn't about to decline, she'd gone overboard as expected.

'Stand on the corner where the fruit and veggie shops are, near the roundabout.' They were his instructions; Eve was looking for the fruit and veggie shop on the corner, exactly which corner, she wasn't sure.

'Where are you?' he asked obviously not able to see her.

'Near a fruit and veg shop.' There were many... she shuffled up to the corner trying to hold her phone to her ear and carry the bags. 'I see you; I see you. Give me a minute.'

As Eve made her way to Marco's car, he got out and rushed to help her. *A gentleman... did he ever do anything wrong? No, not really.* He kissed her and took the bags from her in the middle of the road.

'You're so cute! Who's all this food for?' He asked putting the bags in the back of his car and noticing her little pink dress and white sneakers. It was a warm day with a hot north wind, her hair platted to the side with a neck scarf, she looked like a little French angel, very cute, very sexy.

'Do you often come to the market and pick random women up?' Eve stared up into his eyes as he leaned in for another kiss. He was breathtaking, white shorts, navy T shirt and thongs, Marco loved his thongs, Eve was getting used to his ways.

'Only sexy ones in pretty pink dresses,' he tapped her arse as she got in the car.

Brooke came in from work to the most amazing aromas coming from the kitchen. She loved that Eve had cooked dinner for them every night this week, not to mention she'd cleaned the entire house too. It was like having a live-in housekeeper. Dropping her bag at the end of the bench and going straight to Eve by the stove top, Brooke put a hand to Eve's shoulder. 'This is so what I needed to come home to right now, you have no idea,' Brooke said looking at everything Eve had going on.

There was no welcome home babe or hello kiss from Zach who sat in the living room ignoring his wife's arrival. The tension was awkward and had been all week. Eve had noticed that Brooke seemed to be trying but Zach had been giving her nothing since the lake house. It wasn't in Eve's nature to pry, so she watched on from a distance.

Marco butted his chair up next to Eve's like he always did, so he could be close to her at the dinner table, Zach and Brooked seemed to be miles apart as they began the banquet of seafood. A snapper fish in herbs with lemon, prawns in garlic with pasta and salad. Everyone filled their plates and complimented Eve on her efforts over and over every night… She loved it.

After a long silence of eating, Marco spoke, 'I have a surprise for your birthday this weekend,' he paused with anticipation, 'We're going to Palm Cove,' he was excited.

It took Eve a second to be okay with it. The two of them back where it all began.

It was her birthday on Saturday, and Marco had booked flights for Friday after he finished training. 'You guys should come,' he suggested to Brooke and Zach.

'Yes!' Eve gasped happily.

'You should go.' Brooke turned to Zach. 'I'll be at my parents' all weekend.'

Not what Marco had expected, he and Eve looked on as Zach stared back at Brooke, he pushed out his chair and stood up. 'Dinner was great, thanks Eve, you're amazing.' He glared at Brooke and left the table, stomping upstairs, leaving Marco and Eve stunned along with an anxious Brooke.

'I'm sorry,' she said putting her fork down.

'It's okay. Are you alright?' Eve could see Brooke was bordering on tears. *WTF!* Zach was being so mean to her. It was rude too, she thought feeling sorry for Brooke.

'Excuse me.' Brooke was now leaving the table.

Eve and Marco watched her go and then it was just the two of them left at the table with Pat the dog staring up at them. They were all in bewilderment.

'Do you know what's going on?' Eve asked softly as they sat side by side.

'It doesn't look good.' Marco kept eating; nothing was stopping him from eating.

Changing the subject, Eve had a little smile on her face, 'Palm Cove!' Getting back to his surprise.

'I thought it would be nice to celebrate your birthday there, considering it was where we first got together, it's kind of extra special in more ways than one now, don't you think?'

She knew what he meant, 'You just ooze romance, don't you Marco Rossi?' Eve was watching him enjoy her food, it was so satisfying.

'I try!' he said proudly, putting more pasta in his mouth, 'We can pretend you're a virgin all over again if you want.' The delight on his face priceless.

'Let's do that. This time I'll be better, much better,' Eve said laughing quietly as she turned into his shoulder and took a big breath to breathe him into her lungs. *This is real, not a dream.*

'Imagine you got pregnant again,' he said seriously.

'No,' Eve said. They'd become very comfortable talking about their secret.

'Is it the thought of being pregnant and having a baby, or the fear of-' He didn't finish the sentence.

'Everything.' Eve bit her bottom lip. They'd had a similar conversation a few days ago, they were developing a very open and honest dialog around babies within their relationship since Eve had shared the secret.

'Let's say hypothetically in years to come… would you have a baby?' he looked her, analyzing her.

'I don't know,' Eve huffed, she hated being put on the spot.

'Okay.' It wasn't exactly the answer he had been hoping for, and it wasn't a flat out no either!

Eve saw his face and automatically went into an explanation, 'It's not that I don't want to.' *Fuck*. This was going really deep. A place she didn't go ever – until the past few days that was. 'I was a mother for the slightest moment in time, and when I held him, as excoriatingly painful as it was, it was also the most beautiful moment of my life.' Her eyes suddenly had tears. 'I never stop feeling that pain.'

Marco's hand went to her cheek as he kissed her forehead. He didn't say anymore, he didn't have to.

Friday came and when Eve woke up, she found Pat the dog laying up against her side snuggled on the bed. He was always around; he was such a great dog; Eve was becoming very fond of him. They had been on walks all week together and even napped side by side on the bed in the afternoons. Patty was reclaiming his status on the bed. As Eve got ready to head down to the shops for her morning stroll and coffee, Patty sat in the bathroom doorway and watched her every move with baited interest. He followed her around the house. Eve had a new best friend.

Like with any trip she was looking forward to, Eve did a little shopping to take with her, it had become a ritual, something she enjoyed almost as much as the trip itself. Lingerie was a must for this particular trip. She had never worn lingerie with Marco and thought perhaps it was time, since he was treating her for her birthday, she would give him a treat, and there just happened to be an exquisite boutique on the strip of shops a few blocks away.

Searching the racks Eve looked for something virginally sexy, innocent, and fuckable all in one, she was imagining the role playing in her head. A white lace number that screamed slut, rather than a virgin, something crotchless. Marco would love it… he liked dirty girl sex, which Eve loved about him. He had this straight good guy image, but he was one hell of a lover! She'd also need something a little less slutty, a powder blue bra and knickers with little interesting sequence with a matching satin robe, more sophisticated. Eve liked the idea of the knickers; they were a little different, eye catching, encouraging. Marco would want to put his face to them for sure. *He was masterful when it came to oral pleasure.* Eve bought it all.

On the plane Marco and Eve sat up front enjoying their privacy. Eve settling in next to him, she was excited about being back in Palm Cove with again, spending time alone enjoying each other in the place that had bought them together, they could spend the entire weekend in the bed where it all began.

Reading a book, one hand holding Eve's, Marco was relaxed and content with the way the past week had gone down. As unsettling as it had been, they'd worked through it like a real couple and things now felt different. Better than ever. Gazing over at her head as she sat watching Will & Grace with her earplugs in. Compared to him, Eve was like a tiny little bird. Within a week she would be gone again, back to France... this was the one thing grating on his mind as he sighed. His eyes went to Eve's revealing black camisole top gaping at her cleavage, her legs crossed over on the seat with light black cotton pants that showed her delicate ankles, her expensive mule shoes sat placed neatly on the floor. Marco was consumed by her; he was overwhelmingly content with everything for the very first time in his life. *How was he going to let her go home to France?*

It was just going on dark when they arrived at Cairns airport, Marco walking through the airport pushing Eve's trolley of luggage and his one overnight bag. It was warm and humid the minute the airport doors opened. As the heat hit Eve, she felt that wonderful feeling of excitement and innocence she'd felt all those years ago. That trip had been the end of her so-called innocence in more ways than one.

They got in the hire car and drove the short drive to Palm Cove, where the lights on the beach front lit up like a fairy land, Eve remembering every little inch of this beautiful tropical hideaway. The bar on the corner, the restaurants and the hotels that lined the beach.

They arrived at the apartment and Marco left the car running while he texted a moment. 'I'm just texting mum to let her know we're here. Anyone would think we were still teenagers,' he smiled. Eve thinking it was weird but cute that he was checking in with Jackie.

'Tell your mum, I'm going to take you to her bed and make love to you all night,' Eve joked as she waited for him.

'Mm hm,' he smiled putting his phone away and getting out of the car.

The apartment was ready and waiting for them, lights on, windows and doors open as Eve placed her handbag on the living room table and turned to Marco, he scooped her up in his arms and she flung her arms and legs around him, giving him a lustful passionate kiss. She was happy to have this alone time with Marco, just the two of them, romantically bonding for the entire weekend.

'Here we are again,' he kissed her lips, walking to the stairs heading up to the bedroom with Eve in his arms.

'It's kind of big with just the two of us here, don't ya think?' Eve clung around his neck as he took the stairs two at a time. His strength impressed her; he was so very strong... she was going to screw his brains out!

'I know, it's so peaceful.' Reaching for the door handle, Marco put Eve down to the floor. 'Shall we?' he said looking down at her with a naughty smile as he opened the infamous bedroom door.

'SURPRISE!' Shocking the hell out of Eve, the bed had everyone on it. Zoe, Tessa, Nick, Zach, and Rory laying all over each other on the bed like it was a clothed orgy. Tessa jumped up and ran to hug Eve almost knocking her over. Eve was in shock; she couldn't believe they were all there again.

'Happy Birthday E.' Tessa said hugging Eve, it was such a surprise.

'Happy Birthday,' Zoe sprang at Eve like a jumping jack. Then the boys all hugged her and kissed her happy birthday, she nearly started to cry, it was the best surprise ever.

'What are you doing here?' Eve gushed to Tessa, completely shocked to say the least.

'I had no other place to be, and we thought a reunion gathering for your birthday would be special.' Tessa squeezed Eve tightly, she was so happy to be home with everyone again.

'Oh, my gosh. This is amazing you guys.' Eve hugged Rory and then Nick, Zach stood to the side waiting his turn and then Eve turned to him. 'You came, I'm so happy you're here,' she said putting her arms out to him and giving him a long warm hug. Zach's personal life was in a fray, and he still came all the way to Palm Cove for her birthday weekend. Eve was touched.

'It wouldn't be a reunion if I wasn't here, now would it?' Zach said.

Eve could see an emptiness in his eyes, and that made her sad. She knew it must be bad between he and Brooke and it was weighing heavily on him. Turning to Marco her eyes glistened, he was watching her as she beamed, happy with himself and the surprise he'd successfully pulled off.

'How did you do this Marco Rossi?' Eve smiled tugging at his shirt.

'I just put the idea out there, everyone made it happen.' Hugging her in under his arms as they all congregated in the bedroom.

'Let's get in that spa, just like old times,' Zoe was more than excited.

The guys left Eve and Marco with Tessa and Zoe while they went straight out to the spa on the terrace.

'What happened, why are you here?' Eve asked Tessa with concern, it was a long way to come for only a few nights. 'How long are you here?' Eve's voice urgent.

'I'm home for good... I kind of had to flee New York... Mum and dad don't even know I'm here yet,' Tessa didn't take breath, 'These guys have promised to let me have a few days incognito for your birthday bash, before I have to face Jac and Mars... It's your fucking birthday E!' she was oddly emotional in the weirdest of ways, there was more to the story Eve had no doubt.

'Are you okay?' she asked.

'I'm so fucking good,' Tessa said over doing the fake facade of happiness, 'You have no idea how *good* I actually am, thanks to my big brother.' She seemed relieved beyond words as she hugged Eve. Marco had called her on Monday after the baby secret went down with Eve, they had a long chat and he decided his sister needed to come home, she wasn't in great mental shape, so he flew her home.

'And you?' Eve put her hand out to Zoe. 'This is the best birthday ever.'

The girls went to their room to get ready for the spa, the music was on, and the drinks were flowing. Eve laid on the bed with Marco over the top of her, his elbows at her head and his lips kissing her softly as she unbuttoned his shirt.

'You did this all for me.' Eve took the quiet moment with just the two of them to appreciate this wonderful man she undeniably adored.

'Are you happy?' His mouth gave little kisses to hers, he breathed into her mouth.

'I feel like I've hit rewind and I get to start over again, right from the start. Only this time you will be going back to Melbourne, and I will be going with you, for a few days at least anyway.' Eve felt sad at the thought of leaving Marco, she had to return to France at some point to figure her shit out.

'Let me watch you put your bikini on,' Marco said with a naughty grin.

'You just sit back and enjoy the show Mr. Rossi.' Eve climbed out from under him and rolled off the bed. Unzipping her suitcase and pulling out the first bikini she could find, throwing it at him as he lay back into the bed pillows. Lifting her top off, she flicked it at Marco. She slid her pants down and bent forward to her feet. Standing up again, undoing her lacey bra, letting it roll down her arms, revealing her full round boobs, letting the bra hang at her boobs a few seconds before swinging it to a smiling Marco on the bed.

'You do know they can see in the window, right?' he was sexily smug.

'You do know I don't care, right?' she said sliding her underwear down her thighs.

'I love naughty Eve.'

'Could you two be any cuter? I mean, If I didn't love you both so much, I would actually vomit at how cute you are,' Tessa said as Marco held Eve's hand as she climbed into the spa, she dangled like a little precious spider from her brothers' hand. Eve sat beside Tessa who was neatly tucked in the corner, rather close to Zach... they looked a little too comfy.

Eve had an exotic glow - that freshly just fucked look, where her cheeks were flushed like someone had pinched them and her eyes wide open and her lips puffy and sexy. Her full rounded fuckable boobs covered by a shred of red fabric that showed the hardening of her nipples. The skimpy bottoms barely there at her curvaceous hips, cinnamon skin glistening as she submerged into the warm water.

With a skeptical eye, Eve watched Zoe sipping a glass of champagne, she looked grown up to Eve, and she was. The long blonde bob, she was sophisticated and sexy in a proper way. Sitting comfortably in the middle of Nick and Rory, both of whom she had a sexual entanglement with last time they were all in Palm Cove. Both sat beside her respectively, almost protectively, like they were secretly vying for her attention... oh how things had changed, Eve thought to herself, happy to see Zoe now held the power.

Tessa was downing what looked like straight scotch. Zach was clearly on his way to being drunk; he was understandably way out of sorts. Eve hadn't realized until now, but these people were her *absolute crew*, the people who made her feel her best. Even Nick!

Sitting thigh to thigh with Tessa, Eve could tell her friend was using her best tipsy, flirty laugh and naughty smile on Zach. Tessa was well aware he was married, but given her own dismal personal life, she had little, if no regard for his marital state or her own morals. Watching Tessa at work was making Eve a tad anxious, as much as she loved her best friend, she had become friends with Brooke too. Sure, there were problems in the marriage, but it was not for anyone else to judge or decide. Eve didn't think Zach was in the best frame of mind, he seemed vulnerable, and Tessa was going in for the kill... Eve knew her friend.

Looking over to Rory who caught her eye, Eve had always loved him, he was that guy who could easily become her best male friend, the one she confided in, shopped with, and did coffee dates with. There was something about him that drew Eve in. 'I am so happy you came Rory. Can you believe we're spending two weekends in a row together?' she gloated.

'And thank fuck, there's no Ro here to give you a hard time this weekend. What a bitch!' Rory laughed flicking the water out of his face.

'She wasn't that bad in the end,' Eve laughed it off.

'Ro was a complete bitch,' Marco scoffed as he pulled her into him, 'I won't forgive her for that. She's done it with me.'

'I told you; I've had worse woman than her to deal with,' Eve played it down.

'Who are you talking about?' Zoe piped up wondering who was giving her Eve a hard time.

'Ro, she's Marco's teammates wife, and she gave it to Eve last weekend,' Rory didn't hold back on the dislike in his tone either.

Now Tessa interjected herself into their conversation, 'Ro. She's no one. I'll sort her out.'

'It's fine, I can handle her on my own.' Eve was remembering what the strippers and hookers used to dish out to her over Evan, how jealous they were of her, and how they tried to make her feel insignificant, if she could handle those hard-core bitches, she could handle the likes of Ro.

'My mum will have something to say to Ro - that bitch!' Tessa added.

'Happy Birthday Evie,' Nick said loudly drowning his sister out, 'What time of the day where you born?' Nick asked an innocent enough question, so he thought.

Eve raised her brows, 'I actually don't know.' A smile accompanied her coyness.

'Thanks to James not being able to keep it in his pants. What an arsehole,' Tessa laughed, which was out of character.

Zoe looked at Eve across the spa, thinking it was a bizarre comment from their friend.

'Tess don't say that!' Marco snapped disapprovingly to his sister.

There was no stopping her now, 'Oh, come on… James is a massive womanizer from way back, what he's done to Anna and Eve is atrocious.' Tessa glared at her now edgy brother.

'I don't think Eve needs to hear it thought.' Now Zoe was at Tessa, all Eve needed was Nick to start and then it would be on for sure.

'E. Am I right though?' Tessa scoffed, 'The man should at least have the decency to tell you where the fuck you came from.'

Eve looked at her friend. *What the hell was she doing?*

'Stop it Tessa, that's enough,' Marco said, his patience being measured, he was as shocked as anyone, but he wasn't having it. This was Eve's special weekend; his sister wasn't ruining it.

'Sorry. Too far!' Tessa frowned at Eve who was dumbfounded, just a nod of her head accepting the apology which didn't seem sincere at all.

Then oddly, Nick was the one who got things back on course. 'So, what's the drill for tomorrow, are we running in the morning or what?' he asked changing the subject before it got out of hand, he could see the look in his brother's eyes, Marco was on the edge. *He was like a lion protecting his little lady*, Nick thought with slight amusement. For once it was Tessa and Marco, instead of him.

'Fuck running, I'm sleeping in,' Zach said with a careless tone.

'I'll be running.' A stern Marco was still disgruntled.

'Me too.' Rory wasn't drinking alcohol, not tonight anyway.

'You guys run too far for me; I'll pass,' Zoe said smiling at Nick, she was enjoying the friendship she and Nick had been developing, just being friends was working well. Nick was a much better friend than a fuck buddy.

'You better have a dynamite present for E, her birthday is in the morning.' Tessa was back in the game, and she was targeting Marco.

'Of course, I have,' he snapped at his sister again.

Eve watched Tessa, now convinced she was high on coke.

'Good, considering how she wound up after her last trip to Palm Cove with you... you owe her big time.' It was like verbal diarrhea spilling out of her mouth. Nobody knew what to expect next.

Nick narrowed his eyes, 'What's wrong with you, are you fucking jetlagged or something?' he'd had enough of his sister's strange outbursts, he had been trying very hard to keep himself in check, but even he was annoyed at his Tessa's digs at Eve and Marco. *What was going on!*

'He knows what I mean,' she gave attitude back to Nick.

While Marco counted to ten in his head, Nick had his back.

'I think you should shut the fuck up before I drown you.' The old Nick was back.

'Can you stop, please' Eve asked slowly turning to Tessa who didn't really think she was doing anything offensive or wrong.

'Wow. Gee, I'm sorry,' Tessa said without any sincerity, like Eve was being oversensitive.

'Are you?' Eve's eyes widened, her voice calm and soft as always. Her hand went to Marco's thigh to keep him from saying another word. This was not her Tessa, and she needed to sort her out. Eve held her eyes to her friend's *pinned* eyes. 'Can I have word inside Tessa, you too Zo,' Eve demanded, and all three of them got up and climbed out the spa, Marco putting his big, long arms out for Eve to hold as she got out. Always a gentleman.

It occurred to Eve that Tessa may well be off her face like she had been several times in New York, a combination of drugs and alcohol, or she was for some reason a little jealous perhaps of she and Marco, which Eve doubted, it had to be drugs. Eve marched off to the sliding doors and into her and Marco's bedroom with a towel around her waist, Tessa and Zoe following. She stood with her hands at her hips, dripping all over the floor.

'Are you doing coke?' she asked almost too casually, knowing the answer was yes.

Tessa sighed and huffed with annoyance and amusement.

'Why are you saying those things to Eve?' Zoe questioned her getting uppity.

'This isn't you, what have you done with our friend?' A little humour, it helped Eve stayed calm and unoffensive. In her mind, she imagined slapping Tessa's face.

Huffing, Tessa sighed, 'Marco called me last week to tell me he knew about your baby secret... good for fucking you E... glad you got that one off your chest,' Tessa was flippant. 'He suggested the surprise reunion for you,' Tessa suddenly sounded defeated, 'I moved in with Christopher the week you guys left New York. And yes, the sex was out of this world, how could not move in with him. But he was my last lifeline in New York because I'm fucking broke and I hate my job.' She slumped her wet ass on the bed. 'Can you believe I caught that fucker with not one, but two really, really hot chicks in what I thought was our bed.' Her eyes welled with tears. 'So, yes you caught me, I've been doing coke. Lots of fucking coke.' Admitting what Eve already knew, Tessa was crying.

They all needed a silent minute to digest Tessa's revelations and her tears, she rarely cried.

'Sweetie, you are really, really hot!' Zoe couldn't believe.

Eve was huffed at Zoe, then looked to Tessa, 'Have you taken anything else, some pills maybe?'

'No, I've just had too much coke, I'm sorry,' Tessa said as if it was better to do a lot of coke and only coke.

'Where's your stash and who did you get it from?' Eve was interrogating her in a way that wasn't belittling but stern all the same, so she could keep Tessa on side, find her shit, then flush it.

'It's all gone; I took it all. I'm fine really.' Getting up off the bed and pacing the room.

Zoe wasn't as calm as Eve, 'Who did you get it from?'

'Micah.' Tessa didn't hesitate, she threw her old fuck buddy straight under the bus.

'Oh, of course, he did. You said you're broke; please tell me you didn't fuck him for coke.' Zoe was outraged.

'Okay!' Eve felt that was going too far.

'Of course, I did... I just said I don't have any money,' Tessa shouted as she shook her head at Zoe and looked at Eve waiting for her to say something in her defense. She was crying and very emotional. This was rare.

'Oh, my god. You're like a common druggie.' Zoe couldn't help herself.

'Get off your fucking high horse Zoe, haven't you ever fucked someone for something?' Tessa shouted.

'Right!' Eve interjected, raising her voice, she'd had enough, 'You're going to come back out to the spa. No more coke. And stop being a fucking bitch to me. It's wearing very thin Tessa, believe me.' Eve caught them both off guard with her aggression. 'I'm not sure if you're meaning to drag up every dismal aspect of my entire life, but I'm asking you to stop, because you're going to feel like an arsehole tomorrow.' Eve stepped forward to Tessa. 'F.Y.I. Zach's married.'

'That must be why he just fingered me in the spa.' Tessa looked at Eve triumphantly.

'Oh, my fucking god. Who would believe this shit,' laughed Zoe in total disbelief.

Eve didn't change her expression, she just glared at Tessa, unable to speak for a few seconds. 'Maybe you should call it a night and go to bed - your own bed.' It seemed to Eve the only way to handle it.

'I'm not going to bed, I'm not a child E. You can't tell me to go to fucking bed.'

'Then stay away from Zach because he is married. And don't push it with your brothers, they'll eventually realise you're coked up to the eyeballs,' Eve snapped finally losing her cool.

'Sure.' And with that she headed to the sliding door, 'You should really mind your own business Miss Perfect.'

'And you should go to bed,' Eve said bemused, it was unbelievable, it was actually ridiculous.

'Stop bossing me around E.' Tessa stuck her finger up as she exited.

'Don't let her spoil the night. Let it wear off and she'll be more reasonable.' Zoe glanced over at the spa hoping Tessa could behave herself, though doubting it highly.

'I'll keep her out there Zo, you need to go to your room and go through her things until you find the coke, and then flush it.'

'Don't let her come inside, she'll end up killing me in a coke rage,' Zoe was dramatically humorous. She headed straight to the bedroom and began her search.

Eve went outside and got back in the spa, she sat across from Tessa, so she could see if Zach happened to put his hand between her legs… it was an outrageous accusation! The thing with Tessa was, she was all about the shock factor, she always had been. Her behavior was odd, even for her, though she was loud and outspoken normally, this was over the top. The combination of drugs and alcohol made her completely unpredictable.

The night ended with everyone heading off to bed in the early hours of the morning, nobody wanted to waste the day tomorrow in this beautiful tropical paradise. Tessa had settled down a little, she stopped the bizarre insults. Eve had decided to let it all go, she knew Tessa would never deliberately say those things so flippantly to her in the right frame of mind, it was crazy. Marco on the other hand, ignored Tessa for the rest of the night. Zach still sat close but kept his hands to himself from what Eve could see. Rory and Nick continued to pamper Zoe once she came back from frisking Tessa's luggage for drugs. The guys vying for her attention in a very gentlemanly way. There was something different to how Rory was going about things, as much as he was commanding Zoe's attention, he wasn't trying quite as hard as Nick. Eve didn't feel Zoe was particularly interested in either to be honest, she usually had a strong promiscuous vibe going on, but tonight it wasn't there. If Eve was a gambling girl, she'd put her money on Nick, purely for the way he was looking at her with those handsome Rossi eyes of his, they made most woman weak at the knees. Not forgetting that Zoe had mentioned on many occasions that she loved fucking Nick, he gave her a naughty adrenaline. Tonight, probably wasn't the right time for another friend/brother hook up though, with Tessa being so volatile and out of sorts.

Eve and Marco showered and took a minute to talk before getting into bed. They stood face to face, vertically challenged in the cutest of ways. Letting the water run between them, she touched his stomach gently as she spoke. Marco reached out to push her hair back from her face, he was compellingly captivated by her beauty and the way everything she said was defined by her slow soft voice and way. Eve was feminine and delicate, but interesting too, he was spellbound. She talked about Zoe, avoiding Tessa was a safe bet. Besides Zoe and the way Nick was gallantly trying to make her smile the entire night was more interesting. Marco loved Eve's passion when speaking of her friends and the people she loved, the thoughts behind her words were like expressions, detailed feelings that he felt honored to hear. Her devotion and loyalty to the important people in her life had always been attractive.

Eve had drank a little tonight, so she talked and talked. 'As much as I try to dislike your brother, I can't help but like the new Nick.' Eve soaped under her arms as she looked up at Marco with sparkling eyes. 'Of course, I know it was Nick that told you about the picture of Ferez and I in the paper.' Her cheeky smile forgiving.

'Of course. I knew, you knew it was him. Who else would do that!' Marco and Eve both finding it funny.

'Well, I love the respect he is showing Zoe, it proves he can be a grown up, sort of.' Eve raised her arms to wash the soap the away and Marco ran a lazy hand down the line of her body feeling her smooth cinnamon skin.

The warmth of his now erect cock at her stomach made her shiver. 'I hate to stop you....' Eve pulled back from Marco reluctantly. 'But if you dry off and go to bed, I've got a little something you might just like.' Thinking of her lingerie she had spent the morning buying just for tonight. She was exhausted and didn't really feel like putting her pretty new lingerie on, but her drinking buzz was driving her, disappearing into the bedroom, and dressed in the powder blue set with the robe, she came back into the bathroom with the robe pulled tight around her, so Marco couldn't see underneath – she was a human present.

Standing at the basin cleaning his teeth, Marco wondered what she was up to. He liked the look of the robe, very feminine... very Eve.

'What do you know about Zach and Brooke?' Eve asked, she knew she was missing part of the puzzle. Tonight, Zach had really fallen out of his tree in a big way, he'd been messy drunk, said a few things that where out of character and she'd noticed Marco didn't even try to pull him up or intervein.

'It's serious. It's complicated.' Marco rinsed his mouth of toothpaste.

'So, you know what's going on but you're not going to tell me?'

'Kind of.'

'You don't want to tell me though?' Eve was now more curious than ever because it must be juicy!

'It's private. Really private.'

'Okay. I know Zach's your friend, and your loyalty is admirable.'

'Whilst your sexy little antics are giving me a massive hard on. This is big shit they're going through, and I-' Marco stopped. He was always very loyal and felt like he was betraying Zach by telling Eve, as much as he wanted to tell her.

'That's fine.' *It wasn't really!*

Finally, he caved. 'Brooke had an abortion today. Well, yesterday now.'

'Oh.' It knocked the wind out of Eve's sails. Absolutely not what she was expecting to hear at all.

'You can't say a word Evie. It's not the first time she's had one.' Marco had gone from being extremely tight lipped to spilling it. 'Brooke doesn't want kids. Ever. And Zach does. I don't think she'll be at the house when we get home,' Marco said relieved he'd told Eve. 'He's pretty messed up about it as you could tell tonight.'

'Maybe they can work through it.' Eve didn't like what she was hearing. In the short time she had known Brooke, she had grown to like her. They seemed like such a great couple; this was terrible.

'Like I said. It's not the first time and he isn't taking this one well,' Marco was somberly serious as he pulled the tie on her robe. 'He wants out. It's over.'

'Maybe there's reason behind her actions. Maybe that can work it out.'

Marco was giving her the look, the sexy look, the fuck me look that she loved so much, 'That's very diplomatic of you Evie, but Zach and I are both nearly thirty Evie, we both want kids,' he tried not to sound as desperate as he really was.

Not meaning to be disrespectful, she smiled, 'Well, maybe you should have kids together then.'

It didn't amuse Marco, he got her humour, it was cute, but not right now.

Her hands at his hips, Eve moved him backwards into the bedroom as he untied her robe, he sat down on the bed which lowered him almost to her height. Standing between his legs her robe dropping to the floor and Marco's eyes ran over her body, from the see thru lace bra that her raspberry nipples hardened beneath, to the knickers with no crutch. He thought about where he wanted to start, which part of Eve he wanted to taste first. His salivating mouth was closer to her nipples, so he peeled back the bra from her ripe round pillowing boob, smoothing his hand over bare skin first, letting his eyes look for a moment before rubbing his thumb over her enticing hard nipple. Then his hungry mouth ravish her, holding her nipple between his lips as she sighed impatiently. Marco's eyes glancing up at Eve's, moving the lace from her other boob, both out of the bra... so luscious, big, and intoxicating. Marco went to the other nipple and sucked at her with intensity, he licked at her. Eve's hands going to his shoulders and then up into the back of his neck, pulling at his hair as he went from nipple to nipple, desperately sucking her like she was a delicious desert he'd been waiting for all day.

Eve willing Marco to touch her desperate pussy, his hands at her back undoing the bra clip as she twisted and pulled at his hair. Stradling his knee was the only way she was going to get some kind of pressure to her now throbbing clit. Rubbing her sensitive folds to his leg. 'I know, it's a desperate move, but I need it,' Eve admitted with a sexy sigh, rolling herself over Marco's knee as he took her arms out of her exquisite lace bra. 'I'm very Marco Rossi. Very wet!' The rasp in her voice getting to him.

'Well then, you better lay on the bed and let me taste you.' Such a pleasurable thought, tossing the bra over his shoulder, Marco's cock got harder and harder at the sight of Eve in her little crotchless knickers. She laid on the bed ready for him.

With a hand at each knee as he spread her open wide in front of him. His hungry lips to her tender pink flesh, glistening in its own juices. Eve was like delicious candy to his mouth, sweet and mouthwatering. The intent was to inflict unbearable pleasure on the woman who he desired each and every minute of every waking day. Holding onto the sides of her crotchless knickers, Marco's body stretched out over the bed, he was more than comfortable with his face buried deep in Eve's pussy. A bedside lamp gave him just enough light to see her every crevasse. Soft sensual licks and lips sucking at her as she twitched and writhed to his touch.

Eve put a hand to Marco's head and slowly clenched a clump of his hair into her fist as he stroked the small scar on her belly with gentle fingertips. With one hand at her precious belly, and the other lightly touched at her wet pussy, his tongue licked her pearly cum as she moaned his name. Eve's moans were more than sexual, she was connected to Marco by ways deeper than pure pleasure. Their love story and all it entailed was profoundly beautiful and romantic, yet innocent and heart wrenching all the same.

Marco wanted Eve to be his. The thought of anyone else ever licking this pussy, killed him. Everything about her made him happier within, happier than he had ever been before in his life. Eve had proven her love to him, by travelling halfway around the world, by protecting him from scandal for so many years after he'd left her pregnant at such a young age... Marco had no doubt, Eve's love for him was pure and genuine.

'Tell me if I hurt you,' he said coming up for air, taking each of her ankles in his hands.

His words excited Eve.

Taking her legs out and up, widening her, his mouth returned to her folds of glory. His hands moved slowly down her ankles, then her thighs as Marco felt her smooth skin, pleasing her was his only intention. Eve pleased him sexually without even touching him, a simple look could harden him.

Breathing through the erotic strokes of Marco's magical tongue, his hands meandering down her legs, his wide shoulders holding her knees apart, his fingers at her tender flesh, sliding into her wetness, twirling, and swirling inside her. Pulling at her skin as his mouth sucked and kissed her swelling clit. Eve let herself fade into a sensual bliss as Marco ravished her. His desire for her was enough to make her cum and cum again. Clenching the sheets in her fists, pulling at them, succumbing again Eve groaned his name with pleasure. Then unexpectedly, she reached down and pulled at Marco's hair, pulling him away from her as she gulped for air, for mercy. He sat back on his knees and took her by the hands, bringing her up to his lap, his arms around her soft body. His hard cock was at her entrance of her pussy. She let him glide right on in. Her body fell over him, her cheeks flush with pleasure, her arms around his neck, knees spread at his hips as he kissed her with fiery passion... Eve could taste herself. Another erotic overload evoking her sexuality in all the right ways... cumming again. This was one of those intimate times where she would do anything Marco wanted of her to do... she was under his spell.

His hands rolled Eve's hips into his with a touch of force, moving her up and down and around his large cock. Her mouth opened to his as she let him intoxicate her and command her body. Cumming continuously as he commanded her wet swelling pussy to take all of him into the depths of her stomach. Marco needed more as he pulled at her long dark curls that hung down her back. Hi other hand clenched at her boob, squishing her flesh as he laid her back on the bed, he never left her body, gripping clumps of her hair for traction as he pounded into her, Marco knew it was bordering on too much, yet he kept going.

Eve's body gracefully arching as he went deeper and harder, whimpering a sexy soft cry as his cock penetrated her until there was nowhere left to go. Uncontrollable moans as Eve tried to keep up with his powering strength. It was hard and dominating, she willed herself to take it. This was a side of Marco she liked, he was pushing her boundaries and limitations, he was challenging her physically. She looked up at Marco's face, he seemed lost in his own world of infliction, his own erotic moment of power.

Marco was impressed by Eve Frank's stamina! she was keeping up, he loved her endurance, her physical ability to take all he was dishing out. He knew it was hard work, yet she didn't seem like she was about to falter any time soon. It felt like he was coaching Eve to a triumphant win, with a massive climatic ending as the ultimate prize. The more he gave to her, the more she took, the closer they got. What he didn't know, was that Eve was seasoned when it came to hard core punishing sex, she'd learned from one of the best!

Eve had never told anyone of the testing torment she had sexually endured in what seemed like a past life now. Evan had taught her that pain was indeed the ultimate of pleasures.

Marco didn't want to hurt Eve although he had a competitive nature, and he was beginning to realise she seemed to enjoyed a sexual challenge.

For Eve, this sexual affliction came with complexed feelings that took her back years, it still exhilarated her in the most unethical of ways, to be punished and pushed to near breaking point made her sexually vulnerable, and she literally thrived on it. *Was this normal?* She was sure it was.

Marco pulled out of Eve, lifting her to her knees, he was in front of her as he tried to catch his breath.

'Let me cum in your mouth.' There was always that extra excitement when a woman swallowed. It was the ultimate display of sexual devotion, and Marco wanted Eve to show him just how devoted she really was. He needed her to show him her devotion.

Eve, out of breath too, wary, panting, was willing to do anything for her lover all the same... because she was a downright fucking little sexual trooper... and proud of it!

Taking Marco's pulsing big cock in her delicate small hands, Eve bent to him. Her mouth sucking him as deep as she possibly could into the back of her throat. Her hand clenched him at his base, he was thick and solid. Sucking her hardest, rolling her tongue, she let herself love every inch of him., it wasn't hard to do; she'd loved this man a lifetime. Eve wanted Marco cum, she wanted it to be so fucking spectacular, that it hurt. It had become a sex battle with the best of intentions.

Eve wanted Marco to know, that nobody could, fuck and suck his cock, quite like she could!

Marco's large hands held her head down over him as he exploded into the back of her throat, the force of his cum making Eve gag.

She was committed in every sense of the word. Eve swallowed Marco's cum like she was drinking milk, and in her mind, she had most certainly won the race.

'Fuck Evie... that was fucking awesome!' Marco's flushed frown sexier than ever.

'I play to please.' Eve played the game, cute and sultry, and completely drained.

'Well played, you never give in, do you?' he smiled.

'I had no idea we were competing; I would have tried harder.' The innocent glint in her eyes was cheeky. She knew she had absolutely won.

'Really?'

'Yes, really!' a casual tone to her voice, he couldn't tell if she was for real or not.

Marco gazed into her eyes, he was on a high, he believed he had won that sex battle, 'Are you hungry? I'm starving. Let's go down to the kitchen.'

Eve really felt like just falling asleep in the safety of his arms, but she was learning that if Marco was hungry, he was hungry, and nothing came between him and food. Wearing only his underwear, and Eve wrapped in her sexy silk robe, they snuck down the stairs to raid the refrigerator like mischievous teenagers.

'Would you like ice cream, ice cream or ice cream?' Marco asked as he opened the double doors. There was one tub of ice cream. No milk, nothing, that was it. Vanilla ice cream.

'Will you feed me?' Eve whispered.

Lifting her to the kitchen counter. 'Anything for you.' And he meant it. Eve Frank had him wrapped around her little finger, whilst his finger pushed the silk robe off the edge of her shoulder. Her hardening nipples pointed under the silk fabric, she shrugged the robe, it dropped down her slender cinnamon arm.

'It's time for desert Marco Rossi,' Eve smiled.

'Open your legs for me Eve Frank,' his lips curled with anticipation and Eve immediately complied and spread her legs. Her arms at her sides, she pushed her chest out, Marco settled his hips between her legs.

Eve pulled the tub of ice cream to her side and Marco reached out and put his finger in it, scooping a hunk out and very gently touching Eve's mouth, letting her suck the ice cream from his finger as their eyes held one another with bated breath.

Marco's hand moved down to her nipple, his cold ice cream fingers touching her warm hard nipple.

'More please?' she was encouraging.

'It is officially your birthday.' He stuck his fingers back in the tub and this time he put his hand straight between her legs… cold ice cream fingers to her hot swollen pussy, gently rubbing to her, soothing her. Eve's breaths short and deep. The cold was different and exciting. Marco took his fingers back to the tub and swirled them around in the ice cream, then he put them in her mouth, she sucked his fingers. And again, he swirled them in the tub as she watched on with wondering eyes. Putting her hands at her knees holding them open for him, pushing her chest out as Marco's eyes found hers, his fingers cold and dripping with ice cream back at her pussy, covering her with ice cream as she made a face of agonizing pleasure. A loving kiss to her lips while his freezing fingers pressed up inside her warm luscious pussy. What was not to like? the almost numbing feeling was like an insane aphrodisiac. Eve's hand now in the ice cream tub, scooping it with her fingers, smearing it over her own chest, her arms went up around Marco's neck and she pressed her body to his, cold ice cream boobs pressed at his warm skin. *God she loved this man!*

Their sexualizing of ice cream was playful and sexy as well as very messy. Marco pulled Eve forward to the edge of the kitchen bench, pressing another two fingers up inside her hot and cold folds of flesh, he looked down into her almond eyes as she let him ice cream finger her pussy, it was odd how passionate the cold moment was.

'I love you more everyday Eve Frank,' Marco whispered in a sexy low voice to Eve's ear as he swirled and dug into her flesh. She gasped, her face buried into his shoulder as his fingers and knuckles molded to her sticky wetness, slushing inside her.

'As much as you love ice cream?' shivering suddenly feeling the cold though her body.

'Oh, so much more,' Marco said, his lips at her cheek.

'Good, because I love you too,' Eve whispered tenderly as he touched her clit with his thumb, rubbing her to rousing stickiness of her own… all four fingers inside her moving and probing, his thumb making it impossible to resist his intentions. Wrapping her legs around Marco's hips, digging her hand into the ice cream, and putting it to his mouth, then kissed his cold lips. Marco reciprocated, not wanting to seem like he was eating all the ice cream. He took another scoop of ice cream in his hand and rubbed the cold sensation to Eve's boobs… she gasped at the freezing surprise. He pulled her hips to his, although sticky, Eve slid straight onto his again rock-hard cock.

The man was a machine… her machine!

Clenched with both hands at her arse, he was fucking her cold tight little pussy and he was on the edge of cumming in seconds. Eve had something that made him harden up over and over. Her head dropping back; her long hair dangled at the bench top as Marco stared into her dazed eyes. Panting short and sharply as she felt her body tingle with ecstatic excitement from his fast friction.

Rolling her head back and then to the side with an overload of sensual pleasure. Eve touched her nipples and pinched at them, her orgasm building rapidly. Her face scrunching in magnificent agony, about to explode from the inside out.

Marco's hands pinning her thighs to the bench top as he thrusted, he was at perfect bench height for fucking Eve and going easy now was not an option. He was conditioned to perform at his peak, over and over.

With every pump into her soft silk-like pussy he thrived, she was so beautifully aroused as she slipped in the melted ice cream. Her skin a sheen in the humidity and ice cream, her mouth open, with awe. Watching Eve moan with such pleasure on his cock had become an intriguing part of their love making. The fact that he could do this to her, was enormously satisfying for Marco. Little Eve Frank from up the hill was so erotically carnal and yet so fucking classy and sensual. A rush of cum exit his body to Eve's, it was out of his control. Marco held strong to her and winced with excruciating satisfaction.

Eve fell back onto the cold stone bench top, completely numb, and depleted. The moonlight kitchen escapade would go down as one of the best ever midnight snacks, either had ever had.

Chapter Eighteen

Forgetting to close the blackout drapes, the morning sunlight crept into the bedroom. Eve opened her eyes, she was snuggled into Marco's chest, her hands at her chin and her leg resting at his. Sighing as her eyes flickered, his gorgeous, bronzed chest and nipple the first thing she saw. *What a way to wake up!* Her hand softly touching him as she roused from sleep, this was as close as Eve could get to heaven on earth, she had a soulful sense of belonging. It was going to be a good day.

'Happy Birthday Eve Frank,' Marco's whispered in a raspy morning voice.

'Mmm,' a sighing smile looking up to his eyes. *How could one man be so absolutely perfect!*

'It's all about you today, it's national Eve Frank Day, and I've got a present for you,' Marco paused waking up, 'I don't want you to pretend you like it, if you really don't.' Nudging himself up a little to produce a bag from his side of the bed before Eve had even woken properly, he was bearing gifts.

Moving up the bed so she could sit up, Eve took the card first and opened it.

Dear Evie,
Happy birthday to the most beautiful girl I've ever known.
I'm so lucky to have you in my life again.
Love Always and forever, Marco.
XX

'Thank you, that's so sweet.' She said about his words. *What did it mean exactly... always and forever.*

'I wanted to get you something you could keep. Something just for you,' Marco said hoping his taste wasn't too plain for Eve.

She took the box out of the bag and opened it. 'Oh!' she gasped with surprise. It was a delicate and fine rose gold bracelet with a small flat heart charm. Eve's eyes fixed on the heart for a long moment, then a beaming smile expressing her gratitude. 'Marco, it's beautiful. I love it.' And she did.

'Good.' He was a happy man as he put it on her wrist.

'I love it. I love it so much, it's perfect,' her own morning voice bountiful with emotion. This was her first special gift from Marco. He had known the only special bracelet she had was a handmade platted bracelet from her grandmother, but she never wore it, it was more sentimental. So, Marco wanted her to have one she could wear every day, and a bracelet that reminded her of him.

'I thought it was elegant, like you,' he said admiring it on her wrist.

'It's beautiful. I really love it. Thank you,' Eve said suddenly struck with emotion, tears welling in her eyes.

'Are they tears Eve Frank?' His eyes narrowed; he could always read her through her eyes. 'Absolutely no crying on your birthday... unless it's from an unbelievable orgasm, only then will I allow crying,' Marco laughed as he tried to keep things upbeat.

'I'm not crying, they're just tears of happiness,' Eve began to laugh too, she adored him, and the gift meant more to her than Marco could ever know. She would never take the bracelet off.

'I'm taking you to breakfast, probably not alone. The girls will more than likely want to crash, then the guys will come, and it'll be a breakfast party.'

'That's okay, we can do lunch together, just the two of us.' Eve leaned into him and kissed his cheek. 'Have I mentioned that I love you?'

'You might have said it in the kitchen whilst your mouth was full of ice cream last night, I can't remember.' Marco's was in a playful mood; he was hot and sexy, and he wasn't even trying.

'Well then, I'm saying it again now in case I forget later. I love you Marco Rossi with my entire heart.' Her dream bubble couldn't be burst, not today. This was her special day, and she was the birthday girl.

Following Marco down to the kitchen, Eve had one of his T shirts on, nothing else accept knickers of course. Her cinnamon skin glowing, her hair was bushy and unruly as always. Marco in shorts. They entered the kitchen and found everyone there doing the morning catch up and making coffee.

'It's the birthday girl,' Rory cheered, he was first to kiss and hug her, an all-round nice guy, 'Happy Birthday old friend,' he gushed at her giving her a squeezy hug.

'Thank you, Rory. I'm so pleased you made the effort to be here. I know it's a long way to come for a few nights whilst you're in training, so thank you. It means the world to me,' Eve said as Tessa bound in, never to be outdone on a birthday greeting.

'Happy Birthday E. You look like you've been fucking all night,' Tessa laughed.

Funny that... Eve was thinking the same thing about her! Eve hugged her best friend, happy to see she seemed relatively straight and sober. 'How about you, did you sleep well?'

'You guys ate the ice cream didn't you?' Nick said to Eve as she went to him for a birthday hug. 'Happy Birthday Evie. Tell me he got you a decent gift for your birthday?' Nick couldn't help but tease, he loved his brother very much and he it was great to see him happy with his old flame.

Eve held out her wrist proudly as everyone came in for a closer look.

'Oh, wow! That's beautiful. Happy Birthday Evie babe. I hope this is the best birthday ever,' Zoe said all smiles as she hugged Eve in.

'Of course, it will be, you're all here, how could it not be the best birthday ever?' Eve sparkled, and it truly was the best birthday. She'd never woken on her birthday to a day like this before. She'd never spent a birthday with Marco.

Zach stood on the other side of the kitchen quietly, he seemed so out of sort as Eve gave him a smile. He'd fucked Tessa last night, it was written all over his guilty face, she could see it.

'Happy Birthday,' his croaky voice was a giveaway, he'd hardly slept. He walked around the kitchen bench to Eve with his arms out, a stagger more than a walk.

'I just want to say thank you to all of you for making the trip for my birthday. Tessa you can use this occasion to your advantage when you tell your mum and dad you're home.' Eve gave her knowing smile. 'You can blame it on my birthday and pretend you were my gift from Marco.'

'That's my plan baby,' Tessa winked at her friend.

'Who's coming for a birthday breakfast?' Marco asked clapping his hands together with a sense of celebration, making everyone rushed off to get ready.

The minute they were alone up in the bedroom Marco shut the door behind them and questioned Eve.

'Am I imagining it, or was there something up with Zach and my sister?' He looked at her knowingly.

Eve took a deep breath and rolled her lips then headed straight for the shower. She had to play this one carefully, she couldn't go accusing anyone of anything without knowing for sure. 'Like what exactly?' she asked as she turned the shower water on, keeping it all very cool.

'You don't think they... um, hooked up, do you?' Marco stood in the middle of the bathroom.

Eve was soaping up ready to wash off and get straight out already, 'I don't know.'

He was still there waiting for her response. 'What should I do?' he asked her sounding a bit bewildered.

'You do nothing,' said Eve straight up looking at him. It seemed like the right answer. Marco turned and walked out the bathroom leaving her to ponder the repercussions of Zach and Tessa hooking up yet again here in Palm Cove.

Marco was in the bedroom texting on his phone, Eve came in with a towel around her, he glanced at her before throwing his phone on the bed and going to the bathroom.

'I don't think you should say anything to either of them, it's probably nothing,' Eve said knowing this was going to become something more.

Marco managed to get through breakfast saying nothing to his sister and Zach although he was watching them closely, today was Eve's special day and he had no intention of ruining it with speculation his sister and his married best friend were screwing. Tessa and Zach didn't sit next to each other at the breakfast table, yet they made jokes and laughed at each other like all was fine and dandy. Marco and Eve could feel the sexual tension between them though... it was a complexed situation that neither really wanted to deal with this weekend.

Later down by the pool it was a perfect day with everyone enjoying themselves in the sun. Marco and Eve had gone straight up to the apartment so Eve could change before swimming. They'd been quite a while.

'What took you two so long?' Zoe asked loudly from the pool where she floundered in the middle with Rory.

'Are you two having heaps of sex, catching up on lost time?' Tessa watched them as she lay back relaxing in her skimpy bikini and not so tanned body, she'd come straight from a New York winter.

Marco looked at his sister as he laid his towel down next to Eve's, 'Are you having heaps of catch-up sex?' Point blank, he looked to Tessa then Zach, who also laid on a sunbed.

Everyone looked at Marco. Eve stopped still, Nick's jaw dropped, his eyes going from Marco to Tessa.

'Marco,' Eve said softly, her head tilting to one side as if to hush him.

But he continued, 'I'm taking your silence as a yes,' he said as he sat, still staring at his sister, he tapped for Eve to come and sit between his legs, but she just stood and looked at him with warning eyes.

'Marco mind your fucking business,' Tessa scoffed at her big brother, 'I don't pry into your shit, and you've got plenty of it buddy, you just haven't had to be responsible for it.'

A stunned second of silence filled the air.

'Hang on,' Zach felt the need to intervein right then and there.

Marco didn't hang on though, he went for his sister, 'Mind my business!' a beat, 'That's rich coming from you. His wife happens to be a good friend of mine.' Marco now not holding back. Not even in front of Zach who awkwardly moved on his sunbed to sit up and face his mate.

Eve still stood up with apprehension.

Tessa snapped raising her voice, 'His wife's a fucking moron who doesn't give a fuck about him.'

Eve bit down on her lip nervously, all that could be heard was Zoe's gasp of horror as she watched on.

'You're right. It's not my business, do what you want,' Marco scoffed removing himself from the conversation before he boiled over and said something he couldn't take back.

'Fuck you!' Tessa was up off the sunbed, she dived into the pool making a splash.

'It's over. Brooke moved out this weekend,' Zach said looking to Marco. He wasn't proud of what had happened with Tessa last night. They had spent the night together; it had made him feel remotely better in the moment.

'My sister!' Marco raised his eyebrows; it was a very awkward moment as he stared Zach out.

Eve was now gasping in horror, 'Oh no, that's terrible Zach. I'm so sorry,' she said amidst the awkwardness, she could see Zach was shattered, and Marco wasn't giving him anything. She was a little surprised, it wasn't the first time Zach had slept with Tessa, yet Marco was getting bent out of shape, she understood it was the loyalty to Brooke and the fact he was married.

'Thanks Eve.' Zach looked up at her a little lost, his voice unsure and somewhat confused.

Eve went and sat on the end of his sunbed, she wanted to give him a huge hug and show him some support. Zach was in world of personal pain; she knew exactly how that felt and perhaps Marco didn't.

'Is she really moving out, are you sure?' she asked in her soft voice, sympathetic to his situation, this was a devastating thing to have happen within a marriage, Zach and Brooke had been together for years.

'Yeah, I'm sure. She's moving back in with her parents. It's over.' He sighed, his shaggy blonde locks messed around his fac, he looked terrible.

'Well, I'm really sad for you,' Eve said, she now felt emotionally invested with Zach and Brooke, and it was awful to see him so upset in the midst of despair.

'Eve.' Marco looked at her like he wanted her to stop.

'It's fine, she's just concerned,' Zach said to Marco who gave him a long glare. They played a standoff game of glares for a few seconds. 'You're supposed to be my friend. Why are you taking Brooke's side?' asked Zach.

'I'm not taking Brooke's side. I just don't want you with my sister, you're still married, surely you get that,' Marco explained.

Zach huffed, 'It's Tessa,' Zach looked at Eve and then to Marco again, 'I shouldn't have to explain that to you of all people.' His tone with Marco was not remorseful, it was frustrated.

Nick laid on his sunbed listening to the whole thing play out, Zoe was silently observing.

Marco was in deep thought; he rolled his lips. 'Mate, I'm not judging you. I just don't want you to make a mistake and regret it.' Marco knew how Zach was suffering because of Brooke's decision to have yet another abortion. 'And I need you to respect, that Tessa is my little sister.' Marco stood firm with a hint of compassion.

'I know, I know,' Zach nodding his head. This was there way of apologizing to each other and moving on.

'I'm really glad you're here with us,' Eve said, 'You're with friends who care about you.'

'I'm glad you're here too,' Marco said making his piece, 'It'll be okay.'

'I have no idea what I should be doing or not doing right now,' Zach mumbled as he laid back on his sunbed.

'That's okay,' Eve assured him, 'There's no rules to breaking up.' She smiled to take the edge off the situation.

'Let the dust settle mate,' Marco said now in a calming voice.

'Are you done with your lecture?' Tessa said from the edge of the pool to her brother who was standing up to stretch. 'And please stop telling me what to do? Your names Marco. Not Mario!' She had her cheeky irritating tone going on.

'Ooh, please Tess, just act like a grown up for once.' Marco waved his hand at her, he didn't have the energy for her shit, he loved her, but she was so painful at times.

'You know what asshole!' Tessa saw red. She splashed water with her hand at him. 'I never said a word when you fucked my best friend and left her with a situation. So, I'd appreciate it if you could let me fuck your best friend... he needs no strings sex right now… he's at a crossroads in his fucked-up marriage. For fucks sake, give him a break.' Just when it seemed to be over, Tessa reignited it.

Marco scoffed in disbelief, 'What! You've practically begged me for years to be with your friend. The difference is my friend is married,' he told his sister.

Eve turned quickly looking at Marco who stood at the edge of the pool now, hands on hips about to strangle his sister. Without warning, Eve pushed Marco in the middle of the back, and into the pool he went.

'This friend is going to the beach. When you've cooled off, we can go to lunch for my birthday,' she told Marco, then proceeded to walk off toward the beach, no turning back. Offended mildly at Marco's outburst about Tessa begging him for years. Eve walked bare foot through the grass and down to the water's edge.

Had Tessa really begged him for years?

The beach was beautiful and definitely more peaceful than the pool, her birthday had started out with a little too much tension for her liking, it was supposed to be serene and beautiful, and these nightmare Rossi's were hijacking her day. Neither of her parents had called and it was past midday.

'Eve Frank.' It was Marco. She turned around and looked up at him all wet and one hundred percent gorgeous.

'Did Tessa really have to beg you?' She eyeballed him for the answer as he stood on the sand in his shorts looking super-hot and so exceptionally sexy… no top, blinking those gorgeous eyelashes at her.

'It wasn't like that, and you know it,' Marco smiled to defuse her, 'I shouldn't have said that.'

'I know it was a slip of the tongue. I know you didn't mean it the way it came out. But nevertheless,' Eve said dismissively, 'It's my day today.' Not often did she get uppity, this was a rare moment for her.

'I'm sorry.' Marco reached out to her hand and took it in his.

'I know that underneath that incredibly ripped body, you're upset because Brooke and Zach are your friends. I get it, it's fine.' And she did. Eve took his hand that was holding hers to her mouth and kissed it.

Fine. Marco wasn't sure what fine meant anymore, Eve said fine a lot. *Was it good? Was she okay?*

'Let's get back to your birthday. I feel like it's gone off track. It's not what I had in mind when I planned this weekend for you.'

Eve found it very hard to be anything but Marco's yes girl when he was shirtless and so sexy, tanned, and wet. He had her hook, line, and sinker. She needed to cut him a break, he had been overly emotional about his friends breaking up.

'You just wait until tonight; the best is yet to come,' he said winning her back.

Melting. Completely melting. He was hotter than hot… sex on two magnificently athletic legs. Utterly gorgeous, she wanted to take him there and then into the ocean and have her way with him, there was a possibility they'd be attached by stingers or even eaten by a crocodile, so she reframed. They headed off hand in hand down the beach for a walk instead.

'Are we doing lunch? We've got no shoes and your shirtless,' Eve asked swinging his hand.

'One problem. I don't have any money or my phone.' Marco patted down the pockets on his shorts.

'Lucky for you I've got my bag.' She still had her little bag across her body. She hadn't taken it off at the pool in the commotion. 'Let me buy you lunch for a change. I do have money you know.' She pointed out.

'I know you have money.' It had crossed his mind on several occasions that Eve had money, a lot of money! She bought expensive things without a thought and flew all over the world at the drop of a hat. She was fiercely independent and worldly for a girl her age; she always had been.

'Let's do lunch then.' She took his hand, and they went into the beach café.

'This thing with Zach is a big deal in his life. He needs your support, he's hurting badly right now,' Eve said as they walked up to a table for two right on the front of the deck near the sand.

'He's technically cheating on Brooke with my sister, whether he thinks it's over or not, it's too soon.' Marco didn't feel quite the same as Eve about Tessa and Zach. 'You're accepting it because my sister is your friend.' They sat at the table facing one another, Marco looking around.

'Has he cheated before? Because he doesn't seem the type, so I'm giving him the benefit of the doubt.' This was such a lifechanging event for Zach, she genuinely felt terrible for him, and for Brooke. 'Zach and Tessa are both adults, maybe we need to just leave them to do what they need to do.'

'It's literally just happened; don't you think that's wrong?' Marco wasn't comfortable with it; he was a traditionalist.

'Tessa's a sexual release for Zach. It's really just sex at this point.' Her flippant tone irritated Marco minutely.

'What the hell is she doing sleeping with a married guy?'

'Marco!' Eve sighed with frustration. It didn't thrill her either, but she always tried to be nonjudgmental. 'You need to know she's got her own issues too,' Eve took a breath seeing Marco's mortified face, 'I'm not saying I agree with it, but they obviously need something familiar right now. Perhaps that's all it is.' Eve tried to make her own morals clear.

'Sexual release! You sound like a sex therapist.' The frown on his face was puzzling.

Eve smiled, 'Some people find sex comforting in a time of need,' she said rather seriously. It was as though she had evaluated the situation and diagnosed it.

Marco saw her point and wondered how she knew such a fact; he still didn't like it.

Eve's phone rang in her bag, she hoped that someone had bothered to call her for her birthday, it didn't feel too much like a birthday right at the minute. 'Well, hello,' she said, her face lit up like a Christmas tree. Marco watched her as she glowed. 'Thank you. You're my first birthday caller, believe it or not,' Eve chuckled; she was pleased with whoever it was on the other end of the phone, Marco couldn't help noticing. 'I'm in Palm Cove with Marco.' Her smile was good to see, she sounded pleased to be with him at least, he thought to himself as he listened in on her call. 'He'll call. I'm giving him until six pm before I cut him out of my life for good,' she laughed playfully, 'My dad's preoccupied with more important things at the moment.' She listened to the caller and put her head to one side. 'I wouldn't know that; I don't know her,' Eve lost her smile. 'You'd know more than me about that.' Then her eyes looked down at the table like she'd heard something she didn't like. 'Ha-ha, you're so funny I forgot to laugh.' She was smiling again, which made

Marco curious about who the caller was. 'Thank you for remembering me. Talk soon. Love you. Take care of you.' And she hung up.

Marco didn't want to ask who the caller was, but he was curious. From what he could tell Eve didn't have an abundance of friends. Was that family calling, it must have been, they knew who he was, and she loved them.

'That was Ferez, wishing me happy birthday,' Eve said knowing Marco would be jealous as she put her phone away, but honesty was the best policy. 'He's my friend.' She looked at Marco holding her breath. 'He's one of my only friends... friends call each other for their birthdays.' Marco's silence was uncomfortable for Eve. 'I think you'd like him if you met him. Ferez isn't a bad person,' her soft voice said as she touched Marco's hands.

'Maybe.' He didn't have too much to say about Ferez.

A waitress came and took their order and they continued to look at each other, sizing up what they had in one another. Eve having de ja vu about the restaurant and this very table.

'I feel like we've been here before, like we've sat at this very table.' Her smile demure and peaceful as Marco looked into her eyes.

'We have. Last time we were here together,' Marco said smiled and giving her hands a squeeze.

'Have I changed much since we last sat here?' she was curious as to his answer. The clock was now ticking for them... *What would become of them?* Eve wanted to know how Marco thought of her, a lot had happened in between.

'Parts of you have changed. You're still that cute funny girl I liked talking with. I feel good when I'm with you,' Marco took a big breath in, 'You're more confident now in some ways... sex ways. You speak your mind more now. But mostly you're the same Eve Frank I've always known.'

'Sex ways. How?' Eve knew exactly how. She just wanted to hear him say it.

'You're not that innocent girl anymore that I was so scared of breaking.'

'Mm, hm, I've learned a thing or a two. A lot actually.' Eve's eyes were naughty as she thought of all the experiences she had since being here with Marco her in Palm Cove last time.

'What's the craziest sex you've ever had?' he asked playfully.

Eve was a little taken with the question. *Did he really want to know? She didn't think so… or maybe he did!*

'You really want to know?' her head tilting slightly at the surprise question.

'I think so,' Marco said already wishing he'd never asked.

'You first,' Eve protested thinking it was a dangerous road to go down. Yet somehow, he seemed to think it was intriguing. 'Am I going to regret this? I am, aren't I?' she smiled, 'And it better not be a boring hooker story either. If we're doing this, I want something crazy filthy dirty Marco Rossi,' she laughed.

'Your crazy is probably much worse than mine, isn't it?' he laughed too, thinking about the company Eve had kept in Evan. Marco didn't want to imagine what may or may not have taken place in their sexual relationship. 'Let's not do it.' He suddenly changed his mind knowing it was stupid in the first place to even ask her.

'Good idea. I can however tell my best sex recollection if you like.' Eve's insatiable grin melting Marco, her lips pursing in a love heart shape.

'What have I started!' He threw his head back with a chuckle, then looking at Eve as she took pleasure in his squirming awkwardness… all of which was of his own doing.

'Right here on the beach. On the seat near the chapel, do you remember?' Her smile turned to a soft depth of emotion. They both knew that night was more than likely the very night Eve became pregnant. There was a long meaningful silence between them.

'I remember.' Marco remembered it so well. As time went on, the idea of Eve getting pregnant all those years ago made him feel unsettled. He didn't understand how Eve could just block things out like she did, he wished he could block it out too, but he couldn't. Marco was surprised Eve said it was her best sex.

That night had always been her best sex in her heart, and their first night together would always be her most cherished night. Every second of it was crystal clear in her mind like it was yesterday.

'Our first night was my best ever,' Marco said with a glint in his eye, his head slightly to one side, he leaned back in his chair.

'Are you being sentimental or just polite?' Eve's laugh eased the deepness of their discussion. A waiter came with Eve's big bowl of fruit salad and Marco's burger.

'It's the truth. It was a big deal for me,' he admitted.

Eve realized he wasn't joking. Marco started to eat, her eyes firm on him, she was in awe of this man.

'This is kind of our place then, isn't it,' she said feeling a touch sentimental herself.

'This is definitely our place Eve Frank, that's why I brought you back here.'

The pool side discussion was cheerful when Eve and Marco returned from lunch. Zoe lounged on a blow-up bed in the pool with Rory beside her, they both held cocktails and seemed very relaxed and happy. Tessa was missing, Zach was lying near Nick under the shade of the umbrella's laughing and drinking beers. Eve sat at the edge of the pool, her feet dangling in the cool water, Marco perched himself comfortably on a sunbed with the boys.

'Where's Tessa?' Eve asked Zoe who looked very content floating around the pool like a princess.

'She went up to go to the toilet, that was a while ago now.'

Straight away Eve wondered if Tessa had hidden a stash besides the one Zoe had found and flushed.

Eve looked at Zoe with wonder in her eye, she could tell by Zoe's face she didn't want to take part in today's Tessa saga's, Zoe was busy with the affections of Rory, getting too deep in Tessa shit right now didn't appeal to her, plus Zoe wasn't as suspicious as Eve, she'd learned a lot from Evan, he'd told her stories about Jo's addiction. Addicts lied a lot. 'I'm going up to get my hat,' said Eve casually getting up, she took her bag and went up to the apartment. Her concern for Tessa was that she was well and truly addicted to coke, she was desperate and becoming careless with her daily drug habit. If Marco and Nick found out, they'd freak out. The fact that Eve was in on it and knew what was going on, wouldn't be great either. She needed to see how far-gone Tessa was and try and help her before it all got out of hand.

Her phone rang just as she got in the apartment, she looked around for Tessa as she answered the phone.

'Happy Birthday my darling, are you having a wonderful day?' Anna sounded like she was between things, in a rush or busy. The more she thought about Anna hiding the truth about her biological mother from her, the more she struggled with it.

They chatted for a few minutes about Anna's up coming business trip and how she planed to stop by France to see her grandmother, Anna always had a full schedule.

'I have to go now darling; I'm boarding. I've put your gift in your account.'

'Thank you. Have a good flight.' There was no tone to Eve's voice, the call had lasted all of two minutes. She knocked lightly on Tessa's closed bedroom door and then entered, her focus now on what she considered more pressing issues. Leaving Tessa to self-destruct was not an option, Eve needed to sort her out, straighten her friends crown so to speak.

The bathroom door was closed. 'It's me. Can I come in?' she turned the door handle, but it was locked.

'I'll be out in a minute.' Her fake normal voice came from beyond the door. Eve stood right up close to the door so she could hear. A frantic rustling of what sounded like a makeup bag and then the water running and finally Tessa opening the door to see Eve leaning against the wall, she had a look that wasn't going to take any bullshit excuses or lies. Eve may be the quiet friend, but she was the feared one... not that she knew it. Tessa and Zoe didn't like being offside with her.

'Spying on me are you E?'

'Should I be spying on you?' Eve wasn't letting her best friend do this to herself or her family. Her fears were that if Tessa continued down this reckless path, she would eventually need something more, and then something even more than that, and then she would have lost control of her amazingly beautiful self and become that person who got lost without anyone noticing until it was too late... Eve wasn't letting it happen.

'What are you, a fucking cop or something?'

'Do you get high every day?' Eve asked Tessa who was looking at herself in the long mirror, her hair rustled like she had just been fucked. Not a totally foreign look

269

for Tessa these days, she often had a sexy, slutty look going on. Only now she looked like this because she was strung out, and clearly because she couldn't find her stash. She was anxious and nervous.

'What did you do with it?' Tessa snarled, her hands on her hips, long legs with the beginnings of a tan, she was strung out all right. 'It's not your shit to get rid of.'

Eve didn't say a word.

'I can't believe you fucking took my shit E.'

'And I can't believe you're so desperate for it,' Eve huffed.

'You were married a fucking drug dealer, I thought you'd be down with it,' Tessa spat her words.

'I was never down with it.' Eve took the insult from her best friend without a fuss.

'Whatever. Oh, you liked his cock, not his coke, how stupid of me.' Tessa was amusing herself at Eve's expense as she frantically looked around the bedroom. 'I'd like my shit back E. NOW!'

'Listen to yourself,' said Eve calmly, 'Not in all of our friendship have you ever spoken so horribly to me.' It was like a standoff between them. Eve stood barefoot in her short black kaftan, Tessa in her bikini, face to face.

'Oh, fuck off... you think just because you told Marco about his baby that everything is roses, Princess Eve Frank lives happily ever after.' It came out of her mouth like vile hatred. Eve knew it wasn't really the way Tessa felt about her, her friend was venting, and she was freaking out without her drugs.

'Your mean words won't get rid of me if that's what you're doing. Do you really want Marco and Nick to find out?' Eve was thinking fast, she had to find a way into Tessa's head.

'You're so fucking perfect E,' Tessa exaggerated her words, 'My brother's dick is so far up you; it's effecting your brain.'

Wow! Eve sighed at that one. 'I'm trying to help you. You know how that is, you helped me when I needed you and now let me help you.... please let me help you. Stop being a bitch and let me help you,' Eve was still sounded calm, and it was pissing Tessa off. Inside Eve was devastated that Tessa could say such things to her.

'I don't need your help E, I'm fine... I need my fucking coke. Get the fuck out if you're just going to bitch and moan at me.' Tessa slumped down on the bed and put her hands to her face in desperation, her elbows on her knees. Eve took a few steps forward towards her.

'I'll take you to rehab myself if I have to.' Eve sat next to her on the bed. Tessa wasn't cooperating, she had to do something.

'What!' Tessa sat back and looked at Eve in horror.

'It's the last resort, but I'll do it if I have to.'

'E!' Tessa sighed like she'd suddenly clicked back into being a sane person again. She looked worn out and frazzled, on the edge of tears. 'I've got so much going on. I need to be up not down. There's an audition in Melbourne at the end of the week. I've got a really good chance, but I have to be on my A game.' Tessa's whole mood came down to a strange low.

'You're A game isn't being high on coke. I'm glad to hear you've got an audition. This is your chance to move forward. Imagine you get this job; it could be a whole new start for you,' Eve tried to put a positive spin on it, 'You won't get to the audition if you're in rehab though.'

The devastated frown on Tessa's face was surrendering. 'I'll try,' she said with a soft defeated voice, 'Please don't tell anyone, not Zoe, not Marco. I'm begging you E.'

'Zoe already knows.' Eve shook her head.

'Well, don't tell Marco, I'll get clean, I promise,' Tessa now sounded desperate.

'You have my word, I won't tell anyone, but you have to try,' Eve regretted it the minute she said it.

'How are you so strong and together E?' she sniffed her tears, 'After everything you've been through. Heartbreak with Evan. Losing your baby. Marco's baby. Shit parents… Not Anna, I love Anna,' Tessa questioned Eve in a rambling kind of way as she wiped her tears away.

'I have really good friends.' Eve's smile was full of love. It was true.

Later in the afternoon the girls lounged about under the palm trees on sunbeds in a sun daze, Tessa under the protective eye of Eve, while Zoe entertained them with her self-diagnosis of very early menopause.

271

'The thing is this is so not me. Why do I feel this way? It has to be hormonal; I usually want sex all the time and I'm feeling nothing,' Zoe's voice was full of angst.

Eve sat up quickly covering her boobs with her dress, letting it hang at her front with loads of side boob showing as she moved up closer to Zoe. 'Perhaps you're over thinking it, maybe you just don't want either of them?' Eve suggested.

'No, it's an imbalance, I know it, I love sex with anyone normally.' Zoe shook her head.

Tessa was tired and drained; her attention span wasn't great right now. 'Oh. Fuck. Zo. Fuck my brother... Fuck someone. I personally don't think Rory is interested in pussy, just between us,' Tessa's voice trailed off.

'What do you mean by that?' asked Zoe.

'He's in the closet.' Tessa whispered, she laid with her eyes closed.

'I've been with him. He's pretty good for someone who's in the closet, he knows what he's doing.' Zoe felt obligated to say it, Rory had been memorable in bed.

'That means shit, pussy, arse, what's the difference,' Tessa's words slurred humorously.

'Will you both stop,' hissed Eve.

Zoe sat forward in her sun lounge, 'Evie, how are you going to leave Marco next week?'

'I don't know.' Eve fell asleep with the thought in her head. All three of them had fallen asleep in the shade of the palm trees, they all needed a snooze.

'What are you doing?' Marco said waking Eve, startling her. He threw her kaftan over her body and spun around to faced away from the girls - the second he noticed Tessa was topless too.

Tessa covered up with her towel, she was drowsy but on it, Eve didn't cover up, she was in one of her slow and mellow lazy, moods, the kind of mood that might see how far she could push him.

'It's all clear, I'm good, you can turn around,' laughed Tessa winking at Eve who was still topless and half-asleep laying on her sunbed.

'Eve, you're naked. I'm pretty sure you can get arrested for that here.' He looked down at a relaxed Eve who sat up and held her kaftan at her lap. 'Cover up,' he suggested protectively.

'I've got bottoms on,' corrected Eve, 'I'm not naked.'

'Your phone's been ringing,' he said putting it on her sunbed beside her, but she was so chilled she didn't care.

'Everyone here has seen me without a top before.' Eve casually reached for her bikini top.

'No. Not really,' he looked over at randoms walking down the beach, 'What about him over there?'

'He can't see,' Eve scoffed reached up to Marco, letting her bikini top dangle over her boobs as he came into her embrace. 'Better,' she said as his bare chest pressed against hers.

'Better.' The feel of her soft cushiony breast against his skin made everything better even though he still didn't want anyone looking at her boobs.

'Secretly you like my public nakedness,' Eve whispering in his ear as he tied her bikini top at her back.

'Okay I do,' Marco lied, he didn't like it at all, 'You really should check your phone; it rang a few times. We've got dinner at seven so I'm heading up for a shower. See you soon. Don't take your top off!' He seemed a little edgy Eve thought, she watching him as he walked off, her eyes followed him. Marco Rossi was beyond eye candy, he was that same boy she daydreamed about all those years ago, only he was a man now.

'Earth to E!' Tessa said loudly at her as her phone started buzzing again.

'Hi Dad.' Eve wanted to be pissed with her dad, but she wasn't, her day was on the up.

'Happy Birthday my sweet girl.' James hadn't called her that since she was about twelve, he was either drunk, feeling sentimental or something was very wrong!

'Thank you Dad. How's Aria?' it was the first thing on Eve's mind, she was the caring big sister who had never met her little sister.

James sighed at her question, 'She's okay,' he didn't sound okay, 'How are you darling, how's your special day going so far?' There was so much more he wanted to talk to her about, he needed to talk to her about, but today was her birthday and after all these years and everything that had gone down between them, he didn't want to ruin her birthday.

Eve paused a moment, 'Well, I'm in Palm Cove with Tessa and Zoe, and Marco Rossi.' Her gut sensed James wasn't himself; his tone was off.

'Is that why you've been in Melbourne, because of a guy!' James knew by the way she said his name.

'Yes, actually it is.' Her father could hear her smile through the phone.

'That's nice for you sweetheart. I hope you enjoy your birthday. I'll call you in a few days. I love you Eveline.' Eve couldn't help but think how strange her father sounded and he sounded genuine! It was like he was the old dad she used to know before he left her and Anna, before all the lies and the hurt.

'I always thought James was sexy for an old guy,' Tessa said.

'Yuk. He's my dad. That's not even funny, if he knew, he'd probably ask you out.' Her dad had an eye for younger women… *Why not her best friend?*

'And I'd probably say yes.' Tessa smiled knowing she had horrified Eve.

Eve was the birthday girl, and she looked the part. Her hair was curlier, longer, and fuller than ever because of the humidity, her skin was glowing radiantly, she wore a short tight wrap dress, black cloth that clung to her womanly curves as she sat next to Marco on the deck of the beach front restaurant. He had his arm around the back of her chair as she nestled into his side, her hand resting at his lap close to his crotch, her fingers gently rubbed against the fabric of his linen shorts. It was Eve's new favorite place to be, right next to Marco, so close she could feel his heart beating on her shoulder. Unable to stay apart as they sat talking in separate conversations, their bodies meshed to one another.

As far as birthdays went it had been one of the more enjoyable, despite a few rough moment throughout the day. Eventful and relaxing all in one. Eve was with her favorite people, and she was in one of her favorite places, what more could she ask for.

'So, how long until you head back to France?' Rory asked Eve the dreaded question across the end of the table, she was in a conversation with Rory and Zoe.

'Next week,' Eve said with a heavy heart. She didn't want to leave.

'Will you come back?' Zoe asked Eve quietly, Marco shifting nervously at Eve's side.

'Um… I hope so.' Eve looked confused.

'Oh, so it's like that.' Zoe was surprised that Eve didn't know where she stood with Marco as yet.

Dinner as usual with this bunch was like a king's dinner table, full of food that one would think could never be consumed by a mere seven people, but like always these strapping men managed to wipe the table clean.

Zach and Tessa sat next to each other drinking wine with Nick like it was the last supper. Marco even had a glass or two, unusual for him, but he was on a weekend away. Zoe was having spritzes with Eve and Rory was the disciplined one who drank mineral water. Rory had this way about him that was fun and entertaining regardless of his alcohol consumption. He was becoming someone Eve was growing extremely fond of, the more time they spent together chatting and getting to know each other, the more she knew Rory was her kind of person. They sat around the table laughing and joking amongst themselves as if they were in complete privacy, even though they were not. Eve sat with her hand resting close to Marco's groin, consciously arousing his manhood with gentle movements of her little finger.

Zoe's eyes flickered from Eve's hand on Marco's lap and then to Eve's eyes, she was well aware what was going on, it was one of her own tricks. Eve pursing her lips at Zoe with a glimpse of a smile.

'Enjoying the evening are you Marco?' Zoe's cheeky smile amusing him.

'I am actually, Zo,' Marco said as Eve's hand tensed on him.

She leaned into him, 'Meet me in the bathroom. Soon,' whispering into his ear. Not only had she worked Marco into a hard-thick frenzy in his pants, but she'd also managed to get herself all hot and bothered!

Stepping back into the cubicle, pulling Marco in with her, Eve's heart raced. The door shut and without a word she leaned into him. Hands straight to his zipper and then he was in her mouth. Falling back against the cubicle door Marco let her do her thing, his hands up on his head, focusing on the ceiling light so not to cum immediately. Eve's silk like tongue stroked him with desperate eagerness, her hands at either side holding his hips, her mouth sucking and stroking him. The faster she could get him off, the less chance of getting busted. Long curls fell around her as Marco looked down, how could he not, Eve Frank was literally blowing his cock and his mind.

On the edge of cumming, his sighs were all Eve could hear as she worked him to climax.

How Eve made him feel was unlike anything Marco had ever felt before. Her spontaneity was exciting and random, not to mention beyond sexy... he never knew quite what to expect from her. Besides the incredible sex, she was loyal and grounded and absolutely everything he'd ever wanted in every way. As her beautiful yet purposeful mouth pleasured him, he felt himself about to cum, putting his hands into the mass of curls at Eve's head, Marco held her to him, then erupted volcanically into her precious throat.

Finally, a release of tension that had been building all day. He knew exactly why he'd had this pent-up angst; he just didn't know what to do about it. Conflicted, of course he didn't want her to go back to France, but then he didn't want to pressure her to stay. Either way he needed to do something about it, because even though he'd just cum, he was still on edge.

'You never leave me hanging Eve Frank, you are the best,' Marco sighed.

She stood up and smiled delicately whipping the edges of her mouth, 'It was nothing.' She loved to please him.

Returning to the table, the general consensus of the group was that Marco and Eve had gone for a quickie, they couldn't have been more obvious if they'd announced it to the entire restaurant.

'Really, you two!' Zoe smirked as Eve and Marco seated themselves back in their scats.

'Yes, really,' said Marco casually putting his arm around the back of Eve's chair.

The corner bar had a vibe just as it had years ago, Palm Cove was a relatively quiet place, with only the one bar that stayed open late most nights. It was the gathering place for backpackers and tourist of all ages.

By the bar, Tessa and Zach laughing at each other's silly jokes, the attraction and compatibility between them obvious, even to Marco. Eve and Zoe well aware of

Marco's watchful eye. It didn't seem to bother Nick at all, his sister flirting with a married man, but then he didn't care for Brooke. Marco, however, was uncomfortable, and yet he knew he was ultimately powerless to stop it whatever was going on with his best friend and his little sister.

Eve stood beside her lover at the bar in the same spot they kissed for the very first time many years ago. The corner bar was very special to them both.

Feeling the tension, Eve went to Tessa's side. 'Can you two cool it, just a bit.'

'My big brother needs to chill. We're adults you know that don't you?' Tessa huffed.

Zach gave Eve a smile, 'The Big Fella will come around; he'll get over it.'

'I hope so,' Eve sounded stressed.

'We're really not hurting anyone Eve, my marriage is officially over,' Zach pointed out.

Eve decided that she had said her piece and wasn't going to go on about it, there was only so much she could say and do, and it wasn't her battle to fight.

Minutes later, Rory started to dance with Eve, he had this comfortable thing with her that had developed over the past day in Palm Cove. She made him feel at ease, she understood him. Eve didn't ask him ridiculous questions or try and dig into his private life like other people did, she was completely cool.

'This is like De Ja Vu...' he said as he danced, he had great dance moves even though he was as sober.

Eve laughed, 'I know, I feel like we've been here before,' she was enjoying her birthday.

Rory leant into her, 'Can you believe it all started here. You guys have come a long way.'

'Who would believe it!' Her smile was beaming, she was semi drunk and so very content.

'Could this be it for you two?' Rory delved deeper.

The Rolling Stones, Bitch, filled the bar, it reminded Eve of her mum. *Anna*. 'I have no idea; Marco keeps his cards so close... I mean, I know he wants me, but I don't know that he really, really wants me.'

'I think he really, really wants you, for sure. He's a black and white kind of guy. If Marco lets you sleep in his bed, at his house for more than two nights consecutively, then he's serious about you,' a warm grin as he spoke to Eve, she had a sheen to her cinnamon skin from dancing, the night was humid and still.

'Well, he's being a little mysterious about his feelings then.' Eve raised her brows like she didn't know what to expect, which surprised Rory.

'Oh, he's fallen for you; they guy is balls deep into you, young lady,' laughed Rory.

'Physically, yes,' Eve laughed, 'But he gives me nothing about our future.'

It was strange how people changed; Nick surprised himself with his own behavior. He stood tight in beside Zoe at the bar, she was now wedged in between he and Marco. Two handsome Rossi brothers, she was lapping it up. Nick's eye hadn't left her side since they had arrived in Palm Cove. He felt a tinge of shame when he thought back to how he had treated Zoe the last time they were here. She was a young fun-loving girl back then who he'd taken full advantage of. If there was one thing Nick had learned since then, it was that you couldn't treat woman mean and keep them keen. *Well not the good ones anyway!* The world simply didn't work that way when it came to serious relationships. His youth had been spent using woman for sex, Zoe amongst them. Now, she'd grown into this sophisticated driven young woman who he found mesmerizing. There was something about these girls, his sister, Zoe, and Eve... they had this bond of loyalty to each other that was admirable in Nick's opinion. Each so different in their own way, yet so similar in so many other ways. They loved life even though it had thrown a shit sandwich occasionally... Eve was a downright trooper and although he had given her a hard time over Marco years ago, he appreciated that she still adored his big brother, she was certainly keeping him happy, in every way imaginable. But Nick could see it was more than sex, it was an enduring love story that had been put to the test, and miraculously it had managed to still burn deep for both of them years later.

Marco had a few drinks to settle himself, mindful he was in the middle of the most important preseason of his life. He thought that every year... he'd led his team to a successful premiership, and he knew better than anyone the scrutiny his team would be under for the looming season ahead. It was in his nature to strive for more, to be the best he could be and to make sure his team did the same. Marco was a high achiever and he liked to help other people reach their goals too. Eve had been a surprising distraction; one he'd considered very carefully. The one part of his life he hadn't been successful in, was love. Marco felt Eve was his destiny, he'd never quite got over her. From his very first romantic encounter with her in this very bar, there had been something about her that he just couldn't shake. It had taken months for him to get her out of his system after returning to Melbourne that summer after their little love affair. Then years later, London had been a chance meeting of fate, he couldn't stop thinking about her when he got back to Melbourne, he emailed her, and she emailed back, their communication went back and forwards, like love letters. Confiding in his little sister had been a godsend strangely enough. Yep, Tessa came through, she managed to convince Eve to come to New York for Christmas and New Year, and everything he was feeling was confirmed, Eve still felt the spark too.

'She's waiting for you to take a chance on her,' Zoe nudged against Marco at the bar, her voice had a glint of warmth, Zoe was undoubtably Eve's biggest supporter, she'd been there through thick and thin. Always.

'A chance!' he grinned amusingly at Zoe as they leaned with their backs against the bar.

'Yep. A big old fashion chance,' she said merrily.

'What if I need more than a chance Zo, is she going to give it to me?' Marco sounded vague.

'We're talking about Evie here; she adores the ground you walk on.'

'I want everything,' he said with a cocky edge.

'Everything... Well, I hope you know what you're doing. She doesn't need another heartache, especially not from you Marco.' That was a warning in disguise. Zoe wasn't going to let him hurt Eve again.

'I know. I'm fully aware of that, Zo.'

'Don't get me wrong, she's a tough cookie our Evie, very tough actually,' Zoe gave Marco a demure smile, 'But if you break her heart again... I swear, I'll personally kill you.' It wasn't supposed to come out that harsh, Zoe couldn't help it though, she'd always been fiercely protective of Eve.

Marco smiled, 'There'll be no heart breaking from me. How do you know she won't break my heart? She could go back to France and never come back to me.' Marco felt a sense of uneasiness when he said it out loud, and to Zoe of all people.

'You're it for her, you know that right?' Zoe was so serious she almost teared up, 'It's always been you.' Flabbergasted at the notion Marco still needed convincing. Eve is so in love with him, and why wouldn't she be. He was ever so gorgeous on the eye, a true gentleman, and he adored Eve too, it plain to see.

'I hope you're right.' Marco had a dazed look on his face like he was a million miles away.

Nick moved in on their conversation. 'You know this whole thing is so incestual... look at us all.'

'Incestual! What's incestual about us?' Marco found the comment bizarre.

'We've hooked up with our sisters two best friends. Zach, your best mate, and our sister have hooking up again,' Nick explained the dynamics.

Zoe burst out laughing, 'There's no hooking up with you and I Nick. You fucked that up years ago.'

'Don't say that.' Nick said dramatically.

'It's true,' Zoe said looking up to Marco. 'You have no idea what this Fuckboy has put me through. And to think I used to be madly in love with you.' She turned back to Nick with fire in her eyes, not the sexy kind either. Marco looked on wide eyed, watched it play out.

'What do you mean... really!' Nick was flabbergasted, 'I never knew you were in love with me.'

'I got over you fast,' she snarled, 'Right after you fucked me senseless in ways I'd never been fucked before... in places I'd never been fucked before. Right here in Palm Cove... remember.' Zoe was humorously sarcastic. Marco didn't say a word, he just stood there, unsure what to think or say.

The stroll home down the beach was as amusing as ever. Tessa being piggy backed by a yet again drunk Zach, hanging onto his shoulders, a huge question mark hovered in the air over their heads, as they stumbled laughing.

A very quiet Marco on edge still, everyone else in fits of laughter as the banter went back and forth, he'd been ever so serious tonight. Whilst Nick was still hanging in there with Zoe, especially now that he knew she'd once been madly in love with him. The new Nick didn't want to push himself upon her, he needed to let her find her way back to him, trust him. The new Nick would grant her that.

Rory and Eve were on crocodile watch, she was drunk, and he was escorting her, both laughing and joking as they walked with their shoes off trying not to fall into the water.

Marco walked beside Zoe keeping an eye on everyone, he was always the protector, keeping watch over the herd like it was his responsibility or duty. He couldn't digest the whole Tessa and Zach scenario; Zach was way too comfortable with his sister. Marco didn't know what to do, did he demand they stop seeing each other... forbid whatever was unfolding before his very eyes. His sister was already acting super crazy, if Marco insisted they keep apart, she would without doubt, lose her shit. He was at a loss, he was resigned to the fact that this was the situation, all he could do was ignore them... besides, he had more pressing issues on his mind. Matters of the heart. *His heart.*

As the group got to the entrance to go up to the apartment Marco held Eve back. 'Come for a walk, I want to talk to you.' It was now or never; he knew she was semi drunk, but he had to clear his mind now.

They walked over to the little bench seat by the chapel... *their seat.* They sat side by side, Eve with a gorgeous smile on her face.

'What do you want in life Evie?' Marco asked wonderous as they sat looking out at the dark ocean.

'I want a big life. When I die, I want to know I loved with all of my heart.' She looked up into the stars, her smile joyous and sparkling in the moonlight.

'Deeper than I was expecting, but insightful and beautiful all the same,' his grin super sexy.

'Is that not what you asked me?' she looked up at him with sparkling eyes.

'I'm not sure.' Marco looked at her in a self-induced state of confusion. 'I thought you might have said you wanted to own a hotel in Paris or buy a dog or ski the Dolomites.' But no, Eve went way beyond all that stuff. She had gone all the way to the end and looked back. Surprisingly, what she wanted from life was so simple and humble. Eve just wanted love.

'Your turn, tell me what you want Marco Rossi?'

'Basically, I want a life of love too,' he started, debating whether he would go deeper or not. Fuck it, he would, why not. 'I want to have a house full of noisy kids and a gorgeous wife who loves me with all her heart.' A nervous look in his eyes, he'd laid it all out for her.

Eve's heart began to pound in her chest, 'Wow!'

'Yep,' Marco nodded like he was really sure of his answer.

A few moments of silence went by, both deep in wonder, deep in life.

'Evie do you think it would be weird if I said, I wanted to marry you.'

The way her eyebrows came together made Marco draw a deep breath.

'What!' her voice was soft.

'You think it's too soon?' he was momentarily mortified at her reaction but truly didn't really know what reaction he'd expected.

'Um,' Eve needed to absorb it, 'It's not too soon.' Her heart felt like it was bulging in her chest. It was too soon, but how could it be wrong if her heart was swelling with love to the point of bursting.

'It's consuming me- you're consuming me,' Marco went down on one knee, 'Marry me Eve Frank?' He reached into his pocket and produced a small light-colored box, he opened it and let Eve look at the ring. An exquisite rock sparkled back at her.

Shocked and unprepared, she gasped, 'Wow!' a pause, 'Yes, I will marry you.'

There had been many moments in her life that had been among her best, but this was the ultimate. This was the moment were all her dreams become her reality. *This was it!* Everything she'd ever wanted was standing right there in front of her asking her to be his wife.

Marco took the beautiful ring from the box and placing it on her delicate finger, it slid into position like it was meant to be, it couldn't have been more perfect.

'Stay with me forever Evie, never leave me… not for a single day, ever,' Marco held her hands in his, 'I want to spend the rest of my life with you.' His eyes sparking with emotion. 'I don't want you too ever be alone again.' It wasn't exactly what he'd planned on saying to her, but it was what he needed to say. As her tender almond eyes looked up at his, Marco couldn't read her, this worried him. Eve was holding her breath. 'I love you Eve Frank and I'll never hurt ever you again as long as I live, I promise you.' His tender lips went down to meet hers, picking her up into his arms, her feet left the ground.

She gasped, 'I love you so much I can hardly breathe.' Taking a breath, kissing him as tears fell to her cheeks, grateful that her Marco, wanted to be with her forever. Knowing that he comprehended how he'd impacted her life years ago, also meant the world to her.

Marco sat down on the bench, Eve straddled him, her chest to his, rolling her hips into his, sucking at his lower lip as she felt a wetness seep to her knickers. Her warm breath enticing him as he moved his hands to her front, caressing a boob in each of his large hands. He loved her softness, like warn pillowing flesh put on earth to comfort him. Marco loved everything about Eve, everything she was, her face, her skin, her hair, her heart.

It was true love.

Eve pulled at his shorts desperately as she lifted herself just enough to free him. He sprang out of his shorts, his large thick cock pressed to the wetness of her knickers, she slid the fabric to one side with expertise and fell over him with an engulfing surge of silky tender folds.

Marco's hands pulled her to him, he was now deep and pulsing inside her precious body with one spinetingling thrusts. He'd never felt more connected to another human being in his life. 'I love you so much Evie,' he whisper to the side of her face, he felt her holding her breath in angst, her skin was dewy and soft, she was pure heaven.

'I've always loved you,' she gasped with a breathy pleasure.

'This is it; we're really doing this, we're getting married!' Desire was in Marco's voice as he kissed at her lips feverishly, nipping her bottom lip in his teeth.

'Don't cum... please don't cum yet,' Eve begged, wanting every sweet inch of him for as long as she could on their very special seat by the chapel.

'I can't hold on.' He felt his cock stretching her wide open, her pussy was luscious torture.

'No, no, make it last forever, Marco... Marco.' Numbness spread through her body, she tightened with clenching surges around him.

'This is forever baby, I'm all yours,' Marco assured her with tender lips as they came together.

'I love you so much it actually hurts,' whispering, gripping at his shoulders, Eve surrendered herself.

'I know you do,' said Marco breathing to her mouth as he held her now limp body.

Eve wrapped her arms around Marco's broad shoulders. *She was never letting him go again.* 'This is the happiest night of my absolute entire life, Marco Rossi.' The overwhelming power of her orgasm had left her weak; she could feel his beating heart as she laid to his chest.

They sat together for a long time, watching the moon shimmer over the dark ocean, wrapped in each other's adoring arms on their special seat. Everything felt so very right, it was perfect as Eve had always imagined it would be.

Both agreeing to keep the marriage proposal to themselves for the time being, Eve had her reasons and Marco had his, their mutual respect made it easy to do what was best for the other, they would share their news when the time was right and not before. *Besides, it was nice having their very own secret.* They went straight up to their room and had taken a minute to let themselves consume what had just gone down, before going out onto the balcony and joining the others. She had left her beautiful new ring in its box for safekeeping on her bed side table before they went out to join the others in the spa.

Nobody noticed the extra-long intimate gazes between Eve and Marco, both consumed in the commitment they'd just pledged to the other.

Tessa had sobered up slightly and Zoe was very lively and bubbly, how could she not be with all the extra attention Nick was giving her, Rory seemed to have dropped out of the race... was he ever in it!

In the early hours of the morning as they all sat once again in the spa just like they had done all those years ago. Eve cuddled into the safe and loving arms of her secret fiancé.

'We've got a new housemate, Eve's moving in,' Marco announced to Zach.

'Welcome Eve. It'll be like living with my parents all over again,' Zach joked like it was nothing.

Marco's announcement was music to everyone's ears, they belonged together.

Laughing and enjoyed the night, each, and every one of them felt like coming back up to Palm Cove with the old crew was either an escape or a new beginning. They sought comfort in each other's company again. Everyone was content and in good spirits tonight. Eve and Marco glowing, Tessa was on her best behaviour, maybe because she had Zach at her side, and nobody was stopping their handsy display of affection. Zoe was now at ease with Nick, although not advancing physically. To Nick's credit he'd been trying his very best to win her over like a gentleman, and he would keep trying. And then there was Rory, he was everyone's good friend.

The newly engaged couple stood together in the bathroom cleaning their teeth, chatting whilst checking each other out in the mirror, appreciating one another. Marco stood behind Eve and put his hand at her hip, his toothbrush hanging out the side of his mouth, his fingers massaging softly through her satin robe. He now had no doubt that his wife-to-be adored him from head to toe. For such a complexed person, Eve was also very transparent as a lover and partner. Sometimes Marco still saw the shy seventeen-year-old teenager girl, who he just simply had to fuck... even though he knew it had been wrong to do so. Then other times he saw a savvy sensual woman, who completely captivated his every sense as a man. She was sophisticated and downright sexy.

Eve held Marco's gaze in the mirror, she saw a look in his eyes, he had the greatest fuck me eyes, she could see the want in them, he wanted her, and it was an amazing feeling. With a mouthful of paste and her heart and pussy pounding at his gaze, 'I think I just came.' She smiled at him in the mirror.

Marco chuckled, 'Good, I like it when you're wet.' The toothbrush still dangled from his mouth, both hands at Eve's soft tender body, his face with a naughty expression. He bent to eve, his large hands meandered down her arse and inside her short silk robe. His hardening cock pressing into her back as his fingers tucked inside her white lacey G string teddy that she had bought especially for this very night, well not especially for this actual night, she had no idea this would turn out to be the night that Marco would ask her to marry him.

Eve's hands went out in front of her and rested at the edge of the basin, she spat her toothpaste out and rinsed her mouth quickly. Marco's fingers rimmed her G string and found her moist warmth, he pressed a finger inside her soft flesh and explored her as they stood looking at each other in the mirror.

'More! I need you deeper. Harder,' Eve dared him.

Was this going to be his life, fucking the hottest woman he'd ever know for the rest of his blessed life! The thought was too good, Eve was like having the best sexual dream, like all his porn dreams coming true in this one tiny woman who was going to be his wife. She was his very own little sex goddess, not that he'd ever tell anyone of his good fortune. Real men didn't share intimate details, anyway, it was obvious he was a lucky man, well that was how Marco felt anyway. Besides, he'd seen other men looking at Eve, even his own friends, his teammates, even his own fucking family! They all saw it; he didn't have to tell them a thing.

His wife to be, was super fucking hot!

The fact that Eve wasn't scared to ask Marco for what pleasured her, turned him on bigtime. He chewed down on his toothbrush as it still hung from his mouth, paste on his lips as he pleasured Eve. 'Deep enough?' he plunged his finger up inside her, he knew she liked a little edginess every now and then, Marco had a way of being delicately forceful in the best possible way. He was strong, yet wary of his size and power. He had to watch himself with Eve, he was big in every way compared to her, he was a gentle man by nature and when it came to Eve and fucking her... he knew the boundaries.

Opening her gently with his hand, Marco spat his toothbrush out into the basin so he could kiss her cinnamon skin with his plump toothpaste lips, all the while swirling his fingers in her juices.

'Please fuck me Marco,' Eve's voice a whimper as she caught his eyes in the mirror, 'Or make love to me.' She had an out of it sexy grin as she watched him finger her. Long hair hung over her shoulders and face, her mouth open as she drew breath, transfixed with pleasure. She felt him working her over, touching, pressing, and rubbing in all the right places, it was like he knew her body better than she.

Marco stood up and took his hand from Eve's pussy, taking a good look at her in the mirror, he liked the white lace against her cinnamon skin, he liked that her boobs bulged at the top, and he very much liked that her dark nipples peaked beneath the lace. Lowering his shorts and taking hold of himself, rubbing his huge warm hardness to her back so she could feel what was coming next, her eyes wide and sensual in the mirror looking back at him. Marco lifted her up in the air to his cock, her hands at the edge of the basin, him holding her waist. Eve sliding straight down onto his shaft, gasping as he let her fall all the way onto him, hitting her cervix as he filled her. Eve was a pleaser, and he knew it, she'd do anything he wanted, he'd never take advantage of her willingness… *well maybe not every time!*

Marco was thrusting and bucking to her as he held her in position over him, there was no catching her breath, it was hardcore right off the bat, just the way she wanted it. The angle was deep and sharp as Marco's hands clenched at her body; she was jolting with his movement. Their sex glazed intense at each other again in the mirror, it was like they'd been drugged with orgasmic juices.

Eve pushed herself back into Marco's stomach, his length filling her so it hurt. He pulled her into his front, she was so light weight it was a walk in the park for him. Holding her firm so he could focus on fucking her into a wet crazed madness, her feet dangling, the angle of his large cock penetrating deeper, going in and out, bringing Eve to a sweat in the tropical night heat. Her head rolling back at his shoulder as she tried to handle the sensation. It was furious and intense as she held her arms up to his neck, her boobs moving about at her chest with the motions, she felt herself losing all control and it was utter heaven.

Marco thrusted harder and harder, Eve took it over and over. It was maddening moment of his sheer strength and her unwavering dedication to his cock.

Eve's hands slipped at his neck, 'I can't hold on anymore,' she gasped looking at Marco in the mirror, her arms hurting from hanging onto him. As if she was a light weight, he took her under the armpits and lifted her off his pulsating cock, turning her in the air like she was a tiny child. Eve grabbed at his shoulder, her legs wrapped around his waist for safety, now they were face to face.

Marco lowered her gently back over him as he stood tall, his hands at her back, holding her in place to his body, her soft pillowing chest against his, her nipples swelling and hard at his skin.

Resting his bum down on the edge of the basin, his knees slightly spread, he kissed Eve's mouth. Clenching at her boob and rubbing his thumb vigorously over her nipple.

Eve scrambling and pulling herself up his body, the feeling of him coming out and going back in her pussy was stimulating in all the right ways. Her orgasm was coming back, she was sweating, buzzing as she let herself go numb. Then Marco hand slid down her back to her arse cheek and all the way under to her dripping wet pussy, Eve groaned her approval as Marco's fingers traced over her anus, then her folds, his cock buried deep inside her. All inhibitions had gone as he spread her sticky juices to her behind, his fingers gently rubbing over her anus, she was cumming again. Mid climax, Eve gulping for air, her eyes shut tightly as the erotic sensation took her.

Marco circling fingers at her anus, Eve knew what he had in mind, *and she couldn't wait.*

Still holding her to him, his other hand pulling at her long dangling curls as they hung down her back. Pulling her head back, a firm taught pull that exited her, adding to the amorousness of the act.

'Do it, I want you to,' she gasped.

Her nipples hard bushing over Marco's chest, she was begging for it she was. Marco loved anal sex and Eve knew it… he knew, she knew it too, and that made it all the sexier.

'Lets go to the bed,' Marco gasped carrying her, laying her out in front of him, spreading her legs apart and positioned himself between them. Eve laid back and waited for Marco's next move, she pulled her feet up to her sides as his tongue began to lick over her drenched folds and her anus … she lost her fucking mind!!!

'Are you okay?' Marco came up for moment he heard her cries. Eve's hands covered her face, an exasperated carnal groan told him she was more than okay. A few more slow and tender licks of her velvety pussy, end to end, and she was covered in her own cum. Marco took a precious second to watch her pussy ooze with creamy liquid. On his knees he turned Eve around, she was on all fours. His hand twined in her long hair at her back, his fingers rubbing now over her sensitive folds in a circular motion to taunt her. Inserting one finger and then another, and then a third… fast motions of his large man fingers, his thumb teased her clit.

With fists of bedsheets, it amazed Eve how one man's perfect hand could make her feel so slutty and dirty... in the sexiest of ways, she was unashamedly fucking Marco's hand as she moaned and oozed cum all over him.

Big fingers smoothed Eve's cum to her anus, teasing her. Eve knew what to expect next and she was more than happy for him to go there. *Fuck. Go there, please!*

His masculine body at her back, his arm slid under her waist and lifted her hips into position as she pulled her hair to the side and spread her legs out wide... A soft desperate gasp as Marco's large cock press between her arse cheeks and inside her body. 'Fuck me hard Marco, I'm all yours now,' Eve only ever spoke dirty when she was about to cum... she talked dirty a lot!

Eve was a dream! Marco thought as he slid into her tight arse. Fucking her with deep long slow strokes, barely able to contain himself. The tightness squeezing around his cock told him he needed to take it easy, he needed to ease his way into her. He was a blessed man, making her moan and groan his name, over and over until as he went from gentle pumps to punishing thrust inside Eve arse, all the while his fingers again fucked her saturated pussy as he reached underneath her.

Eve was perplexed as to why men loved anal sex so desperately. She could feel Marco's carnal anal obsession inside his body, the way he moved over her back slow, like a predatorial animal mating. It wasn't so much the feeling for her, it was that Marco loved it so much.

'Oh. Fuck. Evie, you feel so good.' Marco nestled his face into the back of her head trying to keep his cool. Eve looked back at him, a few small harmless bites of her cheek, it was animal like sex, the need for his wife to be taking over. His fingers flicking and fucking her pussy, stimulating her deep inside vigorously. Marco with less care than he would normally taken with Eve, in such a vulnerable position, he penetrated into her arse deeper and harder until her desperate groans filled the room. She was hypersensitive to the sensation of her anus and her pussy being stimulated all at once. Marco absolutely loved it, Eve was a lady on the street and a freak in the bed, the more he demanded of her, the more she begged for it.

The size of Marco's cock during anal sex was overwhelming. The awkward pain made Eve move from him slightly, he was so into it, and she would not be defeated by sex.

'Breath for me baby,' he instructed, realising Eve was holding her breath; her body was tense under him.

'I love you,' she managed a gasp as his fingers dug deep inside sensitive vaginal folds, she felt the craziness of it all taking over her mind and body. Telling herself to surrender to the invasive penetration, then a strange, yet familiar erotic sensation flooded through her like a cocaine rush, her painful apprehension had now become her pleasure as Marco went all the way up inside her arse.

He didn't say a word as Eve softly panted her way through yet another tormenting orgasm, mesmerized by her tightness clenching around his dick, his body responding to her quickly.

'I'm cumming Evie.' Quivering with sweat as he let his senses indulge in the goodness that was Eve's arse, she melted to the bedsheet as he lay over her, emersed in uncomprehensive satisfaction.

For Eve it still felt strange when Marco called her baby… it was what Evan use to call her, all the time, she would get use to Marco saying it, it would just take some time… he said it so fucking sweetly.

Marco didn't pull out of her arse until he had finished cumming. Pinning her to the bed, so he was fully submerged hard and tight up inside her making the most of the awesome sensation. Eve was silent as they collapsed to the bed, hot and exhausted. She laid with her stomach to the bed, her face to the side as she started to cry, a sob alarming Marco.

'What's wrong, did I hurt you, are you okay?' he said moving from her.

'I'm fine,' she sniffed letting a little smile appear. Eve wasn't in pain; she was overcome with love.

'Then what's wrong?' Marco felt a heaviness.

'It's just that I'm so in love with you, I actually can't believe we're getting married,' her cry turned to a smile.

'Yes, we're getting married Eve Frank,' he smiled with relief, 'And I can't wait.'

Eve took the girls to the café on the beach for breakfast, she wanted time alone with them before they went back to Sydney this afternoon, and she went back to Melbourne with Marco.

Tessa was visibly hung over and irritated, even though she'd spent the night with Zach again, there seemed more to that than met the eye, Eve thought as they sat at a shaded table watching the morning unfold amongst the palms.

Zoe was her normal self, 'I for one, am way excited that we're all back home on the same continent. This is the best thing that has happened to me in years,' she said cheery as she sipped her green juice.

'I wish you'd just fuck someone,' Tessa huffed, downing a black coffee and a can of Coke at the same time.

Zoe ignored her rudeness; Tessa's mood was grating on everyone.

'E. You look like you've got something to say,' Tessa was in a strange mood, yet ever so switched on.

'I need to tell you guys something. I know who my biological mum is, and I've known for a while,' she paused, 'Ferez and Marco know too. I need you guys to be really careful with this information because I'm not sure if Anna knows yet,' a pause, 'I think she may know and she's just never told me,' Eve looked hurt, 'I'm really *angry* about that part right now, not that I want to be… I just am. If Anna knows, and she's kept this from me after everything we've been through.' Eve huffed stressfully, 'I'll be really upset.' She was finding it hard to articulate her feelings into words. 'According to my dad, Anna knows… so who the hell knows the truth? Not me that's for sure.' She exhaled and smiled as Tessa and Zoe both sat enthralled.

'Go on. Who is she?' Zoe was eager, putting her juice straw back in her mouth. She loved an Eve drama, there always seemed to be one and they were compelling.

'It's taken a while to come to terms with it, so please forgive me for keeping it from you both.'

'How did you find her?' Tessa asked moving in close to Eve.

It took a few moments for her to begin, 'The night before Evan's funeral I found an envelope in his safe, the one he kept down in his office. The envelope had all kinds of documents regarding me. Doctor reports about my babies.' Eve gave herself a minute. 'There was a title for Villa Rosado in my name. Evan bought the house for me. I've just decided to sell it.' She looked at her friends for their word.

'What the fuck E, he bought you a house worth fucking millions and millions?' Tessa spat her coffee.

'Ssshhh,' Zoe hushed Tessa, 'Keep going Evie.'

'And then there was a copy of my original birth certificate, from when I was born.' A nervous smile came to Eve's face. 'It turns out Evan fucked my biological mum as well as me... by accident... God bless him.' Eve had to laugh, how could she not as Tessa and Zoe's mouth literally dropped open, completely mortified, gob smacked and in shock.

'What the fuck?' Zoe said loudly.

'Who is it?' Tessa screwed her face up impatiently.

'Sam. My dad's girlfriend is my biological mother.' There was no other way to say it.

Tessa stood up in some sort of shocked motion, and then sat back down in her seat, 'Hey didn't she work for Evan's dad. Wasn't she a -' she was right yet confused.

'Tessa!' Zoe silenced her again in horror.

'Yep. My dad got a sixteen-year-old sex worker pregnant, then had twins with her fifteen years later.' Eve had an air of disbelief in her tone, as well as acceptance. It sounded farfetched; she knew.

'Oh, my goodness, Evie,' Zoe how spoke at a whisper.

After the initial shocking few seconds, Tessa cleared her throat 'So, the twins are your full sisters. And your beautiful skin... that's where you get it from, from her.' Tessa was too shocked to be rude again. The girls had seen Sam at Evan's funeral very briefly, she was hard not to notice at James's side, so young and beautiful.

'Yep... I'm a whore's daughter,' Eve scrunched her face up, 'Oh god, I hate that word.'

Zoe gasped, 'No, no you're not... don't say that. You're not a whore's daughter at all!' Zoe put her hand on Eve's for moral support. 'Evie, this is terrible and yet somehow amazing. Are you alright?'

Eve shrugged.

'You think Anna knows your biological mum is Sam?' Zoe asked trying to piece it all together.

'That's what my dad says. Apparently it was part of the deal when Anna agreed to raise me, I was never to know the truth, and Sam was never to have anything to do with me.' Eve shifted in her seat awkwardly; it was hard telling her friends about her very personal and private beginnings.

'Did Evan know who you were from the start, did he know he'd been with Sam and then you from the start?' Tessa asked with suspicion, she was being mature and caring.

'No, of course not. He put two and two together after we ran into my dad and Sam and my dad at the restaurant on Christmas Eve,' Eve explained.

'Wow. This is some heavy shit E,' Tessa was drained just listening to it, 'James has outdone himself this time.' Tessa was in disbelief that James had fucked a sixteen-year-old whore, and that Evan had fucked both Eve and Sam... No wonder James never liked Evan! *This was a scandal of epic proportions.*

'I know, it's outrageous, but it's my life,' Eve said to her friends, 'Please don't tell your mum Tessa until I've spoken to Anna.'

'Absolutely not. Just don't leave it too long, I don't know how long I can sit on this one E,' Tessa teased bring some humor into what was a deep conversation.

Zoe had calmed down, 'You're not the daughter of a whore, and I never want to hear you say that ever again Eveline Frank.' It bothered Zoe. 'You got me!'

'Well, it's the truth,' said Eve as she faced her reality.

'You're a whore's daughter biologically, but not really,' Tessa began, 'The whore gave birth to you, but Anna raised you, and James fucked you all up the arse... Imagine how poor Anna must feel about all this!' There was no stopping Tessa when she had something to say, 'What a woman Anna is. She did such a good job raising you E.' Tessa was having an emotional moment, 'Anna not only took in another woman's baby, who'd also been fucking her very own husband... I personally commend her. Most of all, I thank Anna for giving me a beautiful friend.' Tessa had tears in her eyes, her lip quivered.

Both Eve and Zoe found themselves dumfounded at Tessa's interpretation of Eve's life. She could be sensitive and meaningful when she wanted to, in her own bizarre way.

'We're more than friends Tessa,' Eve said, 'You two are so much more to me than friends to me,' she couldn't help but feel the emotion of the moment, 'The night I found the envelope in Evan's safe, the night before his funeral. I considered ending my life... I actually had Evan's gun in my hand on the floor of his office,' Eve took a breath as she watched her two friends again silenced. 'I'd lost Rafael and the man who I was going to give myself to forever,' her eyes filled with tears, they were tears for her loss. 'I was going to put the gun in my mouth when you came to the door Tessa. Then I thought, how could I do that to the two of you!' Tears fell out of Eve's eyes and rolled down her cheeks, 'Both of you were doing your best to look after me, getting me through the most fucking excruciating pain of my life,' she sniffed a sob, 'Thank you both... for everything.'

Eve held Marco's hand on the flight home to Melbourne, 'I would have thought they might have discussed the whole having children thing before they decided to get married,' she whispered to Marco looking up at him.

He raised his eyebrows; Eve was talking about Brooke and Zach. 'I guess when you're in love with someone, you don't always consider the future that far ahead.' It was the way Marco's eyes sparkled at her, that made Eve realize he was actually talking about them.

'When you commit to marrying someone, you should know how they feel about having a family... It's not for everyone.' Her tone was warning like.

'I don't know babe,' Marco rubbed her hand.

'Are we about to have that conversation... children?' Eve's soft whisper was unassuming.

'You know I want a family Evie.' S

'What if we can't have children together? How would you feel then?' Eve asked.

'We both know we can have children together,' Marco narrowing his eyes.

'I got pregnant to you; I didn't actually have the baby. There's a difference.' She didn't want to be having this conversation, but knew it was needed. 'And then it happened again, so maybe I can't have kids. I don't know.'

'Would you have my baby if you could, that's all I need to know?'

'Of course, I would.' *What the fuck!* She was looking Marco straight in the eye. It had been so easy to just say yes, yet she wasn't sure. Eve was petrified she'd lose another baby. But, and it was a massive *but*, she wanted to give Marco the life he wanted, whether she could do it or not was another thing.

Her therapist in France had told her she would need to deal with these feeling one day, and that day had come.

Marco had come along and swept her off her feet, again! He was her dream, and she didn't want to denying him of anything, but being pregnant was another thing.

It took Eve days to muster the courage up to call her grandmother. The idea of leaving her sanctuary in France was daunting and somewhat deep seeded for Eve. It had been her salvation; it was her safe place and she'd heeled under the watchful eye of her grandmother and Louis. However, she knew they would always be there for her, and leaving Marco even for a minute was not an option. Eve had made her mind up without a second thought, now she just needed to tell her grandmother she wasn't returning. Then there was the conversation she had been going over in her head regarding her biological mother. How was Vivienne going to react, what would be her answer be this time? Eve was filled with anxiety.

'I'm so happy that you are happy, my darling Eveline,' Vivienne gushed when Eve told her she was staying with Marco in Melbourne, she left out the marriage proposal, not even her Gran was going to be privy to that. It was for her and Marco only.

'I know it's fast?' Eve said, wondering why she needed her grandmother's approval.

'Eveline, I've done things fast my whole life, I've made some of my best decision in a second,' Vivienne laughed, she'd always lived life her own way, she had done things that would perhaps shock her granddaughter.

'Mame,' she took a breath, 'Have you told me everything you know about my birth mother?' There was no other way to ask.

'What's happened?' Vivienne sounded unfazed by the question.

Eve noted that she didn't answer *yes or no.* 'I want to know more about her,' Eve said, wondering if her father had told Anna that she knew Sam was her biological mother, and whether Anna had told her grandmother.

Where they all playing her for a fool? It was an awful feeling.

'Darling, the best person to help you with this is your father.'

This alarmed Eve. She was silent after her grandmother deflecting. It felt like they were all in on it together. Every single one of them. Instantly Eve was agitated.

'Right!' It was an almost a narky Eve.

The phone call ended shortly after, and Eve was pissed to say the least, not wanting to be angry at her grandmother, but hurt all the same, Vivienne knew exactly who her biological mother was, and she wasn't telling! They were all treating her like she was incapable of handling the truth.

Stewing on her grandmother's phone call for the entire afternoon until Marco came home, Eve sat in the small courtyard garden out the back with Pat the dog, she drank what seemed like twenty coffees and ate half a packet of Tim Tams, feeding Pat the dog small pieces of each biscuit, she knew dogs and chocolate didn't mix, a little couldn't hurt.

Eve picked her phone up a million times ready to call Anna and have it out with her. Then the impulse to call her father and lash out at him… she thought better of it due to the situation with Aria. She let James off this time. A wave of guilt swept through Eve, she had these two little sisters who seemed like the sweetest little girls, so very much like she had been at the same age, and she didn't even know them. *What a shit big sister she was! And what a terrible dad James had been. Soon she'd have to get over herself and become a big sister.*

Aria was fighting for her life and Eve had never met her. *What if she never got to meet her, what if she left her run too late?* It was a horrible thought. James was father to them all, he'd been trying with Eve of late, she'd been doing the same, they were building a relationship after so long of being offside with one another, he'd been open with her about Sam and Anna demands. After everything, her dad was the only one being honest with her… perhaps!

'The best part of my day is coming home.' Marco found Eve out in the courtyard, Pat the dog at her side, they were now great friends. Eve stood to her tall dark and handsome lover, her arms flinging around his neck, he lifted her feet off the ground as her lips met his. He was very aware Eve was spending all day on her own during the day, and now that Brooke was permanently gone from the house, she didn't have any female interaction at all.

Eve didn't say a word, her feet grounded to the paved floor again as their lips still lapped at each other with passion, her hands going straight up the front of Marco's T shirt to feel him, a sudden surge of lust at the sight of him, he'd always had that effect on her. Sometimes it was stronger than others, sometimes she just needed him, all of him.

Marco leaned down, his arms wrapping around her back, she wore a tiny piece of cloth that was her dress, the weather had been really hot, so Eve wore very little, this made her happy. She had no bra on and a G string as he ran his hands down over her arse thinking this was what he wanted to come home to every afternoon.

Eve's need to fuck Marco hard and wash away her tense afternoon was all she could think about, as her hands moved to the waist band on his sport shorts and pulled them down over his hips, Marco's semi hard bulge sprang to life. She took him in her hand, pulling at him with a soft hand, lowering her mouth over the head of his cock and sucking at him. This was what Eve had become best at, and what she knew Marco liked after a long hard day at training.

'I'm not even going to ask how your day has been, just keep doing what you're doing,' he joked with an amused chuckle, rubbing her hair into her head like he was washing it. Eve's tongue slid along the tender length of his hardening cock. A head massage was the least he could do for her.

It was a stand-up blow job that Eve had become accustomed to giving Marco, he was so tall she didn't have to fall to her knees, she only had to bend forward a little and it gave her more leverage to put her everything into sucking him off in the best way she knew. Lots of tongue rubbing and licking and strong hard sucking.

Marco felt her take him into the back of her throat with more gusto than normal, he was swept away into an erotic sexual coma as Eve sucked him, her hand caressing and kneading at his base and balls.

'Evie this is good.' He couldn't help but press her head gently to him as she continued to take her frustrating day out on him. Gripping him, feeling his veins pulsing as she worked him with a tugging motion, giving him all that she had. Eve's effort was alarming as it was fantastic to Marco. She was on a mission that was for sure, and he was enjoying every second as she worked him over. He knew something was up, she had an abruptness about her that was being masked by her spectacular cock sucking skills.

This was winning nevertheless, Marco thought. He smiled with a cough of satisfaction, his hands to Eve's shoulders, moving her off of him, her sucking was awesome, but she was unusually intense, and as much as he wanted to benefit from her odd mood, he needed to calm her down before she combusted with his cock in her mouth!

His hand reached out to her face and rested at her cheek, 'Evie baby, what's going on?' he asked, his rock-hard cock stood to attention throbbing between them.

Her hair was messed over her face and her dress hung off her shoulders, she was disheveled, 'I need you to fuck away my crap day... can you do that for me?'

Marco was momentarily taken back, and then humored by her forwardness, she was sexy and hot. He went straight to work! 'Get on the table. Spread your legs and touch yourself... I want to see everything.' Marco flung his T shirt off and tapped the side of his leg, then his shorts came off too.

Eve sat at the edge of the table with her legs apart, she rubbed her fingers over her now reactive clit, it was so sensitive she thought she might cum there and then. Secretly, she'd always wanted to cum like in the porn movies, the squirting type of cum. She'd watch porn with Evan on many occasions... and on her own since.

'Finger yourself.' All of the sudden Marco was full of orders, Eve wasn't the only one who knew what she wanted.

She wanted to be in charge, 'I said fuck me.'

'And I said finger yourself.' Marco liked this game a lot, his dominance was doing it for Eve, she plunged two fingers between her legs and deep into her pussy as Marco watched on.

Oh, fuck he loved this woman!

She opened her legs and put on a show, she'd done this before, but not for quite some time. Marco's sheer elation evident on his sweet, gorgeous face. Pulsing a creamy fluid over her fingers, her nipple hurt she was so buzzed. Eve's body craved Marco right up inside her. God, all she wanted was to be fucked good and hard, she didn't want the teasing and the game bullshit. *Just fuck me!* 'Fuck me, now. Please. Please. Please Marco,' Eve insisted like a spoilt child.

'Lick your fingers first,' he huffed with a smile, he was on a sexual roll, she was doing anything he said!

As horny as Eve was, and as desperate as she felt, she loved this Marco who was so sure of his sexuality, her fingers went straight into her mouth without a second thought, she sucked them before putting them back inside herself to stop the crazy beeping sensation from sending her utterly mad. Her face scrunched up and she made a pained noise as her involuntary orgasm felt like it was paralyzing her.

Marco lifted one of her knees, Eve spread them wide in front of him, really slutting it up, doing her best to hurry him up. Her slip of her dress now gathered around her midriff, his eyes widening as Eve now had all her fingers inside her neat little pussy, moving them in a jabbing like motion into herself, panting and groaning.

Fascinatingly mesmerized by what he was witnessing, another layer to the sumptuous woman he was totally besotted with, Marco felt like he was discovering parts of Eve he never knew existed. *And he loved it.*

Both horny as hell and both in a sexual stand-off as Eve dug into her own fleshy wetness. She reached out for his now very large manhood, she had to have him.

'Fuck me, please. Don't make me beg you Marco Rossi... I know you really want to. I know you're holding out on me,' Eve gasping and panting as he moved closer to her, she could tug at him while he watched her fingering herself... not an issue for Eve, perhaps a touch physically awkward, but awesome all the same.

'I will, in good time Eve Frank.' His head went to one side, his eyes fixed to her pussy as he reached for her, his thumb gently teasing her clit as she took her hand away and rested back on her elbows... giving up, somewhat exhausted. Marco began to play with her wet swelling folds, teasing and then teasing some more.

'Marco. Marco. Marco. PLEASE?' Aching for him to be inside her, Eve watched as his fingers explored her now swelling folds, her legs spread wide apart. Her juices lusciously engulfing his hand as he twisted it in and out. Her eyes flickering to his erect cock and then back to her needy pussy.

Eve let out a frustrated moan as Marco stretched her opening with a gentle fisting motion as she began to pant and breathe in rapid puffs, pushing herself to his hand.

Marco's strong hands pulled Eve's hips up to his, rubbing his cock over her before he plunged himself all the way inside her with one harsh and abrupt thrust.

Tears stung her eyes, her cheeks flushed as he hit her cervix, the hardness of him pressing so deep inside her belly was just what she needed. Eve needed to feel pain, physically more than anything. In her own head, it was like a form of self-punishment she'd made Marco bestowed upon her for being upset with her parents.

Or more so for allowing herself to be upset with them. Weird, but true.

'Make me hurt.' Eve's head dropped back as Marco thrusted, slapping into her as he stood and she laid back on her elbows on the tabletop, literally pounding her to the point of no return. His face intense as he pulled her hips carelessly to his, slamming to her almost aggressively as she took him over and over again.

'What's going on with you today?' Marco murmured curiously.

'Harder!' her voice quivered; her face winced to his relentless thrusts.

With all his strength Marco fucked Eve as hard as he possibly could, giving her everything he had, his arse clenching, borderline cramping as he did his best. 'Is it hurting?' he knew it had to be, he could feel his cock hammering into her walls, he was conscious he would hurt her or worse, make her bleed. It was so abruptly carnal that Marco almost needed to stop.

'Don't you dare stop,' Eve said throw clenched teeth like she'd read his mind. Demanding of him as she felt Marco powering her to a different kind of climax. Her stomach and pussy sore, her body struggling to keep up, the numbness overcoming her.

She felt Marco tensing to her as she let out a cry of excruciating satisfaction… finally she was there. Pain. Lust. Satisfaction and cum... Eve sobbed as her body jolted. Marco's cock shot a burst of cum like a missile rocket launcher inside her.

He collapsed over her; her dress still wrapped around her waist; Eve laid back on the tabletop hugging him.

Little kisses to her neck, turning his head to find her soft lips, 'I hope that helped whatever it is you've got going on baby.' His lips moved to hers.

'You have no idea how much I needed you.' She kissed him back softly as his hot sticky body touched hers.

'Me, or my sex?' Marco rubbed his hands up and down the smooth softness of her body that had just given him the most amazing sex once again. *It just got better and better.*

'You and your sex... and just so you know Marco Rossi, that was fucking amazing,' Eve huffed to his lips as she felt his broad shoulders with the palms of her hands as he moved from her. 'Sorry if I'm being weird. I know I'm complexed. I don't want to be,' she felt the need to apologize. The mess between their legs being ignored, it had been so frantically good, neither cared. He pulled her by the hands, so she sat up as he stood.

'I love every little complexed bone in your body Eve Frank. I wouldn't have asked you to marry me if I didn't.' Marco placed his hips between her legs as she sat on the edge of the outdoor table, his arms wrapped around her as he stood up, Eve reached up to his shoulders resting her arms at his.

'I try to keep my complexities to myself. God knows there are so many of them.' Her eyes teary.

'I know you've got things going on. You can talk to me about anything... or you can just do that again, I'm down either way. Whatever works for you,' he smiled placing a kiss on her forehead.

A bothered smile on her face, 'I appreciate you. I hope you know that Marco.' She felt so much better it was amazing. Sore all the same. But it had been well worth it, Marco was like her very own sexual medicine man. *Whatever was wrong, a good Marco fucking was always the answer.*

The night was stuffy and hot, the air conditioner was doing its best, but after a few days of temperatures in the high thirties, it was struggling, so tonight the ceiling fan would have to do.

Marco sat in bed reading a book about a guy who got his arm stuck in rocks and had to chop it off himself to save his own life. Every so often he would stop reading and tell Eve the latest development in the story line, interrupting her as she read her own book about how a woman who found out her older sister was actually her mother at the age of sixteen. Eve's psychologist in France had recommended it a few years ago, and then she stumbled across it by sheer accident at the bookstore around the corner. She didn't feel the need to share updates of her book with Marco though. Patiently she let him fill her in blow by blow of the arm removal which she had absolutely no interest in.

Eve's book focused on the woman's struggle with the betrayal she felt from her entire family and how she felt her mother, really her grandmother, had been the worst perpetrator of all. It was about forgiveness.

Marco slapped his book closed, it was past ten o'clock, and it was sweltering. He turned and laid down so he could watch Eve read. Her hair tied high on top of her head in a ball, he loved her hair like this, her face looked so delicate and small under all that hair. She wore a little cotton singlet and knickers, Pat the dog resting at her feet.

His hand reached out slowly and rest on her stomach, making her glance at him for a second before returning to her book. The hand just at her stomach. Eve glanced again at him, a cheeky glint in his eyes distracting her.

'Do you know what I'm thinking right now?' Marco said as Eve put her book to her lap.

'How you want to go down to the beach and take a night swim because this bedroom is stifling hot! I'm sure there are plenty of people doing it… I'll go with you; Pat would probably love a swim too.' She wasn't being funny; Eve could only imagine the beach would be cooler right about now.

'No, that's not it.' His hand rubbed her stomach softly.

'What are you thinking in that gorgeous head of yours my love?' Eve loved the way the words sounded; Marco was her love. Moments like this when it was just the two of them, alone in bed, in silence, at ease with each other and completely relaxed, she loved more than anything.

'I'm nearly thirty, and I want to be a dad.' It had been playing on his mind since the flight home from Palm Cove. *Did Eve want kids or not!*

'I feel like that's a lot of pressure?' Honesty had to be her policy; she knew exactly what this was all about.

'I know. I know. It's just I want kids; I think about it all the time and I don't want to be an old dad Evie.'

'I know Marco, you keep telling me.' *How had she fallen in love twice with men who wanted her barefoot and pregnant.* 'Marry me first, then we can talk babies.'

Eve's answer was music to Marco's ears. A wave of relief engulfing him, at least she was thinking about it. He was cool with marriage, then babies.

Chapter Nineteen

'This is awesome. You two are fucking crazy,' Tessa gushed, she held Eve's hand from the back seat, Eve sat in the front passenger seat of Marco's car, he was driving. They had picked his sister up from the airport and told her about their wedding plans. It was Marco's idea to tell his sister first, not to mention the fact that it was already early March and she'd been their biggest supporter right from the very start. Tessa was in Melbourne for an audition that had been delayed twice already, it was all very exciting for her, this was a great opportunity.

Eve wore her beautiful diamond ring on her ring finger. Tessa was completely taken by surprise at how fast things had advanced with her favourite love birds, this was the perfect ending to this decade old love story.

Marco spoke with caution, 'You can't tell mum and dad yet,' it was his one stipulation, 'We want to tell them ourselves when they come down to Melbourne.' He glanced at his sister in the rear-view mirror.

'You crazy kids, I just love it, I'm so happy for you both.' Tessa still looking at the engagement ring. Eve's arm bent back into the back seat as Tessa held her hand. Her smiling eyes lifted to Eve's as she looked back.

'We know it's sudden, but in a way it's not,' Eve said smiling back at her best friend who would now become her sister in-law.

'This is amazing. You two really love each other for real... I always knew it.' Tessa had a sense of pride and felt like she'd had a hand in bringing Eve and Marco together.

Tessa took the spare room without a question. Zach was home and he was waiting for her to arrive. He'd had a rough time since splitting from Brooke, the marriage was over, but it was still early days. Part of him still hadn't come to terms with everything, it was going to take time to fall out of love with his wife.

Tessa and Zach respectfully gave each other a hug and short kiss on greeting and kept it low key for Marco's sake, he was her big brother after all, she didn't want to get off on the wrong foot whilst she was staying in his home. Tessa and Zach had cooled it over the past months, they'd had a few chats over the phone and that was about it, but the spark was always there.

The following day, Eve gladly went into the city with Tessa for her audition and snuck into the very back of the theater to watch. She had always been in awe of her friend's ability to move her body so gracefully and so professionally; Tessa really knew how to dance. She had lived and breathed dancing her whole life.

The thought of Brooke and the other girls knowing about Zach and Tessa had played on Eve's mind. What would they think? How would they react? She hadn't met all the wives and girlfriends, and she didn't really want to if she was being honest. It was enough with Brooke, Ro, Louise, and Jules all initially judging her. Eve couldn't see herself being too involved in Marco's football world; she'd never been one to be part of an inner click. The extent of her friendship group was Tessa and Zoe primarily, and then Ferez, Jo, and Kellie... she didn't really have or need any other friends. And after the way Ro took her apart on their first meeting, she was now going to be extremely cautious of all the other wives and girlfriends.

Once Tessa's audition was over, the girls had lunch and did a spot of shopping in the city, Eve bought new bedlinen and shoes of course, she also bought Marco some very expensive underwear, of which Tessa thought was absurd, but Eve could see this becoming a fetish, she was seriously turned-on buying luxury fabric to cover Marco's dick and balls... It really was a kink for her.

Dinner was the four of them meeting up with Rory a local Italian restaurant so Eve and Marco could tell the boys their wedding news, prior to Jackie and Mario's arrival next week. For something that was supposed to be a secret, the news was spreading fast... they were excited.

The girls drank wine while the boys behaved themselves, the season was kicking off in a week, so it was health and fitness like never before. All of this was new to Eve, she admired Marco's dedication and now appreciated his routine and superstitions. God knows his career took up so much of his time with training, meetings, and even compulsory club dinners and functions. Football came first, but then Eve had always known this.

She'd planned to tell her mother and father about the marriage proposal the next time she spoke to them, once Jackie and Mario knew. Of course, she'd already told Zoe, she'd secretly been the first-person to know. Eve and Zoe missed each other tremendously, Zoe was also planning to come to Melbourne next weekend with Nick and his parents for Marco's first game of the season. It was going to be a big Rossi affair. Nick and Zoe were still only friends.

By now Eve had already been in Melbourne for nearly two months, she was curious to see what all this football fuss was all about, seeing Marco play a game in the flesh was something she looked forward to.

Life was good for Marco Rossi right now, he was the captain of the reining premiership team, he was in the best physical shape of his life, engaged to marry Eve Frank from up the hill, who'd surprisingly turned out to be his dream girl. He made love to her every minute of the day he possibly could, one thing he noted blissfully about Eve, she never turned him down, ever! Every morning he woke up and felt blessed because she was in his bed. Every night they talked about the day that was, she always listened and made him laugh when he needed to. Eve's cooking skills were next level and had been a joy to both Marco and Zach, they relished in the fruits of Eve's labor in the kitchen most nights. Having someone make their meals every night was out of this world for the guys. Then there was the fact that Eve was a clean freak, another huge added bonus for Marco who didn't have great housekeeping skills. She magically kept the entire house spotless; the guys didn't expect her to do it at all, she just did it, it gave her something to fill her day with. Little did they realise, Eve loved to potter around the house chatting away to Pat the dog as she cooked and cleaned. She was a loner who liked her own company, she needed it for her sanity, that had changed over the past few days with Tessa around. Eve was unusually domesticated for a girl who had been bought up with a full time housekeeper who literally had done everything for her.

Eve and Tessa sat on towels on the beach relaxing and enjoying the good weather. Tessa was waiting for the phone call to say she was in the show, that she had got the gig in Melbourne. She and Eve had planned the whole move whilst watching the day go by on the sand. Marco was very protective over his personal space in his home, even though it was a biggish house, having Eve come to stay and then asking her to marry him, was a massive change to his lifestyle and routine. So, it would take some hardcore groveling from both the girls to persuade him to let Tessa move into the spare bedroom.

Eve didn't see a problem from Zach's end. Tessa had been up to her old tricks just last night, sneaking into his room and having her way with him. There was something about knowing a woman as an innocent young girl, and then fucking her as a grown woman, that some men found extremely carnal like. Zach's attraction to Tessa was based her being funny and outgoing, and loud by nature, not to mention her sex appeal. She was like a naughty drug, pulling Zach back in for more at his weakest moment. She'd been high on more than life though last night, Tessa had told him so herself; Cocaine was her choice of drug, and she did it to keep up with her chaotic lifestyle apparently.

'Has it been hard keeping away from Zach?' Eve asked prompting Tessa, there had been a lot of eye contact between them in the kitchen this morning, before the boys left for training. Eve knew they'd been together last night; she'd been waiting for it. As if they weren't going to somehow find each other in the middle of the night down the hall... even if Marco had laid down the law to his younger sister, 'NO SLEEPING WITH ZACH' in his home.

Eve saw things differently; they were two consenting adults. She wouldn't judge them, and she had questioned Marco on whether or not he had given Zach the same talking to he'd given his sister, Eve felt sometimes Marco had double standards when it came to his sister and his best mate, or perhaps blaming Tessa was easier than questioning his friend morals!

Tessa stared at Eve from behind her sunglasses as they relaxed on the beach, resting on their elbows watching a swarm of teenagers in the water.

'You can't hide it from me.' Eve teased.

'I might have dropped by his room for a sympathy shag last night.' Frowning as if she had done poor Zach a good deed.

'A sympathy shag!' Eve laughed, 'Zach's a little vulnerable at the moment.' A statement, not a comment or a question, and certainly not judgment.

'It wasn't like I forced him to fuck me... geez E,' Tessa said flicking her long hair to the side.

'Hey, I personally don't give a shit. But your brother can't catch you in the act, he'll freak out,' Eve said casually, 'That's all I'm going to say.' Feeling like she had said her piece, Eve knew there would be no stopping Tessa, she was on a sexual self-destruction rampage with her own emotions... Eve had been there and done that once or twice before herself. Besides, Zach would never say no to Tessa.

'I don't see why it's any of Marco's business,' Tessa said irritated, 'Did I give him a hard time when he had sex with my teenage friend, leaving you knocked up and in a world of fucking pain, and then he didn't want bar of you. No. He's got a nerve butting into my sex life.'

Eve took a breath; she took a second to center herself, 'You have to understand Brooke is Marco's friend too, they've lived together for years. He feels like he's personally betraying her,' Eve pointed out, feeling it was her obligation to defend her fiancé and his feelings.

'Brooke's not like you E, she's not the perfect little wife type of gal,' spat Tessa.

Eve knew this behavior; Tessa was turning on her, this was a classic Tessa mood swing of late, and Eve didn't even think she was high or drunk. But maybe she was wrong.

'What exactly is the perfect wife type?' Eve needed some clarification around that description; she was no wife type. *Or was she?* She didn't see anything wrong with her role in Marco's life, in fact, she loved it.

'You're attentive to Marco and his demanding needs, that's all. You've never had real a job or a career, so you dote on my brother like you did with Evan. I'm not saying that's a bad thing. I'm saying Brooke is not like you. She's a fucking selfish bitch.' Tessa had no idea she was being so offensive.

It certainly sounded like a back handed compliment to Eve, 'Well, at least I know how you really feel about me,' she huffed, trying to keep a lid on it, Tessa was clearly on a tangent.

'You're different to women these days E, you've got like these weird old fashion values... like my mum. Most woman our age are working on their careers, having loads of sex with randoms. You kind of fell into a relationship young and you gave yourself to Evan, and now you're doing the same with my brother. You're a pleaser E.' There was no animosity in Tessa's tone, just loads of judgment.

'Please don't compare how I am with Marco to how I lived with Evan,' Eve feeling herself breathless as she spoke faster than normal. She was on the defense, 'And for your information, I actually had a job and a career in France that I really loved... I'm here because I love your brother, and I don't want to have loads of sex with randoms... I just want Marco.' Eve was rattled at Tessa's version of her life.

'Don't get all fucked up. I was giving you a compliment,' Tessa laughed with a scoffed, well aware that the minute she mentioned Evan, her friend would crack.

'It didn't feel like a compliment. I am different to you Tessa. Very different. My entire life has been different to yours.' Eve sat up to assert herself.

'Is this a money thing?' Tessa sounded condescending, 'You shouldn't feel bad about having money E.' Tessa knew Villa Rosado was for sale for an undisclosed exuberant amount of money, well into double figures of millions... not to mention the trust fund.

'Money has never defined who you and I are Tessa, don't let it now.' Eve never normally spoke about her money or anyone else's. Better than anyone, she knew money was always an underlying evil, no matter the relationship. Everyone wanted it, but not everyone had it.

By the time they walked back to the house, they were back on track walking slowly along the beautiful tree lined streets, both feeling the effects of the lazy day.

'If I don't get this job E, I'm going to have to go back to Sydney,' Tessa said, her mood had mellowed.

'After all our time apart, I'm getting used to having you around. Fingers crossed.' Eve loved her friend so much, even right after she had brutally insulted her. But she wasn't sure how Marco was going to react to his sister moving in if she got the Melbourne job.

'Is it a stupid idea to think that Marco will be okay with me staying?' Tessa gave Eve her sad eyes, she knew exactly how to get what she wanted, 'You know what he's like E.'

'Not at all,' Eve said thinking it would give her a chance to keep a closer eye on her friend, still not convinced Tessa had completely stopped her cocaine use. There had been a few moments over the past few days that Eve thought just maybe Tessa was high… She was definitely having mood swings.

'Will you talk to Marco for me? He listens to you E.' Tessa had done a full turn around, now she was laughing and being sweet and kind. Because she needed Eve on her side. 'I love being here with you.'

'What about Zach?' Eve said, she was onto Tessa, there was an element of sincerity to her groveling, but it was more about her vaginal itch than her friendship, let's face it.

'I can get laid anywhere,' laughing at Eve's suspicion even though it was a major factor in her plight to say in Melbourne. 'I'm enjoying being with you, and Marco. I feel like I've been away for so long.' She genuinely sounded like she was somewhat lost, in need of her best friend and her big brothers love and care. God knows Eve was willing to have her stay, she would never pass up a moment with one of her girls. Eve knew she had to be conscious of Marco, he was starting his season next week and she was well aware of his 'no visitors' rule. He didn't like people staying at the house while he was playing football. It was part of the attraction to him, he had all these little rules and rituals around his football, and now Eve was breaking them down one by one, she smiled at the thought.

'You ask your brother first, and then I will talk to him.' Eve didn't make any promises, she could only try to persuade Marco. She had no idea how he would react to Tessa staying at his house. 'I think between the two of us, we can win him over,' Eve smiled giving Tessa hope.

It was the last weekend before the footy season started, the last chance Marco and Zach would get to go to the lake house until maybe mid-season if they were lucky. So, they committed to a fully loaded, anything goes, no holds barred party weekend. All the usual suspects were invited of course, Eve was never one to shy away from entertaining, she was looking forward to it. In Brooke's absence she was now the go-to girl at the lake house, and Tessa would be her wing woman, so she would have a familiar face around for support this time, providing Tessa could keep her noise clean! Not since France had Eve put her entertaining skills to the test. From the sounds of it, Marco and Zach had put the word out and everyone was jumping at the chance to get way for one last hoorah before round one next weekend.

Marco and Zach rushed home from Friday's training session. Home by two, then back in the car with Eve and Tessa by two thirty. Marco had left his car with Eve for the morning, so she could pack everything they needed. She had shopped in the morning at the market for food, put everything in cooler bags and pre prepared most of tonight's dinner. Eve was on top of everything. Their bags were packed, and they headed off down the highway with all four of them in the car for the three-hour drive, the boys in the front and the girls cozied up in the back seat with Pat the dog between them.

They arrived at the lake house well before sunset and got straight to work putting food away and making beds up with clean linen. Marco and Zach had a thing with the beds, first to arrive, got first dibs. Once the beds were all taken, it was the sofa and the floor.

'And where exactly am I supposed to sleep?' Tessa asked as she helped Eve put sheets in the spare bedrooms.

'You'll sleep were ever you want; we all know that; I don't know why you are asking. Do you want permission from me to sleep in Zach's bed?' Eve laughed as she made the bed.

Minutes later, big brother Marco designated his little sister to the sofa right outside his and Eve's bedroom; her silly shenanigans simply couldn't happen this weekend. No way. He knew she'd been sneaking into Zach's bed all week. It just couldn't happen here!

Marco cooked the BBQ with a small crowd around the delicious aroma, laughing and enjoying the last weekend of freedom as it was. The girls gathered in the kitchen making cocktails, Eve with the help of Tessa and a much friendlier Ro prepared a feast.

311

Tessa couldn't help but be captivated by the double name, Joan Margaret, the latest girlfriend of one of the teammates. The intriguing Joan Margaret was Eve's height; frightfully thin with fake boobs much like tennis balls, long blonde hair all the way down her back, extensions noticeable only to the trained eye. With an uncommon look, fine fair features, Joan Margaret had a prettiness that was compelling. Eve liked her instantly; Tessa was watching them bond over the kitchen bench. Every time Joan Margaret spoke, Eve and Tessa watched her with wide eyes, there was something about her plumped pink lips, and bright blue eyes that reminded them of Zoe. She was friendly and familiar, and they gravitated to her immediately.

After dinner the fires flames kept them all warm in the chill of night air, the day had been a hot one and now the cool evening was very much welcomed. Eve watched as Marco sat across from her, she felt an unusual distance between them, perhaps because she was so used to having him at her side and without all the strangers around who all seemed to want to include him in there conversations… Eve wasn't used to sharing him this much.

Marco had a few beers; he wasn't going overboard one week out from the first game. Eve locked eyes with him just a few times, with long questioning eyes as she sat with Ro, Louise and Joan Margaret talking about an upcoming club social event. Her eyes kept drifting over to Marco as she lost focus on the ridiculous conversation about who should wear what and how. She sensed something, something between her and Marco. He got up from his comfy spot by the fire and went inside, so Eve followed him into the bedroom as he went into the bathroom to use the toilet.

Marco heard the door close behind him and turned to see Eve standing inside the door in one of his oversized Nike sweaters that looked like a dress over her little shorts. Her hair pulled up into a high messy ball atop of her head flopping untidily to the side. They stared each other out for a moment.

'Are you okay?' Eve gave him a pleasant questioning smile as she watched his long lashes blink repeatedly at her.

'I'm fine.' He took a few steps to her as he adjusted his shorts.

'Fine!' Eve let out a slight laugh. *Fine was her thing.* She moved to him once he'd finished with the toilet, putting her hands at his waist, touching him was always heaven. She looked up at Marco with knowing eyes, there was something going on in that beautiful head of his, she could feel it. 'I know somethings on your mind. Tell me.' She tugged at the front of his windcheater.

'I know we're both in the middle.' He tilted his head to the side. 'She's your friend. He's my friend.' Marco was trying to see it from Eve's point of view.

'And you're my lover,' Eve nodded knowingly, she knew what he was trying to say.

'Fiancé, actually.' He took her hand with the exuberant ring and the bracelet he had given her for her birthday, on her wrist.

'Knowing your sister this is how it's going to be forever for us. One of us will always be in the middle... Tessa is my best friend who I will always defend, even when she's wrong.'

Marco leant forward and kissed her, taking her breath away with his sudden passion. His mouth moving over hers softly and persuasively. Kissing him back as she let Marco take her into his arms and pulling her up against his body, her toes off the floor. Her loving arms wrapping around his neck, Eve swung her legs up to Marco's waist as he lifted her to him, their lips still rolling at each other's with a tender kiss.

He was her fiancé, and she did feel terrible guilt for not telling him about Tessa and Zach continuously hooking up or the coke situation, but it was engrained in Eve to be loyal to Tessa above all else. It was how it had always been, and it was very hard to change now.

For Marco it was hard being upset or mad at anyone, let alone Eve Frank, she was delicate and sweet with a gentle nature that he adored. The past few hours after overhearing her and his sister talking about Zach and the sleeping arrangements had been strange. He kept telling himself how difficult it was for Eve, being true to her best friend while keeping something from him that would no doubt upset him. Even though he knew Tessa and Zach were having sneaky catch ups every night in his home, he had just expected that Eve would have mentioned it since she knew too.

The bedroom door flung open, 'We thought we'd find you two in here,' giggling like schoolgirls, Tessa and Ro came stumbling in.

Marco held onto Eve as they both turned to look at the girls, 'And so, you found us. You can leave now,' Marco said to his sister and Ro as they gasped at his unwelcoming words.

'Marco don't be so rude,' Tessa barked, too drunk to know he was pissed at her as she hung off the open door.

Ro smiled with a cheeky eye, 'Eve. Joan Margaret is making Martini's. We thought we'd let you know.'

Ro was actually very beautiful when she let her fake façade down, Eve thought. 'I'll be out in a minute.' Clinging to Marco wishing they would just go so she could take him in the bathroom and make wild love to him. She spoke soft and short, so the girls knew they was in the middle of something.

'Don't be long,' Tessa said pulling the door closed as they left.

'Where were we?' Marco's mouth went straight back to Eve's, he loved her taste, her feel.

'I love you.' Was all she could muster as she sucked at his lips and gasped into his mouth. Her arms squeezed around his neck tight... The bedroom door opened again.

'Do we have any antiseptic cream?' Zach said not sure where he should be looking, 'Taylor's got a fucking huge splinter in his hand from the deck... sorry guys.' He winced knowing he'd interrupted.

Eve and Marco still standing in the middle of the bedroom, Marco still holding her.

'In the bathroom.' Reluctantly Marco let Eve go. 'We'll finish this later.' He kissed the end of her nose and went into the bathroom, Zach followed him.

Eve went out to the kitchen where Joan Margaret was making martinis while Ro was telling a funny a story about someone Eve didn't know. This time at the lake house things were definitely better than the last time Eve had been here. Ro was like a changed person; she was actually charming.

Taylor was one of the younger teammates, and Marco as his captain had taken him under his wing, mentoring him as best he could, the kid had a few issues. The club had asked that Marco keep a close eye on Taylor. So, Marco being Marco took this on with the best of intentions. Every day he checked in Taylor. He was very respectful of the young man's personal issues, his privacy, and his mental state, which was delicate and of a sensitive nature. The kid needed support.

Now here Taylor was, everyone fussing over his splinter, touching him, all leaning in to look and give an opinion on the medical situation at hand.

'We need tweezers and antiseptic,' said Ro, who had poor Taylor in an arm lock on the kitchen bench. Louise had gone to fetch her tweezers. Zach was getting the antiseptic from Marco and Tessa and Joan Margaret sat on the bench top making inappropriate jokes to distract from the humongous splinter!

It was a full theatre for the procedure as Ro performed surgery in the kitchen with Zach as her assistant.

'So, Taylor, tell us about this hot Benny friend of yours out there on the deck... where does he come from?' Ro tried to distract him as she plunged a sterilized needle into his skin.

'Fuck Ro... he's from Ballarat,' Taylor winced as Ro dug deep. Benny was a random, a newcomer.

'He's very sexy, how old is he?' Ro laughed with seductive batter of the eyes to poor little Taylor.

'He's twenty-two,' Taylor looked away as Ro kept digging into his fingers.

'Benny would be perfect for you Tessa,' she said squeezing Taylors hand.

'You think?' Tessa played along, 'I don't know if my brother would approve of me cradle snatching.'

Marco frowning from the sidelines at his sister like she was a moron. Eve was trying not to grin to much at his displeasure. Marco was super cute when he was disgruntled, and he seemed very disgruntled.

'Give me a break will you,' Tessa snapping at her brother, she screwed her face up. Taylor was amused and distracted while Ro pulled at the splinter.

'Is he always so protective?' Louise asked thinking the sibling bickering was a joke.

'You've got no idea!' huffed Tessa, 'It's fine for him to fuck my best friend, even when she was just a girl... Sorry E. But my brother seems to forget this.' Tessa turned and glared at Marco, she knew she was jumping into hot water, she was bored and needed a little controversy, a little sibling banter.

'When did you become such a fucking mole?' Marco was definitely unimpressed; his outburst was unexpected. Everyone held their breath as they watched on. Tessa had struck a nerve; Marco had never called his sister a name like that before, he was always so respectful. To make it worse it only incited her further.

Eve sighed, moving so she was perfectly halfway between the two. She was expecting this to erupt with the need to mediate at some point or pull them apart after Tessa attached him.

'Oh, please. You are such a fucking *mummies* boy, you're so boring Marco,' Tessa slurred as she exaggerated her words, 'Seriously, how did you ever get Eve to fall for you?' she pointed her finger at her friend.

'Tessa,' Eve said trying to jolt her friend back into some kind of sanity.

'Well, it's true E. You like bad boys who treat you like shit and my brothers like Mr. Fucking Perfect, but I think he's an asshole in disguise. Perhaps that's the attraction,' she laughed at herself as Marco turned and walk out the kitchen back outside, baffled at his sister's behavior.

Eve just looked at her friend. 'Not cool,' she said, pointing to Marco's bedroom door, Eve needed to sort her out… *Or kill her – which ever came first.*

The girls and Taylor all looking on.

'E, everyone knows,' Tessa laughed loudly for all to hear, 'She used to live with a sexy arse big-time gangster… and you thought she was innocent!' Tessa scoffed as she followed Eve to the bedroom, closing the door behind herself as Eve stood in the middle of the room.

It wouldn't be too much longer before Marco questioned his sisters state of mind and mental health, something was wrong. This behavior was wrong.

Eve stood with narrow eyes, her arms at her sides and her chest moving in and out with her deep breaths, 'You're out of control,' she said with clear direction as she started in on Tessa, 'How dare you.' A lump in her throat.

'I am not out of control!' Still laughing.

'You just took Marco down in front of everyone,' Eve sounded calm even when she was angry. 'I thought he was supposed to be your precious big brother. Why would you do that to him?' she was actually hurt for Marco.

'Well, I don't know, he-,'

'You embarrassed him and then you embarrassed me.' Eve stared her out.

'I was- '

'No. Tessa,' Eve still didn't raise her voice; she simply changed her tone to be a little more assertive. 'Let me see your bags?' Eve walked to the corner of the room where Tessa had left her large black overnight bag on the floor when they arrived. Unzipping it and pulling at Tessa's things, Eve went right through the bag.

At her side, Tessa was too out of it to give a shit. 'Now that would be the obvious place.' She was amused at Eve's frantic behavior.

Then out of the corner of her eye, Eve s potted Tessa's Nike running shoes with a pair of ruffled socks hanging out of them... she knew Tessa hadn't worn her running shoes today! Tessa realized Eve was looking at the shoes, she leaned over and grabbed the socks from her shoes. If Tessa thought the bag was an obvious place, the socks were more obvious to Eve, she lunged forward and snatched the socks and made a bolt for the bathroom.

'Don't you dare!' Tessa yelled out after her. It all happened so fast; Tessa slammed the bathroom door behind her in a threatening fashion. 'It's my shit, give it back now.'

Shaking the socks like a crazy woman, then out fell a small plastic bag with ten or so coloured pills and another plastic bag full of powder.

'Tess... there's enough here to blow your fucking head off,' Eve was actually shocked.

'What do you want me to say?'

Just then, the door opened, and Marco stood with his arm up at the door frame, he had taken a minute to calm down and thought about how to handle his sister, instead of leaving Eve to fight his battles, Marco was ready to have it out with Tessa. Tension with his sister was the last thing he wanted or needed, they had never fought before, he didn't like that their relationship was changing.

'What's going on?' he asked his two girls at they stood by the bathroom sink.

'I'm just putting some water on Tessa's face. She's not feeling great,' Eve said moving in front of the sink, scrunching the plastic bags up into her fist and let her sleeve fall over her hand. 'We'll be right out babe,' Eve looked back with a smile, defusing him Marco immediately.

Tessa didn't say a word.

Standing a moment looking at them both, not sure if he had interrupted something more, or if his sister was just drunk. Marco was concerned but against his better judgement, he let Eve take care of Tessa.

'We'll be out soon.' Again, Eve appeased him with a confident and calm smile.

Tessa didn't crack so much as a curl of her lip; she was stone faced and Marco assumed it was because she didn't feel well. He back out of the doorway and pulled the bathroom door closed again.

Tessa looked at Eve with big wide eyes, half-gratitude, half-hate. Eve was like a rubber band, it took a lot for her to snap, but Tessa knew she couldn't stretch the friendship much more than she had already.

Emptying the plastic bags into the sink, Eve then washed it clear without a single word. Putting the plastic bag in the back pocket of her shorts and turning to Tessa, she didn't know quite what to say. The silence was thick, to say it was uncomfortable for both of them was an understatement.

Eve sighed; she was stressed. *What the fuck did she do about this now?* She asked herself as she felt a bunch of knots in her stomach. Tessa almost looked ashamed as Eve watched her, growing more emotional with every second. 'How can I help you?' her soft words comforting and caring at almost a whisper. No doubt, Eve was a stayer; she didn't abandon people she loved in their time of need, no matter how bad they behaved.

Tessa's eyes welling up as Eve spoke to her, 'I'll get you help first thing on Monday. If you let me, I'll get you through this, I promise you.' The soothing tone in Eve's voice was reassuring and calm. Tessa felt her tight chest beating again, she had broken a sweat, it was chilling cold.

'Fuck! That was a lot of coke you just washed away,' Tessa said in a dazed and confused state of disbelief, to shocked to be angry about at Eve. 'Thank you for cover for me with Marco?' her voice was shaky, 'He can't know E, he's not that sort of guy. He won't understand. He'll freak out and tell mum and dad.' She was unravelling.

Eve was lying to Marco, 'You have to get your shit together or we'll both go down... he'll never forgive me.' She knew Marco wouldn't understand her loyalty going beyond him to his sister with this particular scenario. Eve was risking everything for best friend, she knew it was wrong, so she laid down the law to Tessa, telling her how it was going to be from this moment on, and making her promise to toe the line.

Tessa agreed to all of Eve's stipulations. She agreed to stop drinking as of that very minute, she agreed to see a doctor on Monday.

A million thoughts ran through Eve's head as she thought about how to convince Marco, to let Tessa move in indefinitely. Zach was also going to be an issue, the last thing Tessa needed was a guy derailing her, or her vagina! Eve knew she had to get Tessa into a day rehab facility pronto. F*uck!*

She flannelled Tessa's hot face as she sat on the edge of the bath completely exhausted as they whispers about how they would get through this together.

'Zoe will have to know. We can't do this without her,' Tessa blinked her big brown eyes to Eve.

'Of course,' Eve agreed dabbing the cold washer gently to her precious friend's gorgeous face. The girls were a threesome, they were better together.

The morning was bright and beautiful, Marco opened the sliding door to the deck, in the distance he could see Eve sitting out on the end of the jetty alone, her feet hanging over the end. She was on the phone as she sat in his jumper from last night and her track pants. He went to the kitchen in his boxers and T shirt to make coffee, the house was in silence as he looked around the living room... *No Tessa! Interesting!* Marco knew where she was, he didn't have the energy to deal with his sister again today.

As he carrying two coffees in his hands out to Eve, the still water of the lake was like glass, the air crisp and fresh in his lungs, this tiny woman had changed his life and he lived it.

'Marco's here mum, and he's made me coffee, I better go.'

The sweetest smile on Eve's face made him harden up. Looking up, pleasantly surprised to see him, her long lashes, those hazel almond eyes and all that messy bed hair, he wanted to carry her back to bed and make love to her in a very indecent way.

'Yes, I will tell him you said hello.' Her eyes looking around at Marco again. 'Thank you mum. Talk soon.' Eve pressed the red button. 'My mum's in London.' The distracted look on her face was telling. The underlying anxiety she'd been having over her mother's knowledge of her birth mother, only Marco had seen. Eve had been trying to figure out just how she would broach the subject with Anna. Every time she thought she might be about to go there Anna, she froze, and the words wouldn't come out or it wasn't the right timing.

'I love your mum,' he smiled, Anna was a distant mother, not smothering in any way whatsoever.

Eve huffed, 'You think she's so great now. There's every chance she's going to crack it when we tell her we are getting married, she'll say we're rushing it.' Eve hadn't told her mother yet, not until Jackie and Mario knew would she tell Anna.

'I think we know they're all going to say, we're rushing into it. I haven't seen your dad in over ten years and now I'm marrying his daughter. He's probably going to hate me for not asking his permission to marry you.' The thought of James Frank made Marco uneasy.

'My dad will be fine. Relieved actually I should imagine because you're the perfect son in law.' Her hand laid gently on Marco's thigh as they sat side by side savoring the morning peace by the lake sipping their coffee. Marco ran his fingers up and down her bare ring finger.

'I feel naked without it on. I hate not wearing it.' Eve had left her beautiful engagement ring at home so as to not let the cat out of the bag, before they told Jackie and Mario the following weekend about the wedding.

'I wish you were naked,' said Marco.

'Mmm, hmm,' Eve sighed.

Their friends who knew about the marriage proposal, could keep their secret. Of course, Eve would tell Anna and her father the same day as Jackie and Mario. James would hate to think he was left out or left to last.

'Mum and dad will be here Friday morning,' Marco said, 'I thought we could have lunch with them and tell them then,' he was very upbeat.

Eve loved that Marco had been thinking about it, planning the moment. This marriage was a huge deal for him, and she knew it would be for his parents too.

'And I've asked them to stay at the house.'

Another rule being broken. Eve smiled, 'Wow. So, they know somethings up already then, you're letting them stay at your house,' she giggled looking up at his loving gaze. He was trying to make it special, and she understood. But Jackie would be wracking her brain trying to figure out why after all these years, her son was inviting them to stay at the house on a football weekend. Eve was surprised she hadn't had a call from Jackie yet!

Tessa had gone into Eve and Marco's bed after breakfast and not come out. She was catching up on sleep and given the state of her personal affairs right now, she needed to zonk out and hopefully wake up feeling remotely better about herself. Mentally she'd evaded her issues by having sex with Zach for most of the night, she now used sex to feel better about her shitty life since there was no coke or pills left.

Popping her head in and out of the bedroom regularly, Eve kept an eye on her friend in the hope that things weren't as bad as they seemed. She couldn't stop thinking about how on earth she was going to keep the enormity of rehab from Marco. She'd been up early, even before she called her mother to research rehab options, finding a place nearby to Marco's in Melbourne that offered a two-week program seemed perfect. It was called day-hab, five days a week and for three to four hours per day, that seemed doable. It was a starting point if anything. Everything else was a twenty-eight day stay, it was a last resort. Eve needed to help and support Tessa. This had to work, Eve had to make it work for the both of them!

Hoping that within the week Tessa would hear that she had the part in the Melbourne theatre show she'd auditioned for, Eve thought that would give her something to look forward to perhaps. Then there was the hope that rehearsals didn't start within the next few weeks so she could do day-hab. Eve had immediately sent off an email to try and book Tessa a spot at day-hab. This felt like the answer. *It had to be!*

The weather was still warm and so it gave the girls one final opportunity to flaunt their summer bikini bodies before the season started, and then their men became the center of the universe. One thing Eve hadn't yet experienced, was just how much of Marco's life would be dedicated to his football career during the season. Then there was his commitment to his club, she had no idea what she was in for or how scrutinized she was about to become. *No idea at all.*

321

The simmering sun made everyone lazily content to lounge around the deck all afternoon, dips in the lake, towels everywhere, relaxing with music playing, the girls' drinking tumblers of Pimm's and lemonade with slices of orange, whilst lapping up the last of the summer sun rays, chatting and enjoying life for what it was in the moment.

The light banter and conversation somehow went to Brooke and Zach's failing marriage, and it seemed everyone had an opinion, which didn't surprise Eve one bit, although it was evident that they didn't have all the facts… Or maybe they did, and they were just judgmental gossip mongers, Eve thought. There was that instinctive feeling as she laid with her back tucked into Marco's stomach on the sunbed, that Brooke may not have been as popular as she once thought with the other wives and girlfriends. Eve wondered who knew what, and she knew everyone else was wondering the same thing. The confusion and apprehension on everyone's face was clear, it was almost as if they all seemed to be talking in some kind of code, and Eve couldn't quite make it out. Was it a weird secretive girl code thing they had going on, or was it because the guys were around, or maybe it was because poor Zach was sitting listening to them decipher his wife's behaviour and his marriage right there in front of him? Whatever it was, Eve had had enough gossip and went to check on Tessa in the bedroom. Marco followed her in a bid to escape too, he hated all the talk and gossip.

In the bedroom Marco looked at Eve for a moment, then at his sister, 'How long has she been asleep?' he asked as they watched over Tessa, quietly surveying the scene.

'About three or four hours. She's very tired,' Eve said moving closer to Tessa thinking it was a little too long. She leaned over her and gently rubbed her arm. 'Wake up Tessa!' Eve said in her soft voice, trying to rouse her.

Marco leaned in when she didn't respond to Eve's words or touch, 'Tessie. Wake Up!' he said with a hint of urgency in his tone, 'Why isn't she waking up?' he looked at Eve for the answer. The panic on Eve's face worried him.

'Tessa. Wake up!' Eve shook her friend by the shoulders with no response.

Was this really happening? What the fuck had she done! In her panic Eve slapped Tessa's cheek harder than she expected to.

'Was she feeling sick?' Marco moved in beside Eve and pushed Tessa's hair back out of her face, moving her head to allow for a clear airway... panic had set in. Then just as Eve was about to tell him about the drug issue, Tessa's eyes fluttered.

'Tessa! Wake up... It's Eve,' she said desperately.

Zach opened the bedroom door and came in, 'What's wrong?'

Standing up Marco spoke sharply to his mate, 'Has she taken something, pills, or medication. She's completely out of it.' Questioning Zach bluntly.

Zach shrugged, 'No, not that I know of.'

Eve spoke louder, 'Wake up for me babe. You have to open your eyes Tessa,' her voice was caring and louder again as she sat right at Tessa's side, willing her to wake. It was clear to everyone that she had taken something, there was no hiding the fact. Her eyes were dazed, glazed, and almost rolling back in her head.

Eve cursing to herself. *This is what happened when you kept secrets from people. Fuck. Fuck. Fuck.* Her hand patting lovingly at Tessa's face desperately. It was as though she was trying to wake up and couldn't.

'Tessie. Come on, open your eyes,' Marco encouraged his sister anxiously.

Tessa flickered her eyes, they fluttered open as she tried to focus on her beloved big brother, then she saw Eve and began to cry, 'I'm sorry,' she said with a soft sob.

'It's okay,' Eve sat forward and felt her forehead, Tessa was clammy, 'You're okay. Take deep breaths.' Looking back over her shoulder she looked at Zach. 'Can you get a glass of water please?' Eve asked him. She had no idea why she wanted to punch him square in the face; but she just did. He had been with her last night and that annoyed Eve now suddenly.

Was he using Tessa, because if he was, she could do without it right now! Had Tessa had more drugs stashed, had she taken drugs last night with Zach?

'What did you take Tessa? I need to know.' Eve rubbed her friends' arms trying to stimulate her back to the land of the living with Marco watching on from the side. *Fuck it, if this was how he had to find out, so be it.*

Tessa said, 'Sleeping pills. I need to sleep E... I'm so tired. I'm sorry.' She started to cry again, still not fully awake, and somewhat incoherent.

'How many pills did you take?' Eve asked softly, she didn't even know Tessa had sleeping pills.

Marco watching on with wide eyes as Zach came back in with the glass of water.

Tessa shut her eyes again, Eve rushed to the bathroom and found two strip of pills just sitting on the bench top. Eight pills per sheet, they were all gone, so it was unclear how many Tessa had actually taken... had the sheets originally been full? *What the fuck was she doing!*

'Tessa, did you take all the pills, tell me, was the pack full?... Zach did you see her take the pills?' Eve rushed back with the pill strips in her hand, shaking them.

'I didn't see her do anything!' he proclaimed his innocents feeling Eve was blaming him.

'I didn't... not all of them,' Tessa laid with her eyes closed mumbling, she was taking deep huff like breaths. She may not have taken all the pills, but she'd taken too many, clearly! It wasn't an attempt to kill herself, it was purely a bid to zonk herself out... To blank out.

'She needs to throw that shit up now,' Marco said pulling his sister up into his arms and taking her to the bathroom, Eve and Zack followed as he manhandled Tessa like she was ragdoll.

It was probably too late for throwing up, but he had to do something, they weren't near a hospital. Marco was taking charge, they couldn't be sure how many pills Tessa had taken, 'We have to make her throw up. I'm going to stick my fingers down her throat.' They swung into full emergencies mode.

Zach helped hold Tessa into position over the toilet bowl while Eve grabbed a face washer from the shelf and wet it with cold water as Marco plunged his fingers into his sister's mouth. Zach now holding her limp body, trying to keep her hair out of the way so Marco could do his thing. It was a frantic scene.

Tessa's body suddenly jolted, and she started to throw up. Eve at her side, Marco holding her head and hair, and Zach holding her body. The panicked trauma only lasted a few minutes, and she was talking; Tessa had literally thrown up everything. Marco sat on the bathroom floor with his sister in his arms. Eve kneeling beside them, dabbing Tessa's face with the cold flannel while Zach held a bunch of toilet paper.

Marco was disheveled, 'What the fuck Tess! You don't take sleeping pills in the middle of the fucking day.'

'Don't yell at me... I took them this morning,' cried Tessa like it made a difference.

'I'm not yelling at you,' he gasped, 'Didn't the box say how many you needed to take?' he looked at Eve like suddenly he knew his sister had a massive problem.

'Can you get out... both of you!' Tessa sniffed through her tears looking at Marco and Zach, 'I just want Eve,' she sobbed, her hands going to her head like she was in pain.

'Are you okay?' Zach screwed his face up as he crouched down beside her.

Eve sighed looking up at Marco, 'Go, I've got it. We'll be okay now,' softly she reassured him. Her eyes begging him to forgive her as she was so torn between her loyalties. Being a true friend to Tessa meant disappointing Marco. And by the look on his face, there was already an element of disappointment, Eve could tell he was starting to wonder what was really going on.

'Can you get the hell out now,' Tessa snapped, she was getting agitated as she slumped forward into Eve's arms, their bond and alliance was like iron.

It was like a death stare, Marco glared at Eve like it was her fault or perhaps she knew more than she was letting on. Her guilt had her catastrophizing at every look he gave her. *Tessa could have died!*

'You should both go. And don't tell anyone, let's keep this between us, this is private,' Eve said with severe warning in her voice. She was upset at Marco's accusing eyes, 'Please don't let the girls come in here, understood?' Eve was stressed, defensive and guilty.

When they were finally alone, Eve took a big deep breath, 'What were you doing?' her voice quivering with sedate anger, everyone knew it took a lot for Eve to reach this point, and between Tessa nearly overdosing and Marco's eyes, she was over it!

'E... I just needed everything to stop. I was just trying to sleep.' And with that she began throwing up again.

'Well, you scared us half to death.'

'I think I'm going to be sick again,' Tessa leaned into the toilet bowl.

It took a good forty minutes for Tessa to stop heaving and dry reaching as her body expelled the foreign toxins. Eve dabbing her head with a cold washer, holding her hear back and caring for her the entire time. Comforting her friend as she went from the basin to the toilet bowl then flat to the cold floor, and back to the basin. It was how Eve imagined a drug addict would behave coming down from a bender, perhaps Tessa was expelling more than just the sleeping pills from her system… honestly who would know at this point. One minute she was boiling hot in a feverish sweat, then shivering cold and completely limp. Then she'd start dry reaching again. Her body squirming with agony and she groaned like she was in awful pain as Eve did her best to see her through it.

Did this mean Tessa was a drug addict? Eve was tired herself, mentally drained, and this was far from over.

Everyone had stayed out on the deck continuing with their day, the boys had said Eve was napping with Tessa to keep them all appeased. When Marco saw Eve eventually go out to the kitchen from the bedroom, he went straight into her. He'd had time to process what had happened and he wanted some answers.

Eve stood at the end of the kitchen benchtop; she looked exhausted as he stood towering over her.

'Is she okay?' Marco asked.

'She's finally resting.' Eve took a big deep breath in and looked up into his questioning eyes.

'Did my sister just try to kill herself?' He looked so upset Eve could barely look at him. She was unclear of his feelings. *Was he directing his tone at her or his sister?*

'No,' she gasped, 'She didn't try to kill herself,' shaking her head like she was absolutely sure, 'Tessa's in a bad place and she wanted to zone out for a while and sleep. She hasn't been herself since she got home from New York, things ended badly for her there.' It was mostly the truth. Eve had debated telling him everything, but she wouldn't sell Tessa out even though it meant lying to Marco. 'I hope you and Zach have kept this private.' Even though Eve knew she was in trouble of sorts, there was still a sting in her tone, she stood strong and loyal to her friend as she always did.

'I said you were both sleeping.' He was pissed off big time. 'I know you think you're doing the right thing by Tessa,' Marco paused, not taking his eyes from eve for a second, 'But she's my baby sister and I need you to tell me if she's in some kind of trouble,' he questioned Eve with every essence of his being, he knew something was up. He knew Eve was holding out on him.

'I'm taking care of it, she's okay.' *Why did she lie, what was she doing? This was the time to tell him. If he finds out down the track, you are fucked!* Eve thought as she bit down on her bottom lip.

Marco knew she bit her bottom lip when she was stressing or anxious, 'Then why do I feel like I'm not getting the full story from you?' he said trying to stay calm. As much as he hated having to push Eve, he also knew unless he pushed, she was a fucking vault when it came to her two best friends.

'Please trust me?' Eve's voice was tender as Marco stepped to her.

'That's' my sister in there, and I know somethings wrong with her, and I can't believe you're not telling me.' Marco's good nature was now being tested; he glared at Eve.

'Don't do this to me. It's not fair. I'm trying to be a good friend.' Eve's teary eyes looked up at Marco.

'You girls are impossible!' he snapped at her gritting his teeth; he hated doing this to Eve. Marco hated being the asshole full stop. With nothing from Eve, he turned and walked off, Eve followed him out to the deck and past everyone, he stopped and lent against the railing overlooking the lake away from the others.

'I don't want to keep secrets from you, really I don't.' She whispered leaning into his body.

'Then don't.' Marco turned, taking her face in his hands gently and leaning down kissing her mouth, taking Eve by surprise, startling her.

'Please don't be angry with me,' she mouthed to his lips, begging for his mercy.

'You're holding out on me Eve Frank.' Marco let her face go, he was a gentle giant, he'd never be rough with Eve. not ever. He was just frustrated and thought he'd kiss some sense into her.

She pulled away a little, 'I love you both so much. I don't want to choose between you. It's not fair.'

'Don't let Tessa come between us.' Marco said softly, but seriously.

'She needs me,' Eve's words urging him to understand.

Marco put a gentle hand at the back of Eve's head and pulled her up to his mouth. The other arm wrapping around her back as he passionately kissed her again, then he stopped. 'Me or her.'

Eve held her breath, an inch from Marco's face, 'Why are you making me choose?' Eve pulled away slightly, tears fell from her eyes at his ultimatum.

'If you want me, you need to be honest with me.' He needed her to choose him.

Eve shook her head, 'I can't. I need Tessa to trust me,' she said as it all became too much for her. *Was she losing him!*

'It's me or Tessa!' Marco said leaving her to contemplate her loyalties.

This was not the perfect Marco Eve was accustomed to.

Sitting on the edge of the bed Tessa pulled her singlet over her head and then put on a pair of snug track pants, Eve sat beside her watching in awe of her long slender body that simply looked spectacular in anything. Her brownish blonde waves messy, Eve had always thought her friend was glorious to look at.

Tessa was at her lowest point; Eve couldn't remember ever seeing her gorgeous bubbly friend so down and out, or so strung out! Yet even at this slump in her life, Tessa could still see the humor in her fucked-up situation. Standing looking out to the deck through the bedroom windows, she turned to Eve and gave her a wink.

'Oh, god. I'm sleeping with a married man and I'm going to rehab. I'm living my absolute best life!' she exhaled with an exhausted chuckle, a pleasure to Eve's ears. Peering out the window, Tessa looked cagey in a tired way. She hadn't had any coke since last night, so she said, and then the sleeping pill ordeal, it was amazing she was even standing up.

Eve leaned back on her hands as she pursed her lips, 'I think Zach's got a lot going on and you're a distraction for him, as he is for you. I just want you to be careful. You don't need any extra pressures or influences.'

'You're very cool E, you know that.' Tessa squinted her eyes at Eve as she slipped her thongs on getting ready to reappear after a day of turmoil, 'You should have been a shrink!'

'Mmm. You might not think so in a minute when I tell you what I really think.' Eve had stewed on it whilst Tessa slept... she was telling Marco the truth as soon as she got the chance.

'What… you think I should stop fucking Zach, don't you?' Tessa said guessing what her always supportive friend had to possibly say next.

'It might be a good idea for a while.' It wasn't the immediate issue on Eve's mind though.

'I know my brother's all bent out of shape about it,' Tessa raised her brow at Eve defiantly, 'But I'll sleep with whoever I want, whenever I want.'

'And that's your prerogative,' Eve not wanting to get into that debate right now, her voice calm as usual as she waited for Tessa to settle just a second, Eve knew what she had to say wouldn't be received well. 'I do have to tell Marco about the coke and the rehab.'

Quick back at Eve, 'You're supposed to be on my side… he won't understand.' Tessa said loudly.

Eve sighed in angst, 'I'm marrying him Tessa; I can't begin our life together with a lie like this.' Eve tried to make her friend see the difficult position she was in.

Getting more agitated by the second, Tessa moved around the room then turned to Eve, 'I can't believe you would do this to me… after all I have done for you. I kept your fucking baby secret from Marco for years,' Tessa shouted at Eve.

Eve sat still on the edge of the bed, 'That secret was to protect him, you know that.'

So much for a relaxing weekend at the lake house!

'I supported you fully when you went off and hooked up with Evan, when everyone was saying how stupid you were, I was always on your side. When you got pregnant to Evan and decided to marry him – again everyone said you were fucking nuts… not me, I was always on your side.'

Tessa's yelling and words had Eve numb, she couldn't speak to defend herself.

'And when Evan died, I was there for you again,' Tessa kept going, 'You've made the most fuck up decisions and I've always had your fucking back E,' a pause so she could take a breath, 'Now you're betraying me.' Finally, she was finished as she stood waiting for Eve to respond.

'This is not the same,' Eve found her words, her eyes full of tears and her chest tight with pain. Her head slowly shock side to side. 'Marco is your brother, and he loves you. I have to tell him or- '

'Or what E!' snapped Tessa condescendingly, she was spinning into an uncontrollable rage that was becoming intimidating for Eve. The bedroom door slowly opened, but Tessa had her back to it and Eve didn't see it open either. It was Marco, who had come to see what all the noise was about.

'Tessa. Please,' Eve tried to calm her.

'You think my brother won't want you, I doubt it!' Tessa sounded evil, 'Poor Eve, her gangster fiancé was murdered. Her babies died…blah, blah, blah. Oh, and my god, how did you get Marco to marry you anyway, he's never committed to anyone ever!' Tessa laughed like she had actually lost the plot, 'No. Don't answer, I know exactly how. You're more like your biological mother than you think if you know what I mean,' Tessa taunted Eve, 'And you're so unlucky, it's actually pathetic. Maybe you should stay away from my brother, you're like a fucking bad luck charm.' Tessa spewed out her evil rathe without taking a breath.

Everything happened at once. Marco stepped into the room. Eve saw him and stood up with Tess turning around, he stared at his sister like he was going to strangle her with his bare hands.

Eve quickly went into the bathroom slamming the door behind her and locking it.

What the fuck! Who the hell are these people? she thought breathing into her hands as she listen to Marco and Tessa have it out in the bedroom.

'Are you in-fucking-sane, what's wrong with you?' Marco's voice projected.

'Mind your business for once, this is not about you,' Tessa yelled back to her big brother.

Even though Eve knew this was not her Tessa, not the friend she loved so very dearly, she was still shocked and devastated by her words.

'Let me tell you,' Marco said with authority and power in his voice, 'You are my business. Both of you are my business. Why would you say those things to Eve?'

'She is my friend; it's always been that way. Now she's choosing you over me,' suddenly Tessa's voice strangely quiet.

Definitely the devil! Thought Eve as she wiped her face, just glad to be out of Tessa's firing line.

Marco spoke loud and very clear, 'She's actually not choosing me, because she's your best friend. Whatever is going on with you, she isn't telling me. BECAUSE SHE'S SO FUCKING LOYAL TO YOU,' Marco yelled and then paused, 'Can you see what you're doing here? You're making her choose between us. She shouldn't have to choose one of us.' Another pause. 'If you would just tell me what is going on, it'd fucking make things a hell of lot better Tess.' Frustration boiling over.

He was the only person who could ever get through to Tessa, she adored him and always had. He was her hero, and it hurt all three of them to be watching this play out.

'I'm having a cocaine issue. There. Happy now? I'm a druggie,' scoffed Tessa with a huff, Eve wasn't sure if she was crying, but it was quieter now, things had come down a notch or two. Eve could almost hear the relief in her crazy tone as she blurted it out. Not expecting her to give it up so easily, Eve stood as still as a statue behind the locked bathroom door listening.

Marco standing, hands-on hips, a knee bent, 'Cocaine!' He had to clarify just in case he hadn't heard correctly.

'Yes, cocaine. Pills. Sleeping pills, alcohol, whatever gets me through the day really.' Her reply was soft and surrendering to her older brother as he stood in front of her listening in horror. Tessa was now quiet and calm, her moods swings were changing by the minute.

Marco took a moment, 'Eve, come out here please,' his voice raised on the last word, which made the girls nervous. He wasn't sure how to handle it, he was upset beyond belief at Eve for keeping something as important as this from him. And as for his sister, how the fuck did a smart girl with everything going for her get into drugs. Marco was baffled, he didn't use drugs or condone drugs of any sort and even though he was aware of them and how prevalent they were in society these days, he was still super naive.

It took Eve a few seconds to muster up the courage to open the bathroom door, when she did she couldn't bring herself to look at Tessa after her verbal abuse, she didn't want to look at Marco either. Her lips twitching with anxiety, she didn't know whether to run out the door or run into Marco's protective arms.

'Drugs,' he huffed, 'You didn't think I needed to know about this?' His face disappointed and irritated.

Tessa stepped in, 'Don't be mad at her,' she interjected defensively, 'I didn't want her to tell you.'

Eve not giving Tessa so much as a look, because she couldn't, looked at Marco momentarily with apologetic eyes, then needed to get out, so she left the room, shutting the door behind her and marching out the front door to escape the craziness of the Rossi's before her mind exploded, it was just all too much on top of her own shit.

Joan Margaret was hiding out the front having a sneaky cigarette, she held her pack of cigarettes in Eve's direction, who in her moment of angst, took one.

'Sometimes it's impossible to be everything to everyone,' Eve said before dragging on the cigarette. Menthol, it was surprisingly nice as the smoke eased out her mouth and nostrils, it felt like a tremendous relief.

Everyone had heard the commotion, but not all of it, just Marco and Tessa yelling at each other.

'Just chill. Give yourself a minute.' Joan Margaret was smooth; she was pint sized and very sure of who she was. Eve liked her a lot. She had no idea what was going on, but she could see Eve was having a moment.

'Thank you.' Eve held the cigarette up in gesture.

'This is a lovely house, do you come here much?'

'It's my second time here. I'm new too.'

'Great, we can be new together,' smiled Joan Margaret.

The door opened, interrupting them and Tessa stood with her arms wrapped around herself like she was tied up, it looked very odd and uncomfortable. Eve looked at her and then looked away, not sure she was ready to speak to her just yet, pissed she had chosen this very moment to come and find her, just when she and Joan Margaret were having a peaceful minute alone and she was enjoying this random cigarette so much.

'I better get back in there,' Joan Margaret said with a smile butting her cigarette in the dirt at her feet, she knew her cue.

'Thank you.' Eve wanted her to know she appreciated her kindness. As Joan Margaret shut the front door Eve could hear Tessa breathing, she hadn't looked at her yet.

'I wasn't going to let Marco blame you.' Tessa had completely disregarded the part before Marco entered the room where she tore Eve to shreds.

'That's big of you,' Eve managed.

'We've sorted it out. I've got the best brother in the whole world. He's going to talk to you about the day rehab and I think he might be on board with me staying too.'

It was like a completely different person had taken over Tessa's body. Again. It was hard to keep up. Now she loved her brother again and they were happy siblings, whilst Eve was outside smoking in despair. She didn't say anything in response to Tessa latest revelations because she didn't have anything to say. Did Tessa have some kind of mental health issue going on too, the moods and verbal abuse were dramatic and hard to tolerate. Tessa's words from earlier still rang in Eve's ears, *'Poor Eve.'* The way it came out of her mouth sounded vindictive. Tessa could never take what she had said back, that was the worst part. Bringing up her biological mother and implying she was a whore too, was a low blow. Speaking of her babies and Evan, really cut Eve deep. She wanted to blame the drugs and detoxing or whatever the fuck it was Tessa was going through. She was not ready to forgive her though. It couldn't be erased; the words had hurt.

Was that what everyone really thought of her, was she stupid and crazy? Because it hadn't felt that way. It had been Eve's life and she was in love; she had loved her life with Evan and their baby.

Who the hell was Tessa to belittle that? Eve was deeply, deeply offended and hurt. She didn't say a word, everything was churning inside like a volcano waiting to erupt.

'E. I'm sorry. I don't know what came over me. I don't know why I said those things to you. It's like my skin is crawling but I can't itch it,' Tessa pleaded for forgiveness, 'I so sorry.'

'It's not the first time you've felt the need to berate me, but it was the worst,' Eve pinned her devastated eyes at Tessa's as her soft words cut the air, 'You've been doing this since New York, it's like you're out to get me… My apologies if I've needed you too much in the past.' A moment of staring before Eve walked up the steps and past Tessa and into the house, leaving her at the front door.

Eve thought about when Evan had been killed, and what a beautiful caring friend Tessa had been back then. *Where had she gone?*

Consciously reminding herself to breath in and out, Eve was getting organised for dinner, the last thing she felt like doing, but the one thing that would occupy her enough to keep her distance from Marco and Tessa. She cut and chopped at the kitchen bench taking her frustrations out. The old Eve would have made a run for it and headed back to Melbourne and boarded the first flight to France. But Marco was within his rights to be pissed at her, and she didn't blame him, as much as it made her feel horrible, she had to deal with it, no running away anymore. It was time to be a grown up. This was the real deal.

Tessa came into the kitchen and stood looking at Eve who just wanted to be left alone, wishing Tessa would just give her space to be disgruntled. Eve ignored Tessa.

'E, I'm sorry,' Tessa begged, her voice desperate. 'I shouldn't have said any of it. I don't even feel that way, I don't know why I said those horrible things to you. They were awful.' The desperation in her voice was clear as was the sincerity. 'I didn't mean to cause you and Marco to fight either, I'm really sorry.'

Eve put her hands on the benchtop, 'The thing is Tessa; you did say all those things,' her chest rose as she sighed, 'I consider myself to be a good friend to you, but I swear if you've fucked this up between Marco and I... I will never speak to you again... ever... I will never forgive you!' The harshness in Eve's voice was unmistakable. For her to say such a thing, Tessa knew she had been pushed to her limit and beyond. There was no mistaking the hurt in her friend's voice.

'I understand,' nodded Tessa in shame.

Ro walked briskly through the living room on her way to the bathroom, 'I'll be back in a sec to help you Eve.'

Tessa moved closer to Eve, 'I promise I will do whatever I have to do, to make things right between you and my brother. I'll do whatever you guys tell me to do, I'll go to rehab, I need to change.'

Still Eve remained silent, she hoped her friend really understood just how hurt everyone was due to her behaviour. In her still very unforgiving mood, Eve took herself into the bedroom and shut the door behind her so Tessa wouldn't come in, she just needed a moment to gather herself. Going back into the bedroom and changing into something lighter and more comfortable for cooking, Eve pulled her T shirt dress out of her bag and began to peel off her clothes. The door opened and she was about to ask Tessa to leave, but it was Marco. He leaned up against the bedroom wall and watched Eve. She didn't stop what she was doing to acknowledge him, complete silence besides the noises coming from the other side of the door in the kitchen where Ro and Tessa continued with preparing dinner.

Every part of her wanted to just fall into Marco's arms and feel his body at hers, but she was emotionally spent, and she knew that one cross word from him would break her.

'You should have told me you know that right?' He hated this tension with Eve, it wasn't how they worked, all the same they needed to talk it through.

'I've just realised how serious the problem is. I've already enquired about her getting into day rehab in Melbourne. I'm arranging it, I'm taking care of it.' Her tone was cold towards Marco.

'Thank you.'

Eve turned and looked at him, 'Why would you thank me, she's my best friend. That's what you do for your best friend, you take care of them when they need you. Your sister took care of me when I needed her most, so now I'm do the same for her.' Still sounding awfully icy.

Moving closer Marco looked down appreciatively at the woman he was marrying, his stomach twisting because she was upset, 'I'm thankful you're helping her, and I'm sorry she said those terrible things to you earlier. I heard most of it from the door before I came in.' The hurt Eve was feeling, was obvious, he didn't know whether to hug her or leave her alone, he didn't know this side of her, it was all new.

She bit down on her lip and her eyes went up to Marco's, 'What do you want me to say?' she tried to hide her devastation by being angry, Marco could see right through her tough façade.

'My sister is clearly fucked up at the moment, she would never want to hurt you like that otherwise. You didn't deserve her bullshit. I know you're in the middle, she's your friend and I'm your fiancé, if you still want to marry me that is.' He needed to soften the vibe between them.

Marco was reaching out; he was being the understanding sweet man Eve loved. She wanted to ignore him but simply couldn't, 'I'm a loyal friend and I always will be.' she tried to look less effected than she was, 'You gave me an ultimatum that was absolutely impossible.' Eve let Marco move into her personal space as they faced each other. 'When I agreed to marry you, I agreed to always put you first - no matter what, because that's what you do in a marriage. I just needed time.'

Marco had never seen Eve so intense. He'd never seen this side of her and didn't know what to do or say to make it right. All three of them managed to get through the night without further commotion. Eve ignored Marco and Tessa, whilst they went on as normal.

Chapter Twenty

Sunday night back in Melbourne was a warm one, the late summer heat was beginning to tire everyone. Tessa and Zach took Pat the dog for a long walk along the beach around eight o'clock, they were on good terms at least, much to Marco's dismay. He and Eve still upholding a somewhat standoff with each other, as hard as that was. When they'd arrived home Eve talked on the phone to Zoe for a while, then her mother called straight after, it was like Anna sensed Eve had something to say the other day, so she followed up with another call. They chit chatted for ten minutes about irrelevant bullshit, while Anna chose the right moment to ask Eve what was on her mind. Eve's lack of meaningful conversation was a dead giveaway that something was bothering her, Anna had no idea her weekend had been awful.

'Have you heard from your father? I believe he's representing that friend of yours. The club owner.' Anna never bought up her father, so Eve was wary.

'Ferez. Yes. He was Evan's friend,' Eve said sounding somber, she wondered where this was going.

'It's tax related from what I hear,' Anna probed. She'd heard all sorts of things about Ferez, she didn't know if she approved of Eve still having a contact in Evan's world. 'How's your fathers little girl doing, any word on her health?' It was very unusual for Anna to talk about James' personal life.

'Aria, she's not doing that well actually.' Eve was hesitant but curious as to her mother's interest.

'Well. She's a little girl, I hope she'll be okay.' Taking the higher ground Anna offered kind words, also unusual. But Aria was a child, so she thought she'd better.

'I've been thinking I might go and meet Aria,' Eve shocked herself with her comment. Another long pause. 'Because she's sick and because we're related.'

'How long have you been thinking about this?'

Immediately Eve knew that tone, Anna had been baiting her the whole time, 'Oh, a long while. I've never met the girls and since I've been in touch with dad so much lately, I've been thinking now would be a good time... they are my sisters after all.' Eve needed to give Anna the opportunity to tell her first but was getting inpatient.

'Right,' Anna was coolly apprehensive, 'Are you ready for that?'

Eve frowned as she sat on the couch watching Marco in the kitchen as he made a bowl of cornflakes for himself. *He was totally eavesdropping on her phone call.*

'I don't see why I wouldn't be ready, and I'd meet Sam of course too.' Eve felt her stomach tensing and her body tingle with anxiety.

The longest pause of all, as Anna considered her next words most carefully, 'Mmm. I guess that's your choice to make darling. It's up to you.'

Was that all she was going to say - was that it? Eve was disappointed, 'It is, isn't it?' Taking a breath at the realization that Anna knew exactly what she was getting at, but chose to let it pass by, Eve was furious, 'By the way, I spoke to Mamie, but I think you already know about that conversation, don't you mum?' The weight of the conversation was upon them both now. It was now or maybe never. *Fuck it!* Eve thought, she'd had about enough for one weekend!

'I do know about that conversation,' Anna managed, 'There's just one thing I want you to know Eveline. And it's the most important thing of all,' she sighed, 'I love you more than anything in this world. I always have and I always will.' It was a statement.

'I don't understand why you never told me,' Eve said with her heart pounding in her chest. 'I really wish you had told me that Sam was my biological mother.' Eve felt like something inside her had died, she wanted to crawl into bed and sleep forever. It felt like she'd just destroyed her mother. *Would Anna hate her!*

Marco gave her a wary glance from the kitchen where he ate his cornflakes.

'Eveline, I wanted you to be old enough to process this properly, it's all very complexed,' Anna's voice was calm, she had an air of confidence that gave Eve some assurance things would be okay between them.

'Mum. I'm twenty-five years old,' Eve tried to see reason in Anna's words, 'I just wish you had told me; I wish it had come from you.' Eve reminding herself to not shut off, speak, use her words, move forward, 'When are you coming home? I'd really like to see you. I've got a few things I need to speak with you about. Some financial things, legal things.' Eve took the conversation on a slight turn to avoid getting over emotional; her eyes darted to Marco who was still pretending to not listen even though it was impossible for him not to.

'I'm home on Friday darling. I've got some important business in Sydney over the next month or so. I'm changing course a little.' A teaser of her own, Anna sounded positive and like she had a few things of her own to tell. She wasn't diminishing the conversation she and Eve had just had, they were both moving forward.

'Okay, well I'll speak to you then... I love you Mum.' After the rough weekend Eve needed some kind of calm, some kind of stability, and Anna was it. Anna was the mother she had always known, and Eve didn't have the energy to cross examine her as much as she would have liked to. Lacking the energy to make Anna see how very wrong she'd been all these years. Not tonight.

'I love you Eveline. Say hello to Marco and Tessa.' Anna knew she'd disappointed her daughter again.

'I will.' She didn't want to speak to either of them, she wouldn't be passing on the message.

Night had come and they still hadn't talked, Eve laid in bed beside Marco as he slept, listening to his breathing, and staring aimlessly out the open window and into the night sky. Her mind questioning the conversation and the things she had said earlier to her mother. It was all very brushed under the carpet, nothing had been resolved, but then she wasn't sure what she expected from Anna. *Did Sam even want to know her, would she even let her meet her sisters?* For some strange reason, all Eve wanted was to be in Sydney, with her father. Right now, in particularly because she felt a closeness to James that had been absent for so long. They spoke almost every day at the moment because of Aria's ill health. It was just like old times. Eve had missed her dad tremendously.

Noise from down the hallway took her mind a moment. Even with the door closed, she could hear Tessa's laughter and playful noises, whilst she herself was in a bed of silence with no talking, let alone touching. Marco had put a wall up as had she. Eve didn't cope well with walls being put up around her by others, it felt like rejection, and she'd had enough therapy over the years to know she didn't do rejection well. As soon as Eve felt it coming she defended herself by putting up an even bigger wall or removing herself completely from the situation.

After the doctors rather intimate interrogation of Tessa first thing on Monday morning, not to mention the very personal questions, she was booked in for the following day to start day-hab. Eve paid upfront so Tessa didn't have to deal with the money side of things, because she didn't have any money left, her habit had bled her dry financially, along with living in New York. Eve didn't want or expect the money back, however Tessa vowed to repay every cent back before they died, which made them both laugh.

'And if I do die before I pay you back, please know that I loved you like a sister E,' Tessa took a breath getting emotional as she and Eve sat at lunch, 'And that I appreciated you more than anyone in my whole entire life.'

'Well, you're not dying... I just want you to be well.'

'I don't want to die yet; I really like fucking Zach again,' Tessa smiled.

'Oh, yeah, I know you do,' Eve laughed, nothing Tessa said should shock her, and yet this did.

The GP had concern's that Tessa's alcohol abuse was as prevalent as her drug abuse, Eve was under strict instructions to rid the house of any alcohol immediately. Marco and Zach had a cupboard full of alcohol, and it all had to go.

'You know your parents are staying at the house this weekend. Marco wants to tell them about the wedding plans, I'm actually not sure he still wants to marry me, but anyway,' Eve smiled as they sat on the deck at the beach café enjoying the sunshine, her lack of spark, noted by Tessa.

'I'm sorry, I've put you in the middle of this E.' Tessa had been struck with a reality check after the doctors. Marco and Eve's relationship had been strained and it was all her fault. 'I'll make it right between you two, I promise you.'

As they walked through the leafy streets back to the house, Tessa's phone rang. Eve listened to her brief conversation, and it was clear that Tessa had got the show in Melbourne. With all her heart, Eve hoped this would be the key to her friend turning things around in her life. At the same time, it meant Tessa would be in Melbourne long term, they had a big few weeks ahead of them.

Zach and Marco sat listened to Tessa's version of what had gone down in the doctor's office. Now that her problem was a household topic, they were both on a need-to-know basis. Tessa of course added her famous animation and over exaggeration to her explanation as only she could, making going to rehab sound like an adventure of a lifetime, which made for an entertaining dinner none the less. Every time Tessa told the boys something, Marco would look at Eve for confirmation.

Since Saturday, there had been something missing from Marco's eyes when he looked at Eve, she tried her hardest to not let it eat at her soul like acid, but how could it not. She felt like they were dissolving day by day, her low moods were like dark cloud, everyone in the house could feel it, even Tessa and she was the one in day-hab.

Eve sat in her chair next to Marco at the table, she didn't have much to say, she barely ate, letting Tessa have her moment, they ordered takeaway steak sandwiches and salad from a local restaurant. Eve didn't even feel like cooking right at the moment.

The boys didn't know it yet, but she had already poured every bottle of alcohol down the sink whilst Tessa had taken an afternoon nap. If Tessa was going to do this, she needed a good healthy environment to do it in. It had been a cleansing ceremony of sorts for Eve pouring the expensive liquids down the drain, she was determined to have a pure and nurturing home for Tessa to get well in.

What had surprise Eve, was Zach's support for Tessa, she wasn't so sure if this thing they had going, was just a filler for him. He looked at Tessa with fascination when she spoke, it was like he savored every word… it seemed very romantic to Eve as she absorbed them across the dinner table.

Again, Eve and Marco went to bed with only a simple goodnight spoken between them. It was ridiculous and they both knew they couldn't go on like this. Something had to change.

The next day Eve sat in the waiting room at the rehab clinic for over three hours. It was a long time to be alone with just you and your thoughts. The quizzical

341

look on Marco's face as he left his car key at her bedside table this morning was plaguing her; he had reached down and touched her head as he said goodbye. *No kiss, no intimacy!*

Only the situation with Tessa was anchoring Eve down as every part of her anxious self, wanted to run away before the ending came and she was left heartbroken... again. The unwelcome feelings were terrifying, the thought of losing Marco again was probably more than she could take to be honest. To think that she had set herself up, so soon, for such a massive fall was tearing her skin off in shreds.

How could you be so fucking stupid? Eve's mind was always awash with self-blame in her dark times. Burning hot tears rolled from Eve's eyes and down her cheeks as she thought about why she should just go back to France and never leave the perimeter of the chateaux, ever again. Working herself up into a thick lather of unnecessary self-pity and loathing, she needed to snap the fuck out of it fast... *Self-sabotage was a bitch!*

Rushing out the main doors and out into the gardens, Eve needed fresh air. Of course, the gardens were serene and calming and reminded her of the smoking area she used to sit in with Jo when she was in rehab. Eve would go and visit Jo with Tia, she missed them, she was homesick this week for the first time in such a long time.

Taking deep breaths, she looked at two men sitting on a bench smoking together, they looked like father and son in the depths of conversation... it that made Eve sad. She settled herself and sat at the other end of the garden, the fresh air was filling her lungs and slowly clearing her head.

'Oh, E. My life is so great compared to some of those poor fuckers in there!' Tessa was energetic and over the top on the car ride home, 'I almost felt embarrassed because I didn't have a solid reason for becoming such a fuck up... I take drugs because I like them and they make me feel good, no other reason.' She made Eve laugh. 'There's one guy in the group who admitted he'd bashed his wife and put her into hospital whilst he was drunk. He's been to jail twice too, and they're still married. And there's this woman who got into fifty thousand dollars of dept in one week at the casino after her husband had killed himself, she's got two little kids... can you imagine.' Tessa took a well needed breath, 'There's this one gorgeous girl who looks so young, she makes porn so she can buy drugs' she was flabbergasted,

'And she's got a black eye. Did you see her?' Tessa was peaking. She had her window right down; she was an adrenaline overload of stories, 'I must have sounded like the dumbest loser ever. All I had to say was that I was away from my family and friends to long while I was dancing on fucking Broadway. What a fuckin idiot!'

It was like Tessa was on acid, high as a kite, full of energy… she kept talking and talking.

Zach was in the kitchen eating a sandwich, he like Marco seriously ate a lot. As soon as he saw Tessa he stood with wide open arms, giving her a big heartwarming welcome home hug as she came in.

'How'd it go, are you okay?' Zach was keen to hear about her day, it was a genuine display of interest, and although Tessa seemed fine on the outside, she needed all the support she could get.

'I'm still breathing, I'm not in dept and I'm not having sex for drugs,' Tessa said wrapping her arms around his waist, 'It was a big session. Let me tell you, there's some fucking awful shit going on out there in the world!'

'I'll leave you to it,' Eve waved her arm and let it drop to her side as she headed towards the stairs.

'The big fella's still at the club, there's a crisis. He said to tell you he won't be home for dinner,' Zach added as she was about to take the stairs. A deep breath and a moment of hesitation.

'Okay,' Eve said glumly, she didn't look back, she didn't stop. Her reaction was completely out of her control as she slumped up the stairs. Before she reached the top, tears fell down her cheeks and her face crumbled. *She got it; this was the beginning of the end.* Marco would normally text her or called her himself to tell her something like this. He was avoiding her in every way possible and it felt awful. Closing the bedroom door and then closing and locked the bathroom door. It was almost six o'clock and all Eve wanted to do was shower and go to bed, she needed to put herself out of the immediate misery she was in.

The softness of the perfect pillow, with the perfect linen was the only comfort Eve had as she dozed off in perfect Marco's bed on her own. Eve's head was heavy, her heart was heavier. It felt like it was all over, and because of nothing… not that she was saying Tessa's drug addiction was nothing, she just couldn't comprehend that it had led to her and Marco being in this position. It was all too much.

Chapter Twenty One

Waking as Marco put his keys on the bedside table again, 'I've got a TV thing on tonight. I'll be home late.' He bent down and ruffled her hair. She opened her eyes to see the most beautiful man on earth looking down at her.

'The car key is here. See ya tonight.' And he left. No kiss. Nothing.

Eve sat out in the waiting room again while Tessa was in her day-hab session. Her mind running away with itself.

Had Marco changed his mind? Maybe he didn't trust her anymore! He wanted out! As much as she didn't want to think the worst, she couldn't help it. Eve was a master catastrophizer.

Finally, she saw Tessa coming towards her with her arms open wide, looking like she'd been attacked by an alley cat, disheveled and crying. Today had been a hard and long day for the both of them. Eve stood to Tessa; it was an emotional embrace. 'It's okay,' Eve's voice muffled as Tessa squeezed her into her body.

Tessa didn't speak, she let out a few dramatic sobs which alarmed Eve, not letting to as she felt comfort in her best friends arms. Today's session had been a difficult one.

'I'm Henry,' said a youngish guy with a mass of curly red-hair standing at their side, 'Tessa's been talking about the consequences of her drug and alcohol abuse today,' he explained as Eve gasped for a breath in the arms of a very emotional Tessa.

'I'm Eve, nice to meet you Henry.'

'All you need to do is listen,' Henry smiled at Eve and walked, she raised her brows and watched him go.

Tessa didn't speak all the way home; Eve was so curious to know what had silenced her friend. When you were used to someone talking constantly it was strange when they didn't.

Eve forgot about her own dramas and let Tessa's mood consume her. Lately her moods seemed to consume everything. 'Cup of tea?' Eve asked Tessa who sat at the dining table like a zombie.

'Please slip some cyanide in it for me?' she said finding a smile for Eve.

'I'm sure there's some here somewhere,' Eve joked pretending to look for it in the cupboard.

'What have I done to my life E?' Tessa asked somberly. Today's mood was a total opposite to how she came home yesterday. One day on top of the world, the next day, not so much.

'You can't change the past,' Eve had to speak positive words, her friend needed them, 'But you've got so much to look forward to, it's a whole new start for you.' Positive and encouraging was not at all how Eve felt, but it seemed the correct thing to say to someone who had just asked you to help kill them.

'Is Marco still mad at you E?'

'Yep. Not a kiss since Saturday.' A troubled grin at the thought.

'Not even one kiss!'

'I'm not sure what we're doing to be honest.' Eve bit down on her bottom lip.

'He'll come around; he never holds a grudge. I don't know why he's acting like this. I've told him he can't treat you like this, or you'll go back to France, and that will be fucked for all of us.' Tessa was nearly in tears, she was so emotional, the fact that Eve didn't deny it, made her feel worse. 'Would you leave?'

Eve was shocked that Tessa really thought she'd do a runner on her brother, 'I don't want to go anywhere.'

'Do you feel like a run? I need to run it out… I feel like I'm going to explode.' Tessa knew it was a whacked thing to ask Eve, she hated exercise. But Eve was down for it, it made sense to expand their lungs and fill them with sea air and get those endorphins happening. *Especially since Eve didn't have any cyanide!*

'Let's go.' *Why not!* Eve thought to herself. She needed to run her angst out too. Sitting around waiting for Marco to forgive her was killing her slowly.

They ran, and they ran… well Eve tried to run… all the way in one direction and then in the other until it got dark, the girls were exhausted looking at the lights of the docked cruise ship.

Tessa had run her angst out; it was that or go on the hunt for a fix, Eve felt momentarily better too. Day after day her heart ached over Marco. Tonight, would be the night though. It was crunch time, it was time to face the music and see if he was her destiny.

With her own turmoil, Tessa needed some time with her brother tonight too. After today's session she had a few things to discuss with him alone, then with Eve on her own, and then maybe both of them together.

'I start rehearsals Monday, eight till one, that gives me an hour to get to day-hab.' On the outside, Tessa seemed positive. 'Will you still come with me next week E?' But she was scared shitless.

'Of course, I will go with you. How exciting for you, a new show,' smiling proudly Eve touched Tessa's leg. For Eve though, it felt like everything was up in the air, she didn't know what she'd be doing tomorrow, let alone next week. Whatever happened, she would see Tessa through her hard times.

'I'm scared E. Really scared. I started doing coke so I could keep up with the shows schedule in New York. I need to find me again, the clean way.'

'You'll find your way, you always do. Plus, you have this thing with Zach, I see the way he looks at you.' It felt nice to talk about the situation between Tessa and Zach with some sort of joy instead of a dirty secret.

'You do?' Tessa pepped up slightly.

'Yes, I do. How's it all going? I've noticed the spare bed doesn't get slept in anymore.' Until now Eve had steered clear of the topic, not wanting to encourage or acknowledge the rekindled love affair.

Tessa shrugged and took a deep breath in, 'I don't want to label it, but it feels okay,' she smiled peacefully, 'You know I used to defend Brooke to people. Football clubs can be awful and bitchy. There's always gossip floating around.'

'What kind of gossip?' Eve was so naive.

'Rumor has it, the first baby she aborted, wasn't even Zach's.'

Eve gasped, 'Wow! That's a pretty serious rumor, that's actually a horrible rumor.'

It was past nine o'clock when the girls got home, Zach's car was parked out the front, this was an indication the boys were home too, they'd both had to do the TV commitment this evening.

Eve's anxiety spiked as they went inside, Tessa had returned home in a better place than she was in when she left. It was no secret she'd never been in love, so with Zach she didn't have anything to compare it to, all she knew was it warmed her heart to find him waiting for her.

'Where have you been? We're on in half an hour,' he said like an excited little boy.

Marco was sitting on the sofa; he gave Eve a smile as he got up.

'We're going to look like two idiots,' said Marco walking past Eve to Tessa, then wrapping an arm around her.

Both guys seemed pumped up in anticipation, their excitement of being on TV puzzled Eve. The two of them played football and were on TV every week, so why was this such an event. Eve didn't get football at all.

'How was today?' Marco asked his sister lovingly.

'Intense but great if you know what I mean. I had to run it out with E,' Tessa seemed energized. 'I needing five minutes of your time… alone if that's okay Marco?'

'Sure. Now?' he said glancing over at Eve who was within earshot, making a Milo and milk at the bench.

'The front room?' suggested Tessa.

'Call me if we come on,' Marco said over his shoulder to Zach as he followed after his sister down the hallway, glancing at Eve, he wanted to walk up to her and grab her face and kiss her right on the precious mouth, but her resistance to him had been going on too long, he didn't know where he stood anymore.

Sitting side by side on the couch, Zach told Eve about the TV hosts having a huge argument behind set right before they prerecorded their segment. Because they had a game the following night, the club didn't want them waiting around the studio all night to be interviewed live, so it was prerecorded. Eve found the whole cross between on-field commitments and off-field commitments hectic, it was nonstop, so it seemed, particularly for Marco. He was forever at training or at a meeting, or doing some kind of media gig, it was never ending, and the season hadn't started yet.

'We're on! We're on!' Zach yelled out loud so Marco would hear him from the front room.

Marco came in, sliding his socked feet along the floorboards, skidding into the space right beside Eve on the couch, close so their legs touched. She could feel the heat from his body for the first time in days, she wanted to touch him, reach out and put her hand on his leg, anything.

'You look really white, almost grey,' said Marco to Zach as they appeared side by side on the screen, Marco so much taller and darker with his summer glow.

'Your hair is messy,' Zach hit back.

They both had eyes fixed to the screen, then came a raucous laugh as the host made a joke about the height difference and about them being best mates and housemates.

It finished and they laughed and poked fun at each other for a few minutes, Tessa then took Zach's attention away by playing with Pat the dog and trying to teach him a new trick.

'I need to speak with you.' Eve turned to Marco, he was still tucked in beside her on the couch, just not giving her an inch of his attention. When she spoke to him, his lips curled up slightly in anticipation.

Marco was in hot demand tonight, first Tessa giving him an apology for the drama she had caused between him and Eve, and for the stress she was causing the household, then she begged her brother to make things better with Eve, claiming their rift was making it hard on the entire house and that included poor Pat the dog according to Tessa.

Marco followed Eve up the stairs, he closed the door to the bedroom behind him. She had just assumed they should talk in the bedroom; it was where they did most of their private things in the house, the place she felt most comfortable and safe.

'Can I go first?' he faced Eve front on as she sat on her hands on the edge of the bed and nodded her approval to him. 'This is killing me Evie,' he said about the standoff between them.

'I know, me too,' she took a breath of relief that his animosity wasn't too punishing.

A cute sexy smirk, 'Does it always take you so long to cool down?'

'Cool down!' gasped Eve.

'How much longer will you be angry at me because I can't do much more of this no talking no touching bullshit?' Marco shifted his weight from one foot to the other doing some kind of leg stretch, liked it was a normal conversation rather than a defining moment in their relationship.

'I'm not angry at you Marco,' Eve felt herself overcome with emotion, 'You've been avoiding me all week.'

'I've been giving you space.'

'I don't need space, I needed you. I know you're upset with me. I thought you'd changed your mind about us,' her voice raising as she stood up.

Marco was astonished that she would think such a thing, 'I haven't changed my mind Eve Frank. I just didnt know what to do, I thought you were angry with me.' *As if he would just call it quits!*

Eve exhaled with what could only be described as pure relief, 'I'm not angry,' she said flopping down on the bed with mental exhaustion. *Had all her angst been for nothing!*

Marco moved into her space and knelt down in front of her. His big protective arms wrapping around her slender waist, she was clad in lycra pants and an oversized T shirt. He kissed her lips slowly, moving his mouth over hers as she sat still. The touch of his lips to hers electrified with passion that had been suppressed for days.

His hand found a fist of her hair at the back of her head, pulling her mouth up to his, taking a deep breath, it had become his signature move. Eve's mouth opening to his wider than she usually kissed, inhaling Marco into her body, it was a raw and intimate kiss that had everything a good kiss should have. Eve pulling herself up his body, her arms around his neck, squeezing him tight to her, it was like they'd been apart for years... full of desire, passion and unraveling nerves as she breathed him into her soul.

'Next time we shouldn't wait five days before we talk,' Marco said still kissing Eve.

'More talking,' she kissed back as she laid back to the bed. Marco stood and pulled her running shoes off and tossed them aside.

He stopped kissing her and peeled her lycra pants down her legs, 'This can't ever happen again Eve Frank. No holding out on each other.' Marco moved over the dop of her.

'No more holding out.' Reaching up she pulled at his T shirt off and his mouth coming back down to meet her soft lips again.

'More talking,' he bit at her lip.

'Definitely more talking,' Eve kissed him feeling the tension leaving her body.

He thought she was angry, she thought he was angry... What a cock up and a waste of time. It may have taken five days, but the standoff was well and truly over as Marco pulled Eve's knickers over her hips. Her hands at his muscular chest, palms to his skin feeling every perfect ripple on his athletic body.

'I love you. Most of all I love how you love me.' Eve felt grateful, relieved, and safe again.

'I'm so glad you still love me,' his voice sexy and low.

'I will never not love you Marco Rossi.'

'Good, because I will never not marry you Eve Frank... I want you to be mine forever,' he chuckled.

'I was yours a long time ago. You just didn't know it,' she said pulling her lips away and looking at his dark eyes, the very eyes that had made her heart flutter as a young girl.

'Timing Baby. It's all timing,' Marco smirked as he looked over her sweet face. 'Now is our time Evie. So, more talking, okay!' He pulled her T shirt over her head with one swift maneuver, then went straight to the clip of her bra.

'I'm not a great at opening up,' she admitted the obvious.

Marco was already firm as he grazed over her body, 'Lucky for you, I'm a great teacher.'

'Mmm, I know you are,' she hummed to his mouth, 'I remember.' Eve finally let herself surrender to his sweetness, smiling as he lowered over her, his bare flesh warmly went to hers, the sensitivity between her legs was beyond madness, she could feel a strong stirring deep in the pit of her stomach. The pounding of her heart was slow and steady in her chest, her hands caressing Marco's face, wandering fingers entwined in his waves of hair as his kisses tenderly trailed off down her neck and then her chest. The cold softness of his lips at her nipples sending a powering surge all the way down to her pussy, she wanted to close her legs together to stop the humming. No such luck! Marco was between her legs. Eve lifted her hips in a bid for some part of him to touch her pussy, anything, she just needed to feel something.

'Tell me how much you want it?' Marco looked at Eve daringly.

'I want it really, really bad,' a desperate gasp, putting her own hand down to herself to ease the explosive sensitivity of sexual pressure building inside her clit. Silk fluid at her fingers, she wanted to bury her hand within herself as Marco's sucks to her nipple stimulated her all over. 'I'll do anything you want,' Eve offered.

He looked at her; he took her hand from between her legs and bought it up to her mouth, placing her own wet fingers inside her mouth. Marco watched as he know knelt over her, his knee pressing to her wet pussy with a movement that stimulated her. 'I don't want you to ever run away from me,' he said seriously, also sucking her fingers as she took them from her mouth. 'There's nothing we can't fix together Evie.' Marco sucked her fingers again as he stared into her large almond eyes, she was sexually intoxicating. Eve was all grown up, but her eyes sometimes still had the innocents of when he'd first fallen for her.

Moving down her body, giving three kisses to her boob, stomach, and hip before he embedded his face in her folds. Puffy lips pressing over her, the friction of his stroking tongue taking her breath away as it ran from end to end.

'I need you inside me?' Eve groaned, trying to wiggle away from his mouth, but he pulled her hips back to his face. Marco began to suck at her swelling clit, tender sucks to tease her.

He made his way up her body again, scrambling to get his pants off. Guided himself straight into her pulsing opening, it felt like he was home again.

Eve took fast and shallow breaths the second he entered her. It was an overload of emotional want that couldn't be stopped. Her arms at Marco's sides as he pressed inside her warmth. working up to a soothing rhythm of tender thrust burying deeper and deeper into her depths.

There was nothing about this woman Marco was prepared to live without! Their sexual connection and energy was raw, more than either had anticipated... their make-up sex was sensually desperate and emotional. A surrendering of souls.

Eve's legs wrapping around Marco, her fingers entwined in his as he took her hands out above her head and pressed them into the mattress, stretching her out so he could get traction as he pounded dominantly to her body.   She fell apart at that very moment, her swelling pussy hot like fire, engulfing his perfect commanding cock.

Tears of joy and ecstasy got the better of her. Without warning or control, she let out a sob of relief to his chest that hovered above her, rolling her head to one side to hide her crumbling face, Eve bit down on her bottom lip.

Looking down at her helpless face, Marco adored everything that this sometimes complexed and delicate woman had become to him. Marco was so in love. Her vulnerability and insecurities fueled his desire to please her, after all she'd been though, he owed her a life of being loved and cherished.

'I need you to know how much I really love you Evie,' he whispered into the top of her head.

'I know... I do know.' Her tears burned at the side of her face as she still tried to hide them from him.

'I'm inside you in more ways than one... I'll always be a part of you,' Marco's unguarded words fell out his mouth. Tensing as he felt the overwhelming urge to cum, he held onto it for Eve's sake. *Ladies first!*

'I will love you until the day I die,' she gasped pulling at his hands as her depths began to tighten around his embedded manhood. He'd pushed to her to the edge emotionally, and physically. This man she'd loved for so long was finally all hers, and even though Eve knew better than most, that this beautiful love they shared could be taken from them in a mere second, she needed to let her walls down and open her heart, Eve needed to trust the process of love completely. Most of all she needed to talk and be open about her feelings with Marco.

'From the beginning... I always wanted to find our way back here, even when you weren't mine,' Marco said softly, his body getting weaker to his will to hold out.

His words were everything she'd always wanted to hear, and yet she had an awful ache in her heart.

If only he'd never let her go, life would have been much less painful, Eve thought, she could only muster a sigh, she pulled her body up to meet his as she felt the intoxicating urge of release taking hold of her. Squeezing her eyes shut as her body relented to his surge of cum, Eve fell back down to the mattress with a thud as she let herself feel every ounce of Marco's satisfaction inside her, she was exasperated and so very emotional.

He couldn't speak either, cumming to Eve with a vengeance, it was like he hadn't cum in months, Marco was depleted and collapsed to her luscious body for comfort. A shaky hand clutched at her face, his head next to hers as he whispered, 'I love you more right now, in this very moment, than I ever have Eve Frank.'

Later that night, Marco and Eve joined Tessa for a chat about how things were going to move forward from here. As her big brother he wanted her close while she was fighting her demons and doing day-hab. Plus, she was doing her show in Melbourne, so she'd need support. Marco was getting used to the idea of her and Zach, even though he tried his damn hardest to ignore the fact. His house was full love which felt better than he ever thought possible. Eve was now part of his life, Tessa was infiltrating her way into his home, Zach was his constant, and he was surprisingly okay with all. Life was changing.

'I want you to stay here with us. We'll make it work,' Marco wanted to make his sister feel welcome.

Tessa was overjoyed at his reaction, 'I don't want to be in your way. I've caused you two enough trouble.' Even thought she was happy, there was a sadness to Tessa that was hard to watch. Her moods and demeanor were now more up and down than ever before as she was detoxing. They'd never seen her this low before.

'You're my sister, you're supposed to cause me grief,' Marco smiled.

Eve put her hands over Marco's as they sat together, 'You know I need you; these two guys are like an old married couple... have you not noticed?' she laughed as she tried to lighten the moment by making a joke about the way Marco and Zach lived. 'Plus, if you're not here, I'll be the third wheel.'

Marco came in with another reason why his sister needed to stay, 'Look at it this way, Eve's just moved here, she doesn't know anyone here and having you around makes me feel less guilty for leaving her here alone all day long… and you just told me you got the show in Melbourne, you're doing the best you can to sort your shit out, and you need our support,' a pause, 'I'm not thrilled about the sleeping arrangements; but I'll get over it.' The boys had aired their thoughts to each other today over a late lunch and they had come to an understanding.

'I promise you both I will never come between you again.'

And so, it was settled, Marco had a full house.

Chapter Twenty Two

Marco and Tessa went to pick up their parents from the airport Friday morning, Zach had gone into the club for a medical check as he hadn't been declared fit for tonight's season opening game yet due to calf tightening.

Eve stayed back at home with Pat the dog busily cleaning, changing the sheets in the guest bedroom for Jackie and Mario, and filling the house with fresh flowers, as Eve did.

'Hi Dad,' her voice pleasant as she answered her father's call. The night of fabulously unforgettable make up sex with Marco had left her feeling radiant and in the best of moods. Marco was breaking all his pre-game rules.

'I haven't got long darling, I'm in Melbourne for a night and I really need to speak with you. Meet me for dinner before I fly home tomorrow?' James didn't ask, he ordered, which was something he did to everyone, not just his daughter. Everything was always on his terms.

'Oh, I'd love to dad, but I can't tonight. It's Marco's first game of the season and I'm going to the game with Jackie and Mario, they're coming down for the weekend, Zoe will be here too. Apparently the opening game is a big deal.'

'Eveline, I really need to see you, it's very important, can't you go to the next game?'

'Dad!' Was he joking? She frowned getting irritated at her father's arrogance.

'I spoke with Martin Li yesterday, I need to speak with you,' James gave her a hint.

The mention of his name made Eve's heart feel like concrete, sinking to the pit of her stomach. An awkward silence lingered. 'What does he want?' She'd never liked Martin; she'd never trusted him.

'There's two issues I need to speak with you about darling,' James sounded like he was speaking with someone's secretary, 'My schedule is tight, I need an answer now.'

Eve huffed at her father's persistence and lack of understanding, 'Can't I meet you for breakfast in the morning? Where are you staying?' a pause, 'Is Aria's alright?' she bounced back at him giving him a little of his own arrogance.

'She's spending a few nights in the hospital at the moment, Sam's with her,' James sounded drained.

'I'll message you the details; breakfast needs to be early so I can be back in Sydney by lunch time.' He caved to her breakfast offer; it was rather urgent he saw his daughter.

'Is Aria okay, she alright isn't she?' Eve was still worried, it was upsetting her in a strange way, this was a feeling she wasn't used to.

'We'll speak in the morning. Don't keep me waiting Eveline.' James made sure he gave the last order before he hung up, leaving Eve completely unraveled, she contemplated calling Ferez to see if he knew what was going on with Martin, but then she doubted he would know anything about it, the two didn't really have anything to do with each other, they weren't friends, they weren't even associates, she hating the fact that her father was, however an associate of Martin Li's.

The phone call had bought on an untimely panic attack… Eve took deep breaths and tried to keep herself calm. It was all very concerning – Martin – Aria. She didn't know who she should be more worried about. Splashing water to her face in the downstairs powder room, Eve took stock of her situation and did something she hadn't done for so very long. She blocked it all out, and pushed it way down, because now was not the time.

Busily putting flowers in the kitchen and the bedrooms before sitting anxiously in the windowsill of their upstairs bedroom, waiting for Marco's car to pull up. Eve needed to get through todays lunch with Jackie and Mario and their wedding announcement, then get Tessa to her afternoon session of day-hab somehow, followed by Marco's game tonight before she could direct her thoughts to the latest issues at hand.

Eve couldn't wait to see Zoe who was arriving with Nick later in the afternoon and staying with him – in separate rooms in a nearby hotel. *Another strange situation!*

The Zoe and Nick saga was a story on its own, one which Eve couldn't work out. Zoe was adamant that she and Nick were only friends, and rather good ones at that. But there had apparently been no sex, not even a sneaky kiss, which Eve found odd given Zoe had always had a thing for Nick and he was now into her in a big way.

Marco's car pulled up and Eve went down to greet everyone at the front door, moving forward from her father phone call. Jackie held her arms out open to Eve, her smile full of warmth and genuine happiness to see her. She squeezed Eve tight into a bear like hug as she inhaling deep, smelling her young friends long dark curls. Marco, Mario, and Tessa stood behind her with all the bags, waiting to come into the house.

'You feel healthy,' Jackie smiled as they shuffled down the hallway together, 'Is it because my sons been taking good care of you?' she asked with a sense of pride.

Eve raised her brows at Marco, oh he took good care of her last night. *Over and over*! 'Yes, he's keeping me in very good health. We look after each other,' Eve exhaled with a demure smile.

'She looks well, doesn't she honey?' Jackie turned to Mario for his opinion as if they'd been expecting her to look awful.

'You're glowing Eve,' Mario said innocently as they gathered in the kitchen.

'No. I'm not glowing,' Eve gushed defensively to squash that idea immediately. She related glowing to being pregnant, everyone used to tell her how she was glowing when she was pregnant with Rafael. She was one hundred percent sure she was not pregnant; nor glowing, she was expecting her period, maybe that was her glow… the comment had alarmed her. She was religiously regimented with her birth control these days, there would be no more mistakes.

'You look well, darling,' said Jackie seeing the instant angst, 'That's what Mario meant,' her words gentle.

Eve nodded, she mentally panicked, it was simply a trigger for her, and after her phone conversation with her father, she was feeling somewhat vulnerable, not quite herself.

Sitting at a curbside table at the pub up the road from the house, Marco had tried to prepare as best he could for his big announcement to his parents, he was nervous and exited.

Jackie was happy to see Tessa, although worried at her appearance she was happy to hear the news of her new job in Melbourne. As a mother, Jackie knew her daughter, and she knew all was not well, but she knew she also couldn't smother Tessa, it simply didn't work. Sitting close to her at the table, holding her hand, it felt like they hadn't had this kind of closeness in a long time.

Jackie observed Marco and Eve across the table, she was fixated on the dynamics of how the vertical orientation worked between them. Her son was a big, tall athletic man, and her gorgeous Eve, tiny and petite. However, it worked for them, it was fine with Jackie, they looked oddly compatible next to one another, yet so very much in love. The attraction was undeniable, unable to separate from one another, it was as much lovely for Jackie to see, as it was weird. Sitting listening to the conversation in the ideal Melbourne weather, she revisited the memories of having all the kids and their friends at the house every summer in the swimming pool, hanging out on the beach, having parties and sleep overs. It had been a wonderful time in her life. Never in her wildest dreams though, did she ever see Eve and Marco falling in love, but then she thought, maybe she should have. They were both similar in nature and personality, it was an extraordinary match regardless of how inappropriate the begin may have been. Jackie felt like a terrible mother for not telling her son about Eve's pregnancy as soon as she had the information in New York, but in her heart of hearts, she knew Eve had to be the one to tell him.

Marco held Eve's hand under the table, he noticed she had her engagement ring turned under her hand, Jackie would have spotted that sparkle within seconds and blown the whole announcement out of the water.

The sun was out, the weather was Melbourne at its best. Eve sat quietly at Marco's side hanging onto his hand for what felt like dear life as the moment grew closer and closer. Her mind kept wandering to her phone call with her father, how could she not. *What the fuck could Martin possibly want from her after all this time?*

Surely it had to be money… the many millions of dollars Evan had bought Villa Rosado with. *What else could it be?*

Eve endured a lengthy conversation about how great it was they were all residing under the one roof in Melbourne, Tessa's new show, Marco's preseason games and of course the breakup of Brooke and Zach, all conversations of which Eve completely zoned out of.

Then, Marco cleared his voice and gave Eve's hand a squeeze, 'I've got some news actually,' Marco began looking and sounding pleasantly calm, taking a nervous breath at his pause, 'Eve's moving to Melbourne… to live with me,' a pause as Jackie and Mario dawned smiles of surprised joy, 'And we're engaged to be married,' he added quickly whilst they were still smiling.

But suddenly, the moment stopped still, everyone's expressions froze still, and silence prevailed for a few extremely tense seconds.

'Engaged!' Mario was the first to draw a breath.

'Isn't it great,' Tessa said with her normal enthusiastic energy as sat between her parents like she was in a vice of unexpected pressure.

The long silence from Jackie making Eve's heart thump in her chest as Marco waiting patiently for his mother to react.

Jackie felt her stomach tighten and her throat swell as her blood pressure skyrocketed. *Eve had to be the most fertile female to grace the earth!* It was the only one explanation for her normally levelheaded son to be rushing into such a lifechanging commitment. Then just as she was about to question them, she saw Eve look up into her son's eyes… almost like they'd done something wrong. The look in their eyes couldn't be mistaken for anything but adoring love, Jackie thought. They comforted one another with a mere look, and at that very moment, Jackie saw a love story that had seen many years of longing and drama, make it to this moment now before her… It was obvious, Eve had been Marco's weakness right from the start in Palm Cove, and she'd been in love with him from the moment she first laid eyes on him as a young girl.

Mario sighed, 'This is fantastic news,' he said slowly, breaking his wife's silence, clapping his hands together loudly as he got out of his seat and went around the table to embrace his son.

Who was he to deny his son of happiness?

Mario hugged Marco tight and patted his back firmly, then went to Eve, giving her an embodied hug as she stood, it felt so familiar, she didn't know if it was because Marco was so like his father, or it was that she had known Mario for so long. Either way she felt the love.

'Welcome to the family Eve. You were always part of us, now it's official.' Mario kissed both her cheeks through her abundance of extra curly hair.

Jackie stood up quickly, still stunned, but then regrouped quickly and moved to Eve and embrace her; it was a long intense hug. Getting over the disappointment of Marco's irresponsible behavior with Eve all those years ago in Palm Cove was not easy for Jackie. Especially because she had seen firsthand the effect it had had on Eve. Her pride for Marco had been tarnished for a brief moment in time when she'd found out he fathered Eve's baby. Her precious son wasn't perfect after all.

'Jackie,' Eve said to her ear at a whisper, 'Are you okay?'

'I'm fine,' her emotions kicking in as she held Eve, 'You know I always secretly wanted you to be my daughter in law,' an emotional chuckle as Jackie stood holding Eve's face in both her hands, 'I just never imagined you would be marrying this one,' she laughed, 'But I'm so very happy you are.' Her teary eyes turning to Marco as she reached for him.

'We want the wedding to be in Palm Cove,' Marco announced, 'It seems like the obvious place to us.'

Jackie's interest peaked, 'Is there a date?' It was like a light switch... there was a wedding to plan!

'Not really, not yet,' Eve was quick to answer.

'October. At the end of the season, it's really the only time.' Marco wasn't being bossy, he was just excited, and it was more to do with his schedule and the off season. Eve didn't know it yet, but she would have to get used to his schedule impacting their life together, this was just the beginning.

'This year?' Jackie sounded surprised.

'It's not a shotgun wedding mum... I know that's what you're thinking,' baulked Tessa to her mother.

'Mum!' Scowled Marco, showing his horror at the notion his mother could think such a thing.

Eve raised her eyebrows and smiled at Jackie, surprise that this was where the conversation had gone.

'I never said that,' Jackie said as she defended herself.

Marco gave a look, 'There's no baby mum, Eve's not pregnant.' It felt like a touchy subject.

Eve could tell by his voice he was just as offended as she was. It was still a sensitive issue for them outside of their own little bubble. Nobody would ever really understand how it felt to have such a history.

Jackie saw Eve's face change; it had hit a nerve, 'Well. Your father and I couldn't be happier for the two of you.' And there it was. As much as it was a surprise, it was a beautiful one.

The whole football game experience was completely new to Eve, she and Zoe sat either side of Tessa with Nick, Jackie, and Mario behind them in the second level of the packed stadium. Ro, Louise and Jules, the other wives and girlfriends sat nearby. A lot of women Eve didn't know smiled at her; she could feel the eyes on her, she could sense the whispering gossip all around her. Some people even introducing themselves, having a chat before the game began, which she thought was nice. *Or was it!* A constant stream of people stopping by to speak to Jackie and Mario who seemed like minor celebrities in their own right Eve thought.

Basically, everyone wanted a closer look at Eve, the new woman in Marco Rossi's life had been a hot topic around the club for weeks, Eve was totally oblivious of course.

The dynamic between Zoe and Nick was weirder than ever, they seemed to be great mates, very convincing and from what Zoe had led the girls to believe, that's all they were, *Mates.* If they believed what Zoe said, they hadn't slept together. Yet. Although they hung out regularly!

Tessa was doing well with her mood swings, she was drilled Zoe for information on the *just mates* relationship, finding it hard to believe that Zoe wasn't banging her brother, she was as sexual being, and Tessa wasn't sold on the no sex. It had taken a while, but she was warming to the idea of her two best friends being with two of her brothers. What could it hurt? According to Tessa, it could hurt a lot, if the relationships went sour, she felt she was the one with everything to lose!

An air of angst was with Eve as she settled herself into the game, watching Marco run around out on the ground was weird, it was like she had to share him with everyone in the entire stadium and she wasn't sure she liked that notion at all. Whenever he went near the play random people in the crowd shouted out his name, which freaked her out just a tad.

Zoe and Tessa whispered nonstop, which Eve found distracting as she felt an obligation to keep her eyes on the game, well on Marco really. She had no idea what was going on and didn't understand the rules, she panicked every time the ball went near Marco. Being at the game was going to take some getting used to, initially, she wasn't sure if she was enjoying the experience as much as she originally thought she might.

Marco's team play well to a solid win, the feeling at the end of the game was exciting and cheerful, with more random people coming up to Jackie and Mario to have a chat and congratulate them like they'd played the game themselves. Eve was wide eyed and intrigued to say the least.

Ro and Louise took the girls and Nick down to the rooms whilst Jackie and Mario stood around chatting. Ro stayed protectively by Eve's side, showing her support, making her feel welcome, introducing her to only those she felt worthy of an introduction. It was so Ro! Nevertheless, Eve appreciated her kind effort.

When Jackie and Mario came down to the rooms, Eve was again surprised by how many people knew the.

'Does your mum really know all those people, who are they?' Eve said hanging onto Tessa's arm in the crowded loud rooms. She'd been watching Queen Jackie work the crowd.

'You're going to know them all too, just you wait and see. By mid-season you will be the one everyone wants to talk to,' said Tessa. Her words unsettling Eve... she was private, she wasn't overly social, and she was actually finding the crowded room rather overwhelming.

Marco appeared as everyone came together again. He hugged his mum and dad first, then gave Nick a brotherly embrace with a big strong pat on the back, followed by a kiss for both Tessa and Zoe. Finally, he found his way to Eve. Standing at her back, he put his arm over her shoulder and gently lifted her face back toward him, giving her a sexy long and sultry kiss, making Tessa and Zoe melt, it was a kiss only Eve and Marco could have. The upside-down kiss was back!

'How'd ya go?' he looked down over her head as she gazed up into his eyes.

'Fine.' She smiled turning around to face him. 'How'd you go?'

'I'm sore and I'm a year older.' Marco gave her an intimate look, she took a step back and looked him over, he was bruised and scratched, dirty and ruffled, and extremely sexy! He touched her cheek lovingly before getting called away.

By the time they got home it was past midnight, Marco and Zach were exhausted and Jackie had the kettle on making toasted sandwiches to order, she was the master of the sandwich press. Tessa was a close second. Apparently, it was all about the butter.

Nick and Zoe had come back for a while to hang out and Jackie made comment on how it was lovely they had become such good friends. 'I think there's something going on between them,' she leaned to Eve at the kitchen bench. Eve rolled her lips in a bid to give herself time to think. 'Come one Eve, surely you know something,' Jackie said looking at her for a clue, 'You'd tell me wouldn't you?'

'They're just friends,' Eve whispered as Jackie gave her narrow eyes of disbelief, 'I really don't know anything,' Eve scoffed with a giggle. Zoe had sworn there was nothing between she and Nick, and they were staying in separate rooms at the nearby boutique hotel.

'Tessa looks like she's lost weight, is she eating okay?' Jackie asked another question Eve would rather not have to answer. 'You know sometimes she doesn't eat, maybe it's the new show and moving home.'

'She's eating alright,' Eve sighed.

'What about Zach, is it really over with him and Brooke?' Jackie took her opportunity to grill Eve whilst everyone was talking.

Eve sighed again, 'I think it's over and done with.' She got more plates out the cupboard.

'Mmm. I never warmed to Brooke; she wasn't faithful you know,' Jackie made comment screwing her face up. 'Is Tessa being nice to Zach, she's always been a little nasty to him I thought?'

Eve couldn't look at Jackie, 'Yes, Tessa's being very nice to Zach actually.'

Tessa was being so super nice to Zach... He was cumming morning, noon, and nigh!

Eve felt the conversation getting too close for comfort, she didn't want to have to lie to Jackie, but once again she felt her loyalty to Tessa taking hold, and then out of know where, Eve came out with it, 'You think Marco and I are rushing things, don't you?' It had been eating at her all day and night along with everything else on her mind.

'Why would you say that?'

Eve's eyes held Jackie's. 'I don't know.' Rolling her lips nervously.

'Is more about how you feel.'

'Not really Jackie,' she said completely disagreeing, she needed Jackie's truth.

'Are you happy with Marco?' Jackie had a nurturing smile on her face.

'Very much so.' Eve broke to a smile that radiated.

Jackie knew this was going to be an epic love story.

An hour later and Eve was sitting on Marco's back giving him her version of a rubdown, he was face down on the bed, she had a G string and a singlet top on, he was naked and beside himself with exhaustion but couldn't sleep.

'It was tense watching you play tonight; I don't understand why they blow the whistle so much,' Eve said as she rubbed her palms firmly up Marco's back to his shoulders.

'You'll get it soon enough,' he chuckled into the pillow under his face.

'Well, I hope so, because it all seems rather complicated... turnover and let me give you my special, post-match happy ending Mr. Rossi,' her voice was cute and sexy, 'It's guaranteed to give you a good night's sleep.' A giggle as she kneeled up beside him, Marco slowly rolled onto his back ready for her, it was about all he could manage, his body was battered and bruised. The first few games were always the hardest to recover from. He was almost fully hard as Eve lowered her mouth over him. Even having a hard on was exhausting, this wasn't his usual post-match routine; he was breaking all the rules for Eve.

365

She came up for a breath, 'I think I might need glasses; I could barely see you on the other side of the pitch. I was looking up at the big screen, then back to the ground and then I couldn't find you.' She was very talkative; he was very tired, she covered him with her warm silk like mouth again.

'Evie - football is played on a field or an oval, not a pitch baby,' Marco sighed amused; he was going to have to teach her his game. She was so not sporty, he kind of thought it was sexy. 'But that's ok, call it what you want... just keep doing that thing with your tongue,' he was breathy and drowsy, stretching his back out over the pillows and letting her climb between his legs as she sucked him perfectly. The softness of her boobs against his inner thighs, tormenting as the smooth rolls of her tongue lapped along the tender side of his cock. 'Fuck Eve Frank, I want this after every game, every week.' Clenched his eyes closed tight and counting backwards in his head from fifty to distract himself from cumming... it was absolute heaven.

Chapter Twenty Three

It wasn't hard to spot her father on Saturday morning in a restaurant by the river… who else would be wearing a suit? Eve had rarely seen him wearing anything else, her entire life. His thick slicked curly hair was now nearly all grey tones, especially at the sides. James as usual looked uptight Eve thought as she headed towards him, he was sitting in the outdoor section, the morning was crisp and beaming with sunshine.

Like always she was initially uneasy greeting her father, the fact that they now talked regularly hadn't changed that. She had good reason this time to be anxious, god only knew what he wanted to speak to her about.

'Is this your special weekend suit?' The soft pleasantness of her voice was sarcastic but loving as she smiled.

'Good morning Eveline.' He stood and gave his daughter a welcoming kiss and a hug, it had been a while, 'You look tired, did that footballer boyfriend of yours keep you up all night.'

She raised her eyebrows, 'Not really your business now, is it!'

'I didn't mean it like that… I watched the game on TV last night, he's good,' James had a rye tone.

'He's actually my fiancé Dad. We're getting married.' Holding her hand out to her father, she flashed her extravagant ring of love.

'Er, already. What's the rush?' he was shocked; his head tilted to one side.

'I've been in love with Marco since I was ten Dad, I'm not rushing.'

'Ten!' James gasped.

'Yes. Ten.' The banter was cute.

'I guess I should congratulate you then.' Still a little sarcastic he smiled and leaned over the table to kiss his daughter on the cheek with congratulations.

'Thank you.' Eve hadn't expected him to be on board so quickly with her news, they talked about Marco a how she was happier than ever and how this was their destiny. James let Eve do all the talking, as he absorbed the news.

'Now put me out of my misery and tell me what Martin wants from me.' She rested her hands on the table.

'Apparently you own some real estate that I don't know about.' James's eyes penetrated her with an accusing glare as he watched his daughters face freeze.

'Villa Rosado.' She'd kept it a secret for years but was now ready to share with her parents now that she was ready to sell.

'You didn't think to tell me Evan bought you a god damn mansion on the harbour,' sounding and looking less than impressed with Eve's secret.

'Don't feel bad, I didn't tell anyone. Mum doesn't know either. You're not special.'

James huffed his disapproval at her attitude, 'I'm serious Eveline.'

'Does Martin want money?' That seemed the obvious reason Martin would go to her father… he'd somehow found out about the house and now he wanted it.

The realter had had two offers for almost double what Evan had paid. It was a matter of days before the deal was done.

'He wants private access to the house for one day. There's something he thinks is still inside the house and he wants it. I would say it's in your best interest to let him into the house for a day Eveline,' James said dismissing a waitress who had come to the table to take their order.

She was suspiciously, surely there was more to it. Martin had to know how much the house was worth. Of course, he did, it was a harbour side home with views of the bridge.

'He thinks there's something inside that's very valuable. If you let him have access to the house for one full day, he will go peacefully… If you don't, we might have a problem.'

If ever she needed her father in her corner it was now. She had no idea what could be in the house, or why Martin suddenly needed it. Maybe it was art or maybe it was something Evan had hidden, who knew. To be completely honest, Eve didn't care, Martin could have whatever he liked, just not the house. The house had been Evan's way of looking out for her.

'Martin can take whatever the hell he wants. He better be quick though, I'm selling it,' she held her nerve, 'I'm surprised he doesn't want money.' It didn't make sense to Eve. *Why didn't Martin want the house? What was so valuable inside it?* Perhaps she didn't really need to know.

'Martin doesn't want the house or money.'

'Are you sure, what if he accidently runs me over!' A dry scoff, she was skeptical of Martin's intentions and with good reason. He was a notorious crime figure.

'He assures me he has no issue with you having the house. Your safety is my priority Eveline. I wouldn't let him hurt you.' James took offence that Eve would think anything else.

'How do I know what Martin would do? This is not a normal person we're talking about here Dad. What if he doesn't find what he's looking for?' worry in her voice as she felt an air of panic, even though her father had assured her there was nothing to worry about. 'It's been five years since I've been in that house. Strangers have been living there. Could I be in trouble?' Eve was catastrophizing.

'You don't need to know what's in the house, the less you know the better,' James appeased his daughter who was getting worked up, 'Just give Martin access for one day, it's simple.' James could see the curiosity on his daughter's face.

'Dad!' She stared at her father with great anxiety.

'Eveline. Nothing will happen to you; I give you my word.'

Wondering if she could take her father's word or not, there seemed no other choice but to trust him on this.

James coached her through the call she made to her property agent. Martin didn't want to hurt Eve, he just needed her to do this one little thing, and he would leave her be. That was the deal James had made with Martin.

His daughter had settled, she'd moved on from Martin and his demands. They'd gone over her keeping the house a secret, and they'd finally found their way back to her marrying Marco. James could see just how ignited Eve was by the mention of Marco's name. This pleased him, he wanted his daughter to be happy in life and finally she had found it with a man who seemingly deserved all her goodness.

'Eveline, I need to speak with you on a personal note, it's about Aria.' James put his second coffee down on the table and focused on his stunning eldest daughter, her beauty had always captivated him.

'Is she okay? She's not, is she?' The sinking feeling of Eve's heart was awful, she'd never met her sick little sister, and yet her connection was strangely intense, there hadn't been a day go by that Eve hadn't wonder, how Aria was or imagine what she was like. Her only vision of her sisters was of them as tiny girls when she had seen then at a glance that Christmas Eve with Evan in the restaurant.

James had been contemplating his words for the past two days, trying to think of the right way to ask such an intimate and personal favor of her. He had always loved Eve, more than she would ever know, nothing that had happened between them, had ever changed that. They had lost their way in the turmoil that was their lives. Eve meeting Evan was a living hell for James. In his eyes, Evan had gone after Eve to get back at him, not because he loved his daughter, and that was unforgivable.

'Dad, tell me,' Eve said. Her father's hesitation was unusual, she knew it was bad.

'The chemo isn't working.' The look on his face was harrowing and full of hurt, regret, a weakness she had never seen. 'I wouldn't ask you Eveline if we hadn't completely exhausted all the other options,' he paused dramatically, 'Aria needs a bone marrow donor, and we can't find one. The doctors tell us the best matches are siblings and Zara isn't a match, we've already had her tested.'

The unreadable look on her face looking back at him, deep with concern and thought, she didn't interrupt, letting her father speak, letting him explain all he and Sam had done to try and help their sick child.

James continued, 'The match is with the tissue type, not blood type and it has to be identical.'

'I'll do it.' Without hesitation Eve made the decision to try and help the sister she'd never met.

'You will!' James hadn't expected the immediate reply, he thought she might string him out, make him pay for all the things he had done to bring pain and misery to her life over the years. This was Eve's perfect opportunity to punish him for being a shitty father… but not his Eveline, she was a pure soul.

'Tell me all about it.' There were no second thoughts, Eve was in, she just needed to hear the details, so she was crystal clear on what she needed to do to help. Eve was in, regardless.

They spent the next two hours going over what was involved, the procedure, the doctors involved in Melbourne with whom James had met with yesterday. Eve would have the test done in Melbourne, then if she was a match, she'd go to Sydney for the actual bone marrow donation. The instant connection she felt to the sister she'd never met was overwhelming for Eve. This child's life felt like it was in her hands, if she wasn't a perfect bone marrow match it would be devastating for everyone. Eve was Aria's last hope.

Arriving home after noon, she'd left early in the morning when Marco and Zach were heading down to the beach for a team recovery session. Eve didn't really understand it, but it sounded like it was therapeutic treatment for their aches and pains.

With Marco sitting beside her, Eve found herself surrounded at the table telling everyone about Aria's bone marrow, she had their full attention as she spoke slowly in her soft voice. Zoe and Nick were there, Tessa and Zach along with Mario and Jackie, all listening to her explain how she'd be tested and hopefully be a match to save her little sisters life. They all listened with bated breath as to how it would all go down.

'Evie does this mean. Um… Will you meet Sam?' Zoe asked awkwardly.

'Yes,' confirming with confidence like she was okay with it, knowing that by now, Jackie and everyone basically knew who her biological mother was.

Marco sat with her, he didn't have to say a word, she knew she had his support, and she knew he was quiet because he was processing it.

Meeting her biological mother wasn't at the forefront for Eve, saving her sister was her main concern, and she wasn't letting anything, or anyone get in her way. They all knew this commitment was one of epic proportions for Eve, she may be pretending the biological mother issue wasn't a biggie… But it was going to be huge for her. If any of them had reservations or doubts for Eve, they didn't say so. Not yet anyway.

She kept the Martin issue to herself. James had made her swear she wouldn't even tell Marco.

A Rossi gathering wasn't normal unless someone had something mega to announce. Eve's bone marrow donation hadn't been the big news story of the day. Mario felt the time was right to make his own more pleasant announcement. He sat with Jackie as they dined at the beachside café under the mild March sun.

'We bought a pad here in Melbourne,' he said with a slight smirk and a hand on Jackie's thigh. They both looked proudly triumphant with themselves.

'And!' Tessa said in her best not a smart as voice.

'Well, it's right over there, you can see it from here.' Mario pointed.

'What!' Marco gushed across the table, it was a mixed gush of shock and disbelief.

'Don't panic. We're not moving here permanently. Not yet,' Jackie said with a proud smile, not sure if her son was happy or mad at them.

Mario began to explain, 'It's an apartment slash penthouse. New and modern. Very us,' he paused, 'We thought Tessa, you could live there while you're working in Melbourne, and we could stay there when we're here for the weekends during the footy season.'

All three siblings looking confused and curious.

'Modern. That doesn't sound very you!' Nick was first with his usual insult.

Jackie took offense, 'We are modern.'

Mario was excited, 'And how good will it be when our family grows,' he looked directly at Marco and Eve who were both still a little stunned at the surprise purchase, 'We'll be here to share everything. We won't miss the important moments and we won't be underfoot either,' He was alluding to the future.

Then Jackie added to Mario's reasoning, 'Until yesterday it was purely so we could be here during the football season, we're so over hotels,' she said with a mild dig at Marco, 'But after your engagement news, we are just so excited. We'll be right around the corner if you need us. We'll be close by when you two start a family.'

'Mum, you're getting a bit ahead of yourself don't you think.' Marco frowned with questioning eyes.

'Well, Eve will need a hand with the house and the babies, and dad can walk Patty for you. You'll be so busy when you become a family man,' explained Jackie like she knew something Eve and Marco didn't. Like she was telepathic and knew exactly what their future held.

Eve was quietly mortified as she sat back and let it all play out.

Marco laughed, 'I can walk my own dog.' He felt like his mother had too many expectations.

'So, will it be my place or yours?' Tessa's mind was ticking over... she hadn't planned on moving out of her brothers, and with Eve there now and of course Zach, she was happy to be there. But it sounded cool.

'It's our place Tessa, you can stay there though honey,' confirmed Mario promptly trying to hang onto the excited vibe he had initially started out with.

'You seem unhappy darling!' Jackie said to Marco with a wide questioning expression, 'We spend most of our weekends here. In hotels mind you. Having a place to call our own here will be very nice,' Jackie tried to not to sound offended, although she was, very offended and taken back by Marco's unexpected reaction.

Eve took the opportunity to engage, 'I think it's wonderful that you'll be nearby,' she said smiling warmly.

'I'm not unhappy,' Marco made it clear sitting forward as he felt Eve pinch his leg softly. He was shocked. He was very used to having his own thing going on here in Melbourne, and he felt like his family were invading, first Tessa, now his parents.

'Well, that's a relief,' huffed Jackie, 'For a moment I thought you were being selfish.' She'd had her feathers ruffled big time and she wanted Marco to stop his ridiculousness. *They'd followed and supported his career beyond what normal parents had... he was acting like a brat!*

Marco sighed, 'You could have moved here ten years ago when I needed you. Why didn't you move then?'

A victory smile from his mother, 'We're not moving darling, it's simply somewhere to base ourselves when we need to be here.' A relief flooded Jackie, for a moment she'd thought her son was being ungrateful.

'We won't cramp your style,' Mario laughed with a touch of nerves, 'We'll simply be here when you need us, when you start a family.'

Marco had to laugh, 'I'm touched you'd move here to be closer to your nonexistent grandchildren,' he made fun of his parents with a sarcastic grin, he'd cooled his jets somewhat.

'We're not moving, we'll just be visiting,' Jackie clarified again.

Banter went around the table, Mario ordered champagne, in which Tessa declined, she was fidgety and anxious the whole time, Eve could see her friend struggling with the fact there was a bottle of alcohol right there in front of her. Eve passing on a glass in support of her friend, which in turn made Jackie curious... she had never known either of them to refuse a glass of anything, ever.

'My goodness, Eve,' Jackie remarked, her face trying to contain her suspicions of maybe being on to something. 'No champagne? Are you feeling okay?'

'I'm fine Jackie. Tessa and I are both on a health kick before she starts rehearsals. There's absolutely no other reason I'm not drinking champagne.' It was half the truth. 'We won't be needing your baby-sitting services.' Eve thought she was being funny.

Marco's house was now Eve's house too, and it had never been so full of life, with all the Rossi clan laughing and being loud in general, everyone had something to say or a story to tell.

Marco had warned Zach and Tessa that this thing between them, was to be kept under wraps well and truly while his parents were staying at the house... no bed hopping under any circumstances! He felt he had to keep Tessa from any scrutiny from their parents, the other part was just him being her big brother and not wanting any more shenanigans from her or anyone else this weekend. There had been enough going on with rehab, the engagement, Eve's bone marrow decision and his parents buying a place literally around the corner from him.

Eve missed Zoe, being home was great and she had Tessa too, but Zoe was still too far away. They had a closeness where they told each other everything and in a private talk upstairs earlier in the night Zoe confided in Eve about her fear of being intimate or too close with Nick.

'Evie, it's just that the friend thing works so well for us.'

'You can just be friends with Nick, there's no law that says because you've have a sexual thing that you can't just be friends.' Eve didn't believe that at all. She knew Zoe adored Nick and that he had fallen head over heels for her. Nevertheless, they needed time, it was just so weird that after all this time. Zoe now had Nick eating out of the palm of her hand, but at the same time her guard was up so high, she had no idea how to let it down.

For now, Zoe was content being Nicks friend, she had completely 'friend zoned' him and that wasn't such a bad thing. Nick had really hurt Zoe all those years ago in Palm Cove, she'd been silently scarred by him, he'd used her for sex and thrown her out like dish water. Nick Rossi had been a shameful lesson in men that she'd carried with her all these years.

As the water washed away the long day, Eve stood under the shower in front of Marco, his athletic body at her back, his hardness pressing against her as she took a deep breath in a bid to clear her head. She'd called Anna and told her about the engagement and the bone marrow, and about how she would be meeting Sam. Not the easiest phone conversation ever, but it had to happen.

For some strange reason, Eve was feeling okay about meeting Sam, it now didn't seem like the main drama in her life, although it was still a huge meet her biological mother. The woman who had given her up, slept with Evan, tore her family apart, and then gone on to have a completely new family with her father... None of that was forgotten, it was just dulled due to the magnitude of Aria's illness.

Marco's hands ran up and down her sides as she let her mind wander for a moment to Vivienne, she needed to tell Vivienne she was engaged to be married to the man of her dreams. Nothing would surprise her grandmother, a staunch supporter and believer in love for all. As Eve reflected she sighed, she was missing France, it seemed the last week in particular had taken a small toll on her. Tessa's drug rehab, the standoff with Marco and the stress of thinking she may lose him again only to have worried all for nothing. And then Martin and Villa Rosado. But the big one was her sister, Aria. This was a matter of life and death, and whichever way she looked at, Aria's life now depended on her. If she wasn't a match with her sister, she would more than likely die. If she was a match, it meant there was a better chance. It was all up to Eve, and it was consuming her.

She let her body relax back to Marco as he held her, his big hands moving slowly in the water over her body, her boobs, and her stomach. His touch was calming and reassuring. He did love her; she could feel it in everything that he did to and for her. He settled her when she needed it, when only he could see beyond her clouded eyes. She'd adored him forever, he'd been her crush, her infatuation, her first lover, her first heartbreak, and now he was the man she was going to marry. Eve put her hands on his arms in front of her as he softly caressed her. They didn't need words as Marco bent to her and began to kiss the side of her neck, her heavy breaths telling him how good he made her feel. Marco kept touching her, running his thumbs over her hardening nipples as she rolled her head into him. His hand softly brushed her chin and went back down her neck. His other hand moved down over her stomach and lower, until he was at her hip, he bent forward so he could reach between her legs, not his usual tender touch that she had become so used to though, it startled her from her daydream. His hand made its way between her thighs, pushing her apart. Marco pressed his fingers up into her *unready* pussy, she gasped.

Pulling her to his front, his hot breath warmed to the side of her face, she looked straight ahead with the anticipation of the unknown. It was a sexual feeling she hadn't experienced in a very long time, the unpredictability of what was to come next. Marco's fingers swirled inside her as she felt her blood warming at his abruptness under the warm water, she'd just started to experience the more dominant side of Marco sexually. It amazed her that he knew what she needed without having to say a word. The fact that she was stressed and had had a day of ups and down meant she needed to release some tension, or rather Marco needed to release it for her... strenuous sex right before bed would help her sleep better.

This was hard and rough Marco sex, which was a whole other kind of arousal that Eve, she knew it would end with a powerful gut-wrenching orgasm. Riding the wave, going with it, Eve moved with Marco to allow him access inside her.

'Want me to stop? Say stop if you want me to,' his voice puffed and sexy from behind her.

The idea of changing up her pleasure had Marco aroused, the more he got to know Eve sexually, the more he wanted to experiment with her. Fisting into her small body with such force felt wrong, but she was loving it! As time went on, he knew Eve needed more from him, she needed it rough sometimes. He was a gentle giant by nature, however, whatever it took to please Eve, he was up for it.

'Marco!' she repeatedly gasped over and over in the heat of the shower every time he plunged his hand inside her tight little pussy. There was no way she was saying stop, she could feel every part of her fucked up angst leaving her body. *Sex was so much better than therapy!* And then, just in the nick of time, she felt herself cumming, erupting just as she'd been expecting into a numbing state of bliss.

Moving to her side Marco took a fist of her hair at the back of her head, pulling her head up to him so he could see her face as she came. 'As much as I know you like it rough, I'm loving you now Eve Frank.' He bent to her and laid his dreamy soft lips on hers; she kissed him back effortlessly, he took his hand from between her legs and held her face at either side, then picked her up. Her arms wrapping around his neck, her legs around his waist, their mouths slowly moving lovingly to each other as the frantic moment became slow and sensually romantic.

Eve hummed as she breathed into Marco's mouth, her heart still pounding in her chest, she began to feel his passion and love in the way she knew so well… the sexy and gentle Marco she loved more than anything in the world. Holding her in his strong protective arms like she was a mere feather, they had gone from hardcore frantic to tender lovers. Eve felt safe and wanted with Marco, all her worries and lonely thoughts vanished in the arms of this beautiful man she would one day call her husband.

'I don't like hurting you baby,' his mouth moved over hers rousingly and tenderly as she recovered from her powerful orgasm.

'You've never hurt me.'

'And I will never hurt you Evie,' his lips curled, making her smile too.

He was getting to know her, every emotion, every feeling, Marco was learning everyday how this gorgeous woman ticked, she had so many layers he wanted to peel them all at once and discover her now, but he knew it would take time, one layer at a time.

Pressing Eve to the wall of the shower, filling her with his hard penetrating girth, slowly grinding into her core as her mouth sucked at his shoulder, her fingernails digging into his biceps as she clung to him. Marco filled her with love. Entering Eve's pussy was like heaven each time they made love. Their vertical challenge work in the shower, he held her up with his hard rod of a cock. Rolling into her hips as she covered his mouth with hers, the intensity of him moving deep inside her stomach had her swelling around him, pulsing over him as he thrusted deeper. Marco could feel her flesh engulfing him, she tightened around him again. They came to each other harmoniously as they did every time they made love. It was like they had been created for one another, their hearts were one aspect, then their bodies although so different, came together as one magnificent union when lovemaking. When they made love it was as though nothing else existed, only their love.

Chapter Twenty Four

By Wednesday Eve was in hospital having her tissue tested by the specialist, James had arranged everything. On Friday morning it was confirmed she was an identical match and there was hope for Aria, Eve was heading to Sydney to be her sisters bone marrow doner.

The phone call Eve made to Anna the previous weekend, had been complexed and long. She had started with the engagement and Anna was of course concerned at first, then emotional and then pleased. As expected, she was worried Eve was rushing into a commitment of marriage, again, even though she more than approved of Marco. Broaching the bone marrow was like peeling her own skin off with a blunt knife, and then her mother's! The conversation had to be had, they discussed how Anna had kept Eve from Sam all these years. Anna heard her daughter out without interrupting, she consumed it with her usual grace and style and thought carefully about her response before delivering it. She knew how hard it was for Eve to talk about, because it was hard for Anna to hear. She had to take the higher ground and admitted she was wrong by keeping Sam's identity a secret. Laying all her cards on the table Anna told Eve she supported her decision to unselfishly help with such a delicate and fragile situation of life and death. Knowing and understanding Eve the way she did, made it easier to accept. Anna ended by telling Eve, she was proud of her decision and her humanity. Anna was proud to have raised such a compassionate young woman, who she would always call her daughter regardless.

A busy week had passed since she had been a positive match to Aria's tissue, there had been nonstop calls from her father and the medical team. Villa Rosado had sold unexpectedly quick, and Martin had his day at Villa Rosado, she presumed that he found whatever it was, that was so very important to him. Now she hoped never to hear from him again.

The financial influx couldn't come at a better time, Eve's trust fund was diminished, she'd been living off the rent from Villa Rosado, which was plentiful. And now she had more money than she knew what to do with, the ease of knowing she would be able to live purely off the interest alone for the rest of her life was comforting… Things had worked out just as Evan had intended, Eve was literally set for life!

Getting Tessa through rehab was a task on its own with all Eve's medical appointments and now going to Sydney. Not great timing, but a chance for Tessa to stand on her own two feet with the help of her brother and Zach.

Marco had driven Eve to the airport, he didn't want her going without him, but he knew he had no choice but to let her go and support her.

'You need to talk to Tessa about things every day, every night. Ask her how she's feeling, what she's thinking, make sure you give her physical contact,' Eve said giving Marco the run down as they stood by the departure gate together, her looking up into his loving eyes, willing him to take in what she was saying.

'Physical contact… You're so cute, you mean like a hug right?' Marco grinned at the gorgeous woman he didn't want to let go. Her long curls tied in an unruly ball on top of her head, stray hairs framing her face, her big eyes dominating his.

'This is important Marco!' Eve huffed, she was super serious, 'I need you to be on it. I'm sick about leaving her, it's such a crucial time for Tessa and I don't think Zach realizes.' Tessa's recovery was very important to Eve, they had come this far, and she felt like she was letting Tessa down by going to Sydney, being everything to everyone wasn't easy.

'I'll report back to you every day like we discussed, and I'll do all the things you've asked me to do. I promise.' Marco leaned down and kissed her. 'I wish I could come with you.' It was killing him that he wasn't able to be with her at such an important time in her life. Not only the bone marrow extraction, but she was meeting her sisters and her biological mother for the very first time. This was huge in Eve's life.

'I'll have Zoe and our mums… I'll be fine,' she said smiling up at him.

It was time to say goodbye, the plane was boarding, and she was dreading their goodbye, they both were. It would be their first time apart in such a long time.

Marco was feeling just as anxious about their time apart, 'Come back to me Eve Frank.' The thought of her being in Sydney left him uneasy.

'Of course, I will, as soon as I can come back, I'll be on the first flight.' Eve had her hands at his waist, her eyes devouring him and every last minute they had together.

'Call me when you get there, so I know you're okay.' He bent down to her for one last kiss, the flight attendants at the gate waited and watched the adoring couple as they parted ways.

Eve reached up and hugged Marco tight with sudden emotion. 'I love you,' she said into his neck as he squeezed her tight.

'I love you too Evie. Call me anytime you need to talk. Keep me updated.' Marco breathed the clean smell of her hair and perfume in for one last time.

Her hands dragged down his arms as she finally let him go. One final kiss and she walked away, turning back at the gate to see him watching her leave.

Being back at her mother's house again was strange, she had a disconnect to it now. The home she had grown up in wasn't her home anymore and it wasn't as big as it used to feel. Now Marco's home felt like her home.

Anna loved Watsons Bay, it was her haven and since her friendship with Jackie had blossomed, she had been enjoying being there more than ever, Jackie's local network of friends had become Anna's too.

'I've been saving this for your visit,' Anna said holding a bottle of red and two glasses as she came out onto the terrace where Eve sat staring out over the harbour, a sight she would never be disconnected from, the beautiful lights of the harbour had mesmerized her from a child.

Anna wore a T shirt and jeans, which was a very casual look for an always professional woman, her hair pulled back in a simple ponytail, Eve couldn't help but notice how relaxed her mother was given the reason for her visit. She had expected a tense Anna and was surprised by the complete opposite.

'How's Nigel, where is he?' Eve asked as Anna poured the wine.

'About Nigel…' she gave Eve an odd look, 'We're over.'

'No more Nigel!' Disbelief as she gasped taking the glass from her mother.

'He took a job in Denmark. The relationship was wearing thin anyway.' Anna seemed perfectly fine with the breakup. 'I'm enjoying being single. I haven't been single since my early twenties. I'm actually very happy,' she smiled as she sat on the opposite lounge and observed her daughter. Eve had grown into a beautiful person, she was so proud and content to see her, Marco made all the difference in Eve's life, and it showed.

'Poor Nigel!' Eve was still coming to terms with no more Nigel.

'Oh, he's fine. It's hard to explain, I needed a change of pace. As much as Nigel was a good man, he wasn't quite the one, if that makes any sense.' Anna had a demure smile on her face.

'Are you having a midlife crisis?' Eve was amused with the change in Anna.

'I don't know. Maybe,' she laughed; it was nice sharing this time with Eve.

'You seem okay with all,' Eve sighed, 'You said you had news for me, are you dating a much younger guy?' Eve teased with a smile.

Anna laid back relaxed, she took big sips of her wine, 'I'm taking a new direction in my career. I've accepted a private role here in Sydney. No more travelling at the drop of hat overseas.'

'Something is going on, I can feel it,' Eve suggested to her mother, 'Are you seeing someone else already? You've got this look about you, like you're having loads of sex,' Eve asked narrowing her humorous eyes.

'Not really.'

'Not really!' Eve gasped, her mother was acting very casual and carefree. *Was it a sex thing?* Eve recognised the sparkle. Her mother looked like she was either having the greatest sex of her life or smoking drugs.

Maybe it was both! Maybe Anna was more like her grandmother after all.

'Eveline. What can I say, it's just time for a change,' Anna said with a flippant smile on her face.

The plan was to spend the day in hospital, being assessed for the bone marrow extraction by Aria's team of doctors. More bloods and tissue samples would be needed, Eve would get a chance to speak with the medical team herself, ask any questions and get acquainted. Next on her agenda was meeting with her father and Sam for dinner at their city apartment. Aria was still in hospital and Zara would be at her friend's house for a sleep over, James was orchestrating the introductions for Eve as he saw fit, he was as usual setting the pace.

Eve wasn't sure how she felt about any of it now. She'd had time to process and found she had gone from being sure about things to being completely unsure. Not the bone marrow part, she was one hundred percent on board with helping Aria, if she didn't help, there was no plan B, she was the only match, the only hope.

James had felt meeting Sam first, before meeting her sisters was the right way to do things.

Sitting in the hospital chair having her blood extracted she put the thought out of her mind, it was only getting her upset although it was a great distraction. Marco had told her not to over analyze the situation. Easy for him to say, he'd met the woman who gave birth to him, and she hadn't given him away! One thing was for certain, James was more attentive than ever as a father, Eve wondered if it was because she was donating her bone marrow to his daughter with Sam... *hang on... she was his daughter with Sam too! Was there a difference? Did he love her the same as he loved the twins? How was this going to play out?* She had to stop catastrophizing.

By the end of the day Eve was drained to say the least. James dropped her home to her mother's house, she laid down for an hour and then called Marco, telling him all about her day at the hospital and all of her strange and insecure thoughts about meeting her biological mother, and how her dad always felt the need to control her any chance given. Marco gave her a pep talk like the angel man he was, then she'd closed her eyes for half an hour more before taking a long hot shower.

Slipping on a pair of tight black capri pants, a black T shirt, black velvet blazer and black Jimmy stiletto's, Eve felt her teeth ache with anxiety, this happened when she was in life changing situations that she had no control over. Her head full of every kind of scenario possible, good, funny, sad, and bad. Her mood uncomfortably black as was her clothing.

Declining Anna's offer to drive her into the city, but accepting the loan of a car, Eve had her bag over her arm as Anna walked her down to the car, she looked like she was being sent off to the slaughterhouse.

Anna fussed over her a little, 'Are you sure you're okay with this? You don't have to go if you don't want to.' It was her duty of care to ask... deep down she really wanted Eve to say she didn't want to go.

A long lunch with Jackie had prepped Anna for this very moment. Sending Eve off to meet the other mother felt like she was relinquishing her parental rights and erasing the past twenty-five years. It was worse than awful!

'I'm fine,' Eve sighed as she hugged Anna goodbye. Even though she wasn't, she felt like she was betraying Anna in the worst way possible. This moment was extremely hard for both of them.

'Am I supposed to wish you good luck?' Anna gave Eve a humorous smile.

'I don't know, I don't think so.' Eve could see the cover up on her mother's face, she was trying to be brave.

Anna took a moment and leaned on the car door as Eve opened it, 'I'll always be here Eveline. Always.'

Eve sighed, 'I know. You always are,' she gave her mum a very needed smile.

'Just be yourself. She's going to adore you,' Anna said offering her last words of support.

Of course, James wouldn't just live in any old apartment, he lived in a penthouse in the clouds overlocking Sydney, in the CBD with views literally all the way to Mars and Venus. The doorman had sent her up in the lift after getting the approval from James. Standing outside the lift, she waited a few moments and regulated her rapid heartbeat, trying not to look too flustered. Straitening herself up, she went over to the door and pressed the buzzer.

Eve would never be ready for this moment!

James opened the door with a saintly look on his face, 'Welcome,' he said kissing her cheek as she stepped forward into the opulence of a large foyer, it was overwhelming even for Eve. Her father had always been excessive with objects, gifts, and style, he loved having good things.

A woman stood in the distance in the next room by the windows... Sam.

Standing beside Eve, James said, 'Eveline come through, this is Sam.' He walked Eve through to the next room and there she was, standing there, looking at her with a demure smile that was so overwhelmingly familiar that Eve forgot to breath. She had gone over this moment a thousand times in her head, and yet she wasn't prepared at all. There in front of her was the woman who had slept with Evan... above everything, that was her very first initial thought as they looked one another in the eye. Then, the woman who had given her away at three weeks old. She'd been her father's mistress and lover all this time. She'd caused her so much anguish and pain, and finally there she was looking right back at her.

Eve held her hand out, very formal, 'Hello.' Her jacket on, bag over her shoulder, she was as stiff as a board.

Sam put both hands out to Eve's and held them.

Her dark lengthy hair wavey, her skin a dark cinnamon, her sparkling eyes intense and exotic as she held onto Eve's hands, 'Hello Eve.'

How did she know not to call her Eveline, only her mother, father and grandmother ever called her that!

The same height, the same body shape, the same eyes, just older, Eve thought. They looked deep into each other's eyes for a few seconds. James stood in silence and let them have their moment.

Eve could feel her heart racing in her chest, her cheeks burning with anxiety.

'Let me take your jacket,' James prompted as they stood face to face evaluating each other for the first time.

'Come in. Sit down,' Sam was breathy, her voice soft and quiet like Eve's. She moved towards a plush lounge, fixated on the delicately gorgeous young woman before her.

James came back, 'Dinner's being prepared; can I get you a drink. Wine, water, vodka?' James offered.

'Water thank you,' Eve said flickering her eyes back to Sam, 'How's Aria?' she found her words.

Sam took a second or two to respond, still absorbing the most amazing creature she'd ever seen, the daughter she'd never known. The missing piece to the puzzle that was her complexed life. 'She's doing her best,' Sam said with a smile, 'She's weak but okay. The conditioning treatment has been hard on her, but she's very brave,' her emotion was unmistakable, 'Aria's ready for the transplant. Thank you,' she tried to hold her tears back, as a mother she was going through such a turbulent time with Aria, and Eve! 'And thank you for going to the hospital today. Dr Simon's said everything went well. I know the test are time consuming and invasive, are you okay how do you feel?' Sam finally took a breath.

Eve had endured more examinations than she'd been expecting, 'I'm fine.' A standard Eve answer, she smiled nervously. 'Dr Simon's said we can harvest tomorrow. I'll spend the night in hospital and then hopefully be good to go home in a few days.'

'Sam and I would like you to meet Aria and Zara in the morning at the hospital if that's okay with you?' James came back with Eve's water and Sam a glass of white wine.

'I'd like that,' she answered looking at Sam, taking her in, wondering what she was thinking.

'Eve,' Sam gasped, 'I've got so much I want to say to you,' overcome with anxiety. She took a minute, pausing. 'Um.. I. I don't know where to start.'

'The beginning might be good.' Eve said with wide eyes, she bit down on her bottom lip super hard, trying to focus, reminding herself to exhale and continue breathing, 'Just tell me how you felt from the start. What's your story?' It was all she wanted to hear, not James's or Anna's version of events, that didn't matter, it was Sam she needed to hear from.

Sam looked at James who now sat next to her and then back at Eve, 'Um. Well... I came to Australia when I was nearly thirteen with my mother who was a single mum,' she paused, 'I haven't seen my dad since I was small, I don't know where he is. I don't have contract with him.' Sam smiled feeling awkward. 'We came to Sydney and my mum worked in a factory and I started school,' a big sigh, 'I didn't like school very much, I kind of didn't fit in. My English wasn't the greatest, I learn fast though.' She still had a slight twang of an accent. A very proper accent, she spoke well and very slowly, like Eve. 'I dropped out of school at fifteen and made friends with some older girls I met at the hair salon I was sweeping hair at. They had lots of money and nice things and I wanted that too,' another pause, 'I lied about my age and ended up working with them, for Martin Li.' Sam looked ashamed.

The name made Eve cringe, she glare at Sam. This was where things started to change!

'James, your father,' Sam corrected herself, 'Was one of my first... um, clients I guess.' Her past was her biggest shame. 'I fell in love with him immediately.' She sighed and looked away from Eve who was determined to not look away.

As much as Eve wanted to shoot her dad a filthy look of disgust, she held her eyes at Sam, unaware of how intimidating she was.

'You need to know Eveline,' James began to speak, 'As much as I loved Anna, we never had a normal relationship. Right from the start we both agreed to live in an open marriage. We had an arrangement.'

Eve ignored him and held her eyes to Sam.

Sam took an uncomfortable deep breath. 'I didn't realise I was pregnant straight away; I didn't understand my body, I had only gained a little weight.' She knew what Eve wanted to hear; the deathly stare was unmistakable, 'I was barely sixteen and my mum was so upset with me when I told her I was pregnant,' The emotion in her voice was building, 'She threw me out, so I went and lived with one of the older girls I worked with, I needed money and I needed to try to put a plan together.' It was like she was reliving it in her voice, Eve could hear the young, scared girl within. 'Um,' blinking her eyes shut tight, Sam got it together, 'Your dad tried to help me, but I couldn't help myself back then, I was very young, and nothing was going to plan... I didn't have a clue what I needed to do,' Sam stopped in thought, 'I was all alone when you were born. Nothing came natural to me; I didn't know how to be a mum. I didn't know how to feed you or how to make you stop crying. I was so scared of what might happen to you because I didn't know what to do.' Sam gave in and she let out a quivery sob. James stayed silent. 'I gave you to your father because I knew he would do the best thing by you.' Her face tensed a little, Eve could see Sam was trying not to cry with everything she had, 'I couldn't do it. I'm sorry. I didn't know how to do it.' She looked at Eve with shameful regret and an aching sadness as tears fell down her cheeks.

Unable to look away, Eve felt her world collapse. All these years she known deep down, as absurd as it was, and as much as she knew it wasn't the only reason, she knew it was because she'd cried too much. It was too hard for a very young Sam to cope with. *Fucking ridiculous. Don't blame yourself, you were just a baby!* Eve wanted to be at home in her bed wrapped in her beautiful Marco's arms, safe in his arms from this world of pain.

'Anna and I made the decision that very first night,' James said, 'We did our best Eveline.'

Her dazed and confused eyes flicked to her fathers; he was the most vulnerable she had ever seen him.

Sam wiped tears from her face with her dainty fingers, 'I never stopped thinking about you for one day,' She was now openly crying, 'Every day of my life, I've thought about you.' she looked at Eve 'I had to respect that I wasn't your mother anymore. And I did... I know you think that sounds like I didn't care about you... but I did.'

Silence past and Eve was lost in her thoughts for what seemed like forever. She sat there wondering why Sam's explanation didn't make her feel any better. This woman who was so clearly her biological mother, didn't feel real, it was unfathomable to think she'd actually given birth to her.

James and Sam sat watching Eve, trying to figure out what was going through her mind as she sat expressionless and still. 'How do you feel?' asked James bidding an end to the uncomfortable silence.

Eve looked at her father, his ridiculous question irritated her, 'How do you think I feel?' she said knowing her father would hate her response. *Was he crazy, did he really want her truth right now?* Finding it hard to speak at all she held his eyes with distain. She didn't want to feel angry, but she was, she was angry at them both, 'You always wanted her,' she said looking at her dad, 'So why didn't you just stay with her when she was pregnant with me, why did you leave her all alone... she was a young girl who needed you?'

The two people who sat before her, were the two very people who had created her, and who had caused her so much grief and pain. None of it made a lot of sense to Eve. It seemed like a lot of time wasted, a lot of heartache.

James raised a brow, 'Because I was married to someone else and because we were raising you.'

'I wasn't always in a great place, he couldn't be with me, he needed to be at home with you,' Sam began to make excuse for him, 'After I had you I was caught up in a lot of self-destructive behavior. I did drugs for a long time, I had to work for Martin to pay for my drug use. Your father tried to help me, but I wasn't easy to deal with, and I'd been the cause of enough chaos in his life.'

Eve looked again at her father who she could tell knew what was coming his way, he knew what was brewing behind her furious eyes. 'How did you think sleeping with a young girl was okay at your age?' Eve's assault came straight out of the barrel, James hadn't expected it to be so loaded and so direct.

He glared at Eve, surprised at her boldness, 'I think you know exactly how I was thinking at the time,' James was cool and measured, he was a lawyer, defense was his expertise, 'Attraction is a very powerful thing; Sam was a young woman.' He looked at Sam for a fleeting second, then returned his attention to Eve. 'Have you forgotten how you looked and felt at sixteen? In your mind Eveline, you were old enough to behave like an adult, and you did need I remind you.' His eyes accusing her.

Oh, he was good! She could tell by her father's face it wasn't what he wanted to say, however he did, and she was horrified that he would use her behavior to justify his own inappropriate behavior. Eve stood up; she wasn't letting him do this to her, 'I can't do this.'

'You should know better than anyone, how things just happen, and they impact on everyone else too,' James said as he stood too. Sam stood to the escalating situation with angst, she looked between Eve and James.

'I can't believe you're comparing my situation with what you did to her.' Eyes ablaze as she took her father on. 'And what are you referring to exactly anyway Dad, tell me I'd like to know?'

'I don't want to go there,' James said like it was shameful and disgusting.

'Go where? What did I do that impacted on anyone else's life, besides my own?' she raised her voice and Sam moved uncomfortably closer to them.

'James, please,' Sam begged visibly stressed, this wasn't how she wanted things to end, she didn't want Eve upset by unnecessary accusations, it wasn't how it was supposed to be.

'Your actions nearly ruined your life! That impacted me,' he said shaking his head with gruff in his voice, 'You got pregnant at seventeen to a thug you shouldn't have even been talking to let alone sleeping with,' his voice raised with hate; it was frightening.

Sam turned away in distress; she didn't like the road they were going down.

Eve gasped at her father's hideous interpretation of events. She let out a semi kind of laugh making Sam turn back to her. As she looked at her father with a bemused grin, Eve realized this was the first time all night she had let herself get emotional. 'I got pregnant at seventeen to Marco, my fiancé; he was the father of my baby.' Her grin had disappeared, she knew her father thought it had been Evan all along. 'So, please don't ever pretend you know anything about me, because you don't,' her tone said everything, she was pissed off hard.

'James! Please don't do this,' Sam was freaking out, 'Eve's not here for this conversation. Can you give us a few minutes alone please? Go out to the terrace and take a break,' she huffed like it was exhausting dealing with him, 'Have a cigarette, drink a scotch,' she dismissed him in her slow calm tone… just as Eve would.

James did leave, and he did go out to the terrace and lite a cigarette.

Sam turned back to Eve, 'Please stay. I'd like to keep talking with you, if you'll stay,' Sam gestured to the sofa and Eve thought a moment before sitting back down, 'I know I don't have to tell you; how unreasonable he can be in times like this,' Sam's face craving Eve's understanding.

Keeping her silence, Eve wasn't really sure if she should stay or go. She so wanted to stay.

'I don't know you Eve,' Sam sat down at her side, 'It's my biggest regret in life,' speaking softly and then paused for a long time, 'I'm sorry he hasn't always there for you, and I'm sorry I wasn't there for you more to the point.' Sam said like it was really hurting her.

Still silent, Eve watched Sam warily, thinking how uncanny it was that they looked so alike. It was like being in a bubble detached from the world, she listened to this woman she didn't know, talk about their lives, it was the most disconnected feeling she'd ever had.

'I've had a good life.' Eve extending an olive branch.

'I know you've had some hard times. Some really painful times. Your dad tells me your engaged now, that's wonderful.' It was time to change it up, Sam wanted to know more about this stunning young woman, she was utterly beautiful in every sense of the word as she sat before her.

'Yes, I'm engaged to Marco.' Eve looked down with a hint of a smile, and then back to Sam, the thought of Marco was always a blessing, just saying his name made her feel better.

'I'm glad for you.' A smile of pleasure, all she'd ever wanted was for Eve to live a good life.

'He makes me very happy,' Eve found it hard to elaborate, it was difficult to string more than a few words together, her body felt heavy, her voice strained, barely there.

'Good.' Nodding eagerly, looking around the room and then back to Eve. A long silence before Sam took a deep breath. 'I hope we can get to know one another. What you're doing for Aria is so very special. I'm so grateful, I'm just...' Sam was lost for words, 'I can't wait for you to meet the girls. I've explain who you are; they know you're giving Aria such a special gift; and they're so excited to meet you. I hope you don't mind that I've told them about you.' Sam wasn't sure how Eve would feel about the girls.

'I really want to meet them too. Who do they think I am exactly?' Eve was relaxing ever so slightly.

'They know you're their big sister. We felt the truth was best, even though they might not understand it completely just yet. I told them I was very young when I had you, and that daddy lived with you and took care of you with your mum,' A spark in Sam's voice as she spoke about the girls, 'It's been a very stressful time having Aria so sick; I can't tell you how much it means to me to have you here tonight Eve,' Sam's emotion was clouding her eyes, her voice was wavering, 'I'm sorry for your father's behavior,' a pause, 'He doesn't do personal very well,' she laughed, 'And he's not coping with Aria being so sick.' Shaking her head, she closed her eyes and tears fell down her face. Sam was doing the silent cry just as Eve did.

'I hope I can help her.' Eve was compassionate by nature.

Sam's eyes opened, 'I wanted to call you, to see you so many times,' her voice a little strained as the tears continued to flow down her cheeks, 'So many times I just wanted to tell you I was here if you, that I was thinking about you and that I… I,' Sam couldn't finish, she couldn't open herself up any further, not yet.

'I understand.' No tears from Eve, no lump in the throat.

'I hope you never make a decision in your life that you regret forever, like I have,' Sam wiped her tears away just as a small thin woman came into the room, she looked like an elderly version of Sam.

'Dinner is ready,' the older woman said with an air to her, like she was announcing so much more than just dinner. She had a tender warming smile.

Sam snapped to attention with a smiled, 'Thank you Lollie,' she spoke gently and kind to the woman, 'Lollie. This is Eve. Eve this is our Lollie… I mean to say Lollie is our everything,' Sam's voice had a loving tone to it. 'The girl's nanny, the housekeeper, our cook, and everything else in-between. Lollie is also my aunt, she's family, and she lives here with us.'

Wow! This was her aunty too. 'Hello Lollie, it's lovely to meet you,' pleasant as always, Eve smiled, knowing the cute little woman knew exactly who she was. She got the feeling Lollie knew everything, and a little bit more.

'I'm so happy to meet you Eve,' said the older lady reaching out and holding Eve's hands in hers, 'I made roast lamb especially for you.'

'I love roast lamb,' Eve couldn't help but feel special.

'I know, your father told me so,' Lollie beamed a huge proud smile, 'It's the first roast I've cooked for the season at your fathers request.' Lollie put her hands together, she was a pleaser, Eve could tell. She was gorgeous. It was the way she talked about food; it was the way she said roast lamb like it was a heavenly delicacy that she'd had the greatest pleasure cooking.

'We won't be long, thank you Lollie,' Sam said with a smile wanting just a minute more with Eve on her own, she waited until the adorable older woman left the room and then turned to Eve, 'I know your father can seem, well… let's say insensitive and overbearing at times,' Sam had a glint of sarcasm in her tone, 'He's actually been very anxious about tonight. He's unpredictable as you know, so I'll apologize now for anything he might say or do at the dinner table that is not acceptable. All the same, you are extremely important to him, he loves you so much.'

Eve didn't speak, she didn't have to. The slow tones of Sam's voice were becoming comforting in a way she had never expected, not to mention, Sam knew her father very well, there was no denying that.

Sitting at the large dining table looking out over the sparkling lights of Sydney, Eve felt strange, here she was sitting with her creators, it was bizarre; she was part of each of them.

'Tell me more about Marco.' James broke Eve's train of thought, she blinked her way back to her father.

'Um… I'm not sure what more I can tell you.'

But James wanted something, 'I think I've met him once or maybe twice at the Rossi's when you were younger. Maybe I should have paid a little more attention to him back then.' He raised his eyebrows at Eve.

'Have you known each other long? Is this a brand-new relationship?' Sam sat forward in her seat as Lollie bought the plates out one at a time. Eve thought it was odd that Lollie wasn't joining them at the table considering she lived here.

'I've known Marco since I was ten. We've just resumed our relationship recently; we had a thing when we were younger. Briefly.'

'Oh, that's wonderful.' Without looking too eager, Sam was dying to ask more questions, just having Eve at the table was more than she had ever dreamt of. 'What's your favorite thing about him?'

'Everything,' smiled Eve.

James chuckled, 'Good answer. I hope he knows how perfect he is.'

'He is perfect actually!' She couldn't keep the smile from her face, which amused her father.

'Well, I can't wait to meet Mr. Perfect again.'

Things had calmed down and as they ate, they chatted about the process of bone marrow transplant, Sam and James wanted to make sure Eve knew exactly what she was in for, it was going to be more painful for her than it would be for Aria. The marrow would be extracted from her lower back via her hip, a night in hospital if she was lucky so the medical team could observe her, and then she would be right to go home.

'How does Marco feel about what you're doing for Aria?' Finally feeling like she could speak more freely, Sam wanted to know everything, and to her surprise Eve was responding to her more naturally.

'He's supportive. He would have come with me, but his football has to come first, it wasn't possible for him to be here,' Eve sighed at the thought of not seeing him for days. It seemed like forever even thought she was talking to him day and night.

'And what about you meeting me, how does he feel about that?' Sam's wide-eyed expression studied Eve as they sat on the lounge now after dinner. She knew this man had a lot of influence over Eve, if he wasn't on board it could pose a threat to her having any kind of relationship with her daughter.

Eve was a little taken by the question, she wasn't sure how to answer, 'I think he's worried.'

James and Sam could see straight through her, they both looked at Eve with their own worry. None of them expected this to be easy, and with James coming straight out the gate earlier, it had taken half the night for Eve to drop her guard with him. Oddly, Eve was more at ease with Sam, she had come tonight with every intention of hating her. But, she had a way that was familiar, the face didn't give much away, the long gazing stares, the poise on certain words. Not quite as reserved as herself, but there was definitely similarities between them, it was eerie.

'Are you okay, sweetheart?' James asked noticing Eve's obvious distress after Sam's last question.

'I'm fine. I'm tired I think. I should probably get going,' she said feeling like she needed to get out of there and inhale some fresh air.

'Good idea, you've got a big few day ahead of you.' His daughter looked like she needed to get a good night's sleep.

'I've got to get back to the hospital now myself,' Sam said, she spent every night at the hospital with Aria.

Eve got up from her seat and stood looking between her dad and Sam who rose with her.

'Thank you for dinner. Thank Lollie, tell her I said it was amazing,' she smiled getting her bag and moving towards the door.

'Thank you for coming to dinner,' Sam said not knowing if she should go towards Eve and embrace her like she wanted to, 'It's been a night I will never forget.' Her emotion was hidden behind her eyes, her tone friendly and somewhat relaxed and satisfied.

'Me too.' All Eve could think about was getting out of there, she'd had enough for one night, it had been one of the biggest of her life.

Driving home feeling like another part of her life was ticked off or completed in a sense, she called Marco the second she could, she needed to sleep, she needed to regroup, she needed to hear Marco's voice.

'Hey, you,' his adoring voice made her wince as tears came to her eyes, hearing his voice was not enough, she wanted to touch him.

'Hey.' She longed for him like she had never longed for him and that was saying something. There had been years and years of comparing her longingness.

'I've been thinking about you all night... how was dinner?' He could tell Eve was emotional.

'Oh god!' She held her breath as she drove slowly in the luxury of her mother's car.

'Are you okay babe?'

This man was a definite fucking keeper! He was perfect.

They talked the whole drive home to Watsons Bay; she told Marco about Sam and about how weird it was to see the person who gave birth to her. He as always her biggest advocate, encouraging her to take it day by day and assuring her that by knowing Sam, it didn't lessen anything she had with Anna. Marco knew this was playing on Eve's mind something terrible, the guilt and pressure was big.

They said goodnight before she got to the security gate. They pledged their love to each other; he made her promise to call him as soon as she woke up. The thought of not being there with her when she had the procedure tomorrow made him feel terrible, missing such a moment in Eve's life was now a big deal to him.

Anna dropped Eve at the hospital early in the morning, she wanted more than anything to be with Eve but knew it was best she didn't want to do that to her daughter, considering James and Sam would be there.

'Call me. I won't come in… unless you want me to.' It was such an awkward situation.

'I want you to.'

'Call me if you need anything, I can bring it to you,' Anna said reached for Eve's hand as she got ready to get out of the car, 'I love you; you know that.'

'I do. I love you too Mum.'

'You're doing a really good thing Eveline. I'm so proud of you,' Anna said not going over the top.

James was waiting for her, she was staying the night and had packed a mid-size suitcase, because she was Eve.

Today was another big day in her life, a huge day by anyone's standards. It was a new day, she was moving forward from last night's turbulence and starting fresh with her father. Eve knew she couldn't keep holding grudges for the rest of her life. Today she was nervous all the same, her sisters were just tiny girls when she'd last seen them that Christmas Eve in the restaurant, they had been little then. Now she didn't know what to expect. Sam and her father had prepared her last night for how Aria would look, no hair, thin and sickly. Eve wasn't ready for any of it, but she was going to face it head on.

James and Eve stood at the door of the room in the children's ward and paused a minute, her eyes went straight to the sick little girl in the bed. Thin and grey, death like. Aria was dying, Eve felt the full weight of her roll in that very second.

The tiny girl had dark rings under her eyes, oxygen tubes up her nose, tubes in her arms and dull skin, she wore a bright pink sparkly T shirt that said, 'Super Star' and matching pajama pants.

Beside her, standing by the bed as if a protector scared of being torn away, a healthier looking little girl, long curly dark hair just like Eve's, her face fuller with long lashed eyes and cinnamon skin. Pretty and smiling at her first glimpse of Eve and her father.

A quiet minute as they all looked at one another. Eve's eyes flickering from one small girl to the other and then to Sam who stood in the corner of the room like she was uneasy or disturbed.

'This is Aria and Zara,' Sam said taking a step forward, she looked drained like a parent with the weight of the world on her shoulders, 'Girls, this is Eve, your big sister.' The first thing Sam noticed was the heartfelt smile that came to Eve's face as she met her sisters for the very first time. It was a surreal meeting that had felt impossible until now.

'Hi,' Eve said softly, smiling, moving toward them, she went straight to the bed and stood at the edge, both girls were looking up at her with big curious eyes.

'Hello,' Zara moved closer to Eve, she was filled with curiosity and excitement.

Eve acknowledging her own flesh and blood. She was looking at her own very mini me, the ultimate in DNA, Zara was just like looking back in time at herself. Then she looked down at Aria who hadn't taken her big dark eyes off Eve, 'It's lovely to meet you Aria,' Eve said to the drawn face, she could see a brightness hiding behind her exhausted eyes.

'I told you she was pretty, like you,' Sam said to the girls from the corner of the room. It was raw emotion at the site of her three daughters all together. The tenderness of Eve towards the girls had taken Sam by surprise, she hadn't expected her to be so warm, so accepting.

'Eve's here to have her procedure today. She's here so she can help you,' James said to Aria.

'Are you scared?' a weak little voice asked from the bed.

'A little,' Eve took a breath, 'I feel much better now I'm here with you.'

'I hope it doesn't hurt you,' said Aria, looking up at Eve, her eyes brightening by the second.

'Oh, don't worry, I'll be fine,' her words soft and caring.

'Do you want to watch Mulan with us?' Zara asked Eve as she picked up the DVD cover from the bedside table, she didn't like sick talk. As the well child, she felt guilty enough without listening or engaging in the daily goings on of Aria's illness.

With surprise, Eve gasped, 'I happen to love Mulan.' *How could this be!*

Zara looked at Eve like she was thinking hard then broke into a smile, before glancing at her mother, 'She is our sister. We love Mulan too.' A crazy little giggle came out as she looked astonishingly around the room, she had a cheeky little personality that was hard not to gravitate to straight away.

'Mulan is our favorite,' Sam let herself smile, 'We've watched it more than a thousand times. You could possibly regret ever confessing to being a fan.'

'Oh, I don't think so, I've probably watched it a thousand times too,' Eve gave a knowing smiled to the two girls who still looked at her like she was a fairy princess. Her love for Mulan started with Tia when she had spent the entire summer with Eve and Evan, they watched it over and over, day and night. Great memories flooded her for a moment. An overwhelming sudden longing for Evan took her breath away. It still hurt like hell!

'Take a seat Eveline, make yourself at home,' James said noticing Eve's demeanor changing, of course he had no idea it was because she was thinking of Evan, he'd be horrified.

Mulan never saw the light of day, they all chatted, laughed, and got to spend some quality time for a while. It was the strangest of vibes in the room, the three siblings in a world of their own with James and Sam watching on from the sidelines, it was somewhat surreal for them all. Even an exhausted Aria was chatty for a child who was gravely ill. Zara was more forward in her fascination of Eve, she was touching her big sister and exploring every aspect she could get her curious little hands on, not to mention asking her a million questions.

'I like your ring Eve.' Zara's delicate fingers brushed over Eve's diamond as she admired it.

'Thank you, I love this ring very much. It's incredibly special to me.' Her smile was warm and comforting. Unlike her first feelings towards Sam, she felt a connection to the gorgeous little angels immediately. Her real sisters! it was hard to believe as she sat at the side of the bed with Aria and Zara.

'Is it a wedding ring, are you married?' Aria sighed with effort as she blinked her dull eyes up at Eve.

'Not yet. I'm getting married later this year.' She wanted to eat this little precious dumpling who was ever so frail, Aria was trying so hard to be part of things, yet she was so ill.

Sam and James sat at a table in the corner of the room, James had taken several quick phone calls and paced around the room from time to time. The girls took their father in his stride, they seemed so used to his ways as Eve was. James was a presence, he always had been, but to them he was just their dad.

'Who are you marrying?' Zara seemed surprised that Eve would be getting married, she sat forward wide eyed in anticipation of Eve's answer.

'His name is Marco. He's tall dark and very handsome. Just like a prince.' The girls both gasped, they loved the animated description. Sam watched on with amusement as the sisterly banter went on and on.

'He's not a real prince though, is he?' asked Zara with intrigue as her face doubted her question.

'No, he's not a real prince. But he could be, he is very special,' Eve said as Zara reached out for one or her long wandering curl of hair.

'Sorry to interrupt the gals club, but we're ready for you Eve.' It was the doctor who had done all Eve's test the day before.

In her gentle but ever so endearing way, Eve leaned to Zara first and kissed her cheek while she touched her shoulder as a show of affection, 'It was so amazing to meet you little sister,' her voice was soft so only the girls could hear her words. She then looked at Aria whose dark eyes became misty. Eve moved in close to her precious face as she leaned in and kissed her forehead gently, 'We have so much to do together,' she smiled holding her own tears back, 'But first we need to get you feeling better.' Aria put a worried hand up to Eve's shoulder, her face filled with concern. 'It's okay, I can do this,' Eve assured her. There was something powerful there, something Eve never felt before, in a matter of hours her heart had opened in a way it had never before.

One last call to Marco, it went to his voice mail. 'Hi. I'm about to go to theater and I wanted to tell you that I love you so much.' Tears filled her eyes at the thought. 'I met my sisters this morning, and they are so amazing and cute, I just wanted to eat them. Anyway, I miss you; I wish you were here.' Hanging up just as her voice started to quiver and the nurse came to get her.

Knowing what to expect didn't help, Eve seemed calm and at ease and yet she was terrified of the unknown. Her will to do right by Aria was stronger than her fear though, now all she had to do was count backwards from ten as the bright lights beamed down on her. Ten, nine, eight...

The silent comfort of the strange bed was warm and nurturing. Rousing as she felt the crisp linen at her face, Eve laid on her side with a puffy soft pillow at her back, she took a deep breath and flickered her eyes open, her head resting at two pillows, the IV in her hand a little stiff as she focused on the person in front of her.

Wake up, breathe! She told herself struggling to open her eyes.

'I got your message. I'm here,' a whisper said from the chair beside her bed.

'Oh, God,' Eve exhaled with a light breath as she woke, an ach in her back.

'No, just me, not God,' said Marco.

'My prince.' She managed a smile.

'Just Marco,' he chuckled.

'You're so good in bed!' Still heavily under sedation, she gave a tired effort at a laugh.

'Okay... I wasn't going to say it, but if you say so,' he gently pushed her hair from her face as he joked. She was drowsy and a little out of it.

'I used to think about sex on the bus,' Eve mumbled. Her eyes closed like she was going to sleep.

'What bus?' confused, Marco went along with it, realising she was out of it still.

She opened her eyes and smiled at him, 'The school bus... I used to imagine laying under you... I don't know... they made me take my jewelry off. I'm sorry,' huffing like she was bothered, 'Can you find my bracelet in my bag, my ring too, in here?' her hand flopped out to the bedside table, her bag was in a cupboard underneath.

'Here they are,' he retrieved them from her bag.

'What are you doing here Marco?' Like she just realized he was there, like she'd just woken.

'I couldn't go another night without you. I got your message when I finished training and drove straight to the airport,' he paused and smiled lovingly, 'I've got a six am flight back so I can get to training in the morning.'

'Are you crazy!' Eve moved her head and winced at the pain now in her hip.

'Are you in pain, are you okay?' Marco moved closer and put her bracelet back on her wrist, her ring too.

'It feels like a horse has kicked me in the arse.'

He laughed, she was still drowsy, and her humor was very entertaining.

'How's Paddy, I miss him.'

'Paddy's good. He misses you too, he's wondering around the house looking for you.' Eve's randomness had a permanent grin on Marco's face, his adoring eyes never leaving her.

'Are you going to be in trouble for coming here?'

'Nobody will know I was ever here. It'll be our secret.'

'I'm good with secrets... ah, but you know that right. You were my biggest secret,' Eve's chuckle was interrupted by another wince of pain.

Marco was starving, and when the nurses got wind of this, they rushed off to find him some food. And they didn't disappoint, returning with a buffet of sandwiches and a tray of hot hospital food, an array of drinks and chocolate ice cream. The nurses knew that Marco was Marco Rossi, and went into full pamper mode, arranging an overnight bed in Eve's room for him, along with all the hospital comforts they could get their hands on.

Eve was coming around, she started speaking sense as she laid watching Marco devour all the food, she knew it wasn't great food, he must have been hungry. Her eyes hovered over his face and hair, she loved the way his hair was lightened by the sun at the very ends, she loved that sometimes his facial features seemed boyish and innocent. He was much older now, not a boy anymore, he was so very handsome, he was a beautiful man.

Eve was now well and truly awake and out of her anesthetic, she was tired and completely blown away that Marco had come to be with her, totally surprised her once again, he was the real deal, and she knew it now without any doubt in her heart or head.

He leaned over the bed and pushed Eve's hair out of her face, it was all around her in its unruly curls, 'You've had a big twenty-four hours.' His head fell to the side as he looked into her eyes closely. 'I love you Eve Frank.' He moved to her as she laid in front of him, she was paler, weaker, her lips lighter, her eyes duller and her energy less. To him she was the most beautiful woman he had ever been in the presence of.

As his lips touched hers tenderly, Eve inhaled him, the wave of completeness that swept over was engulfing every ounce of her soul. She moved her lips to his, he was there for her in every way she needed him to be.

A tap at the door interrupted their kiss, but only enough to make them barely part, they stared at each other a moment, looking deeply into each other's eyes as the door opened.

'Don't let us interrupt you,' said James standing in the doorway, surprised to see his daughter and who was obviously Marco at her bedside, kissing her.

Eve looked past Marco as they both turned to see her father standing there with Sam.

'Hi,' Eve was on a cloud of drugged out bliss that not even this unexpected visit could derail.

'Hello,' Marco said pushing his chair back and standing up.

James at once walked to him, the tall young man looked only mildly surprised to see him. Normally this would have pissed James off, but today he'd give Mr. Perfect the benefit of the doubt. 'Marco, good to see you,' he said extended his hand with narrowed eyes, the two shook hands.

'You remember my dad,' Eve said to Marco, feeling a mild spike in her blood pressure.

'I do, of course I do. It's good to see you Mr. Frank,' said Marco for want of a better name to call James who he hadn't seen since he was a teenager.

'If you're planning on marrying my daughter, you'd better call me James.' It was a jovial James who scoped Marco out in two seconds flat with one glance. 'This is Sam,' James turned to his side and gestured to her, 'I think you know who she is,' he was as cocky as ever.

Sam stood at the end of the bed with a grin as she looked from Eve to Marco, sizing the couple up, her instant take was what a match they made. He was tall and athletically handsome; she was small and delicately beautiful. Adorable to say the least, Sam thought as she then put her hand out to greet Marco.

"Hi Sam, it's nice to meet you.' He was shocked just a little to be meeting Eve's biological mother without warning, thrilled at the same time, and there was absolutely no mistaking the DNA connection between the two, it was like looking at an older version of Eve, and surprisingly, not that much older.

'It's lovely to meet you Marco.' The curiosity in her eyes for everyone to see.

Marco tried not to look at Sam too long but was truly taken by this older Eve. It was unbelievable.

'How's my girl?' James moved in closer, putting his hand on the covers at Eve's leg... just to let Marco know he was there, and Eve was his daughter... she had been his girl first.

Marco felt instinctively protective of Eve in the presence of her father, although he didn't show it.

'I'm good Dad,' she paused and looked up at Marco, 'How could I not be.' Her eyes told the story of how she felt, full of love and adoration for Marco, he was undoubtably her number one man.

'Well, the doctor said everything went well,' Sam gushed moving to Eve's bedside, 'How do you feel, are you alright, are they managing your pain, do you need anything?'

'I'm good, thank you. I was a little out of it when I first woke, but I'm fine now. How is Aria, is she okay?'

Selfless in such a becoming way, Sam thought. 'She's fine, she wanted to see you. She begged us to bring her to you so she could see you. But we didn't know how you would be feeling,' said Sam, becoming increasingly familiar with Eve's reactions and her way.

'I'm all good, you should get her... I would love for Marco to meet her, is it too late, is she still awake? He'll be gone early in the morning,' Eve was eager, her quiet hoarse voice with a slight pep to it.

Aria's ward was close by. James looked at Sam and she gave him a nod of approval, 'Go and get her,' she said giving her permission.

It was clear to Eve and Marco, that Sam was the one who called the shots, *she was the protective mother!*

Eve smiled; she knew Sam absolutely had the upper hand over her father as she watched the exchange.

'Lollie picked Zara up earlier to take her home for the night,' explained Sam to Eve and Marco.

'Oh, that's a shame,' Eve was regretful, she would have loved Marco to meet both the girls.

'I know, she's going to be so envious that she missed out on meeting you,' Sam said to Marco, 'We try to keep her life as normal as we can. Unfortunately, she spends more time in here than she should.'

Minutes later, James carried Aria in, she was in one arm, and he wheeled her IV in the other. Taking her to Eve's bedside, she managed a smile when she saw Eve. James placing the frail little girl down beside Eve on the bed, Marco on a chair at the side, Sam at the other side, and James sitting on the end of the bed.

'Hey, you,' Eve literally sparkled when Aria came in the room, her face was full of joy even though she struggled to hid her own physical discomfort. She was in complete awe of this tiny little girl's battle; how could she ever show her own pain! This child was in the fight of her precious life, and she still had a smile for Eve. Aria was so ill and yet somehow, she found the energy and the will to keep going, Eve was falling in love with her.

'This is Marco the Prince I was telling you about. Marco this is my little sister Aria.'

It was a delight for Sam to witness, Eve calling Aria her little sister. She herself had been introduced without explanation.

Eve held Aria's cold hands in hers as they sat together.

'Hi Aria, I'm so glad I get to meet you.' Marco's words were kind and sincere, he had a way that drew the room in, he was taken by how frail and small Aria was.

'Hello.' The child's dark eyes settled on Marco, she bit on her lower lip as Eve would, what was not to love about this little girl, she was precious beyond words.

'I made it through okay, I told you I would,' Eve said to her sister.

'Did they hurt you?' so softly spoken; the similarities were obvious even in her ill state. It was starting to get weird for Marco, how alike they all were.

'They took good care of me, it doesn't hurt.' Eve had pain, but she knew what she was feeling was miniscule compared to what Aria had gone through and what she had ahead of her. 'Don't you worry, I'm fine,' Eve assured her. The curiosity and underlying guilt on her small face was clear, Eve just wanted to squeeze her in and make it all better.

They talked quietly with James shooting off questions to Marco on the side, he was taking advantage of this time to get a gage on this large and seemingly well-grounded young man who was going to marry his daughter. On his best behavior, James didn't go too hard on Marco, he was interrogating without being too obvious, it was how he operated. Being respectful of how important this man was to his daughter.

Marco wanted to like James, even though he had heard all the not so flattering stories from his mother and Tessa. He was making his own mind up, and he wasn't sure about his future father-in-law.

Aria didn't say a lot, sitting at Eve's side facing her and they quietly spoke to Sam, it was the three of them engaging in what was normal conversation, lighthearted and warm.

'When will you be heading back to Melbourne?' Sam asked Eve as the visit was winding up, Aria was tiring and needed to go back to her room so she could settle for the night.

'Maybe I'll go home Sunday or Monday.'

Marco looked at Aria as she leaned on Eve's legs affectionately, he could tell the little girl was smitten with her big sister, just as Eve was with her. This was her family now; it would soon be his too.

'I've got a game here in Sydney in three weeks. I usually spend a night either side of the game here in my hometown, I'd like to visit you Aria and maybe meet your sister.' Marco was winning them all over with his charm, Aria blushing and nervously biting down on her lip as he spoke to her, just as her big sister did.

'Can you come too?' Aria asked Eve as if she couldn't get enough of her.

'Of course, I will be here any chance I get.' Eve's was totally in love, this tiny girl was the epitome of strength and goodness, the thought of not seeing her through this next part of her journey was playing on Eve's mind.

That night Eve fell asleep with Marco at her side, he was the even keel in her stormy ocean, his fleeting visit was just what she had needed to calm her unchartered waters.

Marco left early and didn't wake her; he kissed her head and watched her for a while before he eventually left.

As Eve's eyes fluttered open, she could hear voices... women's voices! In the doorway she could make out her mother Anna, and Sam. Instantly she had a heavy chest as she watched the two women face to face in the doorway, they hadn't seen her wake.

'Give her time,' Anna said with an assertive tone to her voice.

What the fuck... Eve's heart rate was gaining momentum as she lay still, she closed her eyes, her skin burning with anxious horror and breaking out into a sudden sweat as the enemies faced off.

'Thank you Anna. She's got my blood running through her veins, but you've got everything else.'

'It won't be easy; it was never going to be. Eveline's a closed book, you never quite know what she's thinking,' Anna sounded amicable, 'Give her time, she'll come around. Do right by her. It's the least you can do.'

What!! Eve felt her blood pumping around her body, she was panicked, waking to her two mothers was not awesome! 'What's going on?' she spoke in a hoarse voice and the two women turned to her and came into the room. Anna going straight to her bedside, Sam reluctantly hovering at the door.

'How are you darling?' Anna said with warm concern.

'Fine.' She looked mortified.

'Did we wake you? sorry, we were just getting acquainted.' Anna leant in, kissing Eve on the forehead, touching her arm, and rubbing it. Eve knew her mother's tone, Anna was raw in moments like these.

'Is everything okay?' she said looking at them both, confused, as they stood looking back at her.

'We're okay darling,' Anna had a triumphant sting in her eyes, 'We arrived at the same time. It's about time we knew one another, for your sake.'

Eve could feel her mother's strength as she stood with the air of power in the room. Anna was her mother in every way, and Sam knew it. Words had evaded Eve, she glanced between the two women. Marco had gone, she was alone in a room with these two arch enemies and the air was so thick she could hardly breathe.

Finally, 'How's Aria?' she managed to get out clearing her throat as she steadied her look at Sam.

Awkwardly, Sam stepped forward, but only a few steps closer, still just inside the door, 'She had a good night's sleep. The doctors have confirmed Monday will be the day.'

Eve could see the emotion in Sam's demeanor... she was rattled by Anna's presence her usual impeccably together exterior.

'Oh, okay. That's good, the sooner the better,' Eve raised her voice a little, she knew her marrow would take a few days before it was ready to be transplanted to Aria. It sounded simple enough, it was just like a blood transfusion given via a portal. 'It must be a big relief for you?' Eve could see Sam was on the edge, she wondered what Anna had said to make her so intimidated... *What had they been talking about before she woke up?*

'I'm so very grateful Eve. I will be forever grateful to you,' Sam was suddenly emotional.

'It's my pleasure,' a demure smile came to Eve's lips.

'Thank you, I'll never be able to thank you enough,' Sam took a big breath in, looking at Anna, 'You've raised an exceptional young woman,' Her eyes flickered to Eve full of hurt and guilt, 'Inside and out,' Sam was having a moment, sniffing a sob. Her attention went back to Anna, 'I always knew you'd do it better than me.' Sam took a step back; Anna dipped her head in recognition to Sam's unexpected admission of personal defeat... well that's how Anna took it anyway. Sam may have taken her husband, but Anna had Eve. She would always have the special moments, all the precious years, and the memories of watching her grown into the stunning young woman she was today. Sam had nothing but resemblance and blood.

As Sam backed out of the room Eve said, 'I'll come and see Aria later.'

'Okay,' Sam waved, then left.

A beat, 'And there you have it!' Anna smiled triumphantly.

Chapter Twenty Five

Standing in the bathroom Eve slid her clothes off slowly delicately with Marco inspected the two bruises at her lower back. She was finally home with him were she belonged. He'd picked her up from the airport and not in the pickup area drive thru zone, he was an arrival gate man! With arms full of red roses as she stepped off the plane. Tessa had tagged along; she'd missed Eve too. The three of them had Vietnamese for dinner on the way home so Eve could fill them in on all that had happened in Sydney. Now they were at home, just the two of them.

'Does it still hurt?' Marco asked because it looked sore, he stood in his underwear close to her body.

'No. It just feels like a normal bruise,' she told him standing naked in front of the bathroom mirror.

Taking her by the hand, Marco led her through to their bedroom, he'd changed the sheets and even put fresh flowers in their room, like she would do, he was thoughtful in every way that counted to Eve. Marco had missed her as much as she had him.

'Can I fuck you. I promise I'll be gentle,' a hopeful Marco said pulling the covers back for her.

'I beg of you, please,' she giggled, she'd missed his touch more than anything, she'd missed making love to him, it had only been a few days, but it had felt like a lifetime.

Marco nestled to her under the covers as it was cold. His large frame resting on his elbows at her sides, her legs open as he laid his body to hers, 'I'm so glad your home babe, I've missed you in our bed.' He kissed her soft warm luscious lips as his hands roamed her body.

'There's no place like home,' she kissed him back, 'This is my home right here with you. This is where I belong and where I want to be forever.' Her loving eyes at Marco's as he touched her hair at the side of her head.

'Eve Frank, I love you,' he said feeling so relaxed now she was back with him. Maneuvering over her as he murmured sexily, the softness of her body and large fleshy pillowing boobs under him, his want for her hardening him to a pulsing throb. The girlish Eve who he had fallen for all those years ago, had evolved into this stylish wholesome woman he was now madly in love with and couldn't live without. Marco pressed against her moist folds of flesh, she was opening up to him like a flower in bloom, her wet warmth engulfing him as he moved inside her with care. 'You are everything I've ever wanted and more,' he whispered.

She reached up to him, kissing his chest, 'That's my line,' Eve put her hands to his face.

'And now it's mine. You're the one Evie, all I want is a life with you... a big, beautiful life together.' He slid in and out of her taking the utmost care.

'Oh, God. I love this.' She let him fill her, a hot thick rod of pleasure, sending her into an immediate overwhelming orgasm. Her head pushed back into the bed and then to the side as she felt his big strong body penetrating her, controlling her. Gasping, she was once again lost in desire, 'Promise me Marco, this will never end.'

'I promise you this is forever Evie. You and me,' he exhaled at the tightening of her, 'and Paddy and our babies. That's my dream.'

'Babies!' Eve questioned with a chuckle. She huffed and slight moan at the surprise of babies being his dream!

'Yep, babies and lots of them too... when you're ready of course,' he said casually feeling the pressure building in his cock, it was the best feeling in the world, hands down. And then he was in pure heaven as they came together, a lusting of love for each other that had never faded, they wanted and needed each other more and more as time went on.

Marco's words were innocent enough... Eve knew that. The last thing he would ever do, would be pressure her for children. If being a father was truly his dream, she needed to consider it seriously.

'Let me have you to myself just a little longer, and then you can have your dream... that I promise you Marco Rossi.' Eve rubbed her palms at his strong arms as completeness flooding her. Her life was fulfilled with Marco alone, but now she needed to make his life complete. She had learned that the best rewards in life, came from giving. She would bare Marco's children one day, despite all her fears and apprehensions of failing again, and she would do it with joy and a full heart.

The stars now seemed to be aligning in Eve's world, she had the man she'd longed for nearly all her life. Marco really was as perfect as she'd always imagined, and their life together was just starting, happiness was theirs for the taking.

Marco had proved his loved for her over and over in so many ways… he truly loved her. Throughout all her trials and tribulation, Eve had always given her whole heart, she believed that those who gave, would eventually receive.

The End

Acknowledgements

As always, Anthony you are the first person I will thank. You are my husband and my best friend. This means nothing without you my true love.

My children, Charlie, and Isobel, it's never too late to try new things, follow your hearts and do the things that make you happy.

Sheridan, you have been my writing rock the whole way, I am forever grateful.

Rachel, thank you again, love your work!

My gorgeous girlfriends, you are always there, good, and bad… you are my constants.

To all my family and friends, I love you.

My muse, M.B, I'm sure you'd be amused!

www.ingramcontent.com/pod-product-compliance
Lightning Source LLC
Chambersburg PA
CBHW051328020726
47501CB00013B/1883